Iris Murdoch was born in Dublin. Her parents were Anglo-Irish. She attended Badminton School, Bristol, and read classics at Somerville College, Oxford. During the war she was an Assistant Principal at the Treasury, and then worked with U.N.R.R.A. in London, Belgium and Austria.

She held a studentship in philosophy at Newnham College, Cambridge, for a year and in 1948 returned to Oxford where she was until lately a Fellow and Tutor in philosophy at St Anne's College. In 1956 she married John Bayley, teacher and critic.

Her other novels are *Under the Net, The Flight from the Enchanter, The Sandcastle, A Severed Head, An Unofficial Rose, The Unicorn, The Italian Girl, The Red and the Green, The Time of the Angels, The Nice and the Good, Bruno's Dream, A Fairly Honourable Defeat, An Accidental Man* and *The Black Prince*. Her latest novel is *A Word Child*.

'Not a dull page or a slipshod sentence . . . THE BELL shines with intelligence' – *The Observer*

Also by Iris Murdoch

Iris Murdoch

The Bell

Triad

Panther

Published in 1976 by Triad/Panther Books
Frogmore, St Albans, Herts AL2 2NF

Triad Paperbacks Ltd is an imprint of
Chatto, Bodley Head and Jonathan Cape Ltd
and its associated companies

First published by Chatto & Windus Ltd 1958
Copyright © Iris Murdoch 1958
Made and printed in Great Britain by
Hazell Watson & Viney Ltd,
Aylesbury, Bucks
Set in Intertype Lectura

TO
JOHN SIMOPOULOS

CHAPTER 1

Dora Greenfield left her husband because she was afraid of him. She decided six months later to return to him for the same reason. The absent Paul, haunting her with letters and telephone bells and imagined footsteps on the stairs had begun to be the greater torment. Dora suffered from guilt, and with guilt came fear. She decided at last that the persecution of his presence was to be preferred to the persecution of his absence.

Dora was still very young, though she vaguely thought of herself as past her prime. She came of a lower middle-class London family. Her father had died when she was nine years old, and her mother, with whom she had never got on very well, had married again. When Dora was eighteen she entered the Slade school of art with a scholarship, and had been there two years when she encountered Paul. The role of an art student suited Dora. It was indeed the only role she had ever been able whole-heartedly to play. She had been an ugly and wretched schoolgirl. As a student she grew plump and peach-like and had a little pocket money of her own, which she spent on big multi-coloured skirts and jazz records and sandals. At that time, which although it was only three years ago now seemed unimaginably remote, she had been happy. Dora, who had so lately discovered in herself a talent for happiness, was the more dismayed to find that she could be happy neither with her husband nor without him.

Paul Greenfield, who was thirteen years older than his wife, was an art historian connected with the Courtauld Institute. He came of an old family of German bankers and had money of his own. He had been born in England and attended an English public school, and preferred not to remember the distinction of his ancestors. Although his assets were never idle, he did not speak of stocks and shares. He first met Dora when he came to lecture on medieval wood-carving at the Slade.

Dora had accepted his proposal of marriage without hesitation and for a great many reasons. She married him for his good taste and his flat in Knightsbridge. She married him for a certain integrity and nobility of character which she saw in him. She married him because he was so wonderfully more grown-up than her thin neurotic art-student friends. She married him a little for his money. She admired him and was extremely flattered by his attentions. She hoped, by making what her mother (who was bursting with envy) called a 'good marriage', to be able to get inside society and learn how to behave; although this was something she did not put clearly to herself at the time. She married, finally, because of the demonic intensity of Paul's desire for her. He was a passionate and poetic suitor, and something exotic in him touched Dora's imagination, starved throughout her meagre education, and unsatisfied still amid the rather childish and provincial gaieties of her student life. Dora, though insufficiently reflective to suffer from strong inferiority feelings, had never valued herself highly. She was amazed that Paul should notice her at all, and she passed quickly from this amazement to the luxurious pleasure of being able so easily to delight this subtle and sophisticated person. She never doubted that she was in love.

Once married and installed in the Knightsbridge flat, in the midst of Paul's unique collection of medieval ivories, Dora set about the business of being happy, at first with success. But as time went on, she discovered that it was not so easy as she had imagined to grow into being Paul's wife. She had been beckoned on by a vision of Dora the cultivated woman; but after a year of being Mrs Greenfield she was already finding her ideal too difficult and was even beginning to dislike it. Paul had assumed that she would wish to give up her art studies, and she had given them up with some regret. But since she was lazy, and had in any case shown few signs of talent, she was also relieved. Paul, whose courting had upset the régime of his work, now safely wed resumed his studies with the single-mindedness which Dora so much admired. During long hours when Paul was at the Courtauld or the British Museum Dora found time on her hands. She endeavoured to keep the flat, where she did not dare to disturb any object, meticulously clean. She made long preparations for dinner parties for Paul's friends; on such occasions Paul usually did the cooking. She enjoyed these things, but without feeling that they were really what she wanted to do. The elated confidence which Paul's love had given her at first began to ebb. It seemed to her that Paul was urging her to grow up, and yet had left her no space to grow up into. He wanted to teach her everything himself, but lacked the time and the patience to do so. Though a natural devourer of the women's magazines and an indefatigable tester of 'accessories', she did not even know how to dress herself any more. She abandoned the big skirts and the sandals. But after annoying Paul with a number of mistakes, she purchased one or two safe expensive outfits, which she thought extremely dull, and then stopped buying clothes altogether. Nor was she easily able to spend her money on anything else because of a haunting uncertainty about her taste. She began to suspect that Paul thought her the tiniest bit vulgar.

She liked Paul's friends though they alarmed her. They were all very clever and much older than her and had clever wives who alarmed her even more. They treated her with a protective bantering condescension. She discovered that one or two of them were under the impression that she had been a ballet dancer, and this seemed to her significant. She was invited with Paul to their houses but never got to know them well. When one man, a violinist, had taken a more personal interest in Dora and had delighted her by asking about her childhood, Paul had been very jealous and unpleasant, and they had not seen the man again. Before their marriage Paul had warned Dora that they were likely to quarrel; but he had added that when one was really in love fighting was half the fun of being married. The quarrels, which began soon enough, brought no pleasure to Dora. They left her humiliated and exhausted.

Dora began to see more of her old friends, especially Sally, a girl slightly younger than herself, who was still at the Slade. She began to feel, half apologetically and half defiantly, that she was still very juvenile. It used to delight her that the art students all called Paul 'Sir'; now it seemed upsetting. Sally asked her to join a party going to the Slade dance. Paul detested dances. After some pleading she went alone, and arrived back at six in the morning. Dora was unable to be exact about time or anything else. Paul greeted her with a scene whose violence terrified her. From this moment on she began to be afraid of him. Yet withal she did not judge him. A certain incapacity for 'placing' others stood her here in the lieu of virtue. She learned to coax him or to withstand him mutely, cherishing herself, and although she conspicuously lacked self-knowledge, became in the face of this threatening personality increasingly aware that she existed.

Paul wanted children, or at least a child, in the decisive and possessive way in which he wanted all the objects which he drew into his life. The sense of family was strong in him and he preserved an ancestral nostalgia for the dignity and ceremonial of kinship. He yearned for a son, a little Paul whom he could instruct and encourage, and finally converse with as an equal and even consult as a rival intelligence. Dora however was alarmed at the thought of children. She felt in no way prepared for them; though it was typical of the paralysis which affected her dealings with Paul that she made no effort to prevent conception. Had she been able to examine her lot more dispassionately she might have felt that a child would give her an independence and a status in Paul's *entourage* which she now sadly lacked. It was in her to become a prompt and opinionated mother to whom even Paul would defer. As a child-wife she irritated him continually by the vitality for which he had married her: motherhood would have invested her no doubt with some more impersonal significance drawn from the past. But Dora had no taste for such genealogical dignities, and deliberately to commit herself thus was not in her nature. Though so much under Paul's sway, she depended, like some unprotesting but significantly mobile creature, upon the knowledge of her instant ability to whisk away. To have to abandon this animal readiness by becoming two people was a prospect that Dora could not face. She did not face it. Although to the pain of Paul and his friends the expression 'let's face it', acquired in her student days, was still frequently on her lips, she was not in fact capable, at the moment, of confronting her situation at all.

That Paul was a violent man had been clear to Dora from the start. Indeed it was one of the things which had attracted her to him. He had a sort of virile authority which her boyish contemporaries could never have. He was not exactly handsome, but had a strong appearance with almost black dry hair and a dark drooping moustache which made Dora think of him as Southern. His nose was too large and his mouth inclined to harshness, but his eyes were very pale and snake-like and had fluttered other hearts at the Slade besides Dora's. She had liked to see in him something taut and a little ruthless, especially when he had been at her feet. She had enjoyed her role of a teasing yet pliant mistress; and Paul had delighted her by the revelation of a sophisticated sexuality and a fierceness of passion which made the friendlovers of her student days seem insipid. Yet now she began to see his power with a difference. She was at last disturbed by the violent and predatory gestures with which he destroyed the rhythms of her self-surrender. Something gentle and gay had gone out of her life.

After a while Dora stopped telling Paul everything that she did during the day. She saw friends whom she knew he would dislike. Among them was Noel Spens, a young reporter, who was in fact a slight acquaintance of Paul's, and whose accurate mockery of her husband Dora accepted with vehement protests, knowing it eased something in her heart. Dora did not approve of her behaviour. But the temptation to escape from Paul's elegant and untouchable flat to go drinking with Noel or Sally was simply too great. Dora drank more and enjoyed it. As she was too careless to be a successful deceiver Paul soon became suspicious. He laid traps into which she fell, and there were angry words. Seriously upset, he oscillated between brutality and sentimentality in a way which Dora found frightening and disgusting. She felt ashamed of her erratic behaviour and promised amendment. But the taste for company wherein, as she felt, she could be herself was now too strong. Incapable of consistency or calculation she moved frankly and apologetically from one policy to another and back again.

She saw more of Noel Spens and his circle of easy-going hard-drinking friends. She began to develop, in ways very different from what she had once intended, a certain sophistication. At home, Paul flayed her with reproaches which she knew to be just. She tried to explain to him why she was unhappy, but she was incoherent and he exasperated. Paul knew exactly what he wanted. He told her, 'I want to do my work and be married to you. I want to fill your life as you fill mine.' She felt herself brow-beaten by the energy of his purpose and humiliated by his refusal to understand her complaints. As she was unused to judging others with precision or analysing them in her thoughts she could neither satisfy Paul nor defend herself. At last, obeying that conception of fatality which served her instead of a moral sense, she left him.

She went at first to her mother, with whom she soon quarrelled. When Paul was convinced that she had really gone he sent her a meticulous and characteristic letter. 'You realize I have no legal obligations. But I have arranged for forty pounds a month to be paid into your bank account until such time as you come to your senses and return to me. I don't want you to live in penury. On the other hand, you can hardly expect me to support you lavishly in a state of demoralized and brutish debauch, and shortly no doubt in adultery. You are fortunate to be able to know that my love for you remains unaltered.' Dora decided to refuse the money but accepted it. She moved into a room in Chelsea. It was not long before she began to have a love affair with Noel Spens.

When Dora first escaped from Knightsbridge and from the routine of evening bickering with Paul she felt intense relief. But she soon realized she had no other life to escape into. She became vaguely dependent on Noel Spens, who turned out to be a gentle and considerate person. Noel said to her, 'Darling, come live with me and be my love, on condition that you keep it in mind that I am the most frivolous man in the world.' Dora knew he said this just to calm her nerves, but she was grateful all the same, and her nerves were calmed. She lived in an atmosphere of factitious and self-conscious frivolity, picturing herself as an irresponsible Bohemian. That she had deeply hurt Paul she tried not to remember. Memory was something for which Dora had little use. But she was too conventional a person not to feel painfully guilty and embarrassed at her situation. She struggled to recapture her gaiety. She began to feel frightened that Paul would come and drag her back violently or make a scene with Noel. Paul did not in fact pursue her, but wrote her regular weekly letters of reproach. She felt in these letters, with a certain despair, the demonic energy of his will bent always upon her. She knew he would never give her up. She passed the summer drinking and dancing and making love and spending Paul's allowance on multi-coloured skirts and sandals and jazz records. Then in early September she decided to go back to him.

Paul had been in the country since July. He was working, he told her, in one of his letters which she had never answered, on some fourteenth-century manuscripts of enormous interest which belonged to an Anglican convent in Gloucestershire. He was the guest of a lay religious community which lived beside the convent. It was a beautiful place. Dora who, though touched by his faithfulness, just glanced his letters quickly through to see if they contained threats and tore them up at once so as not to have to see his handwriting any longer, had gathered very little about where he was except the name. The convent was called Imber Abbey, and the house where Paul was staying was called Imber Court. So it was to this address that Dora wrote her laborious letter, half penitent and half aggrieved, to announce that she was proposing to return to her husband.

She received by return of post from Paul a cold and business-like note saying that he would expect her on Tuesday, she should catch the 4.56 stopping train from Paddington and would be met by car at Pendelcote. He enclosed the key of the flat, in case she had lost hers. Would she kindly bring his Italian sun hat and dark glasses, and also the blue note-book which she would find in the top drawer of his desk. Dora, who had been moved by her own letter, felt that not enough was being made of the occasion. She had expected Paul to come running up to London to receive her. She had not expected to be summoned curtly into the country. Alarm overtook her too at the thought of meeting Paul again in such strange surroundings. What, in any case, was a lay religious community? Dora's ignorance of religion, as of most things, was formidable. She had never in fact been able to distinguish religion from superstition, and had given up her own practice of it when she discovered that she could say the Lord's Prayer quickly but not slowly. She lost such faith as she had without pain and had not had occasion to re-consider the matter. She wondered if Paul took part in the religion down there. They had been married very grandly, though amid some ironic glances from Paul's friends, in church. For Paul had followed his father and grandfather in wishing to anglicize himself as much as possible where matters of class and religion were concerned. It had taken Dora some time to realize this, and when she had done so it increased for her the unreality of their relationship. Moreover the contempt of Paul as a Christian was even harder to bear than his contempt as a *savant*, since that aspect of him was for poor Dora even less penetrable. Did Paul believe in God? Dora did not know. As her thoughts now conjured up the reality of Paul and as her imagination played at last upon the fact that he had really existed all through this strange interval, and had continued his life, thinking about her and judging her, her heart sank utterly. She decided not to go.

She returned to her former resolve after discussion with Sally, who disliked Noel, and had always been, Dora suspected, rather sweet on Paul, and with Noel, who was by now thoroughly worried about Dora's state of mind and about what was to be done with her. Dora fetched the things from Knightsbridge, with a fast-beating heart as she opened the door of the flat and saw the familiar accusing scene, florid and unchanged, except for the dust and the smell of absence. She collected some of her own clothes at the same time. Her flight had been not totally unpremeditated but quite unorganized. By the time Tuesday came, fear of seeing Paul again overwhelmed all other emotions. She cried all the way to Paddington in Noel's car.

It was a relentlessly hot day. They arrived in good time for the 4.56 but the train was already in the station and fairly full. Noel found her a corner seat on the corridor side and lifted her large case onto the rack, placing on top of it the paper bag containing Paul's Italian straw sun hat. Dora dropped her smaller canvas bag on the seat and got out on to the platform with Noel. They looked at each other.

'Don't stay,' said Dora.

'Your teeth are chattering,' said Noel. 'At least I assume that's what they're doing. I've never witnessed this phenomenon before.'

'Oh, shut up!' said Dora.

'Cheer up, darling,' said Noel. 'You look the picture of misery. After all, if you hate it you can come away. You're a free agent.'

'Am I?' said Dora. 'All right, all right, I've *got* a handkerchief. Now please go.'

They stood holding hands. Noel was a very big man with a pale unwrinkled face and pale colourless hair. With his look of gentle awkward bland amiability he was like a large teddy bear. He smiled down upon Dora, wanting to be sympathetic without humouring her mood. 'Write to Uncle Noel, won't you?'

'If I can,' said Dora.

'Come, come,' said Noel. 'Don't be tragic. Above all, don't let those people make you feel guilty. No good ever comes of that.' He put his hands under her elbows and lifted her for a moment off the ground. They kissed. 'Give my love to Paul!'

'Hell. Goodbye.'

Dora got into the train. It was now very full indeed and people were sitting four a side. Before she sat down she inspected herself quickly in the mirror. In spite of all her awful experiences she looked good. She had a round well-formed face and a large mouth that liked to smile. Her eyes were a dark slaty blue and rather long and large. Art had darkened but not thinned her vigorous triangular eyebrows. Her hair was golden brown and grew in long flat strips down the side of her head, like ferns growing down a rock. This was attractive. Her figure was by no means what it had been.

She turned towards her seat. A large elderly lady shifted a little to make room. Feeling fat and hot in the smart featureless coat and skirt which she had not worn since the spring, Dora squeezed herself in. She hated the sensation of another human being wedged against her side. Her skirt was very tight. Her high-heeled shoes were tight too. She could feel her own perspiration and was beginning to smell that of others. It was a devilish hot day. She reflected all the same that she was lucky to have a seat, and with a certain satisfaction watched the corridor fill up with people who had no seats.

Another elderly lady, struggling through the crush, reached the door of Dora's carriage and addressed her neighbour. 'Ah, there you are, dear, I thought you were nearer the front.' They looked at each other rather gloomily, the standing lady leaning at an angle through the doorway, her feet trapped in a heap of luggage. They began a conversation about how they had never seen the train so full.

Dora stopped listening because a dreadful thought had struck her. She ought to give up her seat. She rejected the thought, but it came back. There was no doubt about it. The elderly lady who was standing looked very frail indeed, and it was only proper that Dora, who was young and healthy should give her seat to the lady who could then sit next to her friend. Dora felt the blood rushing to her face. She sat still and considered the matter. There was no point in being hasty. It was possible of course that while clearly admitting that she ought to give up her seat she might nevertheless simply not do so out of pure selfishness. This would in some ways be a better situation than what would have been the case if it had simply not occurred to her at all that she ought to give up her seat. On the other side of the seated lady a man was sitting. He was reading his newspaper and did not seem to be thinking about his duty. Perhaps if Dora waited it would occur to the man to give up his seat to the other lady? Unlikely. Dora examined the other inhabitants of the carriage. None of them looked in the least uneasy. Their faces, if not already buried in books, reflected the selfish glee which had probably been on her own a moment since as she watched the crowd in the corridor. There was another aspect to the matter. She had taken the trouble to arrive early, and surely ought to be rewarded for this. Though perhaps the two ladies had arrived as early as they could? There was no knowing. But in any case there was an elementary justice in the first comers having the seats. The old lady would be perfectly all right in the corridor. The corridor was full of old ladies anyway, and no one else seemed bothered by this, least of all the old ladies themselves! Dora hated pointless sacrifices. She was tired after her recent emotions and deserved a rest. Besides, it would never do to arrive at her destination exhausted. She regarded her state of distress as completely neurotic. She decided not to give up her seat.

She got up and said to the standing lady 'Do sit down here, please. I'm not going very far, and I'd much rather stand anyway.'

'How very kind of you!' said the standing lady. 'Now I can sit next to my friend. I have a seat of my own further down, you know. Perhaps we can just exchange seats? Do let me help you to move your luggage.'

Dora glowed with delight. What is sweeter than the unhoped-for reward for the virtuous act?

She began to struggle along the corridor with the big suitcase, while the elderly lady followed with the canvas bag and Paul's hat. It was difficult to get along, and Paul's hat didn't seem to be doing too well. The train began to move.

When they reached the other carriage it turned out that the lady had a corner seat by the window. Dora's cup was running over. The lady, who had very little luggage, departed and Dora was able to install herself at once.

'Let me help you,' said a tall sunburnt man who was sitting opposite. He hoisted the big case easily on to the rack, and Dora threw Paul's hat up after it. The man smiled in a friendly way. They sat down. Everyone in this carriage was thinner.

Dora closed her eyes and remembered her fear. She was returning, and deliberately, into the power of someone whose conception of her life excluded or condemned her deepest urges and who now had good reason to judge her wicked. That was marriage, thought Dora; to be enclosed in the aims of another. That she had any power over Paul never occurred to her. It remained that her marriage to Paul was a fact, and one of the few facts that remained in her disordered existence quite certain. She felt near to tears and tried to think of something else.

The train was thundering through Maidenhead. Dora wished she had got her book out of her suitcase before the train started. She felt too shy to disturb her neighbour by doing so now. Anyway, the book was at the bottom of the case and the whisky bottles on the top, so the situation was best left alone. She began to study the other people in the carriage. Some nondescript grey ladies, an elderly man, and opposite to her, two younger men. Or rather, a man and a boy. The boy, who was sitting by the window, must be about eighteen, and the man, who was the one who had helped her with her luggage, about forty. These two appeared to be travelling together. They were a good-looking pair. The man was large and broad-shouldered, but a little gaunt and drawn in the face underneath his sunburn. He had an open friendly expression and a wide forehead crossed by rows of regular lines. He had plenty of curly dark brown hair, going grey in places. His heavily veined hands were lightly clasped on his knee, and his gaze shifted easily along the row of passengers opposite, appraising each without embarrassment. He had the sort of face which can look full of amiability without smiling, and the sort of eyes which can meet the eyes of a stranger and even linger, without seeming aggressive, or seductive, or even curious. In spite of the heat of the day he was dressed in heavy country tweeds. He wiped his perspiring forehead with a clean handkerchief. Dora struggled out of her coat and thrust a hand surreptitiously into her blouse to feel the perspiration collecting between her breasts. She transferred her attention to the boy.

The boy sat in an attitude of very slightly self-conscious grace, one long leg stretched out and almost touching Dora's. He wore dark grey flannels and a white open-necked shirt. He had thrown his jacket into the rack above. His sleeves were rolled up and his bare arm lay in the sun along the dusty ledge of the window. He was less weather-beaten than his companion but the recent sunshine had burnt his two cheeks to a dusky red. He had an extremely round head with dark brown eyes, and his dry hair, of a dull chestnut colour, which he kept a little long, fell in a shell-like curve and ended in a clean line

18

about his neck. He was very slim and wore the wide-eyed insolent look of the happy person.

Dora recognized that look out of her own past as she contemplated the boy, confident, unmarked, and glowing with health, his riches still in store. Youth is a marvellous garment. How misplaced is the sympathy lavished on adolescents. There is a yet more difficult age which comes later, when one has less to hope for and less ability to change, when one has cast the die and has to settle into a chosen life without the consolations of habit or the wisdom of maturity, when, as in her own case, one ceases to be *une jeune fille un peu folle*, and becomes merely a woman, worst of all, a wife. The very young have their troubles, but they have at least a part to play, the part of being very young.

The pair opposite were talking, and Dora listened idly to their conversation.

'Must keep at your books, of course,' said the man. 'Musn't let your maths get rusty before October.'

'I'll try,' said the boy. He behaved a little sheepishly to his companion. Dora wondered if they could be father and son, and decided that they were more likely to be master and pupil. There was something pedagogic about the older man.

'What an adventure for you young people,' said the man, 'going up to Oxford! I bet you're excited?'

'Oh, *yes*,' said the boy. He answered quietly, a little nervous of a conversation in public. His companion had a loud booming voice and no one else was talking.

'I don't mind telling you, Toby, I envy you,' said the man. 'I didn't take that chance myself and I've regretted it all my life. At your age all I knew about was sailing boats!'

Toby, thought Dora. Toby Roundhead.

'Awfully lucky,' mumbled the boy.

Toby is trying to please his master, thought Dora. She took the last cigarette from her packet, and having peered inside several times to make sure that it was empty, threw the packet, after some indecision, out of the window, and caught a look of disapproval, immediately suppressed, on the face of the man opposite. She fumbled to tuck her blouse back into the top of her skirt. The afternoon seemed to be getting hotter.

'And what a splendid subject!' said the man. 'If you're an engineer you've got an honest trade that you can take with you anywhere in the world. It's the curse of modern life that people don't have real trades any more. A man is his work. In the old days we were all butchers and bakers and candlestick-makers, weren't we?'

'Yes,' said Toby. For some time now he had been conscious of Dora's stare. An anxious smile came and went upon his prominent and, it occurred to Dora, admirably red lips. He moved his leg nervously and his foot touched hers. He jerked back and tucked his feet under the seat. Dora was amused.

'That's one of the things we stand for,' said the man. 'To bring dignity and significance back into life through work. Too many people hate their work nowadays. That's why arts and crafts are so important. Even hobbies are important. Have you any hobbies?'

Toby was reticent.

Dora noticed some children standing on the embankment and waving at the train. She waved back, and found herself smiling. She caught Toby's eye; he began to smile too, but quickly looked away. As she continued to watch him he began to blush. Dora was delighted.

'A problem for our whole society,' the man was saying. 'But meanwhile, we have our individual lives to live, haven't we? And heaven help liberalism if that sense of individual vocation is ever lost. One must never be frightened of being called a crank. After all, there's an example to set, a way of keeping the problem before people's eyes, symbolically as it were. Don't you agree?'

Toby agreed.

The train began to slow down. 'Why, here we are in Oxford!' said the man. 'Look, Toby, there's your city!'

He pointed, and everyone in the carriage turned to look at a line of towers, silvered by the heat into a sky pale with light. Dora was suddenly reminded of travelling with Paul in Italy. She had accompanied him once on a non-stop trip to consult some manuscript. Paul detested being abroad. So, on that occasion, did Dora: barren lands made invisible by the sun, and poor starving cats driven away from expensive restaurants by waiters with flapping napkins. She remembered the towers of cities seen always from railway stations, with their fine names, Perugia, Parma, Piacenza. A strange nostalgic pain woke within her for a moment. Oxford, in the summer haze, looked no less alien. She had never been there. Paul was a Cambridge man.

The train had stopped now, but the pair opposite made no move. 'Yes, symbols are important,' said the man. 'Has it ever occurred to you that all symbols have a sacramental aspect? We do not live by bread alone. You remember what I told you about the bell?'

'Yes,' said Toby, showing interest. 'Will it come before I go?'

'Indeed it will,' said the man. 'It should be with us in a fortnight. We've planned a little ceremony, a sort of christening, all very picturesque and traditional. The Bishop has been very kind and agreed to come over. You'll be one of the exhibits, you know – the first of the few, or rather of the many. We hope to have a lot of you young people visiting us at Imber.'

Dora got up abruptly and stumbled in the direction of the corridor. Her face was glowing and she put up one hand to hide it. Her cigarette fell on the floor and she abandoned it. The train began to move again.

She could not have mis-heard the name. These two must be going to Imber as well, they must be members of that mysterious community Paul had spoken of. Dora leaned on the rail in the corridor. She fingered in her handbag for more cigarettes, and found she had left them in her coat pocket. She could not go back for them now. Behind her she could still hear the voices of Toby and his mentor, and it seemed suddenly as if they must be talking about her. For a short time they had existed for her diversion, but now they would be set before her as judges. Her acquaintance with them in the railway carriage had been something slight and fragile but at least innocent. The sweetness of these ephemeral contacts was precious to Dora. But now it was merely the predude to some far drearier knowledge. It occurred to her to wonder how much Paul had said about her at Imber and what he had said. Her imagination, reeling still at the notion that Paul had actually existed during the months of their separation, now came to grips with the idea that he had not existed alone. Perhaps it was known that she was coming today. Perhaps the sunburnt man, who now seemed to look like a clergyman, had been on the look-out for the sort of woman who might be Paul's wife. Perhaps he had noticed her trying to catch Toby's eye. However had Paul described her?

Dora had a powerful imagination, at least in what concerned herself. She had long since recognized it as dangerous, and her talent was to send it, as she could her memory, to sleep. Now thoroughly roused it tormented her with pictures. The reality of the scene she was about to enter unfolded before her in rows of faces arrayed in judgement; and it seemed to Dora that the accusation which she had been prepared to receive from Paul would now be directed against her by every member of the already hateful community. She closed her eyes in indignation and distress. Why had she not thought of this? She was stupid and could see only one thing at a time. Paul had become a multitude.

She looked at her watch and realized with a shock that the train was due to arrive at Pendelcote in less than twenty minutes. Her heart began to beat in pain and pleasure at the thought of seeing Paul. It was necessary to return to the carriage. She powdered her nose, tucked her untidy blouse back again into her skirt, settled her collar, and plunged back towards her seat, keeping her head well down. Toby and his friend were still talking, but Dora murmured quiet imprecations to herself inside her head so that their words should not reach her. She looked resolutely at the floor, seeing a pair of heavy boots, and Toby's feet in sandals. A little time passed and the pain at her heart became more extreme.

Then Dora noticed that there was a Red Admiral butterfly walking on the dusty floor underneath the seat opposite. Every other thought left her head. Anxiously she watched the butterfly. It fluttered a little, and began to move towards the window, dangerously close to the passengers' feet. Dora held her breath. She ought to do something. But what? She flushed with indecision and embarrassment. She could not lean forward in front of all those people and pick the butterfly up in her hand. They would think her silly. It was out of the question. The sunburnt man, evidently struck with the concentration of Dora's gaze, bent down and fumbled with his boot laces. Both seemed securely tied. He shifted his feet, narrowly missing the butterfly which was now walking into the open on the carriage floor.

'Excuse me,' said Dora. She knelt down and gently scooped the creature into the palm of her hand, and covered it over with her other hand. She could feel it fluttering inside. Everyone stared. Dora blushed violently. Toby and his friend were looking at her in a friendly surprised way. Whatever should she do now? If she put the butterfly out of the window it would be sucked into the whirlwind of the train and killed. Yet she could not just go on holding it, it would look too idiotic. She bowed her head, pretending to examine her captive.

The train was slowing down. With horror Dora realized that it must be Pendelcote. Toby and his companion were gathering their luggage together. Already the station was appearing. The other two were moving towards the door as the train jolted to a standstill. Dora stood up, her hands still cupped together. She must get herself out of the train. She quickly thrust one hand through the handles of her handbag and the canvas bag. and closed it again above the now quiescent butterfly. Then she began to totter towards the carriage door. People were beginning to get into the train. Dora backed her way out, pushing vigorously, keeping the butterfly cupped safely against her chest. She managed to get down the steep step on to the platform without falling, although her awkward shoes leaned over sideways at the heels. She righted herself and stood there looking round. She was on the open part of the platform and the sunlight rose from the glinting concrete and dazzled her eyes. For a moment she could see nothing. The train began to move slowly away.

Then with a deep shock she saw Paul coming towards her. His real presence glowed to her, striking her heart again, and she felt both afraid and glad to see him. He was a little changed, thinner and browned by the sun, and the blazing afternoon light revealed him to her in the splendour of his Southern look and his slightly Edwardian handsomeness. He was not smiling but looking at her very intently with a narrow stare of anxious suspicion. His dark moustache drooped with his sourly curving mouth. For a second Dora felt happy that she had done at least one thing to please him. She had come back. But the next instant, as he came up to her, all was anxiety and fear.

Paul was followed closely by Toby and his companion, who had evidently met him further down the platform. Dora could see them smiling at her over Paul's shoulder. She turned to him.

'Well, Dora –' said Paul.

'Hello,' said Dora.

Toby's companion said, 'Well met! I do wish we'd known who you were. I'm afraid we quite left you out of the conversation! We travelled up with your wife, but we didn't realize it was her.'

'May I introduce,' said Paul. 'James Tayper Pace. And this is Toby Gashe. I've got your name right, I hope? My wife.'

They stood in a group together in the sun, their shadows intermingled. The other travellers had gone.

'So very glad to meet you!' said James Tayper Pace.

'Hello,' said Dora.

'Where's your luggage?' said Paul.

'My God!' said Dora. Her mouth flew open. She had left the suitcase on the train.

'You left it on the train?' said Paul.

Dora nodded dumbly.

'Typical, my dear,' said Paul. 'Now let's go to the car.' He stopped. 'Was my notebook in it?'

'Yes,' said Dora. 'I'm terribly sorry.'

'You'll get it back,' said James. 'Folk are honest.'

'That's not my experience,' said Paul. His face was harshly closed. 'Now come along. Why are you holding your hands like that?' he said to Dora. 'Are you praying, or what?'

Dora had forgotten about the butterfly. She opened her

24

hands now, holding the wrists together and opening the palms like a flower. The brilliantly coloured butterfly emerged. It circled them for a moment and then fluttered across the sunlit platform and flew away into the distance. There was a moment's surprised silence.

'You are full of novelties,' said Paul.

They followed him in the direction of the exit.

CHAPTER 2

The Land-Rover, driven fast by Paul, sped along a green lane. The hedges, rotund with dusty foliage, bulged over the edge of the road and brushed the vehicle as it passed.

'I hope you're comfortable there in front, Mrs Greenfield,' said James Tayper Pace. 'I'm afraid this is not our most comfortable car.'

'I'm fine,' said Dora. She glanced round and saw James smiling, hunched up and looking very big in the back of the Land-Rover. She could not see Toby, who was directly behind her. She was still completely stunned at having left Paul's notebook on the train. And his special Italian sun hat. She dared not look at Paul.

'I tried to get the Hillman Minx,' said Paul, 'but his Lordship still hasn't mended it.'

There was silence.

'The train was punctual for once,' said James. 'We should be just in time for Compline.'

The road was in shade and the late sun touched the great golden yellow shoulders of the elm trees, leaving the rest in a dark green shadow. Dora shook herself and tried to look at the scene. She saw it with the amazement of the habitual town-dweller to whom the countryside looks always a little unreal, too luxuriant and too sculptured and too green. She thought of faraway London, and the friendly dirt and noise of the King's Road on a summer evening, when the doors of the pubs stand wide to the pavement. She shivered and drew her feet up beside her on the seat for company. Soon she would have to face all those strangers; and after that she would have to face Paul. She wished they might never arrive.

'Nearly there now,' said James. 'That's the wall of the estate we're just coming to. We follow it for about a mile before we reach the gates.'

An enormous stone wall appeared on the right of the car.

Dora looked away to the left. The hedge ended, and she saw across a golden stubble field to a feathery copse. Beyond was a shallow blue line of distant hills. She felt it was her last glimpse of the outside world.

'There's a fine view of the house when we turn in,' said James. 'Can you see all right from where you are, Toby?'

'Very well, thanks,' came Toby's voice from just behind Dora's head.

The Land-Rover slowed down. 'The gates appear to be shut,' said Paul. 'I left them open, but someone has obligingly shut them.' He stopped the car beside the wall, its wheels deep in the grass, and hooted the horn twice. Dora could see two immense globe-surmounted pillars and tall iron gates a little further on in the wall.

'Don't hoot,' said James. 'Toby will open the gates.'

'Oh, yes!' said Toby, scrabbling hastily to get out of the car.

As he busied himself with the gates, lifting the huge pin out of its hole in the concrete, two sheets of newspaper blew out of the drive, one wrapping itself round his legs, and the other rearing and cavorting across the road. Paul, whose glance remained sternly ahead, not turning toward Dora, said, 'I wish Brother Nicholas could be persuaded to make the place look less like a slum.'

James was silent. Toby returned and jumped in. Paul swung the car wide into the road and round at right angles into the drive. Dora saw that there was a little stone-built Lodge cottage on the left as they came in. The door stood open and another sheet of newspaper was in process of making its escape. A dog began to bark somewhere inside. A further movement caught her eye and she turned round to see that a thick-set man with long straggling dark hair had emerged from the door and was looking after the car. James was turning round too. Paul, looking into the driving mirror, said 'Well, well.'

Dora turned back to the front and gave a gasp of surprise. A large house faced them, from a considerable distance away, down an avenue of trees. The avenue was dark, but the house stood beyond it with the declining sun slanting across its front. It was a very pale grey, and with a colourless sky of evening light behind it, it had the washed brilliance of a print. In the centre of the façade a high pediment supported by four pillars rose over the line of the roof. A green copper dome curved above. At the first floor level the pillars ended at a balustrade, and from there a pair of stone staircases swept in two great curves to the ground.

'That's Imber Court,' said James. 'It's very fine, isn't it? Can you see, Toby?'

'Palladian,' said Paul.

'Yes,' said Dora. It was their first exchange since the railway station.

'That's where we live,' said James. 'Us straight ahead, and them away to the left. The drive doesn't go right on to the house, of course. The lake lies in between. You'll see it in a moment. Over there you'll get a glimpse of the Abbey wall. The Abbey itself is quite hidden in trees. The tower can be seen from our side of the lake, but you can't see anything from here, except in winter.'

Dora and Toby looked to the left and saw distantly between tree trunks a high wall, like the one which skirted the road. As they looked the car turned away to the right, following the drive, and a stretch of water came into view.

'I didn't realize the Abbey would be so close,' said Toby. 'Oh look, there's the lake! Can one swim in it?'

'One can if one doesn't mind the mud!' said James. 'It's not very safe in parts, actually, because of the weeds. Better get Michael to advise you, he's the lake expert.'

The Land-Rover was running along now close to the water, which beyond a marshy area of bulrushes was smooth and glossy, refining the last colours of the day into a pale enamel. Dora saw that it was an immense lake. Looking back along the length of it she dimly saw what must be the Abbey wall at the far end. From here Imber Court was hidden by trees. The lake was narrowing to a point, and the car began to swing back to the left. Paul slowed it down to walking pace and passed gingerly over a wooden bridge which clattered under the wheels.

28

'The lake is fed by three little rivers,' said James, 'which come into it at this end. Then there's one river leading out at the other end. Well, hardly a river, it seeps away through the marsh, actually.'

The Land-Rover clattered very slowly over a second bridge. Dora looked down and saw the stream, glittering green and weedy, through the slats of the bridge.

'You can't see the far end of the lake from here,' said James, 'because it turns round to the other side of the house. The lake is shaped like an L, an L upside down from here, of course. The house is in the crook of the L.'

They passed over the third bridge. The Land-Rover was turning to the left again, and Dora began to look for the house. It was immediately visible, presenting its side view to them, a rectangle of grey stone with three rows of windows. Below it, and set back a little from the drive, was a courtyard of stable buildings, surmounted by an elegant clock tower.

'And there's our market garden,' said James, pointing away to the right.

Dora saw an expanse of vegetable patches and greenhouses. Far beyond there was park land with great trees scattered upon it. The air was close and dusky. The distant greens were heavy with the final light of day, fading already and hazy.

The Land-Rover ran onto gravel and came to a standstill. They had reached the front of the house. Dora, suffocating with nervousness, felt the blood glowing in her face. Stiffly she began to get out of the car. James vaulted out at the back and came to help her. Her high-heeled shoes crunched onto the gravel. She stepped back and looked up at the house.

From here it looked less huge than it had seemed in the distance. Dora saw that the Corinthian pillars supported a wide portico over a balcony behind which the rooms of the first floor were set back. The twin flights of steps swept outward from the balcony, overlapping the two side wings of the house, and twisted back again to reach the ground not far from each other near the central point of the façade. Stone lions, sitting complacently cat-like, crowned the end of each stone banister, and between them could be seen a line of French windows, put in by some impious late nineteenth-century hand, leading into a large room on ground level. An elaborate stone medallion above these doors contained the message *Amor via mea*. A similar medallion surmounted the tall doorway up above on the balcony, above which a swathe of carved garlands led the eye upward to the stone flowers under the portico roof, dimly alive with the last reflections from the lake. Turning away from the house Dora saw that the gravel drive on which they stood was a terrace which ended at a stone balustrade, surmounted by urns, and a wide shallow flight of steps, cracked and somewhat overgrown by moss and grasses. A gentle grass slope led down to the lake, which lay close in front of the house, and from the steps a roughly mown path, flanked by precariously leaning yew trees, went to the water's edge.

'It's marvellous,' said Dora.

'It's not a bad example of its kind,' said Paul.

Dora knew from experience that nothing put Paul in a good humour so quickly as being able to show her something. He was looking up at the house with satisfaction, as if he had made it himself.

'A pupil of Inigo Jones,' he began.

'Better bustle up if we're going to make Compline,' said James. 'So sorry.' He started off up one of the flights of steps. The others began to trail after him.

James stopped, looking down on them from above. 'I suppose the newcomers would like to join us?' he said.

'Yes, please,' said Toby. This seemed to be the right answer.

Dora supposed that Compline must be some sort of religious service. At least this would put off the moment when she had to meet all those people, and the worse moment when she would be alone with Paul. She nodded.

Paul said nothing, following her silent and preoccupied.

Dora climbed the steps, trailing her hand upon the wide sloping stone banister. It was warm from the sun. She shivered slightly as she touched the house. In a moment she found herself upon the wide paved balcony under the portico. The tall doorway ahead of her led into a large hall. All was rather dark within, as no lights had been turned on yet. Dora followed

James and Toby through the door, and got an impression of a great staircase, and of people hurrying through the hall and out by another door at the far end. There was a stale smell, like the smell of old bread, the smell of an institution.

A woman detached herself from the hurrying figures and came up to them. 'I'm so glad you've arrived in time,' she said. 'Welcome to Imber, Toby and Dora. We all use Christian names here, you know. I feel I know you both quite well already, I've heard so much about you!'

The woman, whom Dora could see now in the gloomy light of the interior, was a middle-aged broad-set person with a round freckled girlish face covered with fair fluffy down which gave her the appearance of an amiable lion. She had pleasant blue eyes and very long faded fair hair which she wore in neat plaits round her head.

'This is Mrs Mark,' said James.

'Would you like to retire anywhere?' said Mrs Mark to Dora.

'No, thank you,' said Dora.

At that moment Dora saw, over Mrs Mark's shoulder, what looked like a rather beautiful girl who was hurrying after the other figures in the direction of the door. She was very slim and had a long downcast pale face, long heavy eyelids, and a weight of dark hair which she wore in a drooping bun. Lost tendrils of hair curled in a short straggly fringe upon her high forehead. She turned a little in Dora's direction before she went through the door and smiled.

Dora felt an immediate twinge of displeasure. She realized that she had been assuming that if she had to decorate so uncongenial a scene she would at least be the only beautiful girl upon it. A woman of the appearance of Mrs Mark was quite in place here. But the figure she had just seen was disturbing, like a portent, menacing almost. Dora remembered that she had forgotten to smile back. The smile appeared on her lips a second or two after the girl had gone.

'Shall we go in?' said Mrs Mark.

She led the way, and Dora followed with Paul. Toby and James came after. James hurried forward to hold the door open and they passed into a wide corridor. Paul took hold of Dora's hand, squeezed it hard, and continued to hold it. Dora was not sure if the pressure was meant as a threat or as a reassurance. She left her hand limp, resenting the hold, overcome with dejection.

A moment later they were stepping quietly into a large long room in which the lights had already been turned on. Three tall uncurtained windows with rounded tops opposite to the door gave a view over the park land, now darkened to a hazy twilight by contrast with the bright naked lights within. Dora blinked. The room was lofty and elaborately panelled. Its pink and white paint had faded to a dusty pallor, blanched now still more by the harsh glare. This, Dora conjectured, must have been the great drawing-room, or banqueting-hall perhaps, of Imber Court, now turned into a chapel. The wall at the end on her right had been completely covered by a curtain of royal blue hessian, fixed to the middle of which was a plain cross of light oak. Below it on a dais stood an altar covered with a white lace cloth and surmounted by a brass crucifix. At the side stood an elaborate metal music stand which served as a lectern. The body of the room was unfurnished except for a few rows of wooden chairs and a scattering of hassocks. A small number of people were already kneeling, and a strong silence, which because of the oddness of the scene seemed to Dora slightly dramatic, made her catch her breath.

James Tayper Pace crossed himself and knelt down at once near the door. Toby knelt beside him.

'We'll pop you in at the back,' whispered Mrs Mark, and pointed Paul and Dora to the back row. Mrs Mark then slipped away to what was evidently her usual station near the front. They went to their places, setting their feet down carefully on the bare floorboards. The silence was resumed.

After a moment's hesitation Dora knelt beside Paul. In the stillness she found that her heart was beating violently. She had released herself from Paul's grip when passing through the door and now clasped her hands determinedly together in front of her. Resisting the pious atmosphere she threw her head well back and looked about the room. She saw now that the ceiling rose in the centre to a round lantern and what must be the inside of the green dome which she had seen from the drive. From inside it appeared quite small. Dora's gaze wandered for a while among pale egg-and-dart friezes and pink scrolls and stucco garlands until it found its way back to the sober scene below.

Kneeling in the front row she could see a man in a black cassock who must be a priest, and near him she now made out with an unpleasant shock a shapeless pile of squatting black cloth that must be a nun. Behind them, in a group with James and Toby, there were three or four men. Mrs Mark was to be seen, kneeling very upright, her head covered by a crumpled check handkerchief which she must have whipped out as she came through the door. The dark girl whom Dora had glimpsed in the hall was kneeling nearer to the back, her face covered in her hands and bent very low. She had cast a scarf of black lace over her head and beneath it there appeared the black knot of her hair, glistening in the bright light. There were no other women.

Someone began to speak and Dora jumped guiltily. She listened, but could not follow what was being said. The speaker appeared to be the priest at the front. After listening for a little longer Dora realized that it must be *Latin*. She was dismayed and distinctly shocked. She had retained her prejudices when she lost her religion. A murmur of voices suddenly surrounded her, and a dialogue was begun between the priest and the congregation. Dora ventured a quick glance sideways at Paul. He knelt with shoulders squared and hands behind him, looking ahead and slightly upward toward the cross at the far end of the room. He had the solemn somewhat noble look which he often wore when he was thinking about his work, but rarely when he was thinking about his wife. Dora wondered whether, happily, his mind was turned to higher things, or whether the religious scene had wrought some change in his feelings. She must remember to ask him, some time when he was in a good temper, whether he believed in God. It was absurd not to know.

Dora suddenly noticed that the nun in the front row had turned round and was looking at her. The nun was fairly young and had a wide ruddy face and strong intent eyes. With the detachment from her devotional surroundings which can best be shown by those whose profession is devotion she scrutinized Dora with unsmiling objectivity for a moment or two. Then she turned away and whispered something over her shoulder to Mrs Mark who was kneeling just behind her. Mrs Mark also turned round and looked at Dora. Dora felt herself becoming red with alarm. There was a cold familiar inevitability about these looks. With the resignation of one who had never in her life got away with anything Dora watched Mrs Mark get up and tiptoe round the chairs to the back so that she could lean over Dora's shoulder. Dora twisted round, trying to hear what it was that Mrs Mark was now whispering in her ear.

'What?' said Dora, more loudly than she had intended.

'Sister Ursula says please would you mind covering your head? It's customary here.'

'I haven't got anything!' said Dora, ready to burst into tears of embarrassment and vexation.

'A hanky will do,' whispered Mrs Mark, smiling encouragement.

Dora fumbled in her pocket and found a small not very clean handkerchief which she laid on top of her head. Mrs Mark tiptoed away, and the nun looked back once more with amiable satisfaction.

Blushing violently, Dora stared ahead of her. She could see that Paul's expression had changed, but she dared not look at him. She clutched the back of the chair in front. The Latin mumbling went on. Dora became conscious that her skirt was intolerably tight and that a ladder was slowly spreading down one of her stockings. Her feet were hurting and she became suddenly aware that it is extremely uncomfortable to kneel with high-heeled shoes on. She began to look distractedly about the room. She could not see it as a chapel. It was a shabby derelict pitiable drawing-room, harbouring an alien rite, half sinister, half ludicrous. Dora drew a deep breath and rose to her feet. She whipped the idiotic handkerchief from her head and walked quietly to the door and out.

She found herself in a corridor which was unfamiliar, but

after trying one or two doors discovered her way back to the stone-flagged hall which opened onto the balcony. She listened for sounds of pursuit but heard none. The hall was spacious, and devoid of decoration: no flowers, no pictures. An open fireplace with a stone carved chimney-piece was swept clean and filled with a heap of brown fir-cones. A green baize notice-board announced times of meals and services, and that there would shortly be a recital of Bach records. Dora hurried on and passed through the tall doorway onto the balcony.

She leaned on the balustrade between the pillars, looking down across the terrace to the lake. The sun had gone, but the western sky to her right was still full of a murky orange glow, glittering with a few feathers of pale cloud, against which a line of trees appeared black and jaggedly clear. She could also see the silhouette of a tower, which must belong to the Abbey. The lake too was glowing very slightly, darkened nearby to blackness, yet retaining here and there upon its surface a skin of almost phosphorescent light. Dora began to descend the steps.

She crossed the terrace and went down the further flight of shallow steps to the path. She paused here because her feet were hurting, took one shoe off, and caressed her foot. Her foot released felt so much better that Dora kicked the other shoe off at once. It fell into some long grass by the side of the steps. Dora tossed its fellow after it and began to run towards the lake. The steps were dry and still warm from the day's sunshine. The path between the yew trees was of clipped grass and slightly damp already with the dew.

At the edge of the water, fringed by reeds, was a little wooden landing-stage and a small rowing boat. The boat had the attentive tempting look that small rowing boats have. A single oar lay within it. Dora loved boats, though they made her nervous too since she could not swim. She resisted the temptation to get into the boat and glide upon the black glass of the lake. She walked instead a little way along the bank, walking now through the longish grass which tugged stickily at the hem of her skirt. The ground was becoming damp and marshy underfoot. The lake began to bend sharply away to the right and she dimly saw that there was another reach of water on the other side of the house, dividing it from the Abbey. She stood looking out into the darkness across the water and reflected that this was the first moment of quietness in her day. She stood so for a little while listening to the silence.

Suddenly a hand bell rang sharply and clearly from the other side. It rang urgently and vigorously shaken for nearly a minute. Then there was complete silence again. It sounded as if the ringer of the bell must be outside on the edge of the lake, so clearly did the high imperative sound reach Dora's ears. She turned and began to run quickly back toward the yew tree path. The bell alarmed her. She hurried panting up the slope and as she put her first foot onto the steps she remembered her shoes. She began to forage in the long grass at the side of the steps. The accursed shoes were not to be found. She looked up at the house, looming up dimly over her in the night sky. She stooped again to fumble helplessly in the grass. It was too dark to see anything. A light went on in the house, somewhere in the region of the balcony. Dora gave up her search and began to trail back across the terrace. The stones hurt her feet.

The room where the light was on opened directly onto the balcony, on the right side, through a pair of large glass double doors, which looked as if they had been recently put in, doubtless by the same vandal that had been active below. Dora could see that there were a lot of people gathered inside the lighted room. She did not dare to hesitate, but blundered quickly in, shielding her eyes as she did so.

Someone gripped her arm and led her further into the room. It was Mrs Mark, who said, 'Poor Dora, I'm so sorry we scared you away. I hope you didn't get lost out there in the garden?'

'No, but I lost my shoes,' said Dora. Her feet felt very cold and wet now. She moved forward instinctively and sat on the edge of the table. People clustered about her.

'You lost your *shoes*?' said Paul in a disapproving tone. He came and stood in front of her.

'I kicked them off somewhere near the edge of the stone steps, the ones down to the path,' said Dora, 'and then I couldn't find them.' The simplicity of this explanation gave her a curious comfort.

James Taypcr Pace came forward and said, 'Let a search party be organized! It shall consist of Toby and me, as we know Mrs Greenfield already. Flash lights will be distributed. Meanwhile Mrs Mark can do the introductions.'

'I'll go too,' said Paul. Dora knew that he was always certain that he could find anything that she had lost. She hoped that he would find her shoes, and not one of the other two. It would put him in a better humour.

Swinging her cold wet legs in their torn and muddy stockings Dora fixed her gaze upon the one remaining familiar face, that of Mrs Mark. A lot of people stood before her, staring at her. She did not dare to look at them; yet everything was so awful now that she was almost past caring what anyone saw or thought.

'You must meet our little group,' said Mrs Mark. 'Toby has been introduced already.'

Dora continued to look at Mrs Mark, noticing how her rosy face, devoid of make-up, contrived to be shiny and downy at the same time, and how exceedingly long her plait of fair hair must be when it was unrolled. Mrs Mark wore a blue open-necked shirt and a brown cotton skirt above the shaggy bare legs and canvas slippers.

'This is Peter Topglass,' said Mrs Mark. A tall baldish man with spectacles swayed in a bow to Dora.

'And this is Michael Meade, our leader.' A long-nosed man with pale floppy brown hair and blue eyes set too close together smiled a rather tired and anxious smile.

'And this is Mark Strafford, with the beaver.' A large man with bushy hair and a ginger beard and a slight sarcastic expression came forward to nod to Dora. He smelt strongly of disinfectant.

'I am Mister Mrs Mark, if you see what I mean,' said Mark Strafford.

'And this is Patchway, who is a tower of strength to us in the market-garden.' A dirty-looking man with a decrepit hat on, who looked as if he did not belong and was indifferent to not belonging, gazed morosely at Dora.

'And this is Father Bob Joyce, our Father Confessor.' The cassocked priest who had just come into the room bustled up to shake Dora's hand. He had a bulging face and eyes glittering with conviction. He smiled, revealing a dark mouth full of much-filled teeth, and then gave Dora a piercing look which made her feel shifty.

'And this is Sister Ursula, the extern sister, who is our good liaison officer with the Abbey.'

Sister Ursula beamed at Dora. She had dark high-arching eyebrows and a commanding expression. Dora felt she would never forgive her for the handkerchief incident.

'We are very glad to see you here,' said Sister Ursula. 'We have remembered you in our prayers.'

Dora blushed with mingled indignation and embarrassment. She managed a smile.

'And this,' said Mrs Mark, 'is Catherine Fawley, our little saint, whom I'm sure you'll love as well as we all do.' Dora turned to look at the rather beautiful girl with the long face.

'Hello,' said Dora.

'Hello,' said Catherine Fawley.

Perhaps she was not really beautiful after all, Dora thought with relief. There was something timid and withdrawn in her face which prevented it from being dazzling. Her smile was warm yet somewhat secretive. Her large eyes, of a cold sea-grey colour, did not sustain Dora's stare. Dora still found her, in some undefined way, a little menacing.

'Would you like a boiled egg or something?' said Mrs Mark. 'We usually have high tea at six and just milk and biscuits after Compline.' She indicated a side table with mugs and a large biscuit tin in which Peter Topglass was now rummaging.

The group around Dora had broken up. Michael Meade could be seen, in converse with Mark Strafford, flashing a nervous smile of irregular teeth, his long hands darting about in Egyptian gestures. 'No more Petit Beurre,' Peter Topglass was saying meditatively to himself in the background.

'No egg, thank you,' said Dora. 'I ate something on the train.'

'A little milk then?'

'No, thank you, nothing,' said Dora. She thought of the whisky bottles. They would be in South Wales by now.

James Tayper Pace came bursting back through the doors, crying 'Eureka! Toby was the lucky one!'

Toby Gashe followed holding Dora's shoes by the heels, one in each hand. He lowered his eyes as he approached Dora and his dusky red cheeks burned a little redder. He presented to her the top of his round dark head as he gave her the shoes with an embarrassed little obeisance.

'Oh, Toby, thank you so much!' said Dora.

Paul came in, his face wrinkled up with irritation.

'Well sought, dear James and Toby,' said Father Bob Joyce. 'There is more rejoicing over what is lost and found than over what has never gone astray.'

'And now,' said James, 'since Mrs Greenfield's shoes have been discovered, we can all go to bed.'

CHAPTER 3

Paul and Dora were alone.

'That notebook is irreplaceable,' said Paul. 'It represents years of work. I was a fool to ask you to bring it.'

'I'm terribly sorry,' said Dora. 'I'm sure we'll get it back. I'll go to the station tomorrow.'

'I ought to have telephoned at once,' said Paul, 'only your antics put it out of my head. Why did you want to take your shoes off anyway?'

'My feet hurt,' said Dora. 'I told you that.'

They looked at each other in the austere light of a strong unshaded electric light bulb. Paul's room was on the first floor, with two large windows looking towards the Abbey side. It had been a grand bedroom in its time, with green panelling and a great mirror set in the wall. It was furnished now with two iron beds, two upright chairs, a large trestle table on which Paul had spread his books and papers, and a small pretty mahogany table which looked like a relic of former days. Paul's suitcase, open and half unpacked, stood in the corner. Two new but cheap mats were on the floor which otherwise was bare. The room echoed as they spoke.

Paul stood with one hand on his hip and stared at Dora. He could scan her in this way for a long time, frowning slightly, and this always frightened her. Yet at the same moment she knew that this was a manifestation of love, of that untiring and relentless love that Paul went on feeling for her, and which held her resentful, fascinated, ultimately grateful. She looked back at him, uneasy, yet admiring the solidity of him, full to the brim with his love and his work and all his certainty about life. She felt flimsy and ephemeral by comparison, as if she were merely a thought in his mind.

To end the stare she went up to him and shook him gently by the shoulders. 'Paul, don't be cross.'

Paul moved away, not responding to her touch. 'Only you,' he said, 'would be simple-minded enough, after betraying me in the way you have done, to paw me and say "Don't be cross"!' He imitated her, and then went to dig in his suitcase and pull out his neat black-and-white check sponge-bag.

'Well, what can I say?' said Dora. 'Here I am, anyway.'

'Nor do I subscribe to the view,' said Paul, 'expressed just now by Father Bob, that the lost sheep is more to be rejoiced over. And if you are expecting me to rejoice you will be disappointed. Your escapades have diminished you permanently in my eyes.' He left the room.

Dora dejectedly opened her canvas bag. Her pyjamas were in the lost suitcase, but at least her toothbrush was here. She was deeply wounded by what Paul had said. How could he assess her like this because of something which had happened in the past? The past was never real for Dora. The notion that Paul might keep her past alive to torment her with, now occurred to her for the first time. She stopped thinking so as not to cry and went to open the two tall windows as wide as they would go. There were no curtains. The night was hot and swarming with stars. From this side of the house the lake seemed very near. It was dark yet somehow to be seen in a diffused radiance of starlight and the not yet risen moon. Other shapes lay beyond.

Paul entered the room again.

'I haven't any pyjamas,' said Dora, 'they were in the suitcase.'

'You can have one of my shirts,' said Paul. 'Here's one that's due to be laundered anyway.'

'Did you tell those nuns all about me?' said Dora.

'I didn't tell the nuns anything,' said Paul. 'I had to say something about you to the other members of the community, and if it was unflattering that is hardly my fault.'

'They'll think their beastly prayers brought me here,' said Dora.

'I respect this place,' said Paul, 'and I advise you to do the same.'

Dora wondered if she would ask Paul now whether he believed in God, but decided not to. Evidently he did. She said instead, 'I can't do anything about the past.'

Paul looked at her hard. 'You can refrain from being frivolous about it,' he said. 'In your case I won't speak of repentance, since I don't think you capable of anything so serious.'

The sharp tinkling of a hand bell, rung on the other side across the water, came in through the window. Dora jumped. 'That bell again,' she said. 'What is it?'

'It's the Abbey bell for the various offices,' said Paul. 'It's ringing now for Matins. If you're awake in the very early morning you'll hear it ringing for Lauds and Prime. They're getting a big bell soon,' he added.

They both began to undress.

'There's a legend about the Abbey bell,' said Paul. 'I found it in one of the manuscripts. It should appeal to you.'

'What is it?' said Dora.

'This is a very old foundation, you know,' said Paul. 'There have been Benedictine nuns here on and off since the twelfth century. The present order is Anglican, of course, but still Benedictine. Anyhow, sometime in the fourteenth century, that was before the dissolution, the story runs that one of the nuns had a lover. Not that that was so very unusual I daresay at that time, but this order had evidently had a high standard. It was not known who the nun was. The young man was seen climbing the wall once or twice and ended up by falling and breaking his neck. The wall, which still exists incidentally, is very high.

'The Abbess called on the guilty nun to confess, but no one came forward. Then the Bishop was called in. The Bishop, who was an especially holy and spiritual man, also demanded that the guilty one should confess. When there was still no response he put a curse on the Abbey, and as the chronicler puts it, the great bell "flew like a bird out of the tower and fell into the lake".'

'Good heavens!' said Dora.

'That wasn't the end,' said Paul. 'The guilty nun was so overwhelmed by this demonstration that she forthwith ran out of the Abbey gates and drowned herself in the lake.'

'Oh, poor thing!' said Dora.

'You, of course, identify yourself with the faithless one,' said Paul.

'She was probably forced into the order,' said Dora. 'People were in those days.'

'She broke her vows,' said Paul.

'Is that a true story?' said Dora.

'These legends usually have some truth behind them,' said Paul. 'There are records of a famous bell here, but no one knows what happened to it. It was cast by a great craftsman at Gloucester, Hugh Belleyetere, or Bellfounder, and it had a considerable reputation because of its fine tone and because it was very good at keeping away plagues and evil spirits. It had some carvings on it too, scenes of the life of Christ, which is a very unusual feature. It would be an object of great interest if it ever did turn up. It's possible that it was in fact thrown into the lake at the time of the dissolution, either by people plundering the Abbey or else, more likely, by the nuns themselves, so as to keep it safe. Bell metal was very valuable. I believe someone once had the lake dragged looking for it, but nothing was found. The bell's name was Gabriel.'

'It had a name!' said Dora. 'How beautiful! But I feel so sorry for the nun. Is her ghost ever seen?'

'That's not recorded,' said Paul, 'but there is a story about the bell ringing sometimes in the bottom of the lake, and how if you hear it it portends a death.'

Dora shivered. She was undressed now and had pulled Paul's shirt over her head. 'Have you told the others this story?' she asked.

'No, I haven't told them,' said Paul. 'Oh yes, I think I told it to Catherine.' He got into bed.

Dora felt a twinge of displeasure. She went over to the window and looked out. The moon had risen now and the lake was fully visible, silvering in ripples caused perhaps by the breeze, perhaps by some night creatures. An air heavy with perfume drifted into the room. Dora saw more clearly now the expanse before her, the gaunt façade of the Abbey wall, wrinkled with light and dark, the trees beyond with their rounded tops catching the pale illumination, and long strange shadows of trees and bushes cast upon the open space of grass underneath the window. Looking a little to her left she made out what seemed to be a low causeway raised upon a series of arches which ran across the nearer reach of the lake towards the wall. Then, with a shock of alarm, she saw that there was a dark figure standing quite near on the the edge of the water, very still.

Dora's heart began to beat violently as she stared down and she checked an exclamation. Then the figure moved, and a moment later she recognized it. It was the boy Toby Gashe who was wandering along on the shore of the lake. He walked there by himself, kicking his feet through the long grass. Dora could just hear the swish of it as he moved. She drew back a little from the window, still keeping him in sight. So that Paul should not think she was watching anything she said, 'They're getting a new bell?'

'Yes,' said Paul. 'A tenor bell is being cast for them, to hang in the tower. It may arrive before we go. My work should take another fortnight.'

Dora saw the boy turning to look back along the lake. Then suddenly he stretched out both his hands and raised them above his head. He looked to Dora at that moment the very image of freedom. She could not bear to look at him any longer and turned away from the window.

Paul was staring at her. He was sitting up in bed with a book in his hand.

Dora looked at him with hostility. 'That was a horrible story,' she said. 'You like telling me unpleasant stories. Like that beastly one by De Maupassant about the dogs that you once made me read aloud.'

Paul continued to stare. Dora realized obscurely that in telling her the story he had released in himself the desire for her which had been quiescent before. The violence of the tale was in him now and he wanted her love. She looked at him with a mixture of excitement and disgust.

'Come, Dora,' said Paul.

'In a minute,' said Dora. Turning from him she caught sight of herself in the long mirror. She was barefoot and wearing only Paul's shirt, with sleeves rolled up and well open at the neck. The shirt just reached to her thigh, revealing the whole length of her long solid legs. Dora looked with astonishment at the person that confronted her. She admired the vitality of the sunburnt throat and the way the flat tongues of hair licked down on to the neck. She threw her head back and looked into the bold eyes. There was a steady and encouraging rejoinder. She continued to look at the person who was there, unknown to Paul. How very much, after all, she existed; she, Dora, and no one should destroy her.

'Come, Dora,' said Paul again.

'Yes,' said Dora. She switched the light out and marched towards his bed.

CHAPTER 4

The moon was rising. Toby Gashe stood with his feet almost in the water looking across the lake at the wall of the Abbey. Behind him various lights had gone on in the big house. He was waiting to be conducted to the place where he was to sleep. It was with some disappointment that he discovered that he was not to live in Imber Court itself, but in the Lodge cottage, with another member of the community whom he had not yet met. He would have liked to stay in the beautiful house and be with the others. He felt shy at the thought of another encounter, and a little alarmed at the idea of being cloistered with one person.

Toby, whose parents lived in north London, had been at a day school, which gave him a slight sense of inferiority together with a thoroughly romantic conception of community life. When James Tayper Pace, who was friendly with one of his masters, had come to give an address in the school chapel and had spoken of Imber, Toby had conceived a passionate desire to go there. He had been, ever since his fairly recent confirmation, a keen practising Christian, and filled with an as yet undirected desire to dedicate his life. He was greatly attracted by the idea of living and working, for a while at least, with a group of holy people who had given up the world. The Imber community, which had not existed for very long and was still in an experimental stage, worked on the land, running the small market garden which supplied the needs of the Abbey and left some produce over for sale. Something clean, simple, and vigorous about the whole conception moved Toby very much. His ecclesiastical experience had been narrow, and he was fired by the dramatic idea, new upon his horizon, of the monastic life. He was also impressed by the personality of James Tayper Pace, with his combination of masculine vitality and Christian candour.

Toby petitioned to be allowed to visit Imber. To his great

joy he had been told that he might come and work there for a month during his final summer holiday before Oxford, where he was due to go in October as an engineering student. His imagination had been busy beforehand, conjuring up some exceedingly close-knit complex of human brotherhood into which he would snugly fit, humble and industrious, edified and strengthened for his life ahead by the company and example of unworldly persons. He was therefore a little dashed to find that he was after all to live apart; but quickly resolved to conquer his disappointment with an ardent cheerfulness. It was not difficult. Gaiety and energy and hope filled him, at this moment in his life, to overflowing.

In a minute or two he would go in again. Michael Meade had asked him to wait for a while until someone was free to take him down to the Lodge. He looked about him in the moonlight, getting his bearings. Over there behind the house must be the market garden. Toby was a town boy, and everything to do with the countryside had for him a profound, almost spiritual significance. Of sun and wind and hard physical work and human companionship he felt he could never have too much. Given a spade and told to dig up an entire field he would think himself in heaven. He stretched out both his arms above his head, extending his body to test its elasticity. He remembered being told that one never sufficiently realizes at the time the wonder of being young. This was not true in his case. He was privileged to be aware of his youth and to enjoy it in a series of present moments crammed full with intense experience.

He looked in the other direction across the lake. His eyes followed the Abbey wall away to the right where it seemed to end or perhaps turned backward into the trees. To his left he could see the old brick-built causeway across the water and the dark hole of the Abbey gateway under its great arch. The moonlight made the high wall look insubstantial and yet somehow alive, with that tense look of deserted human places at night. Toby, as a Londoner, was not used to moonlight, and marvelled at this light which is no light, which calls up sights like ghosts, and whose strength is seen only in the sharpness of cast shadows. He studied the Abbey wall. All was still over there, yet he knew that the Abbey was eternally wakeful. He wondered what the relations were between the Abbey and the Court. He had gathered that the nuns belonged to a strictly enclosed Benedictine order and had very limited dealings with the outside world; but though exceedingly curious, he had not liked to ask more about this for fear of displaying ignorance.

He ought to go in now; and at the thought a shyness overwhelmed him again. He reviewed his day. He had felt rather alarmed at being alone with James Tayper Pace, but thought that he had after all managed all right. James was so simple and gay and easy to talk to. Toby's admiration for him was confirmed. Toby was at an age when he needed to admire, and when admiration was absolute. About Michael Meade, whom he had much looked forward to seeing, he still felt rather uncertain. He had been a little disappointed by Michael's appearance. There was something tired and weedy about him, he lacked the conspicuously manly look of James, and was not so obviously a leader. Toby was rather disappointed too to discover that the community had women members. That, somehow, was not quite right. Still, everyone appeared to be extremely nice, except that that Dr Greenfield man was a trifle rebarbative. (This was a word which Toby had recently learnt at school and could not now conceive of doing without.) It was odd that they should have sat opposite to his wife in the train. His wife was not beautiful, like Catherine Fawley, but she was awfully pretty and rather sort of mischievous. Remembering the train journey Toby felt a slight embarrassment, partly on her behalf and partly on his own. Her husband had not seemed very pleased to see her. But then the behaviour of married people was so unaccountable. Contrary to what Tolstoy seems to maintain in the first sentence of *Anna Karenina* there are a great many different ways in which marriages can succeed. Toby had of late become vaguely aware of this and this new knowledge made him feel sophisticated. He turned back towards the house.

He had come out to the lake by the front way down the steps, and had walked round to the side where the second stretch of water divided the house from the Abbey. He now faced the side of the house and saw that there was a large window illuminated on the ground floor. There was a stone wall which jutted out a little way beyond the window, dividing it from the front of the house, and as Toby approached he saw that there was a rectangle of cobbles and a side door. This must be the old servants' quarters, he decided, and that bright room must be the kitchen. Toby had always been keen on scouting and tracking, and some instinct now made him approach quietly, padding with caution onto the round hard cobble stones and keeping well in the shadow as he came up close to the window. He had been right, it was the kitchen, a huge old kitchen with rough blackened walls and an immense open fireplace, now filled by an Aga cooker. The Aga must be working, since a hot blast of air came out of the open window, perceptible even in the warm night.

A man came into view. It was Michael Meade, dressed in a blue and white striped apron. Toby was shocked at the apron, and conscience-stricken when he saw that Michael was stacking up cups and saucers in a tall wooden rack. He had quite forgotten to offer to wash up. At that moment the inner door opened and James Tayper Pace came in.

'Where's the boy now?' asked Michael.

'He's up on the balcony,' said James.

Toby held his breath.

'Will you take him down?' said Michael.

'I'd rather you did,' said James. 'You know what I think of this idea!'

'I'm sorry, James, I ought to have consulted you,' said Michael, 'but last week was frantic and it went right out of my head. In any case, I still think it's worth trying. We needn't make heavy weather of it. If the boy hates being there, or Nick is unpleasant to him, we'll move him back to the house. But I'm certain it'll be O.K. And it would relieve my mind if someone was there with Nick.'

'Why not send one of ourselves to keep an eye on Nick?' said James.

'Precisely for that reason,' said Michael, 'that he'd know he was being kept an eye on. If we send the boy, Nick'll feel responsible for *him*.'

'You think too well of Nick, and that's the plain truth,' said James. 'If you'd seen as much as I have of that type of person you'd be more suspicious.'

'I don't think too well of him,' said Michael, 'I don't think well of him at all, and I certainly know him better than you do. I think he's a poor fish. I'm afraid of his melancholy, that's all.'

'I'm not afraid of his melancholy,' said James, 'I'm afraid of his capacity to make mischief. The more I think of it, Michael, the more I'm sure we made a mistake when we took him in. I know how one feels about such a case, and I think I agreed with you at the time, at least I let you talk me round. I admit too that I don't really understand his background. But it's obviously a complex business, a bad history there. I doubt if we can do him any good, and meanwhile he can do us plenty of harm.'

'Anyhow, we've got him,' said Michael, 'for better or worse, and we can't chuck him out, just now especially, because of Catherine.'

'I know, I know,' said James. 'It's most unfortunate. All the same, I wish I had your faith. I know faith in people, or perhaps one should say faith *for* people, works miracles. And a miracle's what's needed here. Still, to come down to the common-sense level, I'd rather have kept the boy in the house. We're responsible for him too, you know.'

'He'll take no harm,' said Michael. 'He's got his head screwed on. I like him very much, by the way; you were quite right. That sort of youthful integrity is proof against infections. He'll be working hard anyway, he won't actually be in the Lodge very much – and he may provide just that link with Nick that we haven't managed to make so far.'

Toby began to walk backwards very quietly. When he got off the cobble stones onto the grass he began to run back toward the front of the house. The grass was longish and he had to go leaping through it. He hoped he was not making too much noise. When he reached the terrace he slowed down and walked slowly across the gravel, getting his breath, and up the steps to the balcony. The lights were still on in the hall and in the common room, and the doors stood open but there seemed to be nobody there. Toby stood still on the balcony, tense and irresolute. He was extremely disturbed by what he had over-heard and by having overheard it. The simplicity and curiously pure charm of the scene had disappeared in an instant. He now felt extreme disquietude at the thought of living in the Lodge. On the other hand, he felt very flattered as well as startled at the confidence that was being shown in him, and excited as at the prospect of an adventure. His thoughts were in a turmoil.

Before he had time to reflect any further a shadow fell from the common room doorway and Michael Meade appeared. Toby stepped forward into the light.

'Ah, there you are!' said Michael. 'I'm terribly sorry we kept you waiting. We'll go on down to the Lodge now, if you're ready. Have you got your bag?'

'It's here,' said Toby. He picked it up from beside the door-way.

'Can you manage?' said Michael. 'Let me carry one side.'

They went down the steps together, across the terrace and down onto the yew tree patch. Michael walked with a slight stoop, darting glances at this companion.

'We'll go across by the ferry,' he said. 'We don't use the causeway except for going to the Abbey.'

They stepped onto the wooden landing-stage, and the sound of their footsteps echoed in the hollow space between the planks and the lapping water. Michael put Toby's case into the boat. The moon was still unobscured.

'How does the boat get back,' said Toby, 'after somebody's been across?' He found himself speaking in a low voice.

'There's a painter tied to each end of it,' said Michael, 'and attached to each shore, so that it can be pulled from either side. Here, I'll steady it and you get in.'

Toby stepped into the swaying yielding bottom of the row-ing boat and sat down at once. He wanted desperately to be allowed to row, but kept quiet. The enormous night sky full of stars, the shadows of the moon, the great house brooding behind them, the splashing of the water under the boat, filled him with a breathless inarticulate excitement.

Michael stepped in and pushed off vigorously. He took up the single oar which lay across the seats, slipped it into a rowlock at the stern of the boat, and worked it expertly to and fro. The boat veered quietly and began to move, rolling a little, across the surface of the lake, which remained smooth, scarcely rippled at their progress, black and radiantly glossy. Toby let his hand trail in the water. It was warm.

'All right, Toby?' said Michael.

'Yes!' said Toby, answering the vague question with a sudden inexplicit enthusiasm. He saw Michael looking down at him and caught the flash of his smile. Then Michael freed the oar and drew it smoothly along the side of the boat. The other side came bumping neatly against the landing-stage. Toby hopped out and seized his suitcase. Michael followed, and the boat bobbed away a little on the water.

A grassy path led straight ahead of them and Toby could dimly see the avenue of trees beyond. A bird sang harshly beside the lake. It was not a nightingale.

'I hope you don't mind living at the Lodge,' said Michael. 'You'll be with us for all meals and work and so on. I expect James explained to you. It's just for sleeping.'

'I don't mind a bit,' said Toby. He began to wonder painfully whether he oughtn't to tell Michael that he had overheard the conversation. Perhaps it was dishonest not to. He couldn't decide.

Michael went on. 'I'm sure you'll get on well with Nick Fawley. You may find he's a bit gloomy at times. He's had a difficult life. It'll cheer him up to have a little company, draw him into things a bit.'

'Nick Fawley?' said Toby, surprised.

'Yes, he's Catherine Fawley's brother, her twin brother, in fact. Didn't James tell you? I'm so sorry, we're being very inefficient. You must think we're a proper collection of other-worldly crackpots!'

Toby felt disconcerted, he didn't quite know why, to learn that the man at the Lodge was Catherine's brother. He stole a glance sideways at Michael Meade, but could not see his face. Michael seemed uneasy and embarrassed. Probably he was always rather an awkward man and not easy to get on with like James. Toby felt perplexed. The sense of adventure was gone now and only anxiety remained. He stumbled from the grass on the stony surface of the drive.

'Here we are on the drive,' said Michael. 'You probably remember all this from this afternoon. The avenue of trees from the entrance ends here – it frames the view of the house from the road – but the drive turns away round the end of the lake. It's quite a long walk that way to the house, more than a mile.'

They walked on in silence towards the Lodge. Toby saw that a light was shining from one of the windows. A dog began to bark.

'That's Nick's dog, Murphy,' said Michael Meade. 'Murphy is quite a character.' Michael seemed to be nervous.

'I adore dogs,' said Toby inanely, feeling nervous too.

'Nick used to work in aero-dynamics,' said Michael Meade. 'He knows a lot about engines. In fact, he's by way of being our Transport Officer here. You shall be his understudy. I do hope you'll like it here, Toby,' he added, turning to look at the boy as they neared the Lodge. 'We're all so pleased you were able to come.'

They arrived at the porch. There was no knocker, but Michael knocked briskly with his fist on the wood of the door with an imperious echoing sound. From within the dog's barking was redoubled. Michael slowly pushed the door open and entered. Toby followed.

He shaded his eyes. All the electric lights were so bright at Imber. The door opened straight into what must be the living-room. In a quick dazzled glance Toby saw a large stove in the wall, two sagging wickerwork armchairs, an immense deal table, a wireless set, and a great many newspapers strewn on the floor. There was an unpleasant smell of stale food. The dog was barking and jumping about. A man who had been sitting behind the table had risen and was looking at Michael.

'The great man himself!' said Nick Fawley. 'I didn't expect you. One is not often visited. One is gratified.'

'I brought young Toby along,' said Michael, amid the continued din of barking.

'Shut up, Murphy!' said Nick. '*Shut up!*'

Murphy was a rusty brown dog, of indefinite terrier breed, with a white beard and an intelligent monkey-like face. He had a long sleek mud-coloured tail which hung limply from his rump as if stuck on as an afterthought. Becoming silent, he stood near Toby, legs stiff and fur slightly rising, looking up at him with inscrutable hostility. A long gleaming fang carelessly wrinkled the soft dark skin of his lower jaw. Toby eyed him uneasily.

'You brought young Toby along,' said Nick. 'That was nice of you.'

Toby stole a glance at Nick. He was immediately startled by Nick's close resemblance to Catherine. Here was the same long slightly heavy face, the leaden slumbrous eyelids, the curling fringe of dark hair over the high forehead, the large eyes and secretive expression. Only Nick was wrinkled about the eyes, which were red-rimmed and watery, as if from much laughing, and this, together with a sagging of the cheeks, gave him something of the look of a bloodhound. His nose was large and covered with tiny red veins. He gave the impression of being a little greasy and of having too much hair. Yet he had a certain handsomeness and even a distant touch of that refinement which breathed so chill and sweet in the beauty of his sister.

Nick was younger-looking than Toby had expected, but certainly seemed the worse for wear. Toby, whose imagination was ready for flights where Nick was concerned, immediately conjectured that he might be a drunkard. This would explain the portentous conversation he had overheard. It was a part of Toby's new sophistication to know that there were also many ways of being a drunkard. There were good drunkards. He decided that Nick was probably one, and with that resolved to like him. At the same moment he noticed a whisky bottle standing on the table, which confirmed his view.

Nick and Michael were looking at each other. Michael still seemed embarrassed. He said, 'I do hope you're giving yourself enough to eat down here. I wish you'd come up to the house occasionally for a meal.' He scanned the table. There was an unsavoury-looking dish of meat near the far end.

'That's Murphy's supper,' said Nick. 'I was just going to give it to him. Doggy, your moment has come!' He decanted the meat off the dish on to the floor with a plop. It fell on to one of the newspapers. It was evident that other newspapers present had served a similar purpose. Murphy ceased his contemplation of Toby and began noisily to eat his supper.

'Mrs Mark must have had a fit when she saw this scene,' said Michael.

'She animadverted, as women do,' said Nick. They were looking at each other uneasily.

'She got Toby's room ready?' said Michael.

'She did something upstairs which I assume was that. She was here an unconscionable time,' said Nick. 'Have a drink.' He picked up the whisky bottle.

'No, thank you,' said Michael. 'I think I'd better go. I just came to deliver Toby."

'Don't then, and go then,' said Nick.

Michael Meade still lingered, his eyes straying about the room. He looked as if he felt he had not conducted the encounter very well.

'How is my sainted sister?' said Nick, who also seemed to want to prolong the interview.

'She's very well, very happy,' said Michael.

'When I am told that a person is happy,' said Nick, 'I know that he is not. Of really happy people this is never said. Don't you agree, Toby?'

Toby jumped nervously at being addressed. He had settled into being a spectator. 'I don't know,' he said.

'Toby doesn't know,' said Nick. 'Has the erring wife arrived?'

'Mrs Greenfield has come,' said Michael. 'Well, I hope we'll see more of you up at the house. I must be getting back now.'

'So you keep saying,' said Nick.

'Look after Toby,' said Michael.

Nick laughed, which made him suddenly look pleasanter, and opened the door ceremoniously for Michael, who, with an awkward gesture of farewell, disappeared.

'Incompetent,' said Nick, looking after him into the darkness. 'Incompetent. Oh God!'

He turned to Toby. 'I expect you'd like to go to bed, young man. They've probably told you to get up at a shocking hour. And it must be tiring at your age to meet such a bunch of crazies in a day.'

'I *am* tired,' said Toby. 'I think I'll go up.' He looked Nick firmly in the face, determined not to let him see that he was nervous.

'Up, yes,' said Nick. He turned to where Murphy, who had completed his supper, was standing meditating. 'Up!' he shouted to the dog.

Murphy turned quickly and sprang into the air. Nick caught him in his arms and cuddled him against his chest. The dog's paws and smiling jaws appeared over his shoulder.

'The great thing about a dog,' said Nick, 'is that it can be *trained* to love you.' He leaned over the table to seize the neck of the whisky bottle, went slowly from the room, with Toby following, and began heavily to ascend the stairs, still hugging the dog against him, to a small landing with three doors.

'That's the bathroom,' said Nick. 'My room, your room.' He kicked open the door and turned the electric light on with his elbow.

Toby saw a neat fresh room, an iron bedstead with a white cover, rush mats on the floor, a white painted chest of drawers, the window open wide. The night air, warmer and smelling of flowers, came to them as they entered.

'It's nice up here, isn't it?' said Nick. He buried his face nuzzling in the dog's fur.

Toby was embarrassed. He said, 'Thank you so much. I'll be all right now.'

'Have a drink?' said Nick. 'A little nightcap of whisky and water?'

'I don't drink, thank you very much,' said Toby.

'Ah, well,' said Nick, 'I wish I could say that we would teach you to drink deep e'er you depart. Spiritual draughts, perhaps.' He put Murphy down on the floor. The dog jumped up, pawing his trousers, wanting to be picked up again.

'I think I'll leave you Murphy,' said Nick. 'We're a bit short of blankets. He'll keep your feet warm in the early morning. Nothing like an extra dog on the bed. You stay *here*!' he said to Murphy, pointing.

'Thank you,' said Toby. He could have done without Murphy, who appeared to be a somewhat rebarbative dog. 'I'll be all right now.' He sat down on the bed. He felt exhausted and desperately wanting to be alone.

Nick stood at the door looking down at him. 'I'll tell you something funny before I go,' he said. 'You've been put here to look after me.' He smiled, and looked once more pleasanter and younger.

Toby smiled back, not sure what to say.

'Well, well, we must look after each other, mustn't we?' said Nick. 'Leave your door open, in case Murphy wants to come out during the night. Good night to you.' He disappeared, leaving the door ajar.

Toby felt too tired now even to indulge in surprise and speculation. He went quickly to the bathroom, and returned to find Murphy sitting beside his bed. The monkey-like intelligence upon the dog's face was unnerving, and he stared at Toby with a kind of tense immobility which seemed like the prelude to an attack. Toby thought he had better establish some sort of formal relations, and said 'Murphy, good dog!' holding out a propitiatory hand. Murphy considered the matter and then licked his hand thoughtfully, looking up at him from under what seemed to Toby extremely long eyelashes for a dog. This reminded Toby that his master had extremely long eyelashes for a man.

Toby looked at the half-open door of the room. The landing was dark outside and there were no more sounds in the house. Toby now wanted to say his prayers. He knelt down, one eye anxiously upon the door, but could not collect his thoughts. He got up and crossed the room. There was a bolt on the inside. Very quietly he closed the door and shot the bolt. It went in without a sound. He returned to the side of his bed and knelt again, closing his eyes. There was an immediate scratching noise. Murphy was at the door, his dry blunt claws digging at the crack. Toby jumped up and opened the door again, but the dog would not go out. He stood looking up at Toby with a stare of exasperating amiability; and when Toby went to kneel down for the third time Murphy came and stood beside him with imbecile attentiveness, breathing down his neck. Toby gave up. Too tired to do anything more he put the light out and crawled into bed, leaving the door ajar. He felt the jolt as Murphy jumped up beside him and the warm weight settling down on his feet. The heavy perfumed air blew in a gentle breeze through the room to the half-open door. In a few minutes both boy and dog were fast asleep.

CHAPTER 5

It was the following morning. A rising bell had been rung soon after six, but Dora had learnt that it did not concern her, only those who were going to Mass. Paul had risen early, for work, not devotion. Feigning sleep, she had seen him writing at the trestle table which he had pulled up to the window. The pale sunny light of the early summer morning filled the room and from where she lay Dora could see the cloudless sky, almost without colour, the promise of another hot day. She remembered with distress that her summer frocks were lost with the suitcase and she must put on her heavy coat and skirt again.

Urged by Paul she got up just in time for breakfast at seven-thirty. The refectory of the community was the big room on the ground floor between the two stone staircases, with its doors opening on to the gravel terrace. Meals were taken in silence at Imber. At lunch and high tea one of the community read aloud during the meal, but this was not the custom at breakfast. Dora was pleased with the silence, which excused her from effort, except for such as was involved in the gesturing, pointing, and smiling, a certain amount of which went on, initiated especially by Mrs Mark and James. She consumed a good deal of tea and toast, looking out across the already baking terrace to where the lake could be seen fiercely glinting in the sun.

After breakfast Mrs Mark told Dora that she would find time during the morning to show her round the house and the estate. She would fetch Dora from her room soon after ten. Paul, who had meanwhile been at the telephone, came back with the good news that the suitcase had been found and was being returned to the railway station. Someone in the carriage had observed Dora's forgetfulness. The sun hat, however, was not to be traced. Dora promised that she would go to the station before lunch and fetch the case. This seemed to Paul an appropriate arrangement, and he disappeared in the direction of the Abbey to get on with his work. Mrs Mark would be sure to bring Dora to see him, he said, in the course of her tour. Paul was gentle this morning, and Dora became more positively aware that he was very glad indeed that she had come back. Quite simply and immediately she was pleased to have pleased him, and that and the sunshine and some indomitable vitality in her made her feel almost gay. She picked a few wild flowers in the grass near the lake and went back up to her room to wait for Mrs Mark.

As Dora looked round the room it occurred to her how nice it was to live once more in a confined space which one was free to organize, with small resources, as one pleased. The bare room brought back to her nostalgic memories of the various digs she had lived in in London before she met Paul, shabby bed-sitting rooms in Bayswater and Pimlico and Notting Hill, which it had given her so much pleasure to embellish with posters and more or less crazy items of interior decoration created at small cost by herself or her friends. Paul's flat in Knightsbridge, which at first had so much dazzled her, seemed later by contrast as lifeless as a museum. But on this room at Imber, Paul had made no mark. He had informed Dora that all rooms were to be swept daily and he now delegated this function to her. She had already discovered the place on the landing where the brushes were kept and had swept the room meticulously. She made the beds and tidied Paul's things, with caution, into neat piles. She arranged the wild flowers into a careful bouquet and put them into a tooth mug which she had filched from the bathroom. They looked charming. She wondered what else she could do to make the room look nice.

There was a knock on the door and Mrs Mark came in. Dora jumped, having forgotten all about her.

'So sorry to have kept you waiting,' said Mrs Mark. 'Ready for our little tour?'

'Oh yes, thank you!' said Dora, seizing her jacket which she threw loosely round her shoulders.

'I hope you don't mind my saying so,' said Mrs Mark, 'but we never have flowers in the house.' She looked censoriously at Dora's nosegay. 'We keep everything here as plain as possible. It's a little austerity we practise.'

'Oh dear!' said Dora, blushing. 'I'll throw them out. I didn't know.'

'Don't do that,' said Mrs Mark magnanimously. 'Keep those ones. I thought I should tell you, though, for next time. I feel sure you'd rather be treated like one of us, wouldn't you, and keep the rules of the house? It's not like a hotel and we do expect our guests to fit in – and I think that's what they like best too.'

'Of course,' said Dora, still extremely confused. 'I'm so sorry!'

'You see, we don't normally allow any sort of personal decoration in the rooms,' said Mrs Mark. 'We try to imitate the monastic life in certain ways as closely as we can. We believe it's a sound discipline to give up that particular sort of self-expression. It's a small sacrifice, after all, isn't it?'

'Yes, indeed!' said Dora.

'You'll soon get used to our little ways,' said Mrs Mark. 'I do hope you'll enjoy it here. Paul has fitted in so well – we all quite love him. Shall we go along? I'm afraid I haven't a great deal of time.'

She led the way out of the door. 'I expect you know the geography of the house roughly by now,' said Mrs Mark. 'The members of the community sleep right at the top of the house in this wing, in what used to be servants' bedrooms. The main rooms on your floor are all kept as guest bedrooms. We act, you know, as a sort of unofficial guest house for the Abbey. We hope to develop that side of our activities very much in the future. At present there are still a lot of rooms which we haven't even been able to furnish. The other wing is completely empty. Directly below us on the ground floor are the kitchen quarters at the back of the house, and the big ground-floor room on the corner in the front of the house is the general estate office. Then in the middle, as you know, there's the refectory underneath the balcony, and two little rooms up above, set back behind the portico, which act as offices for James and Michael. And at the back there's the historic Long Room, a great feature of the house, which is two storeys high. We've made that into our chapel.'

As she talked Mrs Mark led Dora along a corridor, past the dark well of a back stairway, into a larger corridor and threw open a large door. They entered the chapel, this time from the end opposite the altar. In the bright daylight the room looked, Dora thought, even more derelict, like an aftermath of amateur theatricals. Though scrupulously clean, it appeared dusty and as if the walls were dissolving into powder. The hessian cloth reminded Dora of school.

'It's not a proper chapel, of course,' said Mrs Mark, not lowering her voice. 'That is, it's not consecrated. But we have our own little regular services here. We go over to the Abbey chapel for Mass, and those who wish to can attend at certain other hours as well. And we have a special Sunday morning service here at which an address is given by a member of the community.'

They went out by the other door and emerged a moment later into the stone-flagged entrance hall. Mrs Mark threw open the door of the common-room. Modern upholstered chairs with arms of light-varnished wood stood in a neat circle, incongruous against the dark panelling.

'This is the only room we've really furnished,' said Mrs Mark. 'We come here in our recreation time and we like to be comfy. The oak panelling isn't original, of course. It was put in in the late nineteenth century when this was the smoking-room.'

They emerged on to the balcony and began to descend the right-hand stone staircase.

'There's the general office,' said Mrs Mark, indicating the windows of the large corner room. 'You'll see my husband working inside.'

They approached one of the windows and looked into the light room, which was furnished with trestle tables and unpainted deal cupboards, and seemed to be full of papers, all neatly stacked. Behind one of the tables sat Mark Strafford, his head bowed.

'He does the accounts,' said Mrs Mark. She watched him for a moment with a sort of curiosity which struck Dora as being devoid of tenderness. She did not tap on the window, but turned away. 'Now we'll cross to the Abbey,' she said, 'and call on Paul.'

Seeing Mrs Mark watching her husband, and seeing her now a little stout and perspiring in her faded girlish summer dress, Dora felt a first flicker of liking and interest, and asked, 'What did you and your husband do before you came here?' Dora, when she thought of it, never minded asking questions.

'You'll think me an awful wet blanket,' said Mrs Mark, 'but, do you know, we never discuss our past lives here. That's another little religious rule that we try to follow. No gossip. And when you come to think of it, when people ask each other questions about their lives, their motives are rarely pure, are they? I'm sure mine never are! Curiosity that is idle soon degenerates into malice. I do hope you understand. Mind the steps here, they're a bit overgrown.'

They had crossed to the Abbey side of the terrace and were going down some stone steps, much riddled by long dry grasses, which descended to a path leading to the causeway. Dora, exasperated, kept silent.

The lake water was very quiet, achieving a luminous brilliant pale blue in the centre and stained at the edges by motionless reflections. Dora looked across at the great stone wall and the curtain of elm trees behind it. Above the trees rose the Abbey tower, which she saw in daylight to be a square Norman tower. It was an inspiring thing, without pinnacles or crenellations, squarely built of grey and yellowish stone, and decorated on each face by two pairs of round-topped windows, placed one above the other, edged with zigzag carving which at a distance gave a pearly embroidered appearance, and divided by a line of interlacing arches.

'A fine example of Norman work,' said Mrs Mark, following Dora's gaze.

They went on down to the causeway. This crossed the lake in a series of shallow arches built of old brick which had weathered to a rich blackish red. Each arch with its reflection made a dark ellipse. Dora noticed that the centre of the causeway was missing and had been replaced by a wooden section standing on piles.

'There was trouble here at the time of the dissolution, the dissolution of the monasteries, you know,' said Mrs Mark, 'and that piece was destroyed by order of the nuns themselves. It didn't help them, however. Most of the Abbey was burnt down. After the Reformation it became derelict and when Imber Court was built the Abbey was a deserted ruin, a sort of romantic feature of the grounds. Then in the late nineteenth century, after the Oxford movement, you know, the place was taken over by the Anglican Benedictines – it was formerly a Benedictine Abbey, of course – and was rebuilt about nineteen hundred. They acquired the manuscripts that interest your husband at about the same time. There's very little of the old building left now except for the refectory and the gateway and of course the tower.'

They stepped onto the causeway. Dora felt a tremor of excitement. 'Will we be able to go to the top of the tower?' she asked.

'Well, you know, we're not going *inside*,' said Mrs Mark, slightly scandalized. 'This is an *enclosed* order of nuns. No one goes in or comes out.'

Dora was stunned by this information. She stopped. 'Do you mean,' she said, 'that they're completely imprisoned in there?'

Mrs Mark laughed. 'Not imprisoned, my dear,' she said. 'They are there of their own free will. This is not a prison. It is on the contrary a place which it is very hard to get into, and only the strongest achieve it. Like Mary in the parable, they have chosen the better part.' They walked on.

'Don't they *ever* come out?' asked Dora.

'No,' said Mrs Mark. 'Being Benedictines, they take a vow of stability, that is they remain all their lives in the house where they take their first vows. They die and are buried inside in the nuns' cemetery.'

'How absolutely appalling!' said Dora.

'Quiet now, please,' said Mrs Mark in a lowered voice. They were reaching the end of the causeway.

Dora saw now that the high wall, which had seemed to rise directly out of the lake, was in fact set back more than fifty yards from the edge of the water. From the lake shore there ran two roughly pebbled paths, one up to the great gateway, whose immense wooden door stood firmly shut, and the other away to the left alongside the Abbey wall.

'This door,' said Mrs Mark, pointing to the gateway and still speaking softly, 'is never opened except for the admission of a postulant: a rather impressive ceremony that always takes place in the early morning. Well, yes, it will also be opened in a week or two. When the new bell comes it will be taken in this way, as if it were a postulant.'

They turned to the left along the path which ran midway between the wall and the water. Dora saw a long rectangular brick building with a flat roof which seemed to be attached as an excrescence to the outside of the wall.

'Not a thing of beauty, I'm afraid,' said Mrs Mark. 'Here are the parlours where the nuns occasionally come to speak to people from outside. And at the end is the visitors' chapel where we are privileged to participate in the devotional life of the Abbey. The nuns' chapel is the large building just here on the other side of the wall. You can see a bit of the tiled roof there through the trees.'

They went in through a green door at the end of the brick building. A long corridor stretched ahead with a row of doors leading off it.

'I'll show you one of the parlours,' said Mrs Mark, almost whispering now. 'We won't disturb your husband just yet. He's down at the far end.'

They entered the first door. Dora found herself in a small square room which was completely bare except for two chairs and the shiny linoleum upon the floor. The chairs were drawn up at the other side of the room against a great screen of white gauze which covered the upper half of the far wall.

Mrs Mark went forward. 'The other half of the room,' she said, 'on the other side, is within the enclosure.' She pulled at the wooden edge of the gauze screen and it opened as a door, revealing behind it a grille of iron bars set about nine inches apart. Behind the grille and close up against it was a second gauze screen, obscuring the view into the room beyond.

'You see,' said Mrs Mark, 'the nun opens the screen on the

65

other side, and then you can talk through the grille.' She closed the screen to again. It all seemed to Dora quite unbelievably eerie.

'I wonder if you'd like to talk to one of the nuns?' said Mrs Mark. 'I'm afraid the Abbess is certain to be too busy. Even James and Michael only manage to see her now and then. But I'm sure Mother Clare would be very glad to see you and have a little talk.'

Dora could feel her bristles rising with alarm and indignation. 'I don't think I would have anything to talk to the nuns about,' she said, trying to prevent her voice from sounding aggressive.

'Well, you know,' said Mrs Mark, 'I thought it might be nice for you to talk things over. The nuns are wise folk and you'd be surprised at what they know of how the world goes on. Nothing shocks them. People often come here to make a clean breast of their troubles and get themselves sorted out.'

'I have no troubles which I care to discuss,' said Dora. She was rigid with hostility, shuddering at these phrases. She'd see the place in hell before she'd let a nun meddle with her mind and heart. They retreated into the corridor.

'Think it over anyway,' said Mrs Mark. 'Perhaps it's the sort of idea that takes some getting used to. Now we'll call on Paul. He works down there in the last parlour.'

Mrs Mark knocked and opened the door revealing a room similar to the first one, only furnished with a large table at which Paul was working. The gauze screen was closed.

Paul and Dora were glad to see each other. Paul looked up from the table and fixed a beaming smile upon his wife. His delight whenever she found him at his studies had always struck Dora as childish and touching. She was pleased now to see him so importantly at work, and immediately felt proud of him, regaining her vision of him as a distinguished man, how obviously superior, she felt, to Mark Strafford and those other drearies. Dora's capacity to forget and to live in the moment, while it more frequently landed her in grave trouble, made her also responsive without calculation to the returning glow of kindness. That she had no memory made her generous.

She was unrevengeful and did not brood; and in the instant as she crossed the room it was as if there had never been any trouble between them.

'These are some of the manuscripts I'm working on,' Paul was saying in a low voice. 'They're very precious and I'm not allowed to take them away.' He was leaning over the table and opening several large leather-bound volumes with thick and brightly illuminated pages for Dora to see. 'Here are the early chronicles of the nunnery. They're unique of their kind. This is called a "chartulary", which contains copies of charters and legal documents. And here is the famous Imber Psalter. See these fantastic initial letters, and the animals running up the side of the page? And this is a picture of the Abbey as it was in 1400.'

Dora saw a complex of white castellated buildings against a background of very leafy green trees and blue sky. 'I suppose it wasn't really so white,' she said. 'It looks more like Italy. However does all that gold stuff stay on? Why, there's the old tower!'

'Sssh!' said Paul. 'Yes, that's the tower that still exists. It's a very formalized picture of course. And here's the Bishop who founded the place holding a model of the Abbey in his hand. You get a better idea of the lay-out from that. The modern Abbey follows the ground-plan of the old one, though of course they haven't attempted to reproduce the medieval buildings. That section still survives as well as the tower. In this old Book of Evidences you can see—'

'We mustn't keep you too long,' said Mrs Mark. 'And I must show Dora the chapel and buzz her round the market garden and get back to my own jobs.'

Paul was disappointed. 'I'll show you more tomorrow,' he said, and squeezed Dora's arm as she turned away.

Dora, who would like to have stayed, gave him a rueful smile behind Mrs Mark's retreating back. She was already determining how she would mock that lady when she was once more alone with Paul. Mockery did not come easily to Dora, and had to be thought out beforehand. Her jests at other people's expense were often a trifle laboured. She followed Mrs Mark now, smiling to herself, and cheered too by the ease of her complicity with Paul.

Mrs Mark took the last few steps along the corridor and entered a little vestibule with two doors, one opening into the garden and the other into the chapel. She opened the inner door and propelled Dora through it into an almost complete blackness. As she strained her eyes to see, Dora was conscious of Mrs Mark vigorously genuflecting beside her. Then she began to be aware that she was in a small box-like room with a highly polished parquet floor, some religious prints on the walls, and a number of chairs and hassocks. A strong smell of incense pervaded the place. The room faced inwards towards an enormous grille which this time stretched from floor to ceiling for the whole width of the room. Some of the bars had been severed to make a door, which was closed. There was a low rail, set a few feet back on the near side of the grille, and behind the bars could be dimly seen, at a higher level upon a dais, an altar set sideways on to the room. Two long white curtains, drawn back now to reveal the scene, hung from a brass rail which traversed the grille. Near the altar a small red light was burning. An annihilating silence came from within.

'This is the visitors' chapel,' said Mrs Mark, speaking now in such a low whisper that Dora could hardly hear her. 'What you see through the bars is the high altar of the nuns' chapel. The main body of the chapel faces the altar and can't be seen from here. By this arrangement we can participate in the services without ever seeing the nuns, which of course would be forbidden. There is a mass at seven every morning which visitors may attend. That's the gate the priest comes through to give communion to anyone who is in this chapel. When the nuns are receiving the sacrament these curtains are closed to cut this chapel off from the main one. This is the place where outsiders like us can come nearest to the spiritual life of the Abbey.'

A soft rustle came from somewhere in the distance, round the corner beyond the bars, and then the sound of a footstep.

'Is someone—?' whispered Dora.

'There is always a nun in the chapel,' murmured Mrs Mark. 'It is a place of continual prayer.'

Dora felt stifled and suddenly frightened and began to re-treat towards the door. The rich exotic smell of the incense roused some ancestral terror in her Protestant blood. Mrs Mark genuflected, crossing herself, and followed. In a moment they were out in the bright sunlight. The tall grasses moved, mingl-ing with the reeds at the water's edge, and the lake flickered quietly in the sun. The wide scene, with a slanting view of Imber Court and a hazy distance of parkland elms, was laid out under a cloudless sky. There was something incredible about the proximity of that dark hole and that silence. Dora shook her head violently.

'Yes, it is impressive, isn't it?' said Mrs Mark. 'There is a wonderful spiritual life here. One just can't help being affected by it.'

They began to walk back across the causeway.

'We'll take that little path to the left,' said Mrs Mark, 'and cut through behind the house to the market-garden.'

The path led them from the end of the causeway a little way along the shore, and then turned away to the right, skirt-ing a thick wood. A glint of greenhouses was to be seen ahead. As they turned by the wood, leaving the edge of the lake, the thin tinkling of the hand bell followed them across the water.

Dora burst out, 'It's terrible to think of them being shut up like that!'

'It is true,' said Mrs Mark, 'that these women lay upon them-selves austerities from which you and I would shrink in terror. But just as we think the sinner better than he is when we imagine that suffering ennobles him, so we do less than justice to the saint when we think that his sacrifices grieve him in the way they would grieve us. Indian file here, I think.'

Mrs Mark led the way along the narrow track which could still just be found in the middle of the encroaching grass, tall and bleached to a faded yellow. Long feathery plumes, brittle with dryness, leaned from either side, touching the shoulders of the two women as they passed. Still stirred and affected by what she had seen, Dora blundered on in her uncomfortable shoes, watching where she stepped, and seeing ahead of her through the undergrowth the intermittent flash of Mrs Mark's well-developed calves, healthily shining, burnished by the sun to a glowing golden brown. The back view of the Court could be seen on the right, from this side a long unbroken façade, with pillars set close into the wall to frame the impressive round-topped windows of the Long Room. They emerged into an open space where the grass had been cut and stacked. The path faded away here and Dora's high heels sank into sharp stubble.

'This is where the market-garden begins,' said Mrs Mark. 'It's still very small, you know. This nearer part is what used to be the flower garden of the Court. We're cultivating that in strips with lettuce mainly, and some carrots and onions and young leeks. Beyond is what used to be the fruit garden of the Court. That's enclosed by the high walls you see straight ahead. We've kept that very much as it was. It's well stocked with apples and pears and plenty of soft fruit. There are some greenhouses in there, and we've added the more modern ones you see on the left. They're all full of tomatoes at present. The wire thing beside them is a chicken house. Just one or two birds, you know. Then we've just started to cultivate a piece of the pastureland beyond the ha-ha. We've got cabbages there, and a good area of potatoes and brussels sprouts. We're only growing the safer vegetables at present till we've gained experience. We shall dig up more of the pastureland in the autumn.'

They came to a concrete path which led between glass frames in the direction of the walled garden. Some figures came into view. A little distance away James Tayper Pace could be seen instructing Toby how to hoe between the rows of plants. A figure, probably Peter Topglass, was moving to and fro in one of the greenhouses.

'Hoeing is an unromantic activity,' said Mrs Mark with a certain satisfaction, 'but it's one's daily bread in a market-garden.'

Patchway approached them along the path, pushing a wheelbarrow. His hat looked as if it had not moved since last night.

'Still no rain I'm afraid,' said Mrs Mark to Patchway.

'Won't see no life in them leeks before the autumn if it don't rain buckets pretty soon,' said Patchway.

They stood aside to let him pass.

'He's going to lift some lettuces,' said Mrs Mark. 'Such a nice simple man. What you can see on the right is the back of the stable block, said to have been designed by Kent. Part of it was damaged by fire about fifty years ago, but as you see it's still very pretty. It figured a lot in old prints. We've made some of the loose boxes into garages, and some into packing sheds where we weigh and pack the vegetables to go to Pendelcote and Cirencester. I supervise that part of the work as well as all the indoor things and the catering. We believe that women should stick to the traditional tasks. No point in making a change just to make a change, is there? We'd be so glad if you ever felt like joining in any time. I expect you're handy with your needle?'

Dora, who was not, was feeling the sun extremely. The reflections of heat and light from the concrete path and the line of glass frames were giving her a headache. She put her hand to her head.

'Poor thing!' said Mrs Mark. 'I've walked you off your feet. We'll just take a quick look at the fruit garden and then I'm sure you should go inside and rest, and I must get on with my jobs.' She pushed open a heavy wooden gate in the wall and they came into the fruit garden.

The old stone walls, dry and crumbling with the long summer, covered over with brittle stonecrop and fading valerian, enclosed a large space crammed and tangled with fruit bushes. A wire cage covered an area in the far corner, and there was a glint of glass. A haze hung over the luxuriant scene, and it seemed hotter than ever within the garden. Disciplined fruit trees were spread-eagled along every wall, their leaves curling in the heat. Dora and Mrs Mark began to walk along one of the paths, the dried up spiky fingers of raspberry canes catching at their clothes.

'Why, there's Catherine,' said Mrs Mark. 'She's picking the apricots.'

They came towards her. A large string net of small mesh had been thrown over a section of the wall to protect the fruit from the birds. Behind the net Catherine was to be seen, almost lost in the foliage of the tree, dropping the golden fruit into a wide basket at her feet. She wore a floppy white sun hat under which her dark hair straggled in a long knot, hazy with wisps and tendrils, which hung down between her shoulder-blades. She was intent on her labour and did not see Dora and Mrs Mark until they had come very close. Her dark head, thrown back beneath the powdery glow of the hanging apricots, looked to Dora Spanish, and again beautiful. Her averted face, without the nervous self-protective look which it wore in company, seemed stronger, more dignified, and more sad. Dora felt that strange misgiving once more at the sight.

'Hello, Catherine!' said Mrs Mark loudly. 'I've brought Dora to see you.'

Catherine jumped and turned about, looking startled. What a jittery creature she is, Dora thought. She smiled and Catherine smiled back at her through the net.

'You must get terribly hot doing that,' said Dora.

Catherine wore an open-necked summer frock with pale washed-out flowers upon it. Her throat was burnt to a dark brown by the sun, but a sallowness in her face had seemed to resist the sunlight and gave her the pale look which Dora had remarked the night before. She pushed the hat back off her head as she spoke to Dora until it rested, held by its strings, upon the great bunch of hair on her shoulders, and she swept the ragged dark fringe back from her brow. She wiped a brown hand wet with perspiration upon her dress, while they exchanged a remark or two about the weather. Dora and Mrs Mark passed on.

'Catherine's so excited about going in, bless her heart,' said Mrs Mark. 'This is such a thrilling time for her.'

'Going in?' said Dora.

'Oh, you didn't know,' said Mrs Mark, as she led Dora back towards the gate. 'Catherine is going to be a nun. She is going to enter the Abbey in October.'

They went out of the gate. Dora turned to take one last look at the figure under the net. At the news which she had just heard she felt a horrified surprise, a curious sort of relief, and a more obscure pain, compounded perhaps of pity and of some terror, as if something within herself were menaced with destruction.

*

'It's time now please,' said the man behind the counter.

Dora jumped guiltily to her feet and returned her glass. She was the only remaining inhabitant of the darkly varnished bar parlour of the White Lion. She went out into the sunshine and heard the sad sound of the inn door being closed and bolted behind her. It was half past two.

After taking leave of Mrs Mark in the morning Dora had rested for about twenty minutes, and then had walked to the village by a footpath which Mrs Mark had indicated to her, to inquire at the station about the suitcase. The walk took longer than she expected, but when she arrived, sweating and exhausted, she was told that the case was due to be returned by a train which came through in about half an hour. Wandering out again into the village Dora was transported with delight to discover that the pubs were open. She patronized in turn the White Lion and the Volunteer, and sat dreaming in the dim light of the bars, enjoying that atmosphere of a quiet pub which was connected with her pleasanter memories of being in church. She went back to the station and found the train was late. Eventually it appeared and the suitcase was unloaded and given to Dora. Her first action was to retire with it to the Ladies' Cloakroom and change into a summer dress and sandals. Feeling much better, she emerged and was about to start out, laden with the suitcase, on the walk back which it had not occurred to Paul, or indeed to herself, to think of as likely to be peculiarly wearisome, when she happened to look at the time. It was a quarter past one. Dora then remembered that lunch at Imber was at twelve-thirty. It was then that she entered for the second time into the White Lion.

Ejected, she trailed off through the village and found the stile and the little footpath which led through two wheatfields and a wood to the main road. The wheat, tawny with ripeness, had been cut and stood in tented stooks about the fields, while a few ghostly poppies lingered at the edge of the path. Dora reached the road, walked a little way along it following the wall of the Imber domain, and went in through a small door. From here a path led diagonally across two of the streams that fed the lake to join the drive at the third bridge. This was a very beautiful part of the walk, and was mainly in the shade, and although very hungry now and somewhat confused at being so late, Dora felt momentarily quite delighted with the soft air and with the green arches of the wood as she reached the plank bridge over the first stream. She was cooled by the shade and her emptiness gave her a sense of energy.

The estate was thickly wooded here and the stream found its way along under a leafy cavern of elder and ash saplings beneath the higher roof of the trees. Grasses leaned into the stream and were spread out in long lines of vivid green, but it was clear in the centre, running over a bed of sand and pebbles. Dora stood for a moment, looking down into the trembling speckled water, and found herself thinking about Catherine. She pictured her attired as a bride, going through the great Abbey door in October, never to emerge again. Then it was in imagination as if she, Dora, were crossing the causeway, her eyes fixed steadily upon the opening door. She woke shivering from the vision, and descending quickly by the side of the bridge walked sandals and all into the bed of the stream. Thank God she was not Catherine.

She climbed scratched and dripping up the farther bank and continued her way. It was a few minutes later that two alarming thoughts struck her almost simultaneously. The first thought was that she must have lost her way, since she had reached the second stream, which was broader and overgrown with brambles, but found no bridge, and was now following a path going uphill parallel to the stream. The second thought was that she had left the suitcase behind in the White Lion. At this second thought Dora gave a wail of despair. It was bad enough to have missed lunch. This second imbecility would make Paul cross for days, even provided the suitcase had not meanwhile been stolen. She turned about, meaning to run back to the village and try to get it at once. But she felt so hot and so tired and so hungry, and it was such a long way and there were so many nettles suddenly all around and anyway she was lost. I am a perfect idiot, thought Dora.

At that moment she heard a rustling of leaves from further down the path, in the direction from which she had come, and a figure emerged from the wood, parting the tangled greenery in front of him. It was Michael Meade.

He seemed surprised to see Dora there and came towards her with a smiling questioning look.

'Oh, Mr Meade,' said Dora, 'I think I'm lost.' She felt shy at finding herself alone with the leader of the community.

'I saw the colour of your dress through the trees,' said Michael, 'and I couldn't think what it was. I thought at first it was one of Peter's rare birds! Yes, if you're making for the house, you've come up the wrong path. I was just visiting the watercress beds. We grow cress on a section of the other stream. It's out of season now, of course, but one has to keep it cleared out. It's pretty up here, isn't it?'

'Oh, lovely,' said Dora, and then to her dismay found that she was starting to cry. She felt a little faint from hunger and the intense heat, more breathless than ever under the canopy of the wood.

'You're feeling the heat, you know,' said Michael. 'Sit down here for a moment on this tree trunk. Put your head well forward, that's right. You'll feel better in a moment.' His hand touched her neck.

'It's not that,' said Dora. Finding she had no handkerchief she wiped her eyes with the hem of her dress, and then rubbed her face with the back of a muddy and perspiring hand. 'I went to fetch the suitcase, you know, the one I left on the train, and I got it, and now I've left it behind again in the White Lion!' Her voice ended in a wail.

Michael looked at her for a moment. Then he began to laugh too, rather ruefully.

'I'm so sorry,' said Michael, 'but it did sound comic, the way you said it! Cheer up, there's no tragedy. I have to go to the village this evening in the Land-Rover and I'll fetch it back then. It'll be quite safe at the White Lion. Did you have any lunch, by the way? We were wondering about you.'

'Well, no,' said Dora. 'I had a drink. But they hadn't got any sandwiches.'

'Let's go straight back to the house,' said Michael, 'and Mrs Mark will find you something to eat. Then you ought to lie down. You've given yourself a strenuous morning. We'll go this way, up the hill, and cross by the stepping stones. It's just as quick from here and rather cooler. Up you get and follow me. I won't go fast.'

He helped Dora to her feet. She smiled at him, pushed the damp hair back from her brow, feeling a little better now, and followed him as he set off along the path. She felt no more anxiety about the suitcase, as if everything had been made simple and settled by Michael's laughter. She was grateful to him for that. Last night he had seemed just a thin pale man, over-tired and inattentive. But today she saw him as a decisive and gentle person, and even his narrow face seemed browner and his hair more golden. With eyes so close together he would always look anxious, but how blue the eyes were after all.

So for a minute or two Dora followed Michael along the path, feeling calm again, looking at her guide's sunburnt and bony neck, revealed above the sagging collar of a rather dirty white shirt. Then she saw that he had stopped abruptly and was staring at something ahead. Without saying anything Dora came quietly up to him to see what it was that had made him stop. She looked over his shoulder.

There was a little clearing in the wood, and the stream had made itself a pool, with mossy rocks and close grass at the edge. In the centre it seemed deep and the water was a cool dark brown. Dora looked, and did not at first see anything except the circle of water and the moving chequers of the foliage behind, unevenly penetrated by the sun. Then she saw a pale figure standing quite still on the far side of the pool. It took her another moment, after the first shock of surprise, to see who it was. It was Toby, dressed in a sun hat and holding a long stick, which he had thrust into the water and with which he was stirring up the mud from the bottom. Dora saw at once, saw sooner than her recognition, that except for his sun hat

Toby was quite naked. His very pale and slim body was caressed by the sun and shadow as the willow tree under which he stood shifted slightly in the breeze. He bent over his stick, intent upon the water, not knowing he was observed, and looked in the moment like one to whom nakedness is customary, moving with a lanky bony slightly awkward grace. The sight of him filled Dora with an immediate tremor of delight, and a memory came back to her from her Italian journey, the young David of Donatello, casual, powerful, superbly naked, and charmingly immature.

If Dora had been alone she would have called out at once to Toby, so little was she embarrassed and so much amused and pleased by what she saw. But the proximity of Michael, which she had for a moment forgotten, made her pause, and turning to him she had a sense of embarrassment, not so much because of his presence as on his behalf, since he would perhaps imagine some embarrassment in her. Michael's face, as she now saw, was indeed troubled as he still looked upon the boy. Then he turned quietly about, and touching Dora's arm led her noiselessly back along the path by which they had come. Toby was not disturbed. All this seemed to Dora to show a foolish delicacy, but she followed, stepping softly.

When they had gone a little way Michael said, 'We gave him the afternoon off. I was wondering where he had got to. I thought we'd better leave him to have his swim in peace. We'll go back the other way.'

'Yes, of course,' said Dora. She looked boldly now at Michael, feeling a complicity between them because of the pastoral vision which they had enjoyed together. Michael seemed to her all at once to have become delightfully shy. She remembered the touch of his hand upon her neck. Their strange experience had created between them a tremulous beam of physical desire which had not been present before. The secret homage was tender and welcome to Dora, and as they descended the path together she smiled to herself over her theory, apprehending in her companion a new consciousness of herself as incarnate, a potentially desirable, potentially naked woman, very close beside him in the warmth of the afternoon.

CHAPTER 6

Michael Meade was awakened by a strange hollow booming sound which seemed to come from the direction of the lake. He lay rigid for a moment listening anxiously to the silence which had succeeded the sound, and then got out of bed and went to the open window. His room faced the Abbey. It was a bright moonlit night and he could see as he looked out, intent and nervous, the great expanse of the lake, and the Abbey wall opposite to him, clearly revealed in the blazing splendour of the moon which was well risen above the market-garden. Everything looked familiar and at the same time rather eerie. He looked further along, his eyes following the wall towards the place where it ended and the Abbey grounds stretched un-walled to the edge of the water, descending to a wide pebbly strand. Here to his surprise Michael saw with extreme clarity that a number of figures were gathered. Several nuns were standing close beside the lake. He could see their black shape-less habits swaying as they moved and the sharp outline of the blue shadows which the moon cast behind them, and by some trick of the light they seemed strangely near. They were leaning down now over something which they were drawing slowly out of the water. It was something large and heavy at which several of them were awkwardly grasping and pulling. He thought he could hear the thing grating upon the pebbles. Then he realized with a thrill of terror that the long limp object which they were pulling out onto the shore was a human body. They were taking a corpse out of the lake. Michael stood chilled and paralysed, not knowing what to do, and wondering what strange disaster it was of which he was witnessing the final scene. Who was the drowned person whose form lay now quite still upon the farther shore? The fantastic thought came to him suddenly that it was someone whom the nuns them-selves had murdered. The scene was so unutterably sinister and uncanny that a suffocating fear came upon him and he pulled desperately at the neck of his pyjamas while trying in vain to utter a cry of alarm.

He turned about and found himself still in bed. The early morning light filled the room. He sat up in bed, still wrenching at his throat, his heart pounding violently. He had been dreaming; but so powerful was the experience that he sat there dazed for a minute, not sure if he was really awake, still overwhelmed by the horror of what he had seen. It was that evil dream again. That was the third time now that he had dreamt more or less the same thing, the scene at night with the nuns pulling the drowned person out of the lake, and with it the conviction that it was their own victim that lay at their feet upon the strand. Each time the dream was accompanied by an overwhelming sense of evil; and each time too Michael had the strange impression that the booming sound which preceded the dream was not a dream sound, but a sound which sleeping he had really heard and which had stirred him towards waking.

His watch said twenty minutes to six. He got up now and crossed to the window, half expecting to see something odd. Everything was as usual, with the derelict and deserted look of the early morning. On the clipped grass near the house a number of blackbirds were running about, following the mysterious activities of newly risen birds. Nothing else stirred. The lake was bland and unbroken, brimming with the pale diffused light of the sun which was risen in a thick haze. It would be another hot day. Michael looked across to where the Abbey wall ended and the lake water lapped among bulrushes along the shore. There was no pebbled strand, and no figures to be seen. Michael wondered what his dream could signify and what it was in the depths of his mind which made him attribute something so terrible to those innocent and holy nuns. He had this thought with an intimation, not so much of the pressure of dark forces upon him, as of the reality within himself of some active and positive spring of evil. He shook his head and knelt down at the open window, still looking towards the scene of the dream, and began wordlessly to pray. His body relaxed. His prayer was no struggle, but the surrender of himself, with all the ill that he contained, to the Ground of his being. Gradually his serenity returned and with it a calm joy, the renewal of the certainty that there existed truly that living God in whom all pain is healed and all evil finally overcome.

It was too late now to go to bed again, so Michael sat down for a while with his Bible. Then he addressed himself to the problems of the day. He remembered with a little distress that it was Saturday, and the weekly Meeting of the community was to take place during the morning. This week there was a rather troublesome agenda. The Meeting was fairly informal and Michael himself usually prepared just beforehand a list of topics to be discussed; and members of the Meeting could then raise their own topics if they wished. He began now to jot down on a piece of paper: *mechanical cultivator, financial appeal, squirrels, etc., arrangements for bell.* His pencil paused as he mused over the list. He glanced at his watch. Still twenty minutes before it was time to go to Mass.

The Imber community in its present form had existed for just under a year. Its beginnings, in which Michael had played a crucial part, had been casual, and its future was uncertain. Imber Court itself had been for several generations the home of Michael's family, but Michael himself had never lived there, and the house, too expensive to keep up, had mostly been let, and during the war and for a few years after was used as offices by a Government department. Then it became empty and the question had arisen of its being sold. Michael, who had always been profoundly attracted by the place, avoided it for this reason. He hardly ever went there, and retained only a vague conception of the house and the estate. As a younger man he had intended to become a priest, but had failed to do so, and had spent a number of years as a schoolmaster. Although he had kept his sense of a religious vocation he had never until very recently made any visit to Imber Abbey; the taboo which rested for him upon the Court had included the Abbey also. It now seemed to him, looking back, as if this ground had been kept sacred, forbidden to him until the time when it should be the scene of decisive changes in his life. He visited the Court in the course of business, when the question of its sale was in the air, and, because it seemed proper, asked to pay his respects to the Abbess. The future destiny of the Court would naturally be of keen interest to the Abbey. Michael was also curious, and now that he was at last close by, very anxious to make the acquaintance of the Benedictine community of whose holiness he had heard so much.

His encounter with the Abbess changed his life and his plans completely. With an ease which at first surprised him and which later seemed part of an inevitable pattern, the Abbess imparted to Michael the idea of making the Court the home of a permanent lay community attached to the Abbey, a 'buffer state', as she put it, between the Abbey and the world, a reflection, a benevolent and useful parasite, an intermediary form of life. There were many people, she said, and Michael was but too ready to credit her since he felt himself to be one of them, who can live neither in the world nor out of it. They are a kind of sick people, whose desire for God makes them unsatisfactory citizens of an ordinary life, but whose strength or temperament fails them to surrender the world completely; and present-day society, with its hurried pace and its mechanical and technical structure, offers no home to those unhappy souls. Work, as it now is, the Abbess argued with a kind of realism which surprised Michael at the time, can rarely offer satisfaction to the half-contemplative. A few professions, such as teaching or nursing, remain such that they can readily be invested with a spiritual significance. But although it is possible, and indeed demanded of us, that all and any occupation be given a sacramental meaning, this is now for the majority of people almost intolerably difficult; and for some of such people, 'disturbed and hunted by God', as she put it, who cannot find a work which satisfies them in the ordinary world, a life half retired, and a work made simple and significant by its dedicated setting, is what is needed. Our duty, the Abbess said, is not necessarily to seek the highest regardless of the realities of our spiritual life as it in fact is, but to seek that place, that task, those people, which will make our spiritual life most constantly grow and flourish; and in this search, said the Abbess, we must make use of a divine cunning. 'As wise as serpents, as harmless as doves.'

Michael, who recognized spiritual authority when he saw it, listened eagerly to the Abbess, coming back day after day to the parlour to sit, his chair tilting forwards, his hands gripping the bars of the grille, to look upon that old pale face, ivory-coloured under the shadow of the white cowl, worn by long-forgotten sacrifices and illuminated by joys of which Michael had no conception. It was an aspect of Michael's belief in God, and one which although he knew it to be dangerous he could never altogether reject, that he expected the emergence in his life of patterns and signs. He had always felt himself to be a man with a definite destiny, a man waiting for a call. His disappointment concerning the priesthood had been the more intense. Now when the Abbess spoke to him in terms which, without any confession on his part, seemed so accurate a diagnosis of his own condition, he took her words immediately as a command. Michael knew the futility of his recent years, eaten by an *ennui* which he had tried to picture to himself as an insatiable thirst for the good. But now the pattern was at last emerging, the call had come.

Michael was made a little sad by the fact that once the plan had been decided on and the arrangements set in train the Abbess ceased to see him. She had never asked him about his past, and through all the excitement of the new project Michael had been waiting for the moment when he could give to her that full account, which he had never yet offered to another human being, of his so far unprofitable and disorderly life. He had reason to believe that the Abbess knew from other sources the salient facts. But it would have eased his heart to have told her everything himself. Yet out of some inscrutable wisdom the Abbess did not ask for the confession which he was so anxious to make, and after a while Michael wryly accepted his enforced silence as something to be offered quietly and as a sacrifice since it was the will of that remarkable lady who certainly knew his desire to tell as well as she doubtless knew all that he had to tell, and more. Since the community had actually been in existence Michael had seen the Abbess only three times, summoned on each occasion by her to discuss matters of policy. All other details which concerned the Abbey had been dealt with in discussion with Mother Clare, or through the intermediary offices of Sister Ursula.

The idea of the market-garden had arisen naturally enough. There was good land surrounding the Court, and the working of it would be the proper and primary activity of the inhabitants of the house. The garden could be begun on a small scale, and grow with the membership of the community. Other types of work could possibly be introduced later. At present it was impossible to foresee the pattern things would take, and undesirable to attempt to plan more than a little way ahead. The nucleus of the community had been Michael himself and Peter Topglass. Peter was an old friend of Michael's from College days, a naturalist, and a man of quiet and undemonstrative piety. Between two jobs he had come to give Michael a hand with his new undertaking. He had settled down at once, doing more than his share of the hard work, and introducing his paraphernalia of bird and animal study into the garden. To Michael's great pleasure he decided, for a while at least, to stay. The next arrivals were the Straffords, whose marriage had been on the point of breaking up. Sent along by the Abbess, they dug themselves in with determination. Catherine had come next and her brother later. Catherine had been for a long time an adherent of the Abbey, and more lately a prospective novice; and the Abbess had judged it profitable, both for the community and for the girl herself, that she should make her entrance to the Abbey by way of the Court. The arrival of Patchway had been unforeseen but as it turned out extremely fortunate. He was a local farm labourer who had appeared soon after Michael had installed himself, and announced that he was going to 'do the garden'. Michael was not sure at first whether Patchway was not under a misapprehension about Michael's return to the Court. Patchway's father, it appeared, had been a gardener at the Court as a boy, in former and far other days. However, undismayed and perhaps unsurprised by explanations, Patchway had determinedly stayed on, working like a carthorse and seeming to have at his disposal an invaluable pool of casual female labour from the village. He even made occasional appearances at Mass. Mother Clare had laughed over Michael's account of him and declared that he was perhaps in the true sense of the word a 'godsend', and must be allowed to stay. The latest and most important acquisition to the community was James Tayper Pace.

James was the younger son of an old military family. His higher education took place upon the hunting field, and he subsequently became known as an accomplished yachtsman, and served with distinction in the Guards during the war. He had had from childhood a strong and simple Anglican faith. The custom whereby in certain families religious faith survived as part of the life of a country gentleman, deeply connected with all the rituals of existence, was for James no empty form. It was fruitful of a deep and unquestioning spiritual life which led him at a more mature age, without any sudden crisis or any emotional rejection of his earlier pursuits, to devote himself more wholeheartedly to the call of religion. He began to train as a missionary, but various encounters and further experience led him to decide that his task lay at home. He went to live in the East End of London where he eventually ran a highly successful settlement and a number of boys' clubs. This excellent venture came to an end when he had a serious breakdown in health owing to overwork. His doctor advised him, and his bishop urged him, to find occupation in the country, preferably in the open air; and it was shortly after this that the Abbess, whose information service had brought her news of James's situation, beckoned him to Imber.

Michael took an immediate and strong liking to James. Indeed some ingenuity would have been required to dislike him, he was a character of such transparent gentleness. Michael was also, and more uneasily, aware in himself of a certain clannish affinity with James, something nostalgic, crystallizing at a moral level distinctly below that at which he aimed at present to live, and tending to exclude the others. His converse with James was easy and laconic, and Michael did his best not to find it pleasing for the wrong reasons. James himself was however touched by no such atavistic memories and his simple and open behaviour soon disposed of Michael's problem. The arrival of James also raised for Michael, as none of the previous arrivals had done, the question of leadership at Imber. When James had come the community immediately took shape as a corporate body. Previously it had been a collection of individuals over whom Michael naturally exercised such authority as was necessary in virtue of his peculiar situation and his priority upon the scene. Michael at once recognized in James a man who was in almost all relevant qualities his superior, and he would have been very happy to be second to such a first. James however was surprisingly supported by the Abbess in a refusal, which his plea of ill-health made conclusive, to allow Michael to retire from his position of unofficial leader; and Michael, with some uneasiness, accepted his role.

Those who hope, by retiring from the world, to earn a holiday from human frailty, in themselves and others, are usually disappointed. Michael had not particularly cherished these hopes; yet he was sorry to find himself so immediately placed in the position of one who by force of personality holds a difficult team together. Michael had always held the view that the good man is without power. He held to this view passionately although at times he scarcely knew what it meant, and could connect it with his daily actions only tenuously or not at all. It was in this sense that he understood, when he understood it, his call to the priesthood. For a creature such as himself the service of God must mean a loss of personality such as could perhaps come about through the named office of a servant or the surrender of will in an unquestioning obedience. Yet these ideals were still for him, while strongly beckoning, remote and hard to interpret. He was aware that, paradoxically, one of the most good people that he knew was also one of the most powerful: the Abbess. He lacked still the insight which would show him in what way exactly her exercise of power differed from his own. He felt himself compelled to remain in a region where power was evil, and where he could not honourably find the means to strip himself of it completely. His lot was rather the struggle from within, the day-to-day attempt to be impersonal and just, the continual mistakes and examinations of conscience. Perhaps this was after all his road; it was certainly *a* road. But he was irked by a sense of the incomplete and ill-defined nature of his role. Thoughts of the priesthood returned to him more and more frequently.

Not that the Imber community, as it so far existed in embryo, was exceptionally problematic. On the surface it was peaceful and reasonably efficient. Yet there were certain stresses of which Michael was continually conscious, he hoped without irritation. James and Margaret Strafford worked too hard, Mark Strafford not hard enough. The tension between Mark and his wife, though muted, remained. Mark Strafford was sarcastic, nervous, and inclined to make much of difficulties. Michael, who did not agree with Kant that feelings of affection cannot be demanded of us as a duty, did his best to like Mark, so far without conspicuous success. The bearded and ostentatiously virile appearance of his colleague was a constant annoyance. James Tayper Pace, without meaning to be so, was inevitably a second centre of authority, and Michael noticed a tendency in both the Straffords to take their orders from James, without consulting him. James, who believed that authority should melt in brotherly love, as would have been the case in a community composed of persons like himself, was careless of such matters. This led to some confusion. Peter Topglass did not improve things by being blindly, and sometimes aggressively, loyal to Michael. There was a faint appearance of two parties.

Michael, who thought that James was often obtuse about the subtler questions of organization, was aware too of serious moral differences between them which had so far scarcely made themselves evident. James was a man of more confident faith and more orthodox and rigid moral conceptions. Michael was not sure how far these things were in him, or ought anywhere to be, connected; but he suspected that James, who was no fool and could judge as well as love those who surrounded him, saw his leader as a man with 'ideals but no principles'. The presence in the community of Catherine, with her highly strung spirituality and her imminent departure, was an inspiration to all; yet it was also undoubtedly a centre of obscure emotional tension, and Michael hoped that he was entirely charitable in his wish to see her soon and securely stowed 'inside'. Then there was the, for him especially, appalling problem of her twin brother.

Michael was called from his meditations by the bell for Mass. After breakfast he repaired as usual to the estate office to cast an eye over the day's correspondence. He enjoyed this part of the morning, during which he could see, as it were, the wheels of his small enterprise turning, and take the numerous minor policy decisions which kept the market-garden from day to day a going concern. Although for other and perhaps higher reasons he had wished to give place to James, he was glad to find himself, in the more purely business side of his work, remarkably efficient. He planned the expanding project delicately, lovingly, like a military operation, and was surprised to discover in himself, after his undistinguished career as a schoolmaster, such a talent for this kind of work. Meticulous timing, careful disposition of labour, quick changes of plan were necessary if the garden with its small and largely unskilled personnel were to yield its best; and Michael found himself experiencing again the curious satisfaction which planning of this kind had given him during his service as a soldier during the war. As a platoon commander, and later a company commander, in a battalion of the local county regiment, he had been conscientious and even, to his surprise, enthusiastic and moderately successful. To his great regret he was never sent overseas. The *métier* of soldiering, with its absolute requirements and its ideals of exactness and devotion had caught his imagination, and when on training exercises he had taken an almost boyish delight in dispatching his men to comfortable beds in the nearest village while he remained by some darkening roadside, to pore over the map with his flashlight and spend the night with his sleeping bag and greatcoat underneath the lorry.

By the time Michael had read the correspondence, made some telephone calls to clients in Pendelcote, and had a word with Mark Strafford who acted in the estate office as his secretary and accountant, it was nearly ten o'clock, the hour of the weekly Meeting. Michael had had no further time to reflect upon the agenda, and sought rather guiltily in his pocket for the scrap of paper on which he had written the items. He wondered who would be present on this occasion. Michael had always taken the view that the Meeting was a regrettable necessity, should be brief and businesslike and attended only by full members of the community. James however had maintained that the Meeting should be an open gathering attended by any guests who happened to be present at the Court and who wished to see the brotherhood in action. Michael had declared that he had no taste, even in so would-be charitable an atmosphere, for washing dirty linen in public. James had replied that the community was not likely to have any dirty linen, and if perchance it had it *ought* to wash it in public. James, it sometimes seemed to Michael, believed that truthfulness consisted in telling everybody everything, whether it concerned them or not, and regardless of whether they wanted to know. This position had however a certain moral force about it. Michael, finding a majority against him, did not care to argue his own more complex views, and gave way. The somewhat tiresome compromise was adopted that visitors, of whom so far there had been very few, were told they might attend, without being given any clear guidance as to whether they would be welcome.

As he left the estate office Michael wondered if Paul Greenfield and his wife would take it into their heads to come along. One or two of the topics for discussion were delicate ones, and he rather hoped to be left in the privacy of his brothers to discuss them. Michael quite liked Paul Greenfield. He was a year or two younger than Michael, who had known him slightly at Cambridge, where he had found Paul's blend of aestheticism and snobbery thoroughly distasteful; and when a strange chance had brought Paul to Imber on the track of the manuscripts Michael had been far from pleased and had wished his old acquaintance could have chosen some less crucial moment for his visit. However, he found Paul much improved or himself less puritanical; possibly both. Paul, who had perhaps had a similar pleasant surprise, showed some tendency to unburden himself to Michael about his matrimonial troubles. But Michael had been too busy for more than the occasional *tête-à-*

tête and had gained only a confused impression of the situation. He had been genuinely delighted at the unexpected announcement of Mrs Greenfield's imminent arrival; and had been astonished, unprepared as he was by Paul's descriptions to which he had paid little attention, at her appearance. He could not yet see, though he found himself interested to know, how Paul could have got himself married to so apparently unlikely a lady.

As Michael entered the common-room he was relieved to hear Margaret Strafford telling Peter that Paul and Dora had gone out for a walk. She had, she said, advised them about a route which should not prove too tiring for Mrs Greenfield. Why, she wondered, had that young woman not brought a single pair of sound shoes with her? Those pretty sandals would be worn out in a few days.

Michael sank into the armchair by the fireplace which was by custom the chairman's position, and took a quick look round as the rest of the community were settling themselves down. There was no sign of Nick. Michael hoped every week that he might come, but he never did. Everyone else was now present. Michael saw young Toby sidling through the door and looking about shyly for a seat. He smiled at the boy and pointed him out a chair. He felt he could have done without Toby's presence; and yet, he thought, as he looked at the boy's face, taut and round-eyed with a sort of warm eagerness, half-smiling as he looked about at his companions, where could be the harm or embarrassment of having such a witness. Perhaps after all there was something in James's theory that privacy has a tendency to corrupt. He saw the boy curl himself into his chair, tucking his long legs under him. He noted his grace.

'All present, I think, with the usual exception,' said James briskly.

The community was disposed in a half circle facing Michael, with James well in the front. The Straffords were beside him. Peter and Patchway made the second row, with Toby. Catherine was on the window-seat, sitting sideways to look out, her thin cotton skirt pulled well down towards her ankles and her hands clasped about her knees. Sister Ursula, who always attended the meetings as a liaison officer, sat by the door, her stoutly clad feet protruding squarely from the habit, her lively and critical eyes fixed upon Michael. He smiled at them all, feeling suddenly at ease and pleased with his crew.

'I've made the usual little list,' he said. Proceedings were quite informal. 'Let me see, what shall we take first.'

'Something nice and easy,' said James.

'There isn't anything easy this week,' said Michael. 'And I'm afraid there are one or two old favourites. For instance, the mechanical cultivator question.'

There was a general groan.

Peter said, 'I think we hardly need to have the discussion again. We all know what everyone thinks. I suggest we just put it to the vote.'

'I'm against voting as a general rule,' said Michael, 'but we may just have to here. Would anyone like to say anything before we vote?'

Michael had for some time been in favour of buying a mechanical cultivator, an all-purpose machine with a small engine which could be used for superficial digging, and also, with various appliances attached, for hoeing, mowing, and spraying. The purchase of this machine, which was light and easily operated even by an unskilled worker, seemed to him an obvious next step in the development of the market-garden. He had been amazed to find himself opposed by James and the Straffords on a curious point of principle. They had maintained that the community, having set themselves apart from the world to follow Adam's trade of digging and delving, should equip themselves only with tools of minimal simplicity and should compensate by honest and dedicated effort for what they had chosen to lack in mechanization. Michael regarded this view as an absurd piece of romanticism, and said so. After all, they were engaged in a particular piece of work and should do it, to God's glory, as well as the frutiful discoveries of the age would allow. He was answered that they had all of them withdrawn from the world to live a life which was, by ordinary standards, not a 'natural' one in any case. They had to determine their own conception of the 'natural'. They were not a profit-making concern, so why should efficiency be their first aim? It was the quality of the work which mattered, not its results. As there was something symbolic, and indeed sacramental, in their withdrawal from the world, so their methods of work should share that quality. Honest spades were to be permitted. Even a plough. But none of these new-fangled labour-saving devices. 'Good heavens!' Michael had exclaimed, 'we shall be weaving our own clothes next!' – and had thereby mortally offended Margaret Strafford whose cherished plan for a craft centre at Imber did in fact include weaving. It was certainly a question with wide implications.

Michael thought that the argument came particularly ill from Mark Strafford, who always discovered urgent work in the office whenever some hard digging was to be done; but he recognized it as a strong one, having more than a merely romantic appeal. They had set themselves outside the bounds of ordinary convention, but without adopting any clear traditional mode of life. They had to invent their own norms. Michael felt sure that his own view was the right one; to be eclectic to this extent about methods of work was a sort of idiotic aestheticism. Yet he found it hard to argue the point clearly, and was distressed to find how emotional he soon became about it. Everyone else seemed ready to become emotional too, and by now the excitement had gone on long enough. In driving the matter to a vote instead of quietly dropping it Michael knew that he was trying to impose his own conception of how the community should develop. It seemed important to him to outlaw nonsense of this kind from the start; but he found his role in doing so a distasteful one.

A silence followed Michael's invitation to speak. It was a subject on which the interested parties had already said rather too much. James shook his head and looked down, indicating that he would make no more speeches.

Patchway said in a tone which was half statement and half question, 'That don't make no difference about the plough.' Patchway had been one of those who looked askance at the cultivator, but for different reasons. He regarded it as an amateur's toy.

'No, of course not,' said Michael. 'This thing won't replace the plough. We'll need that anyway for the heavy work, such as ploughing up that bit of pasture in the autumn.' They had a standing arrangement to borrow a plough from a nearby farmer.

More silence followed, and Michael called for the vote. For the cultiva‧ ‧ were Michael, Peter, Catherine, Patchway and Sister Ursula. Against it, James and Mark. Margaret Strafford abstained.

Trying not to sound pleased, Michael said 'I think that's a sufficient majority to act on. May I be empowered to go and buy the cultivator?' A murmur empowered him. Michael felt there was something to be said for being a leader after all.

Margaret Strafford spoke in a high nervous voice. She was timid of speaking, even in such an informal gathering, 'I don't suppose this is the moment to raise the question about the pottery. But I'd just like to ask people to keep it in mind. I'll raise it again later on.' Margaret was anxious that, even if mechanization should triumph on the agricultural front, at least the Simple Life should be available in other forms.

Michael said 'Thank you, Margaret. You understand that this arts and crafts problem will have to wait until we have more people here and have our finances on a sounder footing. But we certainly won't forget it. And that conveniently raises my next item, which is the financial appeal. Perhaps you could take this one, Mark?'

'I think everyone knows about this item too,' said Mark. 'The point is, we need capital. We've lived so far from hand to mouth, and depended long enough on the generosity of one or two individuals. It seems perfectly reasonable and proper, to get ourselves well started, to make an appeal for funds to a limited circle of persons whom we know to be interested. The only questions are the exact wording of the thing, the list of clients, or should I say victims, and the time-table.'

'Bell!' said James.

'Yes,' said Mark. 'There'd be no harm done if we could

synchronize the appeal with the arrival of the new bell, and got a little innocent publicity.'

'I suggest we appoint a sub-committee to deal with the details,' said Michael. A sub-committee was appointed consisting of Mark, James, and Michael.

'Might I raise the subject of the bell now?' said James. 'It seems to come up. As you know, dear friends, the Abbey has existed since its second foundation without a bell. Now at last, *Deo gratias*, it is to have one. The bell is cast, and should be delivered sometime later this month, in fact in about a couple of weeks from now. The Abbess has expressed the wish, dear Sister Ursula will correct me if I'm wrong, that the whole business be conducted quietly and without undue ceremony. However, since we have this privileged role of camp followers to the Abbey, I think a little merry-making on our behalf would be proper to celebrate the entry of the bell into the Abbey. And as I hinted just now, the tiniest bit of publicity might be welcome for other and more worldly reasons!'

'I'm nervous of publicity,' said Michael. 'This community could so easily be made to look absurd in the press. I suggest we take the Abbess very literally. What do you think, Sister Ursula?'

'I think a *little* merry-making might be in order,' said Sister Ursula, smiling at James. 'The Bishop is coming, you know, and he won't want too Lenten a scene.'

'Gilbert White says,' said Peter, 'that when they had a new ring of bells at Selborne the treble bell was up-ended on the village green and filled with punch and they were all drunk for days!'

'I don't think we can quite emulate Selborne,' said James, 'but then neither need we emulate the old man of Thermopylae who never did anything properly. We could organize a small festival and see to it that we got the sort of publicity we wanted. I gather the Bishop wants to revive the old ceremony of christening the bell. This could take place with just ourselves present on the evening of his arrival, and then we could have a little procession with some of the village people on the following day. The village seems quite excited about the whole business. As I think most of you know, the Abbess has the poetic idea that the bell should enter the Abbey early in the morning through the great gate as if it were a postulant.' He looked at Catherine.

'All right,' said Michael. 'Another committee please. Perhaps a definite plan could be submitted to us next week. And, of course, Father Bob must be consulted about the music.'

'He's got some ideas already,' said James. 'He says he's game for anything except "Lift it gently to the steeple"!'

A sub-committee to deal with the bell was appointed, consisting of James, Margaret Strafford, Catherine, and Sister Ursula. Father Bob was to be co-opted.

Michael looked at his notes. *Squirrels etc.* His heart sank and he was half tempted to leave this item over. He spoke up quickly. 'The next thing, and I think we can't put off discussing it any longer, is this question about shooting squirrels and pigeons.'

Everyone looked glum and avoided each other's eyes. This problem had arisen early and was still unsolved. Soon after arriving at Imber, James Tayper Pace had produced his shotgun and made regular sorties to shoot pigeons, crows, and squirrels in the vicinity. He regarded this both as a normal country pursuit and as a proper part of any farmer's duty; and it could not be denied that the pigeons especially were a menace to the crops. Encouraged by his example, Patchway also took to prowling the estate with a gun and proved singularly adept at slaughtering hares, some of which, it was suspected, went to adorn tables in the village. When Nick Fawley arrived, bringing a .22 rifle with him, he joined in the game, this being indeed the only service which he appeared to perform with any enthusiasm for the community.

Michael, who had had his first unpleasant shock on seeing James armed with a gun, had at last felt that the practice must be put an end to. Again, he felt surprisingly distressed and not able to put his arguments very clearly. It seemed to him improper that a community of this sort should kill animals. Three of its members, Catherine and the Straffords, were vegetarians on religious grounds, and it seemed, to say the least, in bad taste to confront them continually with the spectacle of slaughtered creatures. Michael knew that Catherine especially was thoroughly upset about it, and he found her once in tears over a dead squirrel. She had in any case an extreme horror of firearms. As time went on Michael began to feel far from democratic, and had at last forbidden gunfire upon the estate pending a full discussion. He realized that he was open to a charge of inconsistency. He advocated mechanization because it was natural in that it increased efficiency, but he opposed shooting as improper, although it too increased efficiency. But in this case he was even more sure of being in the right.

James said, 'My view is this. We can't afford to be sentimental. Animals that do serious damage ought to be shot. What we shoot and when and how might need discussing. But after all, as Michael observed a little while ago, we're seriously in business as market-gardeners.' This was as near as James ever came to making a sharp point. He gave Michael a gentle deprecating look as he spoke, to soften the sharpness.

Patchway said, 'A wood pigeon eats its own weight every day.'

Peter Topglass said, 'I think the question is not one of efficiency. We're agreed about that. The fact is that the shooting gives grave offence to some among us.'

Mark Strafford, turning round, said, 'If it's the feelings of the animals that are to be considered one might point out that much more distress is caused to a bird by trapping it and ringing it than by shooting it.' This was a piece of gratuitous polemic, since Strafford was in fact against the shooting too.

Michael, now thoroughly annoyed, said, 'It's the feelings of the human beings we want to consider.'

'I don't see why one side should monopolize the appeal to feeling,' said Mark. 'James and I had very strong feelings about your cultivator.'

There was a disapproving silence. James said 'Come, come,' to dissociate himself from the remark.

Michael was now too angry to trust himself to continue. He said 'Perhaps after all we had better postpone this question again. James has given us his view. Mine is that since a number of people here believe on religious grounds that animal life should be respected we ought, since we profess to be a religious community, to allow this view to prevail, as against a mere consideration of efficiency, even if certain other members don't hold it. I might add that I also hold the view that members of the community ought not to possess firearms at all, and if I had my way I'd confiscate the lot!'

'Hear, hear!' said Catherine in a clear voice, speaking for the first time.

After a silence during which Michael had time to appreciate Catherine's contribution and to regret his use of the word 'confiscate', James said 'Well, well, you may even be right. I for one would like to think the matter over again. Perhaps we could discuss it in a week or two. And meanwhile no shooting.'

'Any other business?' said Michael. He felt tired now and not pleased with himself. He had been catching the eye of young Toby during the last outburst. He wondered what the boy was thinking of them all. How unwise of James to want outsiders at these meetings.

'I would like to remind everybody about the Bach record recital on Friday evening,' said Margaret Strafford. 'I did put up a notice, but I'm afraid people don't always remember to look at the board.'

With various other trivial admonitions the Meeting broke up. James came up to Michael and began to say placatory things. He was obviously regretting his little piece of controversy. Michael felt emotionally exhausted. He patted James on the shoulder, doing his best to reassure him. He could see from the corner of his eye Peter Topglass lying in wait for him. Peter would certainly have been upset by Mark Strafford's attack on his bird-ringing. He was sensitive to this particular charge. Michael, wishing to be alone, excused himself from James, had a word with Peter, and walked out onto the balcony.

The good weather was holding. How very large and peaceful the scene was outside. Michael rested his eyes upon it with relief. The sky was a steady blue, washing paler towards the horizon, and a line of small rotund clouds was stretched above the trees which secluded the Abbey from view. The lake was a brilliant yet gentle colour of which it was hard to say whether it was a light blue or an extremely luminous grey. A slight warm breeze took the edge off the heat. To the left along the drive Paul and Dora Greenfield could be seen returning from their walk, Dora's red dress conspicuous and bright against the grass. They waved. Margaret Strafford, who had been standing down on the gravel with her husband, turned away to go and meet them. Mark Strafford, without looking up, walked slowly the other way towards the estate office. Then suddenly from behind Michael young Toby erupted from the common-room and went past him and down the two flights of steps in three leaps. He set off straight ahead at a run towards the ferry and then slowed to a quick loping walk. He was probably too shy to dally.

Michael walked down the steps. He wanted to avoid the Greenfields who had now stopped and were talking to Mrs Strafford. He began to follow Toby along the path to the ferry. The boy skipped along with an irregular gait, sometimes taking a long jump, his arms swinging wildly. He was wearing his dark grey flannels and an open-necked shirt. His shirt sleeves, escaping from their tight roll, flopped gaily about his wrists. He seemed to Michael a graceful thoughtless animal, without self-knowledge, without sin. Michael quickened his step a little, hoping to come up with Toby before he reached the ferry; but the boy had a long start and had already jumped into the boat and punted violently off before Michael had covered half the distance to the lake. Michael slowed down to a more meditative step, not wishing Toby to think he was anxious to speak with him, for in fact he was not, and had followed the boy half instinctively. Toby, turned now to face the house, waggling the oar vigorously at the back to propel the boat, waved to Michael. Michael waved back and came down to stand on the little wooden landing-stage. The trailing painter of the ferry-boat moved gently in the water at Michael's feet, drooping from its iron ring. The boat itself came abruptly to land on the other side and Toby leapt out; his departing kick sent the boat bobbing away upon the ripples. Michael lifted the painter and began idly to pull it towards him.

A figure emerged from among the trees opposite and was coming to meet Toby across the open grass. Even at that distance there was no mistaking Nick Fawley. He walked with a characteristic stride of rather aimless determination, his dark head thrust well forward. Michael saw that he was carrying his rifle. The dog Murphy followed him from the shade of the trees and ran ahead towards Toby. The boy bent down to greet the dog, who pranced about him, and then walked on to greet its master.

As Nick came up to Toby he turned and saw Michael watching them from the other side. It was too far for speech, and even a shout would have been indistinct. Nick's face was a distant blur. For a moment Michael and Nick looked at each other across the water. Then Nick raised his hand in a slow salute, solemn or ironical. Michael released the painter and began to wave back. But Nick had already turned and was leading Toby away. The boat came lazily to a standstill in the middle of the lake.

CHAPTER 7

Michael had known Nick Fawley for a long time. Their acquaintance was a curious one, the details of which were not known to the other members of the Imber community. Michael did not share James's view that *suppressio veri* was equivalent to *suggestio falsi*. He had first encountered Nick about fourteen years ago, when Nick was a schoolboy of fourteen, and Michael a young schoolmaster of twenty-five, hoping to be ordained a priest. Michael Meade at twenty-five had already known for some while that he was what the world calls perverted. He had been seduced at his public school at the age of fourteen and had had while still at school two homosexual love affairs which remained among the most intense experiences of his life. On more mature reflection he took the conventional view of these aberrations and when he came up to the University he sought every opportunity to encounter members of the other sex. But he found himself unmoved by women; and in his second year as a student he began to fall more naturally into the company of those with inclinations similar to his own. What was customary in his circle soon seemed to him once again permissible.

During this time Michael remained, as he had been since his confirmation, a somewhat emotional and irregular member of the Anglican church. It scarcely occurred to him that his religion could establish any quarrel with his sexual habits. Indeed, in some curious way the emotion which fed both arose deeply from the same source, and some vague awareness of this kept him from a more minute reflection. Toward the end of his student days, however, when the conception of perhaps becoming a priest took shape with more reality in his mind, Michael awoke to the inconsistencies of his position. He had been an occasional communicant. It now seemed to him fantastic that he could, in the circumstances, have come to approach the communion table. He did not, for the moment, alter the mode of his friendships, but he ceased to receive the sacrament and went through a time of considerable distress, during which he continued rather hopelessly to do what he now felt the most dreadful guilt for doing. Even the attraction which his religion exercised upon him, his very love for his God, seemed to be corrupted at the source. After a while, however, and with the help of a priest to whom he had confided his difficulties, more robust counsels prevailed. He gave up the practice of what he had come to regard as his vice, and returned to the practice of his religion.

The change, once he had made up his mind, was attended by surprisingly transitory pains. He emerged from Cambridge chastened and, as it seemed to him, cured. Equally far away now were the days of his indifference and the days of his guilt. His love affairs appeared as the *étourderies* of a much younger man. Michael set his face towards life, knowing that his tastes would almost undoubtedly remain with him, but certain too that he would never again, in any way which could conflict with his now much stricter sense of morality, gratify them. He had passed through a spiritual crisis and emerged triumphant. Now when he knelt to pray he found himself devoid of the guilt and fear which had previously choked him to silence and made of his prayers mere incoherent moments of emotion. He saw himself with a more rational and a more quiet eye: confident of a Love which lay deeper than the contortions of his egoistic and unenlightened guilt, and which worked patiently to set him free. He looked to the future.

After he left Cambridge he spent a year abroad, teaching in a school in Switzerland, and then came back to a post as Sixth Form Master at a public school. He enjoyed the work and was moderately good at it, but after another year had passed he was firmly decided that he wished to be ordained. He consulted various persons, including the Bishop in whose diocese he found himself, and it was agreed that he should complete another year's teaching, while studying some theology in his spare time, and then enter a seminary. Michael was overjoyed.

The presence in the school of Nick Fawley was something of

which Michael had been acutely aware from his first arrival. Nick, then fourteen, was a child of considerable beauty. He was a clever, impertinent boy, who was a centre of loves and hates among his fellows: a trouble-maker and something of a star. His very dark curling hair, which if it had been allowed to grow would have been hyacinthine, was carefully cut to fringe his long face with affectedly waif-like tendrils. His nose tilted very slightly upward. He was pale, with striking dark grey eyes, with long lashes and heavy eyelids, which he kept narrowed, either to increase their apparent length or his own apparent shrewdness, both of which were already considerable. His well-shaped mouth was usually twisted into a mocking grin or pursed in a menacing expression of toughness. He was a master of the art of grimacing and in every way treated his face as a mask, alarming, amusing, or seductive. He put on a sardonic expression in class and hung his long hands ostentatiously over the edge of his desk. The masters doted on him. Michael, while not blind to his qualities, thought him essentially silly. That was the first year.

In the second year Michael saw, owing to the accidents of the time-table, a good deal more of Nick. He became aware too that the boy was directing towards him a more than usual intensity of interest. Nick would sit now in class staring at Michael with an appearance of fascination so bold and unconcealed as to be almost provocative. Yet when questioned he seemed always to be following the lesson. Michael was irritated by what he took to be an impertinent joke. Later on, the boy changed his behaviour, looked down, seemed confused, was less ready with his answers. His expression seemed to have become more sincere, and with that far more attractive. Michael, by now interested, surmised that what Nick had previously feigned for the amusement of his fellows he now perhaps genuinely felt. He was sorry for the boy, thought him now more modest and generally improved, saw him once or twice alone.

Michael was perfectly aware that Nick's charms were beginning to move him in a way which was more than casual. He knew himself to be susceptible without for a second feeling himself in danger, so confident and happy did he feel in his plans for the future. The fact, too, that he had never before felt attracted in this way by a person so much younger than himself contributed to make him regard his affection for Nick as something rather special but in no way menacing. He felt neither guilt nor distress at the pleasure with which he was now filled by the proximity of this young creature, and when he discovered in himself even physical symptoms of his inclination he did not take fright, but continued cheerfully and serenely to see Nick whenever the ordinary run of his duties suggested it, congratulating himself upon the newly achieved solidity and rational calm of his spiritual life. At prayer the boy's name came naturally, with others, to his lips, and he felt a painful joy at the contemplation in himself of such a store of goodwill which asked for itself no ordinary reward.

It chanced that Michael's bedroom, which was also his study, was in a part of the school buildings which was mainly offices and deserted after five o'clock. The door which Michael used opened at the back on to a paddock, now overgrown with small trees and bushes. In this room he kept his books, and boys sometimes came to see him, to continue a discussion or consult a reference. Once or twice after a lesson Nick accompanied him thither, arguing a point or asking a question, and set foot within the door before hurrying off to his next task. He had lately achieved the less restricted status of a senior boy and when free from lessons wandered about at will. It was an evening early in the autumn term, shortly before seven, when Michael working alone in his room heard a knock at his door and opened it to find Nick. It was the first time that the boy had appeared uninvited. He asked to borrow a book and disappeared at once, but it seemed to Michael, looking back, that they had both found it hard to conceal their emotion, and that they had both from that moment known what was bound to happen. Nick came again, this time after supper. He brought the book back, and they talked of it for ten minutes. He borrowed another. It became a custom that he would drop in sometimes in the interval between supper and bed. The gas fire purred in Michael's small room. Outside were the darkening October evenings. The twilight lingered, the lamp was switched on.

Michael knew what he was doing. He knew that he was playing with fire. Yet it still seemed to him that he would escape unscathed. The whole thing was still, in appearance, innocent, and had a sort of temporary character about it which seemed to reduce its dangers. Until half term, until the end of term. Next term the time-table would be different, Michael might have to move his room. Every meeting was a sort of good-bye; and in any case nothing happened. The boy dropped in, they talked of casual matters, they discussed his work. He read assiduously the books which Michael lent him and obviously profited from the conversations. He never stayed very long.

One evening after Nick had come Michael let the twilight linger and darken in the room. Their talk went on as the light faded, and without seeming to notice they talked on into the dark. So strong was the spell that Michael dared not reach his hand out to the lamp. He was sitting in his low armchair and the boy was sprawled on the floor at his feet. Nick, who had stayed longer than usual, stretched and yawned and said he must be off. He sat up and began to make some observation about an argument which they had had in class. As he spoke he laid his hand upon Michael's knee. Michael made no move. He answered the boy who in a moment withdrew his hand, rose and took his leave.

After he had gone Michael sat quite still for a long time in the dark. He knew in that moment that he was lost: the touch of Nick's hand had given to him a joy so intense, he would have wished to say so pure, if the word had not here rung a little strangely. It was an experience such that remembering it, even many years later, he could tremble and feel, in spite of everything, that absolute joy again. Sitting now in his room, his eyes closed, his body limp, he understood that it was not in his nature to resist the lure of a delight so exquisite. What he would do or in what way it would be wrong he did not permit himself to reflect. A mist of emotion, which he did not attempt

103

to dispel, hid from him the decision which he was taking: which indeed it seemed to him he had taken by letting Nick, without comment or withdrawal, lay his hand upon him. He knew that he was lost, and in making the discovery knew that he had in fact been lost for a long time. By a dialectic well known to those who habitually succumb to temptation he passed in a second from the time when it was too early to struggle to the time when it was too late to struggle.

Nick came the next day. Both of them, meanwhile, had been busy in imagination. They were far on. Michael did not rise from his chair. Nick knelt down before him. They stared steadily at each other, unsmiling. Then Nick gave him both his hands. Michael held them tightly, almost violently, for a moment, drawing the boy closer to him as he did so. He was rigid with the effort to prevent himself from trembling. Nick was pale, solemn, his eyes riveted upon Michael, radiant with the desire to beseech and to dominate. Michael released him and leaned back. It was as if a long time had passed. Nick relaxed upon the floor, and a smile which he could not control broke upon his face. The mask was gone now, burnt away by the forces within. Michael smiled too, curiously at peace, as if at some great achievement. Then they began to talk.

The talk of lovers who have just declared their love is one of life's most sweet delights. Each vies with the other in humility, in amazement at being so valued. The past is searched for the first signs and each one is in haste to declare all that he is so that no part of his being escapes the hallowing touch. Michael and Nick talked so, and Michael was continually amazed at the intelligence and delicacy of the boy who throughout contrived to hold the initiative, while at the same time wringing from his status as Michael's pupil and disciple all the sweetness which in this changed situation such a relationship could hold. They spoke of their ambitions, their disappointments, their homes, their childhood. Nick told Michael of his twin sister whom he loved, he swore, with a Byronic passion. Michael told Nick about his parents who had died long ago, his morose father, his clever, fashionable mother, about his life at Cambridge, and with a frankness and suspension of scruple which later amazed him, about his hopes, very distant as he now put it, of the priesthood.

In a week they seemed to live an eternity of passion, although as yet they did nothing but hold hands and exchange the gentlest of caresses. This was a time for Michael of complete and thoughtless happiness. He was strangely set at ease by the knowledge that the term was drawing to its close. This wonderful thing could not last; and so he had no thought of bringing it to an end, and lived in a timeless moment of delight. He would have liked to have taken Nick into his bed; but did not do so, partly from confused scruples and partly because their relationship was for the present so perfect, and indeed the notion that there was so much still reserved was a part of its perfection. Michael did give a sidelong and reluctant attention during this time to the deeper implications of what he was doing. He ceased going to communion. He felt, strangely, no guilt, only a hard determination to hold to the beloved object, and to hold to it before God, accepting the cost whatever it might be, and in the end, somehow, justifying his love. The idea of rejecting or surrendering it did not come to his mind.

He began, hazily, to reflect on how he had formerly felt that his religion and his passions sprang from the same source, and how this had seemed to infect his religion with corruption. It now seemed to him that he could turn the argument about; why should his passions not rather be purified by this proximity? He could not believe that there was anything inherently evil in the great love which he bore to Nick: this love was something so strong, so radiant, it came from so deep it seemed of the very nature of goodness itself. Vaguely Michael had visions of himself as the boy's spiritual guardian, his passion slowly transformed into a lofty and more selfless attachment. He would watch Nick grow to manhood, cherishing his every step, ever present, yet with a self-effacement which would be the highest expression of love. Nick, who was his lover, would become his son; and indeed already, with a tact and imagination which removed from their relationship any suggestion of crudeness, the boy was playing both parts. When he had reflected a little Michael felt even better, as if these bold reflections had done something to restore his innocence. He let his thoughts return again, very cautiously, to his vision of himself as a priest. After all, it would be possible. Everything would turn out for the best. During this time he prayed constantly and felt, through the very contradictions of his existence, that his faith was increased. With a completeness which he had never known before he was happy.

How the idyll would have ended if it had been left to Michael to control he was never privileged to know. The matter was abruptly taken out of his hands. In three weeks his relationship with Nick had grown with a miraculous speed, like a tree in a fairy story, and it seemed to him that developments which in an ordinary love might take years were enjoyed by them in a space of days. Perhaps it was just this that was fatal. Michael never knew. He felt that he had known Nick all his life. Perhaps Nick felt this too and had, as after half a century of knowledge, tired of him. Or perhaps the too great intensity of their love had in some way soured him. Or perhaps there was a deeper explanation, more creditable to the boy. This was one thing they were never fated to discuss.

Towards the end of the term an evangelist came to the school. He was a non-conformist preacher who was taking part in a religious revival campaign sponsored by all the churches, and in connexion with which members of various creeds had already spoken to the boys. He was an emotional man, an excellent speaker. Michael sat through two of his tirades, not listening, thinking of Nick's embraces. Nick evidently had been having other thoughts. On the second day he did not come to see Michael at the time appointed. He went instead to the Headmaster and told him the whole story.

When Nick did not come Michael became worried. He waited a long time, and then left a note and set out looking for the boy. Some premonitory fear had made him, by this time, almost frantic. It was while still on this search that he was summoned urgently to see the Head. He did not see Nick *tête à tête* again. The betrayal, which it was immediately evident had taken place, of something to him so utterly pure and sacred was so appalling that it was not until later that Michael troubled to think of the matter in terms of his own ruin. It was some time afterwards too that, remembering things which the Headmaster had said, it occurred to him that Nick had not given a truthful picture of what had taken place. The boy had contrived to give the impression that much more had happened than had in fact happened, and also seemed to have hinted that it was Michael who had led him unwillingly into an adventure which he did not understand and from which he had throughout been anxious to escape. The picture as the Head saw it, and as Nick seemed to have offered it, was simply of a rather disgraceful seduction.

The term was nearly at an end. Without open scandal Michael took his immediate departure from the school. A carefully worded letter from the Headmaster to his Bishop destroyed completely his hopes of ordination. He went to London and took a temporary job at a University crammer's establishment. He now had plenty of time for reflection. Whereas success and happiness had kept guilt at bay, ruin and grief brought it, almost automatically, with them; and Michael reflected that after all the idea of the matter which the Headmaster had received was not an unjust one. He had been guilty of that worst of offences, corrupting the young: an offence so grievous that Christ Himself had said that it were better for a man to have a millstone hanged about his neck and be drowned in the depth of the sea. Michael was not then concerned to share his guilt with Nick: he was anxious to take all there was, and if there had been more he would have taken that too.

Much later still, when he could at last view the scene, from a distance of many years, more calmly, he did wonder what Nick's motive had been in confessing at all, and in confessing in this misleading way. He concluded that the boy had been sincerely led to confess by religious scruples, together with some perhaps half unconscious resentment against Michael: and that he had told it as he had partly because of his resentment but partly and more explicitly so as to make things seem the very worst since they were already so unpardonably bad. This Michael knew to be a natural instinct in those who confess and he imagined that Nick had turned their love into a dreary tale of seduction without any deliberate malice against himself. But he could never be sure.

The years went by. Michael took a job in the education department of the London County Council. Then restlessly he went back to schoolmastering. Without great difficulty, though sometimes plagued by his inclinations, he avoided amorous adventures. After the emotions and despairs into which the episode had cast him had subsided – and they took long to do so – he began soberly to seek again for what had eluded him, his right place in life, the task for which God had made him. Very distantly the old hopes of becoming a priest dawned again on his horizon, but he would avert his attention from them. At times it seemed to him that the catastrophe which destroyed his first attempt had been designed to humble him; his real chance was still to come. He worked quietly but without satisfaction at various teaching jobs. Then came the call to Imber, the encounter with the Abbess, and the exciting sense of a new life and of the deep and destined pattern emerging at last.

It was very shortly after his first visit to Imber, when the plan for the community was in a vague preliminary stage, that Michael entered a room of some friends of the Abbess in London and was confronted by the head of Nick set upon the body of Catherine. The encounter was so utterly unexpected, the resemblance so close and striking, that Michael had been speechless and had had to sit down and feign a momentary sickness. He had lost sight of Nick completely during the years that followed their severance, though without seeking it he had heard occasional news of him: that he had read mathematics at Oxford, and though thought to be brilliant had missed getting his first, that he had taken a post in aero-dynamic research, but had left this very soon after, when he inherited some money, and bought a share in a syndicate at Lloyds. He was to be seen in the City a good deal, so Michael heard from his few business acquaintances, in the company of the more raffish type of stockbroker. He was mentioned now and then in gossip columns in connexion with women. It was assumed he had taken to drink. Michael had once heard it said, as a vague rumour, that he was homosexual.

Michael had received this information with interest and asked for no more. He packed it away in a part of his mind where he still held and cherished the boy he had known, and commended continually to the Love which comprehends and transforms, the old passion whose intensity had made him think it so pure. But this was at a deep level, where Michael's thoughts were hardly explicit. More superficially he developed, as the years went by, a quiet resentment against Nick for having so efficiently spoilt his life – and thought soberly that though he might be a bit to blame he was certainly not wholly to blame if Nick had gone to the bad. The boy was clearly unbalanced and irresponsible, as had been quite evident to Michael before he fell in love with him. He did not wish to minimize his own guilt, but he knew that at a certain point further reflection on it became mere self-indulgence. He regarded the chapter as closed.

He was overwhelmed by the meeting with Catherine. He did not need to be told that the handsome young lady with the grey eyes and the abundant dark hair whose long hand, in a moment, he limply held, was Miss Fawley. He wondered at once what she knew of him, whether she saw him, with hostility, and a little contempt, as an obscure schoolmaster who had been dismissed for seducing her brother. Contempt in fact it was hard to read into those gentle and evasive eyes, but Michael rapidly decided that if Nick's relation to his sister had been as close as he declared, and somehow those declarations had seemed truthful, he would have given her some, probably fairly accurate, version of what had occurred. She might not remember his name. But a certain confusion and too deliberate kindliness during the first meeting made Michael sure that she knew very well who he was.

It might be thought that since Nature by addition had defeated him of Nick, at least by subtraction it was now offering him Catherine: but this did not occur to Michael except abstractly and as something someone else might have felt. He knew from his first meeting with Catherine that she was destined to be a nun. But it was in any case remarkable how little she seemed to attract him. He liked her, and found appealing a certain pleading sweetness in her manner, but the great pale brow and sleepy eyes, cast now in the unmistakable feminine mould, moved his passions not a whit. It was indeed strange that God could have made two creatures so patently from the same substance and yet in making them so alike made them so different. Catherine's head in repose exactly resembled Nick's, though a little smaller and finer. But her expressions, her smile, gave to the same form a very different animation; and when she inclined her chin towards her bosom, for Catherine was much given to looking modestly down, Michael felt that he was the victim of some appalling conjuring trick. He found her, as he found all women, unattractive and a trifle obscene, and the more so for so cunningly reminding him of Nick.

The people who were introducing them, and who obviously knew of no previous connexion, were busy explaining, with a little help from Catherine, how Catherine was eventually to go into the Abbey and how she hoped she might spend some time with the projected community before she went in. This was an idea of the Abbess's, who had said she would write to Michael, who should by now have had the letter. Michael said he had been divided from his correspondence by a country visit: the Abbess's letter was probably waiting at his flat. He was sure that such a plan would work splendidly; and for him in any case the wish of the Abbess was law. Miss Fawley got up to go. As Michael watched her standing by the door making her good-byes, her long slim umbrella tapping the floor, her grey coat and skirt desperately well cut and inconspicuous, her abundant hyacinth hair held in a firm bun under a small and undeniably smart hat, he wondered at her, and at the strange destiny which had made their paths cross, and which he did not for a second doubt would sooner or later re-unite him with Nick.

This happened in fact even sooner than he had expected. He found the Abbess's letter at his flat: she commended Catherine to him, spoke of her as a 'specially favoured child', a person, potentially, of great spiritual gifts. She hoped he would accept her as a temporary member of the new community. Something in the tone of the letter made Michael feel that the Abbess must know about Nick. Catherine would almost certainly have told her. He could not imagine that that pallid and gentle being, confronted with a personality like that of the Abbess, could have held anything back. In any case, confession ran in the family.

Catherine duly appeared at Imber in the earliest days of the community, when only Michael and Peter and the Straffords were living in the great empty house. Quietly, indeed during the first weeks hardly opening her mouth, she busied herself with the innumerable tasks which confronted the little group. She worked till she was ready to drop and Michael had to restrain her. Seeing her in the country, she seemed changed. There was no appearance of smartness now. She wore old and rather shapeless clothes and her curling purple-dark hair was carelessly knotted or else tumbling down her back. She seemed consumed by a wish to efface herself, to make herself very small and unheeded, while being as busy and ubiquitous as possible. She seemed to Michael at this time a rather strange young person, unbalanced perhaps and given to excess, though as in the case of her brother he soon forgot that he had ever thought this about her. He liked her increasingly and respected her efforts, allowing himself sometimes to look at her, searching for another face, and finding now and then her cool eyes resting upon him.

Patchway arrived, James arrived. The community began very tentatively to take shape. The garden was dug, the first seeds ceremonially planted. Then Catherine spoke to Michael of her brother. She made no reference then or later to the past, except by implicitly assuming that Michael and Nick knew each other. She was seriously worried, she said, about her brother. It seemed that Nick had been living a life of dissipation – Catherine gave no details – from which although he hated it, he lacked the strength to withdraw. He was very unhappy and had threatened suicide. It was necessary that something drastic, something imaginative, be done for him. Catherine thought it possible that if he were asked to come to Imber he would come. Some work could surely be found for him. If he stayed even for a little time it would be to the good, if only from the point of view of his health; and who knows, with prayer, and with the proximity of that great storehouse of spiritual energy across the lake, one might hope perhaps for more than that. So Catherine pleaded, speaking as one that fears a refusal, her face pale and solemn with the force of her wish, resembling her brother.

Michael was extremely dismayed by her request. He had, since he first met her, held it vaguely in his mind, and not without a certain melancholy pleasure, that now some day he would see Nick again: briefly perhaps, in some house in London, as he imagined it. They would give an embarrassed smile and then not meet again for years. But to have the boy here – he still thought of Nick as a boy – here at Imber, at so sacred a place and time, entered in no way into Michael's plans or wishes. He had been very busy, very excited, with his developing project. He had even at times almost forgotten who Catherine was: which was partly perhaps a success on her side. Her proposal struck him as untimely and thoroughly tiresome, and his first reaction to it was almost cynical. In a case like he imagined Nick's to be the proximity of storehouses of spiritual force was just as likely to provoke some new outrage as to effect a cure. Spiritual power was indeed like electricity in that it was thoroughly dangerous. It could perform miracles of good: it could also bring about destruction. Michael feared that Nick at Imber would make trouble for others and win no good for himself. Also he simply did not want Nick at Imber.

However he said none of this to Catherine, but indicated that he would think the matter over and consult the Abbess and the rest of the community. Catherine then said that she had already talked the whole matter over with the Abbess who was thoroughly in favour of the plan. Michael was surprised at this, and ran straight away across to the Abbey: but this turned out to be a time when the great lady for reasons of her own would not grant him an audience. She said if he wrote to her she would answer the letter. By now distracted, Michael wrote several letters which he tore up, and finally sent a brief note which assumed that the Abbess knew the relevant facts and asked her for a judgement. She replied with a sort of feminine vagueness that almost drove Michael into a frenzy that she was in favour of the plan on the whole, but that since he knew, and must know, far more than she did about how it was all likely to work out she must leave the final choice to his wisdom, in which she had, she said, a perfect confidence. Michael stormed about the house and finally called on James. To James, who was never curious or suspicious and who always seemed to believe that he was being told the whole truth, he vaguely indicated that he had known young Fawley as a boy but had lost sight of him since. He described what he knew of his character and career. What did James think?

With a vehemence which did Michael's heart good James said he thought the idea perfectly silly. They had no room, at present, for a passenger of that sort. No one would have time to play nursemaid to him. Perhaps they could give poor old Catherine some help in lodging her deplorable brother (of whom James said he'd heard one or two nasty rumours) in some other place where he'd be out of harm's way; but, heaven preserve us, not here! James was a little shaken to hear that the Abbess was, with qualifications, in favour of the plan, but he appealed to Michael to hold out soberly against her. After all, *he* knew the exact situation of the community and she, as she admitted, did not. It was a mark of James's more robust and unemotional faith that he was not one of those who regarded the Abbess's word as necessarily being law. Michael promised he would hold out and went to bed feeling much better. He dreamt of Nick.

The next day everything seemed different. As soon as Michael awoke he knew with absolute certainty that he could not go to Catherine and tell her that he would not receive her brother. Supposing in a month or a year Nick were to do something really outrageous, suppose he got himself into serious trouble (no unlikely result, according to the details which Michael confidently filled in to Catherine's picture), suppose he killed himself – how would Michael feel then? He could not deny this suppliant, and most especially because of the past. He prayed long and passionately about the matter. He became the more convinced: and with the dawning of a strange joy he apprehended in the way things had gone a certain pattern of good. Nick had been brought back to him, surely by no accident. He did not dare to imagine that he was himself to be the instrument of the boy's salvation; but he thought it possible that he might be destined, in some humble way, to stand by, as one who has a small part in some great ceremony, while this was indeed achieved. He was after all, where Nick was concerned, to have a second chance. He could not be meant to reject it. The thing chimed in so exactly with Catherine's departure from the world. A being of such purity, as he now in exalted mood saw her, might indeed effect the salvation of her brother, and in some way his own as well, and miraculously the redemption of the past.

This highly coloured frame of mind did not last long; yet the essence of the hope and vision which it had brought him remained with Michael and he was now as firmly determined to have Nick as before he had been not to have him. Rather disingenuously pleading the authority of the Abbess he soon brought the others round, although James remained sceptical. Catherine was asked to write to her brother. Michael could not bring himself to do so. She immediately received a reply to say that he would come.

It was a morning early in August that trembling at the knees Michael had gone down to the station to meet Nick Fawley. He had parted from a boy; he was to meet a man. Yet, as happens at such times, the interval was in imagination annihilated, and what chiefly worked in Michael's mind as he drove to the station was his last glimpse of Nick, it seemed yesterday, white as a sheet at school prayers, avoiding his eye. Catherine, who had visited London the previous weekend to see her brother, had tactfully indicated that she was, that morning, unavoidably busy. No one else was much interested in Nick at the moment; the market-garden, producing its first summer crop, was far too absorbing. So Michael, amazed that his agitation had apparently escaped notice, slipped away and stood, far too early, nervously smoothing down his collar, upon the station platform. He had by an effort prevented himself from looking in the mirror in the waiting-room. He reflected with surprise that it was many years since he had had so sharp a consciousness of his external appearance.

By the time the train arrived Michael could hardly stand up. He saw several ladies get off, and then saw a man at the far end of the plaform carrying a rifle and a shot-gun and accompanied by a dog. It was Nick all right. He seemed far away yet very clear, like a figure in a dream. Michael set his feet in motion to walk towards him. He had temporarily forgotten about the dog, though Catherine had warned him, and he felt an immediate irritation as at the presence of a third. Nick, not sustaining his glance as he approached, was leaning down to fuss with the animal. He straightened up as Michael came close to him, a nervous smile breaking involuntarily upon both their faces. Michael had wondered if he would be able not to embrace him. But it was quite easy. They shook hands, babbling trivial remarks, although they could not conceal their emotion. The dog provided a useful diversion. Michael took Nick's large suitcase from him, which Nick in a dazed way surrendered, keeping the firearms slung over his shoulder. They walked out to the car. Michael drove back to Imber in a state resembling drunkenness. He was unable later to recall the journey with any clarity. The conversation was not so much difficult as mad. They talked constantly but completely at random, sometimes both starting up a sentence at the same time. Michael made imbecile remarks about dogs. Nick asked banal questions about the countryside. On two occasions he asked the same question twice. The car swept onto the gravel in front of the house.

Catherine was waiting. The brother and sister greeted each other in a muted and deliberately casual way. Margaret Strafford bustled up. Nick was taken inside. Michael went back to his office. Once alone he put his head down upon the desk and found himself shuddering: he did not know whether he was glad or sorry. Nick had seemed at first dreadfully changed. His face, once so pale, was now reddish and fatter; his hair was receding over the tall brow and grew untidily down his neck, curling vigorously, but looking greasy rather than glossy. The heavy eyelids had thickened in layers, the eyes were vaguer, less full of power. He was a handsome man, but heavy, florid, almost coarse.

Michael quickly pulled himself together and turned back to his work. The encounter had been, on the whole, less upsetting than he had expected; and he was rather relieved than otherwise to find Nick now so devoid of the taut pallid charm which he had possessed as a boy and which dreamily survived in his sister. Michael had already resolved to see as little as possible of Nick during his sojourn at Imber; he did not feel, now that the first shock was over, that this would be difficult. Nick was, at his own urgent request, given a room outside the main house. Michael did not like leaving him there alone, but it was not immediately easy to find him a companion. Catherine had not proposed herself, Patchway had refused, the Straffords were impossible as there was only a small room available, an egotistical delicacy prevented Michael from asking Peter (who knew nothing of the story), and James had taken an instant dislike to the newcomer. So it was that until the arrival of Toby Gashe three weeks later Nick was by himself in the Lodge.

In so far as Michael had had serious hopes that any individual other than Catherine might be of any genuine help to Nick at Imber he had thought that James Tayper Pace was the man. He was disappointed in James's reaction. James showed himself, where Nick was concerned, stiffly conventional. 'He looks to me like a pansy,' he said to Michael, soon after Nick's arrival. 'I didn't like to say so before, but I had heard it about him in London. They're always troublemakers, believe me. I've seen plenty of that type. There's something destructive in them, a sort of grudge against society. Give a dog a bad name, and all that, but we may as well be prepared! Who'd believe that thing was twin to dear Catherine?'

Michael demurring a little, wondered what James would think if he knew a bit more about his interlocutor, and marvelled once again at this curious naïvety in one who had, after all, seen plenty of the world. James was certainly no connoisseur in evil; a result perhaps of a considerable pureness of heart. Could one recognize refinements of good if one did not recognize refinements of evil, Michael asked himself. He concluded provisionally that what was required of one was to *be* good, a task which usually presented a singularly simple though steep face, and not to recognize its refinements. There he left the matter, having no time for philosophical speculation.

As the days went by Nick's presence, somehow, began to seem to Michael less remarkable. Nick was given the nominal post of engineer, and did in fact occasionally attend to the cars and cast an eye over the electricity plant and the water pump. He seemed to know a lot about engines of all kinds. But most of the time he just mooched about, accompanied by Murphy, and until asked to stop, shot down with remarkable accuracy crows, pigeons, and squirrels, whose corpses he left lying where they fell. Michael watched him from afar, but felt no urge to see more of him. Half guiltily he began to see Nick a little through the eyes of James and Mark Strafford; and once in conversation he found himself calling him a 'poor fish'. Nick on his side seemed passive, almost comatose at times. Once or twice, when opportunity offered, he seemed to want to talk to Michael, but Michael did not encourage him and nothing came of these half explicit gestures. Michael felt curious about Nick's relations with his sister, but this curiosity remained unsatisfied. They seemed to meet infrequently, and Catherine continued her work, seemingly unobsessed by the proximity of her eccentric brother. As for the lines of force from the power house across the water, in which Catherine had had so much faith, they were apparently impinging without effect upon the thicker hide of her twin.

Michael did not altogether give up hope that Imber might work some miracle. But he could not help seeing, after a while with some sadness, and some relief, that Nick was neither inspired nor dangerous but simply bored; and it was hard to see how he could escape boredom on a scene in which he chose to participate so little. Michael, who was exceedingly busy with other things, did not at present see how he could be further 'drawn in', while, congratulating himself on his good sense, he avoided *tête-à-têtes* with his former friend. Nick lingered on, looking a little healthier, a little browner, a little thinner.

Doubtless he was drinking less, though his seclusion in the Lodge, chosen perhaps with just that in mind, made it difficult to know. Michael guessed that he would hang around, taking Imber as a cheap rest cure, until Catherine had gone into the Abbey. Then he would return to London and carry on as before. It looked as if the strange tale would have, after all, a rather dull and undistinguished ending.

CHAPTER 8

It was Saturday evening, the same day as the Meeting recorded above, and the afternoon heat had lingered on, becoming thicker and hazier and seemingly undiminished. The sky was cloudless now, rising to a peak of intense blue that was almost audible. Everyone trailed about quietly perspiring and complaining of being stifled.

Work was supposed to end, subject to the more urgent seasonal requirements of the garden, at five o'clock on Saturday, and Sunday was supposed to be kept as a day of rest. In fact, work usually encroached on these times; but there was, from Saturday evening onward, a sense of deliberate *détente*, a somewhat self-conscious effort at diversion, which Michael found tedious. He managed unobtrusively to busy himself in the office, and indeed the time was badly needed to catch up on the paper work of the previous week; but he was forced to some extent to support the fiction of being on holiday. The Straffords were particularly keen on this idea, and Michael suspected that they thought the time should be devoted to getting on with one's hobbies. Michael had no hobbies. He found he was not able to divert himself; even books were unattractive to him now, though he kept steadily to a modest programme of devotional reading. He was restless to be, officially, back at work.

It was also that this leisure period was too full, sometimes, of disturbing thoughts. He worried now about Nick, imagining various plans for his welfare, and tormented occasionally by a desire, which he rejected as a temptation, to go and have a long talk with him alone. No good would come of that for either of them. Michael prided himself on having lost at least certain illusions; and he felt, from this austerity, an increase of spiritual strength. He resolved, however, to speak to Catherine seriously about her brother. He had surely been right to wait, before making more solemn efforts, to see if Nick would be able to find for himself a place in the picture. He was reluctant to appear, in the eyes of his former friend, either as censor or as benefactor, or indeed to appear as officiously concerned with him at all. He was also reluctant to broach any serious or intimate matter with Catherine, who seemed surrounded at this time by an electrical field of emotion and anxiety. But things had drifted for long enough.

Michael, when he had leisure to reflect, was disturbed too by the thought, which was both distressing and delightful, that he must soon begin to explore again the possibility of ordination. He had a strong sense of the due time having elapsed. His premature approach had been, rightly and fruitfully for himself, rejected; and he could not resist a conviction of being deeply held in God's purposes for him, which although to chasten him had been for a time obscured, now were again become clear and demanding. He had digested and re-digested his old experiences, and he thought that he had reached a sober enough estimate of himself. He felt now no excessive or blinding sense of guilt about his propensities, and he had proved over a long time that they could be held well and even easily under control. He was what he was; and he still felt that he could make a priest.

On this day, however, no such solemn thoughts were in his mind and for some reason, after the agitation caused by the Meeting had died down, which it did surprisingly quickly, he felt almost light-hearted and quite glad to be at leisure. After high tea on Saturday it had become the custom for some of the little band to accompany Peter Topglass on his evening visit to his traps. Peter trapped birds at various places on the estate for purposes of study and in order to ring them. There was always some excitement in coming to the traps and finding what was there. Michael gladly accompanied his friend, and the women, Catherine and Margaret, usually came too. Once Nick came, brought along by Catherine, but had very little to say and seemed vague and rather bored.

On this occasion Catherine and the Straffords were pledged to sing madrigals with James and Father Bob Joyce. Father Bob, who sang a fine bass, was a serious musician and often swore that when he had time he would take the singing of the community in hand. He had hopes of plain song chant. The Abbey used plain song and had achieved quite a high standard. To Michael's relief, he had so far not had time. James sang in somewhat tremulous tenor which Michael teased him by terming 'Neapolitan'. Mark Strafford provided a more solid baritone, Catherine a thin but very pure soprano, and Margaret an energetic and adequate contralto. The singing group was already established on the balcony, fanning themselves with white sheets of music, when Peter and Michael were ready to set out. Toby, who had heard about the traps and had already inspected them on his own account, was eager to come, and Paul and Dora had asked to come too. Toby said that Nick Fawley had gone into the village. So after exchanging some badinage with the musicians they straggled down the steps and began to make for the ferry.

Dora Greenfield was wearing a spectacular dress of dark West Indian cotton and carrying a white paper parasol, which she must have purchased in the village, and, for some reason, a large Spanish basket. She wore the sandals deplored by Margaret Strafford. At Mark's suggestion, she had drenched herself in oil of citronella to keep off the midges, and the heavy sweetish perfume gave to her person an allure both crude and exotic. Michael watched her, as they ambled along, with irritation. He had seen her, similarly attired and accoutred, in the market-garden that afternoon, and her presence had seemed to make their labours into some absurd pastoral frolic. There was something a little touching all the same about her naïve vitality. Her arms touched by the sun were now a glowing gold and she tossed her heavy tongues of hair like a pony. Michael saw dimly how Paul might be in love with her. Paul himself was in a restless excited state and fluttered about his wife, unable to keep his eyes and his hands off her. She teased him with a slightly impatient tolerance.

They reached the ferry, and began to crowd into the boat which, much weighed down, would just accommodate them all. Helped by Paul, Dora settled herself in the bows with a little scream, and as she arranged her skirt admitted to the general amazement that she could not swim. Lazily Michael propelled the heavy boat very slowly through the water, which was warm and seemingly oily with summer idleness. Dora trailed her hand. As they neared the other side Toby exclaimed and pointed. Something was to be seen swimming in the water near the boat. It turned out to be Murphy. Everyone looked, tilting the vessel dangerously to one side. There was something strangely exciting in the spectacle of the dog, his dry furry face kept well above the surface in the rather anxious attitude of a swimming animal, his eyes bright and attentive, his paws beating as it seemed wildly in the water.

'Is he all right, do you think?' asked Dora, worried.

'Oh, he's all right,' said Toby with authority. He seemed, Michael noticed, to regard himself by now as part owner of Murphy and able to answer for his peculiarities and well-being. 'He often swims in the lake, he likes it. Hey, Murphy! Good boy!'

The dog gave them a quick sidelong glance and returned to his paddling. He reached the land before them, shook himself vigorously, and ran away in the direction of the Lodge. Everyone seemed curiously elated at having seen him.

Disembarked, they began to trail along to the right across the grass and into the woodland that lay between the lake and the main road and which was bordered at the far end by the high Abbey wall as it curved back at right angles from the waterside. Dora, partly as it seemed to tease Paul, began to monopolize Peter Topglass, and was asking him questions about the birds. She was astonished at the variety of creatures which could be seen on even the most casual stroll about the estate. She felt the slightly scandalized surprise of the true town-dweller that all these beasts should be here, displaying themselves, quite free, and getting on with their own lives perfectly unmindful of human patronage and protection. She had been much upset that morning, on the little walk with Paul, to see a magpie flying off from the lake with a frog in its beak.

'Do you think the frog knew what was happening? Do you think animals suffer as we do?'

'Who can say?' said Peter. 'But for myself I believe with Shakespeare that "the poor beetle that we tread upon in corporal sufferance feels a pang as great as when a giant dies".'

'Why can't the animals all be good to each other and live at peace?' said Dora, twirling the parasol.

'Why can't human beings?' said Michael to Toby, who was walking beside him.

The other three were drawing ahead. Peter swung along light-heartedly, the sun glinting on his spectacles, his field-glasses and camera bumping on his back, setting now a more vigorous pace. His bald spot was shining, burnt to a glowing red. Looking at him affectionately Michael marvelled at his detachment, his absorption in his beloved studies, his absence of competitive vanity. He lacked that dimension of the spirit which made James formidable as well as endearing; but he was a person who, like Chaucer's gentle knight, was remarkable for harming no one.

They had now entered the wood. Dora kept step with Peter, and the two of them occupied the narrow path, while Paul, who insisted on holding onto Dora's arm, had to stumble along in the undergrowth, falling over brambles and tufts of grass.

Toby, now quite at his ease, and obviously very happy, kept up a desultory chatter, stopping every now and then and dropping behind to inspect wild flowers, investigate fugitive rustlings, or peer into mysterious bolt-holes in the earth. Michael paced along evenly, feeling pleasantly older and protective and unusually cheerful. He wondered if anything would come of his having lodged Toby with Nick. The idea had seemed to Michael when he first had it, which was before he had met Toby, a brilliant conjecture. Toby was in fact the only person available; and Nick had been alone quite long enough. But apart from that, Michael had felt that the presence of a younger person might constitute a sort of challenge to Nick, might stir him into some sort of participation. At worst Toby could keep an eye on the black sheep, and perhaps his proximity would reduce the drinking which Michael had no doubt went on. It had to be admitted that James had been right; the present organization at Imber simply had no place for a sick man such as Nick. It was no one's business to look after him. For himself, Michael felt that reminiscing with Nick was a self-indulgence he ought definitely to avoid. He recalled the way the Abbess had declined to hear the story of his life. No, he would have to rely here on Toby and Catherine. It did not seriously enter his head that Nick might do Toby any harm. Michael could not now see Nick, as James so dramatically saw him, as a destructive force. The designation 'poor fish' was after all nearer to being the truth. Nick's vague dejected appearance, his watery eye, his comatose behaviour were not those of a tiger waiting to spring. Moreover, although not in any way warmed by the atmosphere of Imber, he had shown a due respect for the place, and Michael could not imagine that he would dare seriously to misbehave or to upset the boy by any grossness of speech or conduct. Nick was by now far too subdued for any such outbreak.

Since making the acquaintance of Toby, Michael had reviewed his thoughts on this subject. The fact was that Toby was exceptionally attractive. He watched him now as he bounded about near the path, running up to Michael and away again like an exuberant dog. His long limbs had still the sprawling awkwardness of youth, but there was something neat and clean in his whole demeanour which took away any suggestion of untidiness. Michael noticed the freshness of the pale blue open shirt which he was wearing; and reflected ruefully upon the filthiness of his own. He guessed that as an undergraduate the boy would be something of a dandy. Above the firm and now darker flesh of his neck the dark brown hair ended in a clear furry line, and similarly fringed his brow, carefully cut, and showing the finely rounded head. His cheeks and lips bulged ruddy with health. His eyes retained the shy searching look of a boy; he had not yet become the confident or self-assertive young man. He seemed electrical with unused energy and hope. Michael reflected how much less complex an entity he seemed at eighteen than Nick had seemed at fifteen. All the same, it must be admitted that he was charming. Michael's mind reproduced with a vividness amounting to violence the image of the pale body of the boy naked beside the pool. How startling and in a way how utterly delightful that had been. At the time Michael had been upset to find how greatly the sudden vision had moved him. Now more gently he put the image aside. Perhaps he ought to insist on both Toby and Nick coming to live in the house; it was difficult to find a pretext for moving Toby alone. But somehow the idea of having Nick so near to him was not acceptable. He dismissed the problem for the moment and returned to his enjoyment of the evening.

A further scandal had arisen in the group ahead, to whose conversation Michael had been vaguely listening. Peter had been asking Dora whether she was going to paint any landscapes while she was at Imber: a question which she seemed to find surprising. It had evidently not occurred to her, or to Paul, Michael noted, that she might do any painting. After a few more exchanges about country life and the observation of nature it emerged that Dora had never heard the cuckoo. Peter found this almost inconceivable. 'Surely, in the country, as a child?' He seemed to imagine that all children naturally lived in the country.

'I was never in the country as a child,' said Dora, laughing. 'We always took our holidays at Bognor Regis. I can't remember much about my childhood actually, but I'm sure I never heard the cuckoo. I've heard cuckoo clocks, of course.'

Toby and Michael came up with them as, still disputing, they approached the grassy clearing where the traps were laid. Peter hushed them to silence. They came cautiously up to where the path opened out, and Peter went forward to survey his catch. He had laid three old-fashioned sparrow-traps, dome-shaped wire structures about three feet long and eighteen inches high, which stood upon the grass. Each trap was divided into two compartments. One end wall of the trap sloped gradually inward to a small opening fringed by projecting wires which led into the first compartment at ground level. A similar opening, wide at the near end and narrow at the far end, led a little above ground level into the second compartment, on the other side of which, in the farther wall of the trap, there was a small door to admit the trapper's hand. It appeared at once that there were several small birds in each trap. There was a good deal of fluttering as Peter approached.

Michael had seen this operation performed many times, but it never failed to fill him with uneasy excitement. Once or twice, under Peter's direction, he had even handled the birds; but it made him too alarmed, it too much moved him with distress and pity, to hold in his hand those exceedingly light, exceedingly soft and frail bodies, and feel the quick terrified heart-beat. The only exhilarating moment was releasing the bird. But Michael was too much afraid that one might die in his hand, as they sometimes did if one held them too tight; and Peter reluctantly let him off any further lessons.

Peter came back and motioned his companions forward. 'Come and look,' he said, 'only don't come too near. There's one splendid catch. The little goldcrest in that cage. See him, the little fellow with the red and yellow streak on his head. The rest are sparrows and tits, I'm afraid. And one nuthatch in the far one.'

The birds were inspected while Peter photographed the goldcrest through the netting.

'Why ever do they go in?' Dora wondered.

'For food,' said Peter. 'I lay down a little bread and nuts as bait. Then they try to get out by flying what seems the easier way into the second compartment, and then its still harder for them to escape. Some birds will even enter an unbaited trap out of sheer curiosity.'

'Again, like human beings,' said Michael.

'I won't bother with the tits and sparrows this time,' said Peter. He lifted up one of the cages from the ground and in a quick flurry the birds rose with the wire and darted away. 'I'll ring the nuthatch and the goldcrest. Perhaps, Michael, you wouldn't mind photographing the goldcrest while I'm holding him.'

Michael took the camera. Peter knelt down and opened the door at the end of the cage and put his hand in. The birds in the small compartment began to flutter madly. Peter's brown hand seemed very large beside them. Fingers spread wide he cornered the little bird. His hand gently closed, folding its wildly agitated wings to its body and drawing it out. The small gold striped head appeared between Peter's first and second fingers. Dora gave an exclamation of alarm, excitement, and distress. Michael knew how she felt. He got the camera ready. Peter took the light metal band from his pocket, so small that a magnifying glass would be needed to read its legend. He juggled the bird carefully in his hand until one tiny scaly leg and claw appeared between his fourth and little fingers. Then with his left hand he bent the flexible band around the bird's leg, and lifting it up to his mouth closed the band deftly with his teeth. At the sight of Peter's strong teeth closing so near to that tiny twig of a leg, Dora could bear it no longer and turned away. Michael took two photographs. Peter rapidly tossed the bird into the air and it vanished into the wood, bearing with it forever after to all whom it might concern the information that on that particular Saturday it had been at Imber. Peter then ringed the nuthatch and released the other birds. Dora was full of wonderment and distress and Paul was laughing at her. Michael looked at Toby. His eyes were wide and his lips moist and red where he had been biting them. Michael now laughed at Toby. It was extraordinary how affecting the whole business was.

While they examined the traps at closer quarters, turning them on their backs, Peter wandered away into the wood. Under the trees the light was fading faster, and great clouds of midges drifted about the clearing. Dora was waving her parasol and complaining of being bitten in spite of the citronella. Then a moment later everyone was electrified to hear clearly and unmistakably at quite close quarters the call of a cuckoo. They straightened up and looked at each other – and then burst out laughing. Peter was called back.

'Oh dear!' cried Dora. 'I thought it really was one. What a shame!'

'I'm afraid the real cuckoo is in Africa by now, wise bird,' said Peter. He showed Dora the little instrument he used to make the sound. Then he took from his pocket other toys made of wood and metal, and reproduced in turn the song of the skylark, the curlew, the willow warbler, the turtle dove, and the nightingale. Dora was enchanted. She demanded to see and to try, seizing the small objects from Peter with little cries and self-conscious feminine twittering. Michael observing her thought she epitomized everything he didn't care for about women; but he thought this with detachment, liking her all the same, and feeling too good-tempered at present to feel distaste for anyone.

'It's as good as the real thing!' cried Dora.

'Nothing's as good as the real thing,' said Peter. 'It's odd that even a perfect imitation, as soon as you know it's an imitation, gives much less pleasure. I remember Kant says how disappointed your guests are when they discover that the after-dinner nightingale is a small boy posted in the grove.'

'A case of the natural attractiveness of truth,' said Michael.

'You're full of pious remarks today, isn't he?' said Peter. 'You must be practising for your sermon tomorrow.'

'It's James tomorrow, thank heavens,' said Michael. 'I'm next week.'

'I think the moral is don't be found out. Don't you agree, Toby?' said Peter, laughing.

They began to walk back. Paul asked Peter if he would mind taking a photograph of Dora. Peter was delighted, and finding an opening in the trees began elaborately to pose her sitting on a mossy stone and fingering a flower.

'Paul doesn't realize what he's in for!' said Michael to Toby. 'When Peter gets hold of a human subject he's at it for hours. It's a revenge for the frustrations the birds are always making him suffer!'

Michael and Toby walked on together. From behind them they could hear the laughter of the other three and Dora's voice protesting. Paul seemed quite restored to good humour now. Michael felt suddenly very happy. He felt as if he had gathered all these people benignly about him and as if he were in some way responsible for the beautiful evening, for the gaiety and innocence of it all. He found the word 'innocence' coming naturally to his mind, and did not pause to ponder over it. How rarely now he had this sense of being, in the company of other people, at leisure and at ease. His thoughts then turned to Nick: but the sadness that followed seemed purged and sweet even, unable to break the spell of his present mood.

He was glad to be walking along with Toby, talking idly and intermittently about nothing in particular. He felt on holiday.

'There's an avenue in these woods,' said Michael, 'a bit farther on from where we were, where you see nightjars sometimes. Ever seen a nightjar?'

'No, I'd love to!' said Toby. 'Could you show me?'

'Surely,' said Michael. 'Some evening next week we'll go along. They're very strange birds, hardly like birds at all. They make one believe in witches.'

They came quite suddenly out of the wood onto the wide expanse of grass near the drive. The great scene, the familiar scene, was there again before them, lit by a very yellow and almost vanished sun, the sky fading to a greenish blue. From here they looked a little down upon the lake and could see, intensely tinted and very still, the reflection in it of the farther slope and the house, clear and pearly grey in the revealing light, its detail sharply defined, starting into nearness. Beyond it on the pastureland, against a pallid line at the horizon, the trees took the declining sun, and one oak tree, its leaves already turning yellow, seemed to be on fire.

They both stopped, taking a deep breath, and looked in silence, enjoying the great space and the warm expanse of air and colour. Then from across the lake came sharply and delicately the voices of the madrigal singers. The voices plied and wove, supporting and answering each other in the enchanting and slightly absurd precision of the madrigal. Most clearly heard was Catherine's thin triumphant soprano, retaining and re-asserting the melody. It was too far away to catch the words, but Michael knew them well.

> The silver swan that living had no note,
> When death approached unlocked her silent throat.
> Leaning her breast against the reedy shore
> She sang her first and last, and sang no more.

The song came to an end. Toby and Michael smiled at each other and began to walk slowly toward the ferry. It was too magical a time for hurrying. Then as they neared the lake another sound was heard. Michael could not at first think what it was; then he recognized it as the rising crescendo of a jet engine. From a tiny mutter the noise rose in an instant to a great tearing roar that ripped the heavens apart. They looked up. Gleaming like angels four jet planes had appeared and roared from nowhere to the zenith of the sky above Imber. They were flying in formation, and at this point still perfectly together turned suddenly upward and climbed in line quite vertically into the sky, turned with an almost leisurely move-ment onto their backs and roared down again, looping the loop with such precision that they seemed to be tied together by invisible wires. Then they began to climb again, standing upon their tails, absolutely straight up above the watchers' heads. Still roaring together they reached a distant peak and then peeled off like a flower, each one to a different point of the compass. In another second they had gone, leaving behind their four trails of silver vapour and a shattering subsiding roar. Then there was complete silence. It had all happened very quickly.

Michael found himself open-mouthed, head back and heart thumping. The noise and speed and beauty of the things had made him for a moment almost unconscious. Toby looked at him, equally dazed and excited. Michael looked down and found that he had fastened both his hands onto the boy's bare arm. Laughing they drew apart.

CHAPTER 9

'The chief requirement of the good life,' said James Tayper Pace, 'is to live without any image of oneself. I speak, dear brothers and sisters, as one who is most conscious of being remote from this condition.' It was the next day, Sunday, and James was standing on the dais in the Long Room, one arm resting lightly on the music stand, delivering the weekly talk. He frowned nervously and swayed to and fro as he spoke, tilting the stand with him.

He went on. 'The study of personality, indeed the whole conception of personality, is, as I see it, dangerous to goodness. We were told at school, at least I was told at school, to have ideals. This, it seems to me, is rot. Ideals are dreams. They come between us and reality – when what we need most is just precisely to see reality. And that is something outside us. Where perfection is, reality is. And where do we look for perfection? Not in some imaginary concoction out of our idea of our own character – but in something so external and so remote that we can get only now and then a distant hint of it.

'Now you will say to me, dear James, you tell us to seek perfection and then you tell us it is so remote we can only guess at it – and where do we go from there? The fact is, God has not left us without guidance. How, otherwise, could our Lord have given us the high command "Be ye therefore perfect"? Matthew five forty-eight. We know in very simple ways, ways so simple that they seem dull to our subtle moral psychologists, what we ought to do and what avoid. Surely we know enough and more than enough rules to live by; and I confess I have very little time for the man who finds his life too complicated and special for the ordinary rules to fit. What are you up to, my friend, what are you hiding? I should say to that man: A belief in Original Sin should not lead us to probe the filth of our minds or regard ourselves as unique and interesting sinners. As sinners we are much the same and our sin is essentially something tedious, something to be shunned and not something to be investigated. We should rather work, as it were, from outside inwards. We should think of our actions and look to God and to His Law. We should consider not what delights us or what disgusts us, morally speaking, but what is enjoined and what is forbidden. And this we know, more than we are often ready to admit. We know it from God's Word and from His Church with a certainty as great as our belief. Truthfulness is enjoined, the relief of suffering is enjoined, adultery is forbidden, sodomy is forbidden. And I feel that we ought to think quite simply of these matters, thus: truth is not glorious, it is just enjoined; sodomy is not disgusting, it is just forbidden. These are rules by which we should freely judge ourselves and others too. All else is vanity and self-deception and flattering of passion. Those who hesitate to judge others are usually those who fear to put themselves under judgement. We may remember here the words of Saint Paul – Michael will correct my Latin – *iustus ex fide vivit*. The good man lives by faith, Galatians three eleven. I think we are meant to take this remark quite literally. The good man *does* what seems right, what the rule enjoins, without considering the consequences, without calculation or prevarication, *knowing* that God will make all for the best. He does not amend the rules by the standards of this world. Even if he cannot see how things will work out, he acts, trusting in God. He does the best thing, breaking through the complexities of situations, and knows that God will make the best thing fruitful. But the man without faith calculates. He finds the world too complicated for the best thing, and he does the second best thing, thinking that this in time will bring forth the best. Ah, how few of us have the faith spoken of by Saint Paul!'

Dora was beginning to lose interest. It was all too abstract. She had come to the little service out of curiosity and placed herself at the back where she could see all the congregation. Paul was sitting beside her, which was unfortunate. She would have liked to be able to survey him too. He kept glancing at her, and at one point drew his foot up to hers till she could feel his highly polished shoe touching her instep through the sandal. She saw from the corner of her eye the soft blur of his moustaches, the bird-like movements of his head. She kept her gaze resolutely forward.

Dora felt restless and dejected. In spite of certain moments of satisfaction, when the warmth of the weather and the beauty of the scene lifted her above her anxieties, she had not been able to settle down at Imber. She still felt nervous and shy and as if she were acting a part. It was not that she disliked anyone, though she did find Michael and James, especially James, a bit alarming. Everyone was nice to her, she had an easy time, she didn't even have to get up at what James called 'shriekers', which she discovered to mean crack, or shriek, of dawn. She ambled down a minute before breakfast. Sometimes she missed breakfast and scrounged a bite later on from the larder. She did nothing all day quite agreeably, without anyone looking askance. Even Mrs Mark seemed to have forgotten about her, and was quite surprised when Dora offered to help with this or that. Her only regular duty, besides doing her room, was washing up, and she could do this quite serenely in a dream. What nagged her however was a certain new sense of her inferiority; that, and the prospect of going home with Paul when all this, unnerving as it was, was over. Dora was not unused to feeling inferior. A vague sense of social inferiority, an uneasy lack of *savoir faire*, was normal to her. But what she felt at Imber bit deeper, in a way which she at times resented. Often it seemed to her that the community were easily, casually even, judging her, placing her. The fact that so little was expected of her was itself significant. This was distressing. The sense that the judgement occurred without their thinking about it, that it happened automatically, simply as it were by juxtaposition, was still more distressing.

On the other hand, the prospects of escape were not rosy either. Dora missed London. She was surprised to find that she felt no urge to smoke or drink at Imber. She had slunk down to the White Lion once or twice in the first days; but it was a long way and the weather was forbiddingly hot. She had drunk a little of her whisky from the tooth mug in her bedroom. But these little celebrations had a surreptitious and dreary quality which had her soon discouraged. She did not like drinking alone. She noted with pleasure, and it was her only solid consolation, that as a result of this abstention and because of the sobriety of her diet she was becoming a little thinner. The trouble was that the return to London would be so far from gay. Paul was within sight of the end of his work. He was speaking of going home; and he glowed with a palpable determination to take his wife back with him and instal her as one does an art treasure, clearing the scene, locking the door. His will arched over Dora like a canopy. It was not that she had any thought of not returning with Paul. After all, she had come back to him, and although their reunion was far from successful the calculations that had led to it remained solid. It was just that she could make no vision of herself back in London with Paul. She saw the flat in Knightsbridge, meticulous, exquisite, glowing with stripy wallpaper and *toile de Jouy* and old mahogany and *objets d'art*, utterly alien and utterly dreary. She could not see herself in it. It was not that she intended anything at all. She simply did not believe in that future.

At this moment, however, Dora was not obsessed with thoughts such as these. She was studying the male members of the congregation to decide which were the most handsome. It was James, certainly, who bore the closest resemblance to a film star, so big, so curly-headed, and with that open powerful face. Toby had the best features and the most grace. Mark Strafford was rather striking, but men with beards had an unfair advantage. Michael had a very sweet face, like a worried dog, but was not dignified enough to be handsome. In the end, she concluded Paul was the best-looking of them all: distinguished, dignified, noble. His face lacked serenity, however, it lacked radiance. It often looked distinctly bad-tempered. But then, as she sadly reflected, her husband was not a happy man.

Dora turned her attention to the women and got as far as Catherine. Catherine was sitting at the side near the front, easy to survey. She wore a neat grey Sunday frock, rather smart it occurred to Dora. The sort of frock that might be worn with an expensive hat at a luncheon party. Only here, somehow, it just looked simple. She had combed her hair, which made a spectacular difference to her appearance. The bun was worn low, firmly knotted, and the hair, pulled smoothly behind the ears, was glossy, undulating, refusing to look demure. Catherine was looking down and drooping her eyelids in a customary pose which seemed at times modest and at times secretive. Dora could see the bulge of the brow, the high arch of the cheek, the gentle yet somehow strong upward tilt of the nose. The natural pallor of the skin looked today more ivory than sallow. Dora looked at her with an admiration and a pleasure which were not untempered by the knowledge that this splendid piece was so soon to be withdrawn definitively from circulation.

The unconscious part of Dora's mind which was still listening to James advised her that this bit was getting interesting again. She began to attend. 'I cannot agree with Milton,' James was saying, 'when he refuses to praise a fugitive and cloistered virtue. Virtue, innocence, should be valued whatever its history. It has a radiance which enlightens and purifies and which is not to be dimmed by foolish talk about the worth of experience. How false it is to tell our young people to seek experience! They should rather be told to value and to retain their innocence: that is enough of a task, enough of an adventure! And if we can keep our innocence for long enough, the gift of knowledge will be added to it, a deeper and more precise knowledge than any which is won by the tawdry methods of "experience". Innocence in ourselves and others is to be prized and woe to him who destroys it, as our Lord Himself has said. Matthew eighteen six.

'And what are the marks of innocence? Candour – a beautiful word – truthfulness, simplicity, a quite involuntary bearing of witness. The image that occurs to me here is a topical one, the image of a bell. A bell is made to speak out. What would be the value of a bell which was never rung? It rings out clearly, it bears witness, it cannot speak without seeming like a call, a summons. A great bell is not to be silenced. Consider too its simplicity. There is no hidden mechanism. All that it is is plain and open; and if it is moved it must ring.

'If we think here naturally of our own bell, the great bell of Imber which is so soon to make its triumphal entry into the Abbey, our thoughts will turn to one of our number who is also shortly to cross the lake and enter by that gateway: one in whom, and although she blushes I know she will forgive me, we so resplendently see the merits of which I have been speaking, the worth of innocence which is retained until it becomes knowledge and wisdom. She will doubtless chide me by saying that I speak of the beginning as if it were the end: and indeed the contemplative life is a way so endlessly transforming that it can scarcely be spoken of by an outsider: and he who asks for the contemplative life does not know what he is asking. But we who are merely, if I may put it so, camp-followers or fellow-travellers of holiness, must be excused our moments of enthusiasm. At such times as this one may well feel that the purposes of God are visible in this world. One may even feel that the age of miracles is not over. Certainly it will be, for this community, a most vital and perhaps decisive inspiration to know that someone who has so completely belonged to us, who has been one of ourselves, has taken that other path; and although we may rarely see her again, we shall know that she is near us and that we shall have her prayers. I had not meant to make this personal digression, but, as I say, I know dear Catherine will pardon me. And I think it no harm to say what, in this matter, we have all been thinking. And now, my friends, I must bring my remarks, which I fear have been awfully rambling and lengthy, to an end.'

James stumbled from the dais, looking rather shy and awkward now that the flow of his eloquence had ceased. Father Bob Joyce exhorted the company to pray, and with much pushing and scraping of chairs everyone knelt down. James hid his face at once in his large hands and drooped his head very low. Catherine knelt with her eyes closed and her hands folded, her face revealed and contracted with an emotion which Dora could not read. Michael had laid one hand, fingers spread out, lightly upon his brow, his eyes screwed up, frowning a little as he bent his head. Then Dora divined that Paul was watching her, and closed her eyes too. The prayer ended, the service was over, and the little congregation began to shamble out.

As they came out into the sunlit hall Mrs Mark detained Paul with some question. Catherine, who walked out just ahead of Dora, was smiling at James who was chaffing her in a rather ponderous way which was no doubt supposed to be a sort of apology. Dora felt he *had* laid it on rather thick, but was certainly right in thinking that he would be forgiven. His sincerity was monumental, and, in the light of his own remarks, Dora was ready to see his *gaucherie* as a remarkable spontaneous candour. Moved by him, she was even ready to imagine she believed in brotherly love. She smiled vaguely in his direction, and then found herself walking out onto the balcony with Catherine, James having vanished into the common room. He thinks a little talk with her will do me good! was Dora's immediate reaction; but she looked at Catherine at that moment with interest, almost with affection.

'I liked your service,' said Dora, for something to say. She wanted to get into the sun, and began to walk slowly down the steps. Catherine walked with her.

'Yes,' said Catherine. 'It's quite simple, but it suits us. It's difficult, you know, for a lay community where nothing's ordained. It all has to be invented as you go along.'

They began to walk across the grass, taking the path towards the causeway.

'You've tried different things?' said Dora vaguely.

'Oh yes,' said Catherine. 'At first we had it that everyone said the whole Office privately every day. But it was too much of a strain.'

Dora, who had very little conception of what the Office was, heartily agreed. It sounded awful.

They walked out a little on to the causeway. The sun cast their shadows onto the water. The bricks, overgrown with moss and small plants, were warm underfoot; Dora could feel the warmth through her light shoes. The strong sense she now had of her companion's shyness and nervousness set her at ease. She felt less afraid of Catherine, glad to be with her.

'It's so hot,' she said, 'it makes one want to swim. I can't swim – I wish I could. I expect you can. Everyone can except me.'

'I never go into the water,' said Catherine. 'I can swim, but not at all well, and I don't like it. I think I must be afraid of water. I often dream about drowning.' She looked rather sombrely down at the lake: in the shadow of the causeway it was obscure and green, the water thick, full of weeds and floating matter.

'Do you? How funny. I never do,' said Dora. She turned to look at Catherine. It came to her how very melancholy she looked; and Dora, her imagination abruptly set in motion, wondered for a moment whether Catherine could possibly really want to be a nun.

'You can't really want to go in there!' said Dora suddenly. 'To shut yourself up like that, when you're so young and so beautiful. I'm sorry, this is very rude and awful, I know. But it makes me quite miserable to think of you in there!'

Catherine looked up, surprised, and then smiled very kindly, looking straight at Dora for the first time. 'There are things one doesn't choose,' she said. 'I don't mean they're forced on one. But one doesn't choose them. These are often the best things.'

I was right, thought Dora, triumphantly. She doesn't want to go in. It's a sort of conspiracy against her. They've all been saying for so long that she's going in, and calling her their little saint and so on, and now she can't get out of it. And stuff like what James was saying this morning.

She was about to reply to Catherine when to her irritation she saw Paul coming towards them across the grass. He couldn't leave her alone even for five minutes. Catherine saw him and with a murmur to Dora and an apologetic wave she turned and walked on across the causeway, leaving Dora standing.

Paul came up to her. 'I couldn't think where you'd got to,' he said.

'I wish you'd leave me alone sometimes,' said Dora. 'I was having an interesting conversation with Catherine.'

'I can't think what you and Catherine could find to say to each other,' said Paul. 'You seem to have rather different interests!'

'Why shouldn't I talk to Catherine?' said Dora. 'Do you think I'm not worthy to, or something?'

'I didn't say so,' said Paul, 'but you evidently feel something of the sort! If you want my view, I think Catherine is everything that a woman should be – lovely, gentle, modest, and chaste.'

'You don't respect me,' said Dora, her voice trembling.

'Of course I don't respect you,' said Paul. 'Have I any reason to? I'm in love with you, unfortunately, that's all.'

'Well, it's unfortunate for me too,' said Dora, starting to cry.

'Oh, stop it!' said Paul, 'Stop it!'

Catherine had reached the other side of the lake and walked along under the Abbey wall. She passed the first door into the parlours, and went in by the door that led into the visitors' chapel. It seemed to Dora afterwards that she closed it behind her with a bang.

CHAPTER 10

Toby pushed open the door of the Lodge. There was ample time after the Service and before lunch to have a swim. When he had opened the door and stepped half inside he paused, as he always did, wondering where Nick Fawley was. Murphy came forward wagging his tail and jumped up rather lazily, presenting his two forelegs to the boy to hold. Toby held him for a moment, nuzzling down onto the soft warm head, and then straightened up. No sign of Nick. He was probably out. With a feeling of relief Toby bounded noisily up the stairs and got his bathing trunks. Admonished by James he had got some cheaply in the village. He took his towel, which was rather grimy and rebarbative by now with the mud of frequent swims, but still serving.

As he emerged onto the landing he heard Nick's voice calling him from the next room. He went to the door and looked in. Nick was in bed. This was not unusual; he ought to have thought that Nick might be in bed.

'Who was spouting?' said Nick. He was propped up on his pillows and had been reading a detective story.

'James was,' said Toby. He was impatient to be away.

'Any good?' said Nick.

'Yes, jolly good,' said Toby. He felt embarrassed talking about this to Nick.

'What was it about?' said Nick.

'Oh, innocence and all that,' said Toby.

Nick, still in pyjamas, his plump face puffed out on the pillows, the long greasy wig of his hair descending on either side, suddenly looked to Toby like the Wolf pretending to be Grandmamma in the story. He smiled at the thought and felt less embarrassed.

'I'll give you a sermon one day,' said Nick. 'They haven't asked me to spout, so I'll give you a private one.'

Toby could think of nothing to say to this. He wondered

how to take his leave, and said 'Shall I take Murphy swimming with me?'

'If Murphy wants to come,' said Nick, 'he'll come even if you don't want him, and if he doesn't want to come he won't even if you do.'

This was true enough. Toby said 'Ah, well,' and rather ponderously raised his hand in a vague salute. Nick continued to stare at him till he turned and departed. It could not be said to have been a successful conversation.

Released, Toby ran quickly downstairs and out across the grass, calling to Murphy who seemed only too eager to come. Toby had with him his underwater swimming gear, the mask and the breathing tube, which he hoped he might find some chance to use somewhere in the lake. The river pools where he had swum so far, though deliciously clear, were rather shallow. Today Toby thought he would go toward the farther end of the lake, beyond the Abbey, where he had not yet explored. From the causeway he had seen in the distance what looked like a gravelly beach, on the Court side of the lake. Round about there the water might be clearer. He decided he would make a reconnaissance before lunch and come back again for longer later on. He had been saving up this expedition. He did not want to exhaust the mysteries of Imber too quickly.

He crossed in the ferry. Murphy elected on this occasion to ride in the boat, walking around boldly in the bottom of it, and making it rock by planting his paws on the edge. On reaching the other side Toby began to run across the open grass by the Court, and passing the end of the causeway, took the lakeside path towards the wood. He was longing to be in the water and didn't want to be delayed by meeting anyone. As he neared the wood he saw Dr and Mrs Greenfield. They seemed to be disputing about something, and when they saw him they turned away along the path that led inland toward the kitchen garden. Once inside the wood Toby ran even faster, but now for sheer delight, jumping over the long strands of bramble and the hummocks of grass which were growing freely on what used to be the path. Evidently no one came along this way.

The path followed the lake side, divided from the water by an irregular hedge of greenery, finding its way through a tunnel dappled by circles of sunshine and shifting watery reflections. Deeper in the wood the dog was running parallel to the boy and could be heard blundering through the undergrowth and scuffing the dead leaves. Toby slowed down at last, and walked along panting, looking to see where he was. Through the bushes at the water's edge he could see the other shore of the lake, the part where the Abbey enclosure was unwalled. He paused and looked across. There was a wood over there, very like this wood. And yet, he thought, how very different everything must be over there. He wondered if, in that wood, there were neat well-kept paths, along which the nuns walked in meditation, their habits dragging on the grassy verge. As he was watching, suddenly on the other side two nuns came into view. Toby froze, wondering if he was well hidden. The nuns took what must be a clear path fairly near the water. They were a little screened by bushes and tall reeds, but every now and then they emerged into full sunlight and he could see that their skirts were hitched up a little to reveal stout black shoes, as they walked at a brisk pace along beside the lake. They turned to each other and seemed to be talking. Then the next moment, as clear as a bell, he heard one of them laugh. They turned away from him and back into the darkness of the wood.

That laugh moved Toby strangely. Of course there was no reason why nuns shouldn't laugh, though he never normally imagined them laughing. But such a laugh, he thought, must be a very very good thing: one of the best things in the world. To be good *and* gay was surely the highest of human destinies. With these thoughts he recalled James's talk of this morning. What James had said about innocence was surely in a way meant for him. Naturally he could not claim, as Catherine could, to have kept and guarded his innocence. How well old James had struck off just that thing that one felt about Catherine, what made her so exceptional: a sense of something retained. He himself had not been tried yet; how true what James had said about the keeping of innocence being enough of a task! Yet, Toby reflected, would it really be so difficult if one were fully *aware*? The trouble with so many young people nowadays was that they were not *aware*. They seemed to go through their youth in a daze, in a dream. Toby was certain of being awake. He was amazed, when people said that youth was wonderful, only one didn't realize it at the time. Toby did realize it at the time, was realizing it now as he paced along close to the water, his shirt wet with perspiration, feeling already the cool emanations from the lake. He was glad he had come to Imber, glad he had surrounded himself with all these good people. He was full of thanksgiving to God and a sense of the renewal of his faith. A conviction overpowered him of the almost impersonal power within him of his own pure intent. This was perhaps what was meant by grace. Not I, but Christ in me. He felt, remembering the sudden gaiety of the nun's laughter over the water, a sense of joy which seemed both physical and spiritual at the same time and almost lifted him off the ground. When one was so favoured it was not difficult to be good.

As he reflected he had been walking slowly on, and looking ahead now he realized that he had reached his destination. He saw at once with interest that what he had taken to be a gravelly beach was in fact a wide stone ramp which led gently down into the water. His lofty thoughts forgotten, he examined the scene. A few rotting stumps in the lake beyond the ramp suggested that there had once been a wooden landing-stage; and the woodland for a little distance around had been cleared, though now weeds and grass had plentifully covered the area. There were traces of stone and gravel, and in the midst a wide pathway led back into the wood. Toby threw down his swimming things and started along the path. He saw in a moment or two that there was a building of some sort ahead of him. He was confronted by what seemed to be a very old tumbled-down barn. The roof, which had once been stone-tiled, was partly fallen in, and the roof timbers, made of fir wood, with bark and ragged branch ends still showing on them, could be seen at one end, pointing upwards in gaunt empty arches. The walls were of thick roughly hewn stone, piled together in mortarless intricacy. Toby decided it must be a medieval barn. He approached the gaping entrance with caution and looked in. A huge door opened on the other side towards the pasture, but the place was twilit within. It was quite empty except for some old rotting sacks and boxes. It echoed a little. The mud floor was as hard as cement, though cracked here and there under the broken part of the roof by grass and thistles. Looking up Toby saw the great cross beams, immensely thick, each one made long ago from the stem of a huge oak. Enormous cobwebs entangled the beams and made a textile net under the peak of the roof. Up there something, perhaps a bat, was stirring in the lofty darkness. Toby hurried through and out the other side.

He could now see through the trees the wider light of the pastureland. He walked on. By the edge of the pasture a concrete path, used perhaps for the transit of logs, ran along beside the wood in the direction of the Court. Once perhaps the barn had stood on the verge of the grass, but now the wood had captured it and it was derelict and useless. Excited by his discovery Toby bounded back toward the shore of the lake and the cheerful open sunshine which he could see ahead of him along the path. He found Murphy sitting on the ramp, guarding his things, his long tongue drooping in the heat, with the patient smiling face of a panting dog.

It had been chilly in the barn. The sun warmed Toby now with a luxurious zeal. He looked at the water and desired intensely to be in it. Glancing across the lake he saw that the land opposite was just outside the enclosure wall. He had been told never to swim opposite the enclosure. He decided that, although he would still be visible from within the wall, he would follow the letter of the law and swim from the ramp. He liked the place and did not want to go any farther. Indeed, looking on along the lake shore it seemed that the banks were increasingly muddy and weedy, and the lake ended in a sort of rebarbative bog. Toby undressed quickly and went to sun himself on the sloping stones before going in. The sun warmed his flesh deeply.

First he tried lying flat on his face with his feet down the slope. But the human body is not so constructed that when in that position the neck and chin can rest comfortably upon the ground. Our awkward frames deny us the relaxed pose of the recumbent dog. Convinced of this truth, Toby turned over and reclined on one elbow. In this more inviting position he was accosted by Murphy who came and laid his head against his shoulder. In a kind of physical rapture Toby sat up and took the furry beast in his arms and cuddled him as he had sometimes seen Nick do. The sensation of the hot soft living fur against his skin was strange and exciting. He sat there motionless for a while, holding the dog and looking down into the lake. It was deep there by the landing-stage; and suddenly his eyes made out a large fish basking motionless where the sun penetrated the greenish water. From its narrow length and its fierce jaws he knew it to be a pike. His head nodding a little over Murphy's back he watched the quiet pike. Then his eyes began to close and only the hot sparkling of the lake pierced through the fringe of his eyelids. He felt so happy he could almost die of it, invited by that sleep of youth when physical well-being and joy and absence of care lull the mind into a sweet coma which is the more inviting since its awakening is charmed no less, and the spirit faints briefly, almost sated with delight.

Toby woke up and pushed Murphy off. He hadn't been asleep more than a moment, to be sure, but now it was time to swim, his body so baked that it seemed it must sizzle as it entered the glossy water. The pike had gone away. The water lazed thickly at the foot of the ramp and the pale stones were not visible under it. There would be little point in underwater swimming here; the water would be too opaque to see anything. He stood, poised on the brink, looking down. The centre of the lake was glittering, colourlessly brilliant, but along the edge the green banks could be seen reflected and the blue sky, the colours clear yet strangely altered into the colours of a dimmer and more obscure world: the charm of swimming in still waters, that sense of passing through the looking-glass, of disturbing and yet entering that other scene that grows out of the roots of this one. Toby took a step or two and hurled himself in.

For a while he swam quietly about, waiting for the ripples to subside and the surface to re-form as a taut silky sheet touching his chin, enjoying as he did so the exquisite sensation of his body continuing to be hot in the cool water. It was as if a silver film covered him, caressing his limbs. He came back and lay like a stranded fish upon the ramp, his head and shoulders out of the water; and he could feel his skin being dried at once by the burning sun. The mask and breathing tube were within reach, and lying where he was he slipped them on and turned to crawl down the ramp, holding onto the edge of it, his head submerged. It was difficult to keep under water as the mask was buoyant and the stones provided no good hand-hold. He could see very little, but apprehended that the ramp extended at least eight feet under the surface. He threw the mask and tube back, and sank into the water again. This time he tried walking down the ramp but found himself out of his depth before he reached the end of it. He was joined by Murphy who swam round him in a dignified fashion, contriving to keep his fluffy side-whiskers and most of his brown beard high and dry out of the water.

Toby was sorry it was too dark to see under the water. He thought he would swim down all the same and see if he could touch the bottom of the ramp, to find whether it ended before it reached the floor of the lake. He did not know how deep the lake was just here. Toby was a strong underwater swimmer. Upending himself he dived vertically and found the side of the stone slope with his hand as he began to straighten out under the water. He opened his eyes and saw the opaque green sunlight-penetrated water and the paler stone of the ramp, speckled with moving light from the ripples on the surface. In a moment the ramp had ended, disappearing into the ooze of the lake bottom. Toby's hand plunged into the mud. He withdrew it quickly and shot up to the surface again. After all, the lake was not very deep.

He swam a little farther out and then dived again so that

he went vertically down to where the ramp ended and then swam out along the soft lake floor. He opened his eyes, but now there was nothing to be seen except an obscure green light. Fascinated, he clove the very soft ooze with his hands as he glided along. It was so soft, almost as soft and giving as the water, and yet somehow sinister. Supposing he were to find a corpse or something, a human form half buried in that deep ancient deposit? As he thought this thought Toby's hand encountered something hard and rough. Half alarmed he rose to the surface and swam in a circle, panting. He had been under for quite a long time. He got his breath back. What he had touched was doubtless an old tin can, and he examined his hand to make sure he hadn't cut himself. He knew from experience that one can wound oneself quite seriously under water without noticing it. He seemed to be intact. It must be nearly time now to go back to lunch.

He thought he would dive just once more to see what it was that he had touched. He went down like a plummet, opening his eyes and spreading his hands wide over the bottom. He shovelled the ooze about a little and then felt a hard projecting surface. He got his fingers underneath it and pulled. The thing, whatever it was, must be quite large and deeply embedded in the mud. The water, even thicker now with the disturbance of the bottom, was entirely opaque. Toby held on to the thing with one hand, keeping himself down, while with the other he explored it. He felt a thick arc-shaped rim raised above the ooze and descending into it on both sides. It might be a large vase; only the arc was too wide for a vase. The thing must be big: an old boiler perhaps. He felt the outside surface of it cautiously behind the rim. It seemed to be pitted and fretted, perhaps with rust or with some watery vegetation. His breath gave out and he had to surface again.

As he trod water, quietly inhaling, he heard across the Abbey grounds the hand bell ringing the Angelus. That meant that he ought to go almost at once if he didn't want to have to run all the way back. He determined to dive just once more and try to dig the thing out. He dived, and found it at once this time, and began to shovel away the ooze from all round it, holding onto the massive rim with one hand. The upper half of it seemed to emerge quite easily from the mud. The rim to which he had attached himself was the widest part, and now he could feel more of the arc he reckoned it must be several feet across. It appeared to be circular, the lower part of the circle being still submerged. Within the rim it seemed to be hollow, becoming narrower. It occurred to Toby that it might possibly be a large bell. By this time he was breathless again and had to let go.

He swam in to the ramp and rested for a moment. The investigation had been quite strenuous. He reached a dripping hand up to his clothes and fished his wrist watch out of his trousers pocket. Heavens, it *was* late! He scrambled quickly out of the water, dried himself summarily, and began to dress. It had been a splendid expedition; he would certainly come back again soon. It would be fun to explore that thing down in the water, though it probably wasn't really anything very exciting. Meanwhile, he resolved he would say nothing to the others about this delightful place but keep it privately for himself.

CHAPTER 11

It was James Tayper Pace who suggested to Michael that he should take Toby with him in the Land-Rover. Michael was going in to Swindon to buy the mechanical cultivator. Though several days had elapsed since the Meeting, and Michael was longing for his toy, he had not had time to make the journey. Now it was Wednesday, and he was determined to go, come what might, in the late afternoon. The shop would be shut by the time he arrived, but he had made his arrangements by telephone and the shop people, with whom he had already done a lot of business, said he might pick the thing up any time before seven.

'Why not take young Toby with you?' said James. They were leaving the estate office together. 'It'll just mean his knocking off half an hour early. Let him see a bit of the countryside. He's been working like a black.'

This would not have occurred to Michael; but it seemed a splendid idea, and when he was nearly ready to go he went to look for Toby in the kitchen garden.

He found him, with Patchway, hoeing the brussels sprouts.

'Don't be so careful wi' 'em,' Patchway was saying. 'Knock 'em around! Does them good.'

Toby straightened up to greet Michael. The boy was well bronzed now and oily with sweat. Patchway, stripped to the waist, was still wearing his redoubtable trilby.

'I was wondering if Toby would care to come with me into Swindon, just for the ride,' said Michael to Patchway, 'if you can spare him.'

Patchway grunted and looked at Toby, who said, 'I'd love to, if that's all right!'

'Pigeons haven't troubled us so far, have they?' said Michael to Patchway.

'Why should they?' said Patchway. 'Little buggers have

plenty else to eat. But you watch 'em when the cold weather starts!'

Toby ran off to change and Michael stood around for a while with Patchway. Patchway had the enviable countryman's capacity, which is shared only by great actors, of standing by and saying nothing, and yet existing, large, present, and at ease.

This silent communion ended, Michael went to fetch the Land-Rover from the stable yard, and drove it round to the front of the house. The fifteen-hundredweight lorry would have been better for the trip, as the cultivator would have a tight squeeze in the Land-Rover, but the lorry was still laid up with an undiagnosed complaint and Nick Fawley, though asked twice, had not yet condescended to look at it. This was the sort of muddle which lack of time, lack of staff, brought about. Michael knew he ought either to see that Nick fixed it, or else get the village garage man on the job. But he kept putting the problem off; and meanwhile the Land-Rover, perilously over-loaded, had to take the vegetables in to Pendelcote.

Michael felt good-humoured and excited. He had great hopes of the cultivator; it would save a great deal of hard work, and it was so light that it could be used by the women: well, by Margaret, anyway, since Catherine would soon be gone, and by any other women who turned up in the community. Michael's heart sank a little at the thought of the arrival of more women, but he reflected that he had got perfectly used to the two that were there. The enlarging of the community was from every point of view essential, and the shyness one felt at the breaking of an existing group was after all soon got over. With more staff and more machinery the place would take shape as a sound economic unit, and the present hand-to-mouth arrangements, which were nerve-rending although they had a certain Robinson Crusoe charm, would come to an end. Michael was pleased too at the thought of a trip to Swindon. It was weeks since he had been any farther afield than Cirencester; and he felt a childish pleasure at the thought of visiting the big town. And it was delightful to have Toby with him; the more so since he had not proposed it himself.

The drive, during which Michael answered Toby's questions about the countryside, took a little over an hour. Once they stopped briefly to look at a village church. Arrived at Swindon, they went straight to the shop, and found the cultivator packed up ready in the yard. With the shopman's help, Toby and Michael heaved the wonderful thing into the back of the Land-Rover and made it fast with ropes so that it should not shift about on the journey. Michael looked upon it with love. Its great toy-like yellow rubber-covered wheels jutted out below, and its square shiny red body had burst the packing paper at each corner. The sensitive divided handle thrust its gazelle-like horns toward the front of the van, reaching to the roof between the driver and the passenger. Safely stowed, Michael admired it. He was sorry to see that Toby, whose present ambition was to drive the tractor, seemed to share Patchway's view that the cultivator was rather a sissy object.

'Now, what about something to eat?' said Michael. By their early start they had missed high tea. Sandwiches in a pub seemed to be the solution; and Michael recalled a nice-looking country pub he had seen a little way outside Swindon on the road home.

By the time they arrived there it was about half past seven. The pub turned out to be rather grander than Michael had thought, but they went into the saloon bar, which had kept its old panelling of much-rubbed blackened oak and its tall wooden settles, together with a certain amount of modern red leather, coy Victorian hunting prints, and curtains printed with pint mugs and cocktail glasses. The bottles glittered gaily behind the bar, against which leaned a number of cheerful red-faced men in tweeds of whom it would have been difficult to say whether they were farmers or business men.

Michael installed Toby, to the latter's amusement, in a big cosy settle near the window from which they could see the inn yard and keep an eye on the Land-Rover with its precious cargo.

'It's practically illegal, my bringing you in here!' said Michael. 'You are eighteen, aren't you? Only just? Well, that's good enough. Now, what'll you drink? Something soft perhaps?'

'Oh, no!' said Toby, shocked. 'I'd like to drink whatever the local drink is here. What do you think it is?'

'Well,' said Michael, 'I suppose it's West Country cider. I see they have it on draught. It's rather strong. Would you like to try? All right. You stay here. I'll get the drinks and the sandwiches.'

The sandwiches were good: fresh white bread with lean crumbling roast beef. Pickles and mustard and potato crisps came too. The cider was golden, rough yet not sour to the taste, and very powerful. Michael took a large gulp of the familiar stuff; he had known it since childhood. It was heartening and full of memories, all of them good ones.

'This isn't the West Country here is it?' said Toby. 'I always thought Swindon was rather near London. But perhaps I'm mixing it up with Slough!'

'It's the beginning of the West,' said Michael. 'At least I always imagine so. The cider is the sign of it. I come from this part of the country myself. Where did you grow up, Toby?'

'In London,' said Toby. 'I wish I hadn't. I wish at least I'd been away to boarding-school.'

They talked for a while about Toby's childhood. Michael began to feel so happy he could have shouted aloud. It was a long time since he had sat in a bar; and to sit in this one, talking to this boy, drinking this cider, seemed an activity so perfect that it left while it lasted no cranny for any other desire. Vaguely, Michael reflected that this was an unusual condition; he knew that it was one which he did not especially miss or yearn for: yet, in a little while, he was, even in his enjoyment of it, conscious too of things missed, things sacrificed, in his life. At one moment, somehow connected with this, he had a vision, which had at one time haunted him but which he rarely had now, of the Long Room at Imber, carpeted, filled, furnished, its walls embellished with gilt mirrors and the glow of old pictures, the grand piano back again in its corner, the cheerful tray of drinks upon the side table. But even this did not diminish his enjoyment: to know clearly what you surrender, what you gain, and to have no regrets; to revisit without envy the scenes of a surrendered joy, and to taste it ephemerally once more, with a delight undimmed by the knowledge that it is momentary, that is happiness, that surely is freedom.

'What do you want to do after you leave College?' said Michael.

'I don't know,' said Toby. 'I'll be some sort of engineer, I suppose. But I don't know quite what I want to do. I don't think I want to go abroad. Really, you know,' he said, 'I'd like to do something like what you do.'

Michael laughed. 'But I don't do anything, dear boy,' he said. 'I'm a universal amateur.'

'You do,' said Toby. 'I mean you've made something marvellous at Imber. I'd like to be able to do that. I mean, I couldn't ever *make* it like you have, but I'd like to be part of a thing like that. Something so sort of pure and out of the modern world.'

Michael laughed at him again, and they disputed for a while about being out of the world. Without showing it, Michael was immensely touched and a little rueful about the boy's evident admiration for him. Toby saw him as a spiritual leader. While knowing how distorted this picture was, yet Michael could not help catching, from the transfigured image of himself in the boy's imagination, an invigorating sense of possibility. He was not done for yet, not by any means. He looked sideways at Toby. Toby had put on a clean shirt and a jacket but no tie, for his trip to town. He had left the jacket in the van. The shirt, still stiff from the laundry, was unbuttoned and the collar stood up rigidly under his chin while a narrow cleft in the whiteness revealed the darkness of his chest. Michael remarked again the straightness of his short nose, the length of his eyelashes, and his shy wild expression, tentative, gentle, untouched. He had none of that look of cunning, that rather nervous smartness, that is often seen in boys of his age. As Michael looked he felt hope for him, and with it the joy that comes from feeling, without consideration of oneself, hope for another.

'I can't finish this, I'm afraid,' said Toby. 'It's nice, but it's too strong for me. No, nothing else, thank you. Would you like it?' He poured the remains of his pint of cider into Michael's almost empty pint pot. Michael tossed it off and got himself another pint. He saw that there was chocolate displayed on the counter, and got some for Toby. Returning to their corner he noticed with some surprise that it was quite dark outside.

'We must be off soon,' he said, and began to swallow his drink quickly while Toby ate his chocolate. How rapidly the time had passed! In a moment or two they rose to go.

As they came out into the yard Michael felt an extreme heaviness in his limbs. It was foolish of him to have had that second pint; he was so unused to the stuff now, it had made him feel quite tipsy. But he knew he would be all right once he got into the van; the driving would sober him up. They packed in and Michael turned up the lights and set off on the homeward road, the cultivator bumping comfortably behind him, one soft rubber handle just touching his head.

The road looked different at night, the grass verges a brilliant green, the grey-golden walls of tall-windowed houses looming up quickly and vanishing, the trees bunched and mysterious above the range of the headlights. Every now and then a cat was to be seen running in front of the car or deep in the undergrowth, its eyes glowing brightly as it faced the beam of light.

'You're a scientist,' said Michael. 'Why don't human beings' eyes glow like that?'

'Are you sure they don't?' said Toby.

'Well, do they?' said Michael. 'I've never seen anyone's eyes glow.'

'It may be that human beings always turn their eyes away,' said Toby. 'I remember learning at school that Monmouth was caught after the rebellion, when he was hiding in a ditch near Cranborne, because his eyes were gleaming in the moonlight.'

'Yes, but surely not like *that*,' said Michael. An unidentified animal faced them at some distance down the road, a pair of greenish flashes, and then was gone.

'I believe there's something about special cells behind the

eyes,' said Toby. 'But I'm still not completely sure that our eyes mightn't glow too if we really faced the headlights. Let's try it! I'll get out and come walking towards you facing the light, and you see what my eyes look like!'

'You *are* a scientist!' said Michael, laughing. 'Well, not now. We'll wait till we arrive home, shall we? Then you can make your experiment.'

Toby fell silent and they drove along for a while without speaking. Michael could hear him yawning. At last he said, 'That cider has made me quite sleepy.'

'Well, go to sleep then,' said Michael.

'Oh, no,' said Toby. 'I'm not as sleepy as all that.' In a few minutes he was asleep. Michael could see from the corner of his eye the boy's head hanging forward. Days of hard physical work followed by the dose of potent cider had knocked him out completely. Michael smiled to himself.

The Land-Rover proceeded more slowly than on the journey out. Michael still felt a bit drunk though perfectly capable. The exaltation and delight which he had felt in the pub had faded into a purring contentment combined with a most luxurious heaviness of the whole body. He leaned upon the steering wheel, turning it with the length of his forearm, and singing inaudibly to himself. Toby hung forward, obviously dead asleep. Then on a corner he slumped quietly sideways and Michael could feel his weight against him. The boy's head descended gently on to his shoulder.

Michael drove on in a dream. He could feel Toby's knee touching his thigh, the warmth of his lean body against his side, his hair brushing his cheek. The unexpected delight of the contact was so great that he closed his eyes for a moment and then realized that he was still driving. He tried to breathe more quietly so as not to disturb the boy, and found that he was taking long deep breaths. He slowed the Land-Rover down a little, and calmed his breathing. He could feel distinctly, as if his frame were suddenly magnified, the rise and fall of his ribs and the corresponding movement of Toby's body. He was afraid his heart-beat alone might wake the sleeper.

He drove on slowly now at an even pace. If he didn't have

to stop there was no reason why Toby shouldn't sleep all the way to Imber. He manoeuvred the Land-Rover gently round corners. Fortunately the roads were clear. That Toby should just go on sleeping seemed the most desirable thing in the world. Michael felt an ecstasy of protective joy; and for a moment he remembered an old peasant he had once seen high in the Alps sitting on a green bank and watching his cow feeding. The absurd comparison made him smile. He went on smiling.

On a piece of straight road he ventured to look down at Toby. The boy was curled against him, his legs drawn up, his hands touchingly folded, his head lying now between Michael's shoulder and the back of the seat. The white laundered shirt hung open almost to his waist. As Michael looked at him, and then returned his gaze to the road, he had a very distinct impulse to thrust his hand into the front of Toby's shirt. The next instant, as if this thought had acted as a spark, he had a clear visual image of himself driving the Land-Rover into a ditch and seizing Toby violently in his arms.

Michael shook his head as if to clear away a slight haze which was buzzing round him. He began to realize that he had a headache. He really must control his imagination. He was surprised that it could play him such a trick. He was blessed, or cursed, with a strong power of visualizing, but the snapshots which it produced were not usually so startling. Michael felt solemn now, responsible, still protective and still joyful, with a joy which, since he had taken a more conscious hold on himself, seemed deeper and more pure. He felt within him an infinite power to protect Toby from harm. Quietly he conjured up the vision of Toby the undergraduate, Toby the young man. Somehow, it might be possible to go on knowing him, it might be possible to watch over him and help him. Michael felt a deep need to build, to retain, his friendship with Toby; there was no reason why such a friendship should not be fruitful for both of them; and he felt a serene confidence in his own most scrupulous discretion. So it would be that this moment of joy would not be something strange and isolated, but rather something which pointed forward to a long and profound responsibility, a task. There would be no moment like this again. But something of its sweetness would linger, in a way that Toby would never know, in humble services obscurely performed at future times. He was conscious of such a fund of love and goodwill for the young creature beside him. It could not be that God intended such a spring of love to be quenched utterly. There must, there must be a way in which it could be made a power for good. Michael did not in that instant feel that it would be difficult to make it so.

He realized with intense disappointment that they were nearing Imber. He must have been following the road without noticing it. He wondered how drunk he still was. Thank heavens there had been no mishaps. He turned smoothly onto the main road and in a few minutes the high stone wall of the estate appeared on the right. Michael was deeply sorry to arrive. Toby was still heavily asleep. It was a shame to wake him. The Land-Rover began to slow down. Following some instinct Michael did not drive it as far as the Lodge gates. He stopped some hundred yards short of the Lodge and turned off the headlights. Then he switched off the engine. A terrible silence followed.

Toby stirred. Then he rolled back in his seat and opened his eyes. He became at once wide awake. 'Good heavens, was I asleep?' he said. 'I'm so sorry!'

'Nothing to be sorry for,' said Michael. 'You had a good sleep. We're home again now.'

Toby exclaimed with surprise. He stretched, yawning. Then he said eagerly, 'Look, we can do that thing with the headlights now. Do you mind? You turn them right up and I'll come walking towards you looking straight into them.'

Michael obediently turned the headlights full up, while Toby jumped out of the Land-Rover. He saw the boy running away down the road until he was nearly beyond the range of the beam. Then he turned and began to walk slowly back, keeping his eyes steadily fixed on where Michael was behind the blaze of the lights. His brightly illuminated figure approached at an even pace. His dark eyes, wide open and strangely like those of a sleepwalker, were unblinking and clearly visible.

They did not gleam or glow: he walked with a graceful slow stride, very slim, the white sleeves of his shirt uncurling on his arms. He was a long time coming.

When he reached the van he leaned his head in through the window towards Michael. Michael put one arm across his shoulder and kissed him.

It happened so quickly that the moment after Michael was not at all sure whether it had really happened or whether it was just another thing that he had imagined. But Toby remained there rigid, where he had stepped back, pulling himself away from Michael's grasp, and a look of utter amazement was to be seen on his face.

Michael said, and found his voice suddenly thick and stumbling, 'I'm sorry. That was an oversight.' The remark was idiotic, not what he had meant to say at all, that was not the word he wanted. There was a moment's silence. Then Michael said, 'I'm sorry, Toby. Just come round the other side and get in and I'll run you to the Lodge. We're still a little way away.'

Toby came round the front of the car, averting his face. As he had his hand on the door on the other side, someone came into view on the road, another figure vividly revealed and walking slowly up into the beam of the lights. It was Nick. As soon as Michael saw him, following an instinctive desire for concealment, he switched the lights off again. Nick's form loomed up near the car. Toby was still standing in the road.

'Hello you two,' said Nick. 'I thought you were never coming. What's the game, stopping such a long way from the gates?'

'I made a mistake,' said Michael. 'Perhaps you'd see Toby in. I'll be off now. Cheerio, Toby.' He put the lights up, started the car with a jolt, and moved off down the road and in through the Lodge gates which fortunately were open. He and Toby had been behind the headlights; but Nick might have seen something all the same. As he drove up to the house, which was by now entirely in darkness, it was this thought which tormented him most.

CHAPTER 12

It was lunch-time on the following day. As was customary, the meal was taken in silence, while a reading was made by some member of the company. Lunch usually took about twenty minutes, during which the reader sat at a side table, while the others sat at the long narrow refectory table with Michael at one end and Mrs Mark at the other. Today the reader was Catherine and the book from which she read was the Revelations of Julian of Norwich. Catherine read well, in a slightly trembling voice, with deep feeling and patently moved by the matter of her reading.

'This is that Great Deed ordained by our Lord God from without beginning, treasured and hid in His blessed breast, only known to Himself: by which He shall make all things well. For like as the blissful Trinity made all things of nought, right so the same blessed Trinity shall make well all that is not well.

'And in this sight I marvelled greatly and beheld our Faith, marvelling thus: Our Faith is grounded in God's word, and it belongeth to our Faith that we believe that God's word shall be saved in all things; and one point of our Faith is that many creatures shall be condemned: as angels that fell out of Heaven for pride, which be now fiends; and man in earth that dieth out of Faith of Holy Church: that is to say, they that be heathen men; and also man that hath received christendom and liveth unchristian life, and so dieth out of charity: all these shall be condemned to hell without end, as Holy Church teacheth me to believe. And all this so standing, me thought it was impossible that all manner of things should be well, as our Lord showed in the same time.

'And as to this I had no other answer in Showing of our Lord God but this: *That which is impossible to thee is not impossible to me: I shall save my word in all things and I shall make all things well.* Thus I was taught, by the grace of God, that I should steadfastly hold me in the Faith as I had aforehand understood, and therewith that I should firmly believe that all things shall be well, as our Lord showed in the same time.'

Toby, who had soon finished with his meal, sat crumbling his bread and pushing the crumbs into cracks in the old oak table. He did not dare to turn his head in case he caught Michael's eye. He felt tired and listless after a bad night. His morning's work had been irksome. He was not listening to the reading.

Toby had received, though not yet digested, one of the earliest lessons of adult life: that one is never secure. At any moment one can be removed from a state of guileless serenity and plunged into its opposite, without any intermediate condition, so high about us do the waters rise of our own and other people's imperfection. Toby had passed, it seemed to him in an instant, from a joy that had seemed impregnable into an agitation which he scarcely understood. He could not, during the long night and when he awoke from intermittent sleep in the morning, quite make out whether anything very important had happened or not; at least, at the surface of his mind he debated this. Deeper down he knew that something extraordinary had occurred though he did not yet know what it was.

As he walked back with Nick to the Lodge, after Michael's abrupt departure, he had felt extreme confusion, but had managed all the same to speak calmly to Nick and answer with cheerful casualness his questions about their journey. He wondered if Nick could possibly have seen the incident, but decided that he had not. Toby and Michael had been well behind the headlights, and Nick, even if he had emerged from the gates in time, would have been dazzled by the strong beam. He might have guessed from Michael's odd manner that something was up; but there was no reason why he should guess it to be something as remarkable as *that*. Nick was possibly curious: and showed, Toby observed, during their conversation that followed, a sharpened interest in him and a desire to keep him talking. But Toby maintained his composure, and cut their talk short, though not too short, and hurried up to bed. He wanted passionately to be by himself.

When he was alone he sat down on his bed and covered his face. His first emotion was sheer amazement. He could hardly think of anything he would have expected less. Toby's knowledge of homosexuality was slight. His day school had yielded him no experience of this sort, nor even the remotest approach to such experience. The matter had been the subject of certain simple jokes among his school-fellows, but their ignorance was as great as his and little information could be obtained from this source. As his education had included Latin but no Greek his acquaintance with the excesses of the ancients was fragmentary; but in any case it was all different for them. What he did know came mainly from the more popular newspapers, and from remarks he had heard his father make about 'pansies'. In so far as he had up to now reflected on this propensity at all he had regarded it as a strange sickness or perversion, with mysterious and disgusting refinements, from which a small number of unfortunate persons suffered. He also knew, and differed here from his father, that it was more proper to regard these persons as subjects for the doctor than as subjects for the police. And there his knowledge ended.

Like all inexperienced people, Toby tended to make all-or-nothing judgements. Whereas previously he had regarded Michael as a paragon of virtue and had not dreamt of speculating about whether his life could contain blemishes or failures, he now attributed to him homosexuality *tout court* with all that it involved of the unnatural and the nameless. At least this was his first reaction. He found that his thoughts moved fast and in the direction of greater complexity. His immediate emotion had been surprise. It was soon succeeded by disgust and an alarming sort of fear. He felt a definite physical repugnance at having been touched in that way. He felt himself menaced. Perhaps he ought to tell someone. Did the others know about it? Obviously not. Oughtn't they to be told? Yet it was certainly not for him to speak. Besides, it was a matter also of protecting himself. He was thoroughly alarmed to find that he was the sort of person who attracted attention of that sort. He wondered if that showed that there was something wrong with him, an unconscious tendency that way which another person so afflicted would divine?

It was at this point that he began to accuse himself of exaggeration. Surely the thing wasn't as important as all that; and was he not, by becoming so idiotically upset, just displaying his naïvety and lack of sophistication? Toby had a horror of being thought naïve. He began to undress and resolved to think no more about it till the next morning. He turned the light out. But sleep did not come. And as he lay there in the darkness Toby found that after all what had happened had its interesting side. It certainly constituted an adventure, though a somewhat rebarbative one. And what he then experienced, though he did not at the time recognize it as such, was a feeling of pleasure at being suddenly in a position of power *vis-à-vis* someone whom he had so unquestioningly accepted as his spiritual superior.

This thought led him back toward considerations which were more humane: and it was here that the complexities began in earnest. He began really to envisage Michael. What was it like to be Michael? What was Michael thinking now? Was he lying awake, miserable, wishing that that hadn't happened? What would he do tomorrow? Would he speak to Toby about it? Or would he ignore it completely and behave as if it hadn't been? Toby felt he couldn't bear that. The sense of something needing to be completed began already to be strong in him. He was feeling, for the first time, intensely interested in Michael. He felt too, as he conjured up the image of that obviously rather complicated person, a new emotion about him. He found himself feeling, towards Michael, curiously protective. And with this thought at last he fell asleep.

The next morning he just felt wretched. His disgust had returned, but now it was directed for some obscure reason against himself. He felt as if he had taken part, on the previous night, in some exhausting orgy. Yet although he recalled with undiminished repugnance the incident in question, it seemed that what had constituted the orgy was chiefly his own thoughts. Yet he was far from wanting to turn his mind to other things. Whereas before he had wholeheartedly enjoyed his work in the garden, it seemed today burdensome and time-wasting in that it distracted him from thinking about Michael. He would have liked to spend the morning walking in the woods. Instead he had to sustain a conversation with James, and then with Patchway, and then with Mrs Mark, with whom he was detailed to spend the last part of the morning packing vegetables into nets and boxes. Michael avoided him.

It seemed possible that Michael might take an opportunity at lunch-time to call him aside. But the meal passed off without their having even looked at each other. Toby was anxious not to appear to invite a *tête-à-tête*, and he vanished during the short interval after lunch to a remote corner of the fruit garden where there was a job of attaching wires to the wall which he had been asked to do when a spare moment came. But when he got there he could not bring himself to do the job. He sat on the path, turning the little stones over with his fingers, until it was time to start work officially again.

In the afternoon he was employed once more on the perennial hoeing. At least here he was alone. The weather had continued very hot and his vigorous efforts soon made him perspire freely. He worked on doggedly with his head down. From farther away he could hear the purr of the mechanical cultivator, which had gone into action immediately under the control of Patchway, who had experienced in its respect a lightning conversion. As the afternoon wore on Toby began to feel totally miserable, and the confusion of his thoughts was resolved into one intense need: to talk to Michael.

He went through high tea in a daze, and after sitting about for some time conspicuously in the common-room, forced himself to return to the fruit garden to do the wiring. It was here that Mrs Mark found him round about eight o'clock with the message that Michael would like to see him at once.

*

When Michael reached his bedroom he immediately lay down on the floor, and for a while it was as if, in a sheer desire to be hidden, all sense of his own personality left him. The shock of what had occurred and the intensity of his regret for it left him quite stunned. To have thought it, to have dreamed it, yes – but to have *done* it! And as Michael contemplated that tiny distance between the thought and the act it was like a most narrow crack which even as he watched it was opening into an abyss. Covering his face he tried to pray: but he soon realized that he was still thoroughly drunk. His present prostration was fruitless and ignoble. He was not even in a condition properly to recognize his own wretchedness. He uttered some words all the same, conventional and familiar words, put together for such purposes by other men. He could not find any words or thoughts of his own. He got up from the floor.

He went to the washstand and sponged his face over with a wet flannel. His skin was burning. He must pull himself together and do some decent thinking: but as he stood there with the dripping flannel in his hand what came back to him with a pain more searching still was the desire that Nick might not have seen, and the fear that he might. When he wondered why this seemed now to matter so desperately the answer was a strange one. He did not want Nick to feel himself betrayed or abandoned by Michael's preference for a younger man. But this was, he knew, a perfectly crazy emotion, since it assumed that time had stood still. That he should not want Nick to think him corrupt or wicked was proper enough, and that for Nick's sake as well as his own. But what seemed to distress him so profoundly was the notion that Nick might think him unfaithful.

Michael found this thought so surprising that he did not know what to do with it. He threw down the flannel. The cold water was trickling across his neck and down his back. He was conscious again of his headache and unpleasant sensations in the stomach. He sat on the bed making a violent effort to be calm. When he had to some extent succeeded he recognized it as appalling that his first concern had not been for Toby. His prior instinct had been that of a sort of self-preservation: a fear for himself, which he had not yet dared fully to examine, together with this insane reaction about Nick.

Whereas what he ought to be considering was the damage done to the boy.

Thinking about Toby was at first less painful, since it was possible here to see the thing as a problem and to attempt at least to circumscribe it. Michael began soberly to estimate Toby's state of mind. He was certain from what he knew of the boy and his background that Toby would have no experience and very little knowledge of homosexuality and probably regarded 'queers' as contemptible, mysterious, and disgusting. The effect of Michael's embrace would probably be considerable; and even if Michael himself were to decide it wisest to pass the incident off as something best not discussed, Toby would hardly be able to cooperate. He would want an explanation. He would require a sequel. To say no more about it would be to leave the boy in a state of unrelieved anxiety and tension. Something would have to be done.

As Michael now seriously considered Toby he began for the first time, and noted wryly how late this came, to recognize that he had damaged somebody other than himself. He pictured Toby's reactions: the shock, the disgust, the disillusionment, the sense of something irretrievably spoilt. Toby had come to Imber as to a religious house, as to a retreat. He had looked for an inspiration and an example. That Michael's own halo had abruptly vanished mattered less: but the whole experience of Imber would now be ruined for Toby. Bitterly and relentlessly Michael explored the implications of what he had done. That something so momentary and so trivial could have so much meaning, could achieve so much destruction! In a sense, Michael knew what had happened: he had drunk too much and yielded to an isolated and harmless impulse of effection. In another sense, he did not yet know what had happened. Our actions are like ships which we may watch set out to sea, and not know when or with what cargo they will return to port.

With an effort Michael composed himself for sleep. For a while he prayed, endeavouring to direct his intent towards Toby. There would be time enough for self-examination later on. He was aware, seeing them as it were with the corner of his eye, that there were demons within himself which his action had set loose. The insane tormenting thought about Nick was still present to his mind. As he crawled into bed and began at last to lose consciousness his final reflection was that though he had done something bad to Toby he had done something worse to himself. What that thing was remained to be seen.

The next day he addressed himself to deciding what to do. It was then that he noticed another feature of the situation. He found himself intensely anxious to see Toby again and to speak to him about what had occurred. At breakfast-time they both sat with downcast eyes and Michael escaped immediately afterwards to his office. He was frantic to talk to Toby. He remembered how yesterday, during the journey home, he had felt his heart heel over in tenderness for the boy, and had been sure that such a spring of feeling could not be wholly evil. Today, with more cynicism, he wondered if he had not better play what was safest for himself, regardless of Toby's puzzlement and anxiety, and just let the matter drop completely. An emotional talk, anything resembling an apology, would only prolong the incident. Michael also found himself wanting to be reassured about Nick; while at the same time the thought of questioning Toby about Nick agitated him extremely. If he did speak to Toby he must be very cold and reserved; but would he be capable of it?

During the morning he found time to go over to the visitors' chapel and sat there for a while in the darkness and the silence. It was not difficult in that place to be persuaded of the nearness of God. The purer striving of so many others had carved, as it were, a path, a chasm. Here at last the fever of his mind was calmed and he felt with his whole being the desire to do only what was pleasing to God, and the confidence that this was something which he could both know and do. At the same time, in this recollected state he was more able to judge the poverty of the thoughts which had afflicted him last night and this morning. How quick he had been to take fright, how far from any sort of true repentance, how unready to seek for that *real* goodwill towards Toby which should be his guide. He prayed now for that most remote and difficult of insights, the sober realization that one has sinned; and as he looked through the grille towards the altar he felt calmed, helped, and supported. There was work for him to do and God would not ultimately let him suffer shipwreck. He decided that Toby must be spoken to.

His desire to see the boy was still extremely keen. As he left the chapel he decided he would postpone the interview till the following day. This small abstinence would cool him yet further, and in any case he hoped to be generally much calmer on the morrow. At lunch-time, still avoiding Toby's eye, he listened attentively to the reading, touched by Catherine's obvious devotion to her author, and remembering how she had once told him that Dame Julian had had an influence in her decision to become a nun. How many souls indeed had not this gentle mystic consoled and cheered, with her simple understanding of the reality of God's love. Michael took the reading to himself, reflecting that his innumerable hesitations, his inability to act simply and naturally, were marks of lack of faith.

In the afternoon he went to a remote part of the garden and occupied himself with hard physical work. The delights of the mechanical digger he surrendered to Patchway. His pleasure in that gaily coloured toy was in any case quite spoilt. Turning over the earth, he found himself a prey to many thoughts. At tea-time he was nervous and listless and without appetite. After tea he tried to settle down in his office and make a draft of the appeal for financial help. But his mind was blunted. The earlier complexity of his thoughts began to collapse. It began to seem to him absurd and gratuitously mystifying to Toby, to postpone the interview. He felt dully and violently, with a mixture of pain and pleasure which was not itself unpleasurable, the desire to get it over. He needed above anything to rid himself of a craving which made all other activity impossible.

Michael decided not to interview Toby in his office or bedroom. Reflective, now that he had decided to wait no longer, he wanted the interview to be business-like, not intimate. He found himself planning it and deciding what he was going to say, even with a sort of satisfaction. He recalled his promise to show Toby where the nightjars haunted, and he thought that to speak to the boy while fulfilling that promise would strike the right note of ordinariness. He would thereby make clear to Toby that nothing much had changed and there was no fearful discontinuity between the time before and the time after that unfortunate moment last night. He discovered from Margaret Strafford that Toby was in the fruit garden; and as she was going there herself she bore him the message.

Michael waited for him on the other side of the ferry. He wanted to shorten the part of the journey they would make together. He also wanted to make sure that Nick was not in the vicinity. Fortunately there seemed to be no sign of him in the field or in the wood. As Michael walked back to the lake side he saw Toby running down the grassy slope from the house. He jumped into the boat, almost sinking it, propelled it across as fast as its sluggish weight would allow, and arrived breathless on the wooden landing-stage where Michael was now standing.

'Hello, Toby,' said Michael coolly, turning at once to lead him along the path to the wood. 'I'm going to show you the nightjars. You remember I said I would. It's not very far from here. Do you know anything about nightjars?'

Toby, who was looking resolutely at the ground while he walked, shook his head.

'The nightjar,' said Michael, 'is a migrant. It should be leaving us any time now, and it always sings with particular vigour just before it goes. It's a most unusual bird, as you'll see. Its Latin name is *caprimulgus*, goat-sucker, as it was once thought to feed on the milk of goats. Its main call, which I hope you'll hear, is a sort of bubbling sound on two notes. It only flies in the twilight and it has a very odd flight, exceedingly fast, yet rather irregular and bat-like. It has another peculiarity too, which is that when it's sitting on a branch it often claps its wings together over its back.'

Toby said nothing. They were well into the wood now, and although it was still daylight outside, here it was already quite obscure. The weakened light of the setting sun could not penetrate the trees, which seemed to generate their own darkness.

They turned into a wide grassy alley where many coniferous trees had been planted among the oaks and elms. Here it was a little lighter, but still shadowy, and even as they looked growing darker. The alley led towards the wall of the Abbey which could be seen in the distance, pierced by a small gate, the sun still lingering upon it.

Near the middle of the alley Michael stopped under a tree. They stood there in silence, listening to the inaudible yet somehow living and stirring quietness of the darkening wood. They stood there for a long time, not looking at each other, lulled at last in a kind of coma. Then from nearby among the trees, seeming like a signal, there came a hollow clapping sound. The clapping was followed shortly by a low bubbling churr, then by more clapping; and in the thickening twilight of the alley the birds were suddenly present. They flitted to and fro between the trees, turning and returning in an insistent bat-like circular dance. It was impossible to see how many there were, but it seemed like a multitude as they fluttered and poised in the granular darkness, making a very soft whirring noise with their long pointed wings. Deep in the wood the hollow clapping continued.

Soon it was almost too dark to see. The birds could still be vaguely apprehended, close overhead, like great leaves that fluttered but never fell, until at last they disappeared, gathered up into the obscurity of the coming night. Michael began to pace slowly back down the middle of the avenue. He did not turn towards Toby, who kept step with him, putting his feet down softly in the longish grass. Michael felt now an extraordinary peace in which he felt sure that Toby shared. It was as if they had been present together at some esoteric and liberating rite. In a way, it was a pity to break the spell by vulgar explanations. But at last he spoke, seeming to utter something that he had learnt by heart.

'Toby, about what happened yesterday evening. I did something foolish and wrong – and something I assure you that I'm not at all in the habit of doing. I was almost as surprised at it as you were. I don't want to make a drama about this. I won't say "forget it" because we can't do that; but I suggest we set it aside and don't brood on it or give it an exaggerated importance. In so far as it was a wrong action, that concerns me and not you. I just wanted, well, to apologize to you and to ask you to bury the matter. I know I needn't appeal to your discretion. But I was anxious in case you should be worrying about it. I'm deeply sorry that you've been upset and bothered in this way – and I hope you'll make a real effort not to let this thing spoil your time at Imber.'

They stopped and turned to face each other. It was almost completely dark now, even in the more open space of the avenue, and the trees were almost invisible, opaque presences of deeper black on either side. Toby looked at the ground and then with an obvious effort raised his head to look at Michael. He said in a low voice, 'Of course, it's all right. I'm sorry. It's all right. It was good of you to talk to me like this. I quite understand. As far as I'm concerned, I'll bury the matter completely.'

Looking at his darkened countenance Michael had suddenly a strange sense of *déjà vu*. Where had this scene, with its inevitable ending, happened before? And even as he spoke and moved he remembered the fading light in his room at school when he and the boy had sat for so long quite still and face to face.

'Thank you,' said Michael, also very softly. No power on earth could have prevented him at that moment from touching Toby. He reached his hand out blindly toward the boy – and as if drawn magnetically Toby's hand met his in a strong grip. They stood silently together in the darkness.

CHAPTER 13

It was the next morning. The sun was still faithfully shining, but a certain chillness and bleakness in the air at breakfast-time made known the season, and then the eye was more quick to see the signs of autumnal decay. Toby spent the earlier part of the morning with Patchway, who was anxious to teach him how to use the cultivator. Toby found himself surprisingly uninterested in the thing and clumsy with it. After eleven he was dispatched, as usual, to the packing shed, but found there was nothing for him to do there. Mrs Mark, rushing off herself to the house to do the laundry, told him to go back to the garden. But instead Toby slunk away by himself. He wanted to think.

He decided to go and sit for a while in the visitors' chapel, and crossed the causeway, careless of observation. He had never been in the chapel except during Mass, and he found it now, empty and silent, an awe-inspiring place. The curtains were drawn back and the altar and the dim sanctuary light could be seen through the grille. The visitors' chapel was lighted by two small windows of greenish glass and was rather dark. The nuns' chapel, or what could be seen of it, was darker still, lit no doubt by late Victorian stained-glass windows. Inside there it was desperately silent and yet somehow attentive.

Toby stood for a while near the door of the visitors' chapel, listening. He had been told that, between the hours, day and night, there was always a nun at prayer in the main chapel. He could hear nothing. He advanced on tiptoe towards the grille and stopped at the low communion rail which was about three feet in front of it. There was something very odd about being placed sideways on to the altar and not being able to see the body of the chapel which faced the altar. He did not venture to step inside the communion rail; but, looking nervously behind him, he edged up as far as he could toward the left wall of the chapel, and peered through the bars from there. He could see very little more of what lay beyond: only the altar steps, some coloured tiling on the floor, and a further piece of the opposite wall. The nave remained relentlessly hidden.

Looking through into the greater darkness Toby was suddenly reminded of the obscurity of the lake, where the world was seen again in different colours; and he was taken with a profound desire to pass through the grille. When he had had this thought he was immediately shocked at it and rather frightened. Here he stood, and in a way, nothing prevented him from opening the little gate in the grille and walking through into the chapel and standing there, just for a moment perhaps, looking down the nave. He wondered what he would see. A great expanse of empty benches and a solitary nun, perhaps, kneeling somewhere near the back, regarding him sombrely; or, and the thought made his flesh creep, perhaps the entire community was in there at this moment, a few yards from him, sitting in complete silence. In a way nothing prevented him from going through. In a way it was something entirely impossible, and he could not even bring himself to step over the rail.

He retired quickly to the back of the visitors' chapel, feeling shame at the idea of being caught peering, and sat down. He felt irritated and confused and upset. Yesterday he had felt shock and a sort of horror, and then that feverish need to talk to Michael. But at least yesterday he had felt detached, yesterday he had been a spectator. Today he felt involved. He had suffered violence and then somehow been made privy to it; he was no longer a victim but an accomplice. He realized that in a way he was being unfair to Michael. What Michael had *said* yesterday had been perfectly sensible and cool; and after that very brief conversation in the alley they had walked back to the house, talking with careful casualness about other matters. But what lingered chiefly in Toby's mind was the way in which Michael had seized his hand, and the long moment when they had stood with their hands tightly clasped. If only it hadn't been for that; for the fact was that Toby knew that he himself had been just as anxious for the contact as Michael had been.

He too had been brimming over with emotion. In spite of the words, it had been like a scene between lovers; and looking back, it seemed as if the words were merely straw, flying upward to destruction in the fierce heat of the encounter. Toby felt himself caught in something messy and emotional and he hated it.

He felt however no dislike for Michael. Even the sense of physical disgust with which the whole business filled him remained turned against himself. What Michael had done was to Toby a tremendous revelation. His whole conception of human existence was become in a moment immensely more complex and even in a brief space had made progress. Toby was already less inclined to label Michael or to circumscribe what he was. He was filled rather with an immense curiosity. Whatever could it be like to be an almost priestlike figure and yet go round kissing boys? He wondered if, in spite of what he had said, Michael did this often? Perhaps he just had sudden irresistible inclinations of this sort. Did he suffer torments of remorse? The sense which Toby had had of the agreeableness of knowing the sordid side of so venerated a person was with him still. For all his distaste for the situation he was sensible of a sort of pleasure in having gained power over Michael: power which in his mind he scarcely distinguished from an instinct to protect. He found himself dwelling with tenderness upon the idea of Michael's frailties.

Toby was not in the habit of sitting and brooding. Usually, he was active, practical, and without a care in the world. With the simplicity which goes with a certain sort of excellent upbringing he had regarded himself as not yet grown up. Men had never troubled him nor women neither. 'Falling in love' he regarded as something reserved for the future, for that, it still seemed to him, fairly remote future in which he would become acquainted with the other sex. It was a shock to him now to find how rapidly his vision of the world had altered. He felt an extreme reluctance to work. He wanted most of all to do as he was doing now, to sit and think, remembering endlessly things that had been said and done and conjuring up continually in his mind the pale golden head and narrow worried hawk-like face of his friend. He wondered with alarm if just *this* was falling in love.

Toby was far from the sophistication of holding that we all participate in both sexes. He believed that one loved either men *or* women, and if one was unfortunate enough to develop homosexual tastes one would never be able to live a normal life thereafter. This thought filled him with an insidious fear. Michael had told him not to exaggerate the importance of what had happened; but what had happened had happened to *him* and was still going on happening, and he had as little control over it as over the progress of digestion. He wondered, and the thought, after last night, had more substance, whether he was a natural homosexual.

Was he attracted by women? The fact that he had not so far been had bothered Toby, till this moment, not a whit. Now it worried him and he began to want to be immediately re-assured. Toby had one brother, much younger than himself, and no sisters. He had scarcely met any girls of his own age. Images he had none to conjure up to test his inclinations. He pondered for a while rather generally upon the conception of Woman. A shapely yet maternal being arose before him. Shyly he began to unclothe her. And as he contemplated the vision, slyly observing his own reactions, he gradually became aware that this immense incarnation of femininity was taking on the features of Dora Greenfield.

Toby was both surprised and gratified at this development. He had not been especially conscious of finding Dora attractive, but now that he positively searched his mind, encouraging declarations which he would before have regarded as improper, it seemed to him that he had for some time been sensitive to her charms. She had, certainly, a magnificent head, with those flat tongues of golden brown hair shaping it, like something in an Italian picture; and for the rest, she was well rounded, buxom you might say. Toby's imagination shied for a while about the more expansive image of Dora. But most of all he saw her face, with its full mouth and gentle features and that maternal and encouraging look in the eye. Whereas from the colder image of Catherine, for all its sweetness, Toby's thoughts fled as from the figure of Artemis, he found in his memories of Dora's mien and gestures a warm encouragement and an invitation.

These imaginings were interrupted by the sound of movement within the nuns' chapel. Soft footsteps were heard and the frou-frou of heavy skirts. Toby jumped up in alarm. It must be time for sext. He stood listening to the footsteps and the suggestive rustling. They continued for some time; and then there was a subsiding sound as of a great bird settling into its nest. Silence followed, and was ended at last by a single soprano voice breaking into a plain-song chant. Toby was shaken. There was something monstrous, provocative almost, in the invisible and impregnable closeness to him of so many women. The taboo quality of the enclosure could no longer be taken for granted; he found it now irritating, tantalizing, exciting. The nun who was chanting had a very thin true voice, not unlike Catherine's. The chant continued until the hideous purity and austerity of the song became intolerable to him. He turned and stumbled out of the chapel.

Out in the dazzling sunlight he felt unutterably sick and disconsolate. He was conscious of an obscure wish to do something violent. The knowledge that he was playing truant from the market-garden troubled him and yet pleased him too. With deliberation, he turned away from the causeway, following the wall of the Abbey in the direction of the still distant main road. He walked close to the wall, trailing his hand against it. It was a very high wall built of small square stones, granite and ironstone, and had a mottled golden appearance. The dust from the dry surface came off on Toby's hand like pollen. He walked on, head down, thoroughly cross with himself and the world.

The wall, turning away from the lake, was soon fringed on both sides by tall trees and Toby found himself in the wood. A little further on he realized that the scene was familiar. A wide coniferous alley opened out to his left, leading towards the lake, and at the far end of it he could see the sun shining on the open ground not far from the Lodge. Memories of the previous evening returned to him vividly, and he had a curious sense of being unfaithful, followed by a feeling of the utter messiness of everything. Violence is born of the desire to escape oneself. Toby looked up at the wall.

A day or two ago he would not even have conceived of the possibility of climbing the Abbey wall. Now suddenly it seemed that since everything was so muddled, anything was permitted. The sense of this was not altogether unpleasant. An enormous excitement filled Toby and he realized then how much he had been, for the last half-hour, physically upset. He moved back into the cover of the trees and looked about him. His heart struck fiercely in his breast. He remembered the little gate he had seen leading into the alley; but that would certainly be locked. He examined the wall. It was a very old wall, loosely put together, full of irregularites and projections. He chose a place where the stons jutted and receded in an inviting way and began to mount, his hands searching for holds in the crevices towards the top of the wall.

It was harder than it looked. The soft stone crumbled at the edges and with grazed wrists Toby fell back to the ground. He was now frantic. The desire to see inside the enclosure had taken violent hold upon him. He had once more, and to an unprecedented degree, the disturbing sense of being about to pass through the looking-glass. The wall presented just the right degree of difficulty. It was an obstacle but not an insuperable one. Toby tried again.

This time he found a strong foothold, and spread-eagled half-way up the wall explored above him for a reliable place for his fingers. He found one, and edged one foot up further. He reached out blindly over his head, hoping now to get a grip upon the top. His groping hand encountered the clear edge, and thrusting his fingers through a soft fringe of moss and stonecrop he held on. The other hand followed as his foothold below began to give way. He got one elbow over the top of the wall and his feet scrabbled for holds on the crumbling surface. In another moment, panting and straightening his arms, he pulled himself up until, leaning on his front, one leg could be curled over the top. He rested, astride the wall.

Exhausted and triumphant, Toby surveyed the scene. He saw, rather to his surprise, that the alley of conifers continued on the other side. He could not, from where he was, see down it. Within the enclosure the wood was just as thick, and no buildings were to be seen, except for a glimpse of the Norman tower far away on the right. Toby felt immediate disappointment. After all, it looked pretty much the same inside as outside. He swung his legs over onto the inside of the wall and sat looking about him. Perhaps something would happen, perhaps a nun would pass by. But he sat for a while, and the wood remained impenetrable and silent.

When climbing the wall Toby had not meant to do more than look into the Abbey grounds. Now that he was on the wall he began to feel, tickling and torturing him as a physical urge, the desire to jump down into the enclosure. A moment or two after feeling the urge he knew it to be irresistible. He might delay, but sooner or later he *must* jump. When he realized this he became so agitated that he jumped immediately, landing with a good deal of noise and damage to his clothing among some brambles. He picked himself up and stood still, breathing hard and listening. As everything remained quiet he moved cautiously away from the wall and walked softly towards the alley where he hoped he might get a view of the Abbey buildings.

Trembling a little and feeling that at any moment a stern voice might call him to account, Toby came into the open ground at the end of the alley. The alley was smooth and well kept. It led however not to a building but to another smaller wall in which there was a door. Nothing more could be seen. Toby stood still for a while looking. He wondered what would happen if he were found; and his imagination hesitated between a picture of nuns fleeing from him with piercing screams and nuns leaping upon him like bacchantes. He did not know which picture was the more alarming; or indeed, he was amazed to find himself reflecting, the more delicious. Gradually as he stood there in the unnerving silence of the place his dismay at what he had done increased. He decided he had better start climbing back again. However the repetition, further down the alley, of the wall and the door constituted too fascinating a challenge. He could not take his eyes off the door; and in a moment he found himself gliding between the trees towards it.

When he reached it he looked back. Already the high wall of the enclosure seemed far away. He reflected that he might yet have to return at a run. He faced the little door. The wall here was lower, but too high to see over. It disappeared into the shade of trees on either side; but there were no trees beyond the wall. The avenue ended at this point. Toby put his hand on the latch and took a deep breath. He pressed the latch down and the bar rose with a loud click. He pressed the door which groaned a little and began to open slowly. The noise alarmed him, but he went on pushing the door which opened onto a carpet of close-cut grass. He stepped through the opening and found himself in a cemetery.

The unexpectedness of the scene made Toby rigid in the doorway, his hand still on the door. He was in a green space enclosed by a rectangle of walls, within which there stretched neatly row after row of graves, each with a small white cross above it. A line of rather gaunt black cypresses against the sun-baked wall on the far side gave the place a strangely southern aspect. His alarm at the vision was hardly increased by seeing quite near to him two nuns who were apparently tending the graves. One of them had a pair of shears in her hand. A lawn mower stood by but had evidently not been in use or Toby would have heard it. Toby looked at the nuns and the nuns, who had straightened up from their labours at the sound of the opening gate, looked at Toby.

The nun with the shears laid down her tool and said something in a low voice to the second nun. Then she came towards Toby, her long habit sweeping the grass. Paralysed with shame and alarm he watched her approach.

When she was near enough for him to focus his distracted glance upon her face he saw that she was smiling. His hand dropped from the gate and he stepped back automatically out of the cemetery. She followed him, closing the gate behind her, and they faced each other in the alley.

178

'Good morning,' said the nun. 'I believe you must be Toby. Have I guessed right?'

'Yes,' said Toby, hanging his head.

They began to walk slowly back together between the trees. 'I thought so,' said the nun. 'Although we never meet, we seem to know each one of you, as if you were our dearest friends.' The nun seemed quite at her ease. Toby was in an agony of embarrassment and alarm.

'I expect our little cemetery gave you quite a surprise?' said the nun.

'It did!' said Toby.

'It's a beautiful place, don't you think?' said the nun. 'It's so cosy and enclosed, rather like a dormitory I sometimes think. It's nice to know that one will sleep there oneself one day.'

'It's beautiful, yes,' said Toby, desperate.

They passed under a large cedar tree from whose spreading lower branches Toby noticed something hanging. It was a swing. Involuntarily he reached out his hand as he neared it and touched the rope.

'It's a fine swing,' said the nun. Her voice was by now betraying her as Irish. 'Why not try it? It would cheer the old swing up. We sometimes do ourselves.'

Toby hesitated. Then blushing violently he sat in the swing and urged himself several times to and fro. The nun stood by smiling.

Mumbling something Toby got out of the swing. He was ready to run, to dive into the ground. Averting his head he walked on beside the nun, who was still talking, until they reached the gate in the enclosure wall.

The nun opened the gate.

'It wasn't locked!' said Toby with surprise.

'Why, we never bother with locking the gates!' said the nun. 'I expect you enjoyed your climb. Young boys are forever climbing things.' Beaming she swung the gate open. Toby stepped through and for a moment they looked at each other through the gateway. Toby felt he ought to apologize and struggled for the words.

'I'm sorry,' he said, 'I know I oughtn't to have come in.'

'Don't be after worrying,' said the nun. 'They say that curiosity killed the cat, but I never believed it when I was your age. Besides, we have a special rule which says that children can sometimes come into the enclosure.' She closed the gate between them and it seemed to Toby that her smile lingered on the outside of the gate for a second or two after it clicked shut. He turned to face the avenue.

All was silent. No one had seen his entry and no one had seen his ignominious exit. He began to run down the avenue, anxious to get as far away as possible from the dangerous and it now seemed to him even more impregnable enclosure. He felt ridiculous, humiliated, and ashamed. He ran with his head down saying, 'Damn, damn, damn' to himself as he went along.

He emerged panting into the open grassland by the drive, and as he crossed it he saw the Land-Rover come sweeping in through the gates. His heart had time to give one violent jump; but the next moment he saw that it was Mark Strafford and not Michael who was at the wheel.

When he saw Toby, Mark slowed down and called out, 'Give you a lift? We're nearly late for lunch.'

Toby climbed in beside Mark and tried, as they drove round towards the house, to make coherent replies to his remarks about the tiresomeness of people in the market at Cirencester. They stopped on the gravel in front of the steps and Mrs Mark at once came bustling up to them, asking her husband if he had remembered all the shopping.

Toby said to her, 'You don't happen to know where Dora is just now, do you?'

Mrs Mark turned her round shining face on him portentously. 'You don't know?' she said. 'Mrs Greenfield has left us. She's gone back to London.'

CHAPTER 14

Dora Greenfield was lying in bed. It was the morning of the same day. Paul had been making love to her. Now he was gone to his work. Dora had submitted to his love without enthusiasm, and after it she felt tired and unreal. Breakfast-time was past and there was no reason to get up now rather than later. She lay looking at the open window where a clear sky was once more displayed. She contemplated this depth of space, wondering whether to call it blue or grey. The sun must be shining and the sky must be blue, only since her room faced north and she could see nothing sun-lit from her bed, the colour eluded her. She pulled the bed-clothes more closely round her and lit a cigarette. It was a chilly morning all the same with an autumnal dampness in the air.

With Paul, nothing had gone right since he had made that little speech about Catherine. It was not that Dora was jealous, or that Paul was really infatuated with Catherine. It was just that Dora had then estimated, with a devastating exactness which was usually alien to her, how much of sheer contempt there was in Paul's love; and always would be, she reflected, since she had few illusions about her ability to change herself. It did not occur to her to wonder if Paul might change, or indeed to hope from him anything at all. She felt his contempt as destructive of her, and his love, consequently, as unwelcome. Yet all the time, in a shy roundabout way, she loved him herself, rather hopelessly and gloomily, as one might love someone to whom one had never spoken.

They had started quarrelling again. Dora had gone round to the parlours, several times, to look at Paul's books; but, apart from one or two pictures, they seemed to her dull, and Paul exclaimed bitterly about boring her, which made it all the harder for her to show interest. She left him alone now during the day, and mooched about by herself, or else performed small tasks in the house under the direction of Mrs Mark. She felt herself watched. Everyone, she imagined, was covertly observing her to see if she was cheerful, to see if she was settling down again with her husband. She felt organized and shut in. Mrs Mark had now suggested three times that it would be a good idea if she had a talk with Mother Clare; and on the third occasion out of sheer inertia Dora had said perhaps she would sometime. Today, no doubt, Mrs Mark would try to pin her down to a definite appointment. Dora stubbed out her cigarette carefully on the back of a matchbox and began to get up.

On the way to the window she looked at herself in the tall mirror. She was wearing her blue nylon pyjamas which had been lost with the suitcase. She looked at herself gravely, wondering if she was really thinner, and whether cutting down on alcohol had improved her complexion. But she could not interest herself in what she saw or quite believe in it. She could not even focus her eyes properly upon the stupefied face of her image. She went on and leaned out of the window. The sun was shining, the lake was hard and full of reflections, the Norman tower presented to her one golden face and one receding into shadow. Dora had the odd feeling that all this was inside her head. There was no way of breaking into this scene, for it was all imaginary.

Rather startled at this feeling, she began to dress and tried to think about something practical. But the dazed feeling of unreality continued. It was as if her consciousness had eaten up its surroundings. Everything was now subjective. Even, she remembered, Paul this morning had been subjective. His lovemaking had been remote, like something that she imagined, like a half-waking fantasy, and not at all like an encounter with another real human being. Dora wondered if she was ill. Perhaps she ought to borrow Mark Strafford's thermometer, to ask for something from the medicine chest. She went again to the window, and an idea occurred to her of trying somehow to break into the idle motionless scene. She thought that if she threw something very hard out of the window it would fall into the lake with a splash and disturb the reflections. She opened the window wider and looked for something to throw. The match-box was not heavy enough. She took her lipstick, and leaning well back, hurled it out. It vanished, falling presumably far short of the lake, somewhere in the long grass. Dora felt almost tearful.

It was then that she began to want to go to London. Since her arrival at Imber she had not for one second seriously contemplated leaving. But now, driven by this fit of solipsistic melancholy one degree more desperate, she felt the need of an act: and it seemed that there was only one act which she could perform, to take the train to London. The idea sent the blood rushing to Dora's head. She felt her cheeks hot, her heart beating: at once more real. She put on her coat and examined her handbag. She had plenty of money. Nothing stopped her from going, she was free. She sat down on the bed.

Ought she to go? Paul would be very upset. But in fact her relations with Paul had been so wretched lately, they could hardly be worse, and she reflected vaguely that the shock might do him good. More deeply, she felt a wish to punish him. He had been, during the last two days, consistently unpleasant to her. Dora felt the need to show him that she could still act independently. She was not his slave. Yes, she would go: and the idea, now it existed more fully for her, was delightful. She would not stay long of course – perhaps not even overnight. She would make no drama of it. She would come back, jauntily, casually, almost at once. She needn't plan that now. But what a tonic it would be for her – and what a slap in the face for Imber! She packed a small bag and set off unobtrusively on foot for the station, leaving a note saying 'Gone to London'.

Dora had of course not troubled to inform herself about trains. It turned out, however, that she was lucky and no sooner had she arrived, rather breathless, at the station than a fast London train came in. She was amazed to find, when she stepped out onto the platform at Paddington, that it was not yet midday. She stood for a while and let the crowds course round her, delighting in the rush and jostling, the din of voices and trains, the smells of oil and steam and dirt, the grimy hurly-burly and kind, healing anonymity of London. Already she felt more herself. Then she went to a telephone box and rang Sally's number. Sally, who was now teaching at a primary school, was at home at irregular times and might just be caught. But there was no answer. Dora felt both glad and sorry since she could now with a clearer conscious telephone Noel.

Noel was in. His voice over the wire sounded delighted, ecstatic. She must come to lunch, she must come round at once, the place was full of delicious things, he had no work that afternoon, nothing could be nicer. Overjoyed, Dora jumped into a taxi. She soon arrived at the house where Noel lived, a great cream-coloured early Victorian mansion with an immense portico in a tree-shaded cul-de-sac near the Brompton Road. Noel lived in the top flat.

The meeting was enthusiastic. Dora could hardly get through the door fast enough. She hurled herself into Noel's arms. He swung her round, lifted her off her feet, threw her onto the sofa, and bounded about her like a large dog. They were laughing and talking at once at the tops of their voices. Dora was quite astounded at how pleased she was: 'Gosh!' she cried, 'All that noise does me good.'

'No wonder,' said Noel, 'after that ghastly convent. Let me look at you. Yes, paler, thinner. Dear darling, I *am* so glad to see you!' He pulled her to her feet and kissed her boisterously.

Dora looked up at him. She touched his plain, irregular features, pulled his floppy colourless hair, and squeezed his enormous friendly hands. How very large he was. And my God, he was easy on the nerves. 'Give me a drink,' she commanded.

Noel's flat was modern. A grey fitted carpet covered all the floors. White painted book-cases contained books on economics and foreign travel. Three walls were yellow and the fourth covered with a black and white paper that looked like a grove of bamboos. Everything was shining and very clean. A hi-fi gramophone in light walnut, piled high with a glossy litter of long-playing records, occupied one corner. The enormous divan was covered with a Welsh bedspread of geometrical design and garnished with innumerable cushions of different greens. The chairs were made of curly sagging steel and exquisitely comfortable. As she heard the chink of ice cubes and smelt the aroma of the lemons which Noel was slicing with a sharp knife Dora spread out her arms. Noel made her feel that it was no scandal to go on being young. She announced, 'I'm going to have a bath.'

'Darling, you do that small thing!' said Noel. 'I'll bring you your drink in the bathroom. I suppose the sybaritic practice of bathing was forbidden at the convent.'

At Imber the immersion heater was turned on twice a week and a bath list, pinned to the notice board by Mrs Mark, made known the order of priority. Dora, who was only interested in baths as a luxury and not as a necessity had missed hers. Now in Noel's pink and white bathroom she was running the steamy water, pouring in the odoriferous bath salts, and seeking in the airing cupboard for a warm and downy towel. She was already in when Noel arrived with the cocktail.

'Now tell me all about it,' said Noel, sitting on the edge of the bath. 'Was it hell?'

'It's not too bad actually,' said Dora. 'I'm only up here for the day, you know. I felt I needed a change. All the people are nice. I haven't seen any nuns yet, except one that lives outside. But there's a horrible feeling of being watched and organized.'

'How's dear old Paul?'

'He's fine. Well, he's been beastly to me for two days, but I expect that's my fault.'

'There you go!' said Noel. 'Why should everything be your fault? Some things are perhaps, but not every damn thing. The trouble with Paul is he's jealous of your creative powers. As he can't create anything himself he's determined you shan't.'

'Don't be silly,' said Dora. 'I haven't any creative powers. And Paul's terribly creative. Could you hold my glass and pass me the soap?'

'Well, don't let's start on Paul,' said Noel. 'But about those religious folk. Don't let them give you a bad conscience. People like that adore having a sense of sin and living in an atmosphere of emotion and self-abasement. You must be a great catch. The penitent wife and so forth. But don't give in to them. Never forget, my darling, that what they believe just isn't true.'

'You're drinking my drink!' said Dora. 'No, I suppose it isn't

185

true. But there's something decent about them all the same.'

'They may be nice,' said Noel, 'but they're thoroughly misguided. No good comes in the end of untrue beliefs. There is no God and there is no judgement, except the judgement that each one of us makes for himself; and what that is is a private matter. Sometimes of course one has to interfere with people to stop them doing things one dislikes. But for Christ's sake let their minds alone. I can't stand complacent swine who go around judging other people and making them feel cheap. If *they* want to wallow in a sense of unworthiness, let them; but when they interfere with their neighbours one ought positively to *fight* them!'

'You sound quite passionate!' said Dora. 'Pass me the towel.'

'Yes, I am a bit worked up,' said Noel. 'Don't get cold, sweetie. I'll make you another drink and put on my new longplayer. It's just that I hate to think of those people making you feel a miserable sinner when in fact it's not all that much your fault at all. And the idea of old Paul playing the aggrieved and virtuous spouse makes me want to vomit. I wonder has that place got any news value. Potty communities are good for a feature. Shall I come and give it the once over?'

'Oh dear no!' said Dora, shocked. 'You certainly mustn't! They're getting a new bell soon, the Abbey, that is, a big bell to hang in the tower, and I think there'll be a statement to the press about that. But otherwise nothing happens at all and they'd be awfully upset if anyone came to write them up. They really *are* nice, Noel.'

'Well, if you say so,' said Noel. 'Listen to this, angel.'

As Dora slipped into her clothes she heard the steady expectant beat of a drum. Then into the deep rhythmic sound were woven the unpremeditated and protesting cries of a clarinet and a trumpet. The beat, more insistent than ever, was hidden in the increasingly complex golden nostalgic din. The music flowered, rampageous, irresistible. Dora issued eagerly from the bathroom and joined Noel who was already pacing panther-like about the room. They began to dance, very slowly at first, solemn, holding each other's eyes. Slight movements of head and hand and hip expressed their communion with the rhythm. Then their feet began to move faster, weaving a complicated pattern upon the carpet as Noel, moving to the beat, expelled the chairs and tables from the middle of the room. Then he reached out his hand to Dora, swung her towards him, tossed her away again, turned and twirled her until she was a kaleidoscope of rippling skirts and flashing thighs and golden brown hair tumbled across the face.

When the record ended they fell exhausted to the floor, laughing with triumph after the ritual solemnity of the dance. Then when their laughter ended they regarded each other, sitting entwined upon the floor, still hand in hand. 'Fight!' said Noel. 'Don't forget, fight! And now, dearest creature, I must leave you to go and get the only thing which is missing, which is a bottle of wine. I won't be a moment. You know, the off-licence is just round the corner. Let me fill your glass again. You can amuse yourself meanwhile getting the things out of the fridge.'

He kissed Dora and went away down the stairs singing. When he had gone she sat for a while on the floor, sipping her replenished drink and enjoying the sense of sheer present physical being which the dance had given her. Then she got up and went to the kitchen and opened the fridge. A delicious meal seemed to be pending. She took out several kinds of salami, stuffed olives, pâté, tomatoes, pickled cucumber, various cheeses, a hand of bananas, and a large thin piece of red steak. Dora, who liked her meals to tail away in a series of small treats, looked at the scene with satisfaction. She put the things on the table, and assembled round them the garlic, pepper, oil, vinegar, French mustard, sea salt, and all the apparatus she knew Noel liked to cook with. At his simple and appetizing repasts he was always the chef and Dora his admiring assistant. She felt extremely gay.

The telephone began ringing in the living-room. Absently Dora went back and lifted the receiver. Her mouth full of a handful of cocktail biscuits, she was not able to enunciate at once, and the caller at the other end had the first word. Paul's voice said: 'Hello, is that Brompton 8379?'

Dora froze. She swallowed the biscuits and held the phone away from her, staring at it as if it were a small savage animal. A silence followed.

Then Paul said, 'Hello, could I speak to Mr Spens?' Dora could just hear him speaking. Cautiously she brought the phone back to her ear. 'This is Paul Greenfield. Is my wife there?'

Dora knew that voice of Paul's, stiff, trembling with nervous anger. She hardly dared to breathe in case it should be audible. It seemed that Paul must know that she was there at the other end of the line. She couldn't bring herself to put the phone down. If she kept quiet perhaps Paul would think the number was unobtainable.

Then Paul said 'Dora.'

As Dora heard her name her eyes closed, and her face wrinkled up in pain. But she kept icily still, scarcely breathing.

'Dora,' said Paul again, 'Dora, is that you?'

Suddenly in the silence that followed another sound could be heard along the wire. For a moment Dora could not think what it was. Then she recognized it as a blackbird singing. The bird uttered a few notes and then was quiet. The telephone box at Imber was downstairs in the hallway by the refectory. The blackbird must be just outside on the terrace. It sang again, its song sounding clear and intolerably remote and strange in the silence after Paul's voice. Dora put the phone down noisily on the table. She went into the kitchen. She looked with a sort of amazement at the collection of food, at the half-open door of the fridge, at her own half-finished drink. She went back and replaced the receiver.

She returned to the kitchen. The piece of steak, uncurling from its frozen state, lay raw and oozing, its wrapping paper, stained red, adhering to it. The garlic, the olives, the oil, suddenly looked to Dora like part of some dreary apparatus of seduction. Here too, she felt, she was being organized. The sense of unreality returned; after all, there were no meetings and no actions. She stood for a while miserable and irresolute. She no longer wanted to stay and have lunch with Noel. She wanted to get away from the telephone. She picked up her coat and her bag, scribbled a note to Noel, and began to trail down the stairs. She knew Noel wouldn't mind. That was a wonderful thing about Noel, and made him so unlike Paul; he never bothered about little things such as one's coming to lunch with him and then suddenly deciding to go away.

Dora reached the corner of the road and hailed a taxi. As the taxi was turning round to join her at the kerb she saw Noel running towards her with the bottle in his hand. He reached her just as the taxi drew up.

'What's got you now?' said Noel.

'Paul rang up,' said Dora.

'My God!' said Noel. 'What did you say to him?'

'I said nothing,' said Dora. 'I put down the receiver.'

'Is he on his way here?'

'No, he rang from the country. I heard a bird singing. And I didn't reply so he can't know.'

'Well what about our lunch?' said Noel.

'I don't feel like it any more,' said Dora. 'Please forgive me.'

'I thought you were a fighter,' said Noel.

'I can't fight,' said Dora. 'I never could tell the difference between right and wrong anyway. But it doesn't matter. Sorry to rush away. I enjoyed our dance.'

'Me too,' said Noel. 'All right, off you go. But don't forget, what these people believe isn't true.'

'O.K.,' said Dora. She turned to the taximan and said the first thing that came into her head, 'National Gallery.'

Noel called after the taxi, 'Don't forget! No God!'

Dora hadn't especially intended to visit the National Gallery, but once she was there she went in. It was as good a place as any other to decide what to do. She no longer wanted any lunch. She wondered if she should try telephoning Sally again; but she no longer wanted to see Sally. She climbed the stairs and wandered away into the eternal spring-time of the air-conditioned rooms.

Dora had been in the National Gallery a thousand times and the pictures were almost as familiar to her as her own face. Passing between them now, as through a well-loved grove, she felt a calm descending on her. She wandered a little, watching with compassion the poor visitors armed with guide books who were peering anxiously at the masterpieces. Dora did not need to peer. She could look, as one can at last when one knows a great thing very well, confronting it with a dignity which it has itself conferred. She felt that the pictures belonged to her, and reflected ruefully that they were about the only thing that did. Vaguely, consoled by the presence of something welcoming and responding in the place, her footsteps took her to various shrines at which she had worshipped so often before: the great light spaces of Italian pictures, more vast and southern than any real South, the angels of Botticelli, radiant as birds, delighted as gods, and curling like the tendrils of a vine, the glorious carnal presence of Susanna Fourment, the tragic presence of Margarethe Trip, the solemn world of Piero della Francesca with its early-morning colours, the enclosed and gilded world of Crivelli. Dora stopped at last in front of Gainsborough's picture of his two daughters. These children step through a wood hand in hand, their garments shimmering, their eyes serious and dark, their two pale heads, round full buds, like yet unlike.

Dora was always moved by the pictures. Today she was moved, but in a new way. She marvelled, with a kind of gratitude, that they were all still here, and her heart was filled with love for the pictures, their authority, their marvellous generosity, their splendour. It occurred to her that here at last was something real and something perfect. Who had said that, about perfection and reality being in the same place? Here was something which her consciousness could not wretchedly devour, and by making it part of her fantasy make it worthless. Even Paul, she thought, only existed now as someone she dreamt about; or else as a vague external menace never really encountered and understood. But the pictures were something real outside herself, which spoke to her kindly and yet in sovereign tones, something superior and good whose presence destroyed the dreary trance-like solipsism of her earlier mood. When the world had seemed to be subjective it had seemed to be without interest or value. But now there was something else in it after all.

These thoughts, not clearly articulated, flitted through Dora's mind. She had never thought about the pictures in this way before; nor did she draw now any very explicit moral. Yet she felt that she had had a revelation. She looked at the radiant, sombre, tender, powerful canvas of Gainsborough and felt a sudden desire to go down on her knees before it, embracing it, shedding tears.

Dora looked anxiously about her, wondering if anyone had noticed her transports. Although she had not actually prostrated herself, her face must have looked unusually ecstatic, and the tears were in fact starting into her eyes. She found that she was alone in the room, and smiled, restored to a more calm enjoyment of her wisdom. She gave a last look at the painting, still smiling, as one might smile in a temple, favoured, encouraged, and loved. Then she turned and began to leave the building.

Dora was hurrying now and wanting her lunch. She looked at her watch and found it was tea-time. She remembered that she had been wondering what to do; but now, without her thinking about it, it had become obvious. She must go back to Imber at once. Her real life, her real problems, were at Imber; and since, somewhere, something good existed, it might be that her problems would be solved after all. There was a connexion; obscurely she felt, without yet understanding it, she must hang onto that idea: there was a connexion. She bought a sandwich and took a taxi back to Paddington.

CHAPTER 15

By the time Dora arrived back at Imber she felt considerably
more subdued. She had caught a train at once, but it was a
slow one. She was vastly hungry again. She was afraid of Paul's
anger. She tried to keep on believing that something good had
happened to her; but now it seemed that this good thing had
after all nothing whatever to do with her present troubles. It
had been a treat and now it was over. At any rate, Dora was
tired and couldn't think any more and felt discouraged,
frightened, and resentful. The village taxi took her most of the
way down the drive; she would not let it come right up to the
house as she wanted the fact of her return to dawn quietly on
the brotherhood. She was also afraid that, unless she could first
see him alone, Paul would make a public scene. She saw from
a distance the lights of the Court and they looked to her hostile
and censorious.

It was well after ten o'clock. As Dora approached along the
last part of the drive, stepping as quietly as possible on the
gravel, she saw that there were lights on in the hall and the
common-room. She could not see the window of her and Paul's
room, which faced the other reach of the lake. The Court
loomed darkly over her, blotting out the stars; and then she
heard a sound of music. She stopped. Quite clearly on the soft
and quiet warm night air there came the sharp sound of a
piano. Dora listened, puzzled. Surely there was no piano at
Imber. Then she thought, of course, a gramophone record, the
Bach recital. This was the night for it and the community must
all be gathered in the common-room listening. She wondered if
Paul would be there. Leaning carefully on the balustrade so as
to step more lightly she glided up the steps on to the balcony.

The lights from the hall and from the modern French windows of the common-room made a brightly illuminated area in
the space at the top of the steps. Dora could see the flagstones
clearly revealed. The music was now very loud and it was plain

that no one could have heard her approaching. Dora stood for a moment or two, well out of the beam of light, attending to the music. Yes, that was Bach all right. Dora disliked any music in which she could not participate herself by singing or dancing. Paul had given up taking her to concerts since she could not keep her feet still. She listened now with distaste to the hard patterns of sound which plucked at her emotions without satisfying them and which demanded in an arrogant way to be contemplated. Dora refused to contemplate them.

She slithered round, still well in the darkness, until she reached a place from which she could see into the common-room. She trusted that the sharp contrast of light and dark would curtain her from the observation of those within. She found, with something of a shock, that she could see in quite clearly and that by moving round she could inspect the whole room. The music had seemed to make, like a waterfall, some enormous barrier, and it was strange now to find so many people so close to her. They were, however, people under a spell; and she felt she could survey them as an enchanter surveys his victims.

The community were gathered in a semi-circle and seated in the uncomfortable wooden-armed common-room chairs, except for Mrs Mark who was sitting on the floor cross-legged, her skirt well tucked in under her ankles. She was leaning back against the leg of her husband's chair. Mark Strafford, his hand arrested in the act of stroking his beard, was turned towards the corner where the gramophone was, and looked like someone acting Michelangelo's Moses in a charade. Next to him sat Catherine, her hands clasped, the palms moving slightly against each other. Her head was inclined forward, her eyes brooding, the heavy expanse between the lashes and the high curved eyebrows slumberously revealed. Her gipsy hair was thrust carelessly behind her ears. Dora wondered if she was really listening to the music. Toby sat in the centre, opposite to the window, curled gracefully in the chair, one long leg under him, the other hooked over the arm, a hand dangling. He looked absent-minded and rather worried. Next to him was Michael who was leaning his elbows on his knees, his face hidden in his hands, his faded yellow hair spurting through his fingers. Beside him James sat with head thrown back in shameless almost smiling enjoyment of the music. In the corner was Paul, sitting rigid and wearing that somewhat military air which his moustache sometimes gave him and which went so ill with the rest of his personality. He looked tense, concentrated, as if he were about to bark out an order.

Dora was sorry to find Paul at the recital. With any luck he might have been more easily accosted, moping upstairs; as indeed he ought to be, she reflected resentfully, with the mystery of his wife's disappearance still unsolved. Dora watched him for a while, nervously, and then returned to scanning the whole group. Seeing them all together like that she felt excluded and aggressive, and Noel's exhortations came back to her. They had a secure complacent look about them: the spiritual ruling class; and she wished suddenly that she might grow as large and fierce as a gorilla and shake the flimsy doors off their hinges, drowning the repulsive music in a savage carnivorous yell.

Dora had now watched for so long that she felt herself invisible. She moved slightly, about to withdraw, and as she did so she saw that Toby was looking straight out of the window towards her. She wasn't sure for a moment whether he had seen her and she stood quite still. Then a change in his expression, a widening and focussing of his eyes, a slight tensing of his body told her that she had been observed. Dora waited, wondering what Toby would do. To her surprise he did nothing. He sat for a moment giving her a look of intense concentration; and then he dropped his eyes again. Dora slid quietly back into the darkness. No one else in the room had noticed anything.

She stood at the far corner of the balcony dejected, apprehensive, wondering what to do. She supposed she ought to go up to their bedroom and wait for Paul; but the prospect of this gloomy vigil was so appalling that she could not bring herself to mount the stairs. She wandered down again to the terrace and began to walk slowly along the path that led to the causeway. The moon was just rising and there was enough light to see where she was going. The silhouette of the Abbey trees and the tower could be seen, as on her first night at Imber. She reached the lake which seemed to glimmer blackly, not yet fully struck by the rays of the moon.

As she looked back towards the house she was alarmed to see that there was a dark figure following her down the path. She felt sure it must be Paul, and her old deep fear of him suddenly made the whole night scene terrifying. She was ready to run; but she stood still, her hand at her breast, as if to take a physical shock. The figure came nearer, hurrying soundlessly along the grassy track. When it was quite near she saw it was Toby.

'Oh, Toby,' said Dora with relief. 'Hello. You came out of the music.'

'Yes,' said Toby. He seemed breathless. 'I came out before the last movement.'

'Do you like that music?' said Dora.

'Not terribly, actually,' said Toby. 'I was going to come out anyway. Then I saw you through the window.'

'Did you say I was back?' said Dora.

'No, I thought I'd better not talk between the movements. I just slipped out. They're good for another three-quarters of an hour in there,' he added.

'Ah well,' said Dora. 'It's a nice night.'

'Let's walk along a bit,' said Toby.

He seemed pleased to see her. Thank heavens somebody was. They walked along the path beside the lake opposite the Abbey walls. The moon, risen further, was spreading a golden fan across the surface of the water. Dora looked at Toby and found that he was looking at her. Dora was glad to be with Toby. She felt a natural complicity with him which convinced her of the abiding strength and wholeness of her youth. Here was one who was not concerned to enclose or judge her. The rest of them, however, she gloomily reflected, Paul in one way and the brotherhood in another, would make her play their role. A few hours ago she had felt free and she had come back to Imber of her own free will, performing a real action. Yet *they* would make of it the guilty enforced return of an escaped prisoner. Contemplating the inevitability, whose nature she scarcely understood, of *their* superiority over her, and the impossibility of ever getting even with them, Dora was beginning to regret that she had come back.

They walked on, exchanging a word or two about the moonlight, until the path entered the wood. The cavern of darkened foliage covered them, illuminated here and there by glimpses of the gilded water. Toby plunged on confidently and Dora followed, finding silence easy in his company. She had decided to let the three-quarters of an hour which Toby had said they were 'good for' elapse, and then a little more time, to allow the company to disperse to their rooms; then she could be sure of finding Paul alone.

'Why, here we are!' said Toby.

'Where?' said Dora. She came up beside him. The trees stood back from the water and the moonlight clearly showed a grassy space and a sloping stone ramp leading down into the lake.

'Oh, just a place I know,' said Toby. 'I swam here once or twice. No one comes here but me.'

'It's nice,' said Dora. She sat down on the stones at the top of the ramp. The lake seemed quite still and yet made strange liquid noises in the silence that followed. The Abbey wall with its battlement of trees could be seen on the other side, some distance away to the left. But opposite there was only the dark wood, the continuation across the water of the wood that lay behind. It seemed to Dora that the wide moonlit circle at the edge of which she sat was apprehensive, inhabited. An owl called. She looked up at Toby. She was glad she was not there alone.

Toby was standing quite near the head of the ramp, looking down at her. Dora forgot what she was going to say. The darkness, the silence, and their proximity made her quite suddenly physically aware of Toby's presence. She felt a line of force between his body and hers. She wondered if at this moment he felt it too. She remembered how she had seen him naked, and she smiled. The moon revealed her smile and Toby smiled back.

'Tell me something, Toby,' said Dora.

Toby, seeming a little startled, came down the ramp and

squatted beside her. The cool weedy smell of the water was in their nostrils. 'What?' he said.

'Oh, nothing in particular,' said Dora. 'Just tell me something, anything.'

Toby sat back on the stones. After a pause he said, 'I'll tell you something very strange.'

'Go on,' said Dora.

'There's a huge bell down there in the water.'

'*What?*' said Dora. She half rose, amazed, scarcely understanding him.

'Yes,' said Toby, pleased with the effect he had produced. 'Isn't it odd? I found it when I was swimming underwater. I wasn't sure at first, but I came back a second time. I'm certain it's a bell.'

'You saw it, touched it?'

'I touched it, I felt it all over. It's only half buried in the mud. It's too dark to see.'

'Had it carvings on it?' said Dora.

'Carvings?' said Toby. 'Well, it was sort of fretted and worked on the outside. But that might have been anything. Why do you ask?'

'Good God!' said Dora. She stood up. Her hand covered her mouth.

Toby got up too. He was quite alarmed. 'Why, what is it?'

'Have you told anyone else?' said Dora.

'No, I don't know why, but I thought I'd keep it a secret till I'd visited it once again.'

'Well, look,' said Dora, 'don't tell anyone. Let it be *our* secret now, will you?' Dora, who felt no doubts either about Toby's story or about the identity of the object, was suddenly filled with the uneasy elation of one to whom great power has been given which he does not yet know how to use. She clutched her discovery as an Arab boy might clutch a papyrus. What it was she did not know, but she was determined to sell it dear.

'All right,' said Toby, rather gratified. 'I won't utter a word. I suppose it is very odd, isn't it? I don't know why I wasn't more thrilled about it. At first I wasn't sure – and, well, a lot of other things distracted me since. Anyway, I *might* be wrong. But you seem so specially excited about it.'

'I'm sure you're not wrong,' said Dora. Then she told him the legend which Paul had told her, and which had so much seized upon her imagination, of the erring nun and the bishop's curse.

By the end of the tale Toby was as agitated as she was. 'But something like that *couldn't* be true,' he said.

'Well, no,' said Dora, 'but Paul said there's usually *some* truth in those old stories. The bell probably did get into the lake somehow, and there it is.' She pointed at the smooth surface of the water. 'If it is the medieval bell it's very important for art and history and so on. Could we pull it out?'

'We, you mean you and me?' said Toby amazed. 'We couldn't possibly. It's a huge thing, it must weigh an immense amount. And anyway, it's sunk in the mud.'

'You said only half sunk,' said Dora. 'You're an engineer. Couldn't we do it with a pulley or something?'

'We might rig up a pulley,' said Toby, 'but we haven't any power. At least, I suppose we might use the tractor. But what do you want to do?'

'I don't know yet,' said Dora. Her face was cupped in her hands, her eyes shining. 'Surprise everybody. Make a miracle. James said the age of miracles wasn't over.'

Toby looked dubious. 'If it's important,' he said, 'oughtn't we just to tell the others?'

'They'll know soon enough,' said Dora. 'We won't do any harm. But it would be such a marvellous surprise. Suppose – oh, well, I wonder – suppose, suppose we were to substitute the old bell for the new bell somehow, you know, when the new bell arrives next week? They're going to have the bell veiled, and unveil it at the Abbey gate. Think of the sensation when they find the medieval bell underneath the veil! Why, it would be wonderful, it would be like a real miracle, the sort of thing that makes people go on pilgrimages!'

'But it would be just a trick,' said Toby. 'And besides, the bell may be all broken and damaged. And anyway it's too difficult."

'Nothing is too difficult,' said Dora. 'I feel this was meant for us. I should like to shake everybody up a bit. They'd get a colossal surprise – and then they'd be so pleased at having the bell, it would be like an unexpected present. Don't you think?'

'Wouldn't it be – somehow in bad taste?' 'said Toby.

'When something's fantastic enough and marvellous enough it can't be in bad taste,' said Dora. 'In the end, it would give everyone a lift. It would certainly give me a lift! Are you game?'

Toby began to laugh. He said, 'It's a most extraordinary idea. But I'm sure we couldn't manage it.'

'With an engineer to help me,' said Dora, 'I can do anything.' And indeed as she stood there in the moonlight, looking at the quiet water, she felt as if by the sheer force of her will she could make the great bell rise. After all, and after her own fashion, she would fight. In this holy community she would play the witch.

CHAPTER 16

'The chief requirement of the good life,' said Michael, 'is that one should have some conception of one's capacities. One must know oneself sufficiently to know what is the next thing. One must study carefully how best to use such strength as one has.'

It was Sunday, and Michael's turn to give the address. Although the idea of preaching was at this moment intensely distasteful to him, he forced himself dourly to the task, thinking it best to maintain as steadily as possible the normal pattern of his life. He spoke fluently, having thought out what he wanted to say beforehand and uttering it now without hesitations or consulting of notes. He found his present role abysmally ludicrous, but he was not at a loss for words. He stood upon the dais looking out over his tiny congregation. It was a familiar scene. Father Bob sat in the front row as usual, his hands folded, his bright bulging eyes intent upon Michael, devouring him with attention. Mark Strafford, his eyes ambiguously screwed up, sat in the second row with his wife and Catherine. Peter Topglass sat in the third row, busy polishing his spectacles on a silk handkerchief. Every now and then he peered at them and then, unsatisfied, went on polishing. He was always nervous when Michael spoke. Next to him was Patchway, who usually turned up to hear Michael, and who had removed his hat to reveal a bald spot which although so rarely uncovered contrived to be sunburnt. Paul and Dora were not present, having gone out for a walk looking irritable and obviously in the middle of a quarrel. Toby sat at the back, his head bowed so low in his hands that Michael could see the ruff of hair at the back of his neck.

Michael was aware now, when the knowledge was too late to do him any good, that it had been a great mistake to see Toby. The meeting, the clasp of the hands, had had an intensity, and indeed a delightfulness, which he had not foreseen – or had not cared to foresee – and which now made, with the earlier incident, something which had the weight and momentum of a story. There had been a development; there was an expectancy. Michael knew that he ought to have managed the interview with Toby differently, yet that, being himself, he could not have done so: and since this was the case he ought to have written Toby a letter, or better still done nothing whatsoever and let the boy think of him what ill he pleased. He was ready to measure *now* how far the interview had been necessary to him in order that he might somehow refurbish Toby's conception of him, so rudely shaken by what had occurred.

The trouble was, as Michael now saw, that he had performed the action which belonged by right to a better person; and yet too, by an austere paradox, a better person would not have been in the situation that required that action. It would have been possible to conduct the meeting with Toby in an unemotional way which left the matter completely closed; *it* was only not possible for Michael. He remembered his prayers, and how he had taken the thing almost as a test of his faith. It was true that a person of great faith could with impunity have acted boldly: it was only that Michael was not that person. What he had failed to do was accurately to estimate his own resources, his own spiritual level: and it was indeed from his later reflections on this matter that he had, with a certain bitterness, drawn the text for his sermon. One must perform the lower act which one can manage and sustain: not the higher act which one bungles.

Michael was aware that to over-estimate the importance of what was going on was itself a danger. He sighed for some robust common sense which should envisage his action as deplorable but now at least completed without disastrous consequences. He felt, rather pusillanimously, that a sturdy, even cynical, confidant could have helped him to reduce the power which the situation had over him, by seeing it in a more ordinary and less dramatic proportion. But he had no possible confidant; and he remained continually and miserably aware of one consequence which his action had had. He had completely destroyed Toby's peace of mind. He had turned the boy from an open, cheerful hard-working youth into someone anxious, secretive, and evasive. The change in Toby's conduct seemed to Michael so marked that he was surprised that no one else seemed to have noticed it.

He had also destroyed his own peace of mind. An unhealthy excitement consumed him. He worked steadily, but his work was bad. He found now that he awoke each morning with a feeling of curiosity and expectation. He could not prevent himself from continually observing Toby. Toby, on his part, avoided Michael, while being obviously extremely aware of him. Michael guessed on general grounds, and then read in the boy's behaviour, that a reaction had set in. When he had spoken with Toby in the nightjar alley he knew that the emotion which he had felt had received an echo: the memory of this moved him still. The sense that Toby's feelings were now ebbing, that he was perhaps deliberately hardening his heart and regarding with disgust that impulse of affection drove Michael to a sort of frenzy. He longed to speak to Toby, to question him, once more to explain; and he could not help hoping that Toby would sooner or later force such a *tête-à-tête* upon him. He wished that somehow he could pull out of this mess the atom of good which was in it, crystallizing out his harmless goodwill for Toby, Toby's for him. But he knew, and knew it very well, that this was impossible. In this world, it was almost certain, Toby and he could never now be friends: and hardening of the heart was perhaps indeed the best solution. He prayed constantly for Toby, but found that his prayers drifted into fantasies. He was tormented by vague physical desires and by the memory of Toby's body, warm and relaxed against his in the van; and his dreams were haunted by an ambiguous and elusive figure who was sometimes Toby and sometimes Nick.

The thought, when he let his mind dwell upon it, that Nick and Toby were together at the Lodge, added another dimension to Michael's unrest. He returned, fruitlessly, again and again, to the question of whether Nick could possibly have seen him embracing Toby. On each occasion he decided that it was impossible, but then found himself wondering afresh. Such a cloud of distress surrounded this subject that he was not sure what it was, here, that he was regretting: the damage to his own reputation, the possible damage to Nick, or something far more primitive, the loss of Nick's affection, which after all he had no reason to think he still retained and certainly no right to wish to hold.

The only result of these agitations was that it became more impossible than ever to 'do anything' about Nick himself; though he was still resolved to speak to Catherine. When his imagination, with its cursed visual agility, conjured up possible scenes at the Lodge, he was tormented by a two-way jealousy which also prevented him from reconsidering his plan, so desirable from many points of view, of moving Nick or Toby or both up to the Court. His motives, he felt, would be so evident, at any rate in the quarters which at present concerned him most, nor could he bring himself to act on such motives, even though supported by other good reasons. His only consolation was that Toby would be leaving Imber in any case in another couple of weeks; and Nick would probably leave when Catherine had entered the Abbey. It was a matter of hanging on. Afterwards he would, with God's help, set his mind in order and return to his tasks and his plans, which he was determined should not be altered by this nightmarish interlude.

Michael was continuing with his address. He went on, 'It is the positive thing that saves. Can we doubt that God requires of us that we know ourselves? Remember the parable of the talents. In each of us there are different talents, different propensities, many of them capable of good or evil use. We must endeavour to know our possibilities and use what energy we really possess in the doing of God's will. As spiritual beings, in our imperfection and also in the possibility of our perfection, we differ profoundly one from another. How different we are from each other is something which it may take a long time to find out; and certain differences may never appear at all. Each one of us has his own way of apprehending God. I am sure you will know what I mean when I say that one finds God, as it were, in certain places; one has, where God is concerned, a sense of direction, a sense that *here* is what is most real, most good, most true. This sense of reality and weight attaches itself to certain experiences in our lives – and for different people these experiences may be different. God speaks to us in various tongues. To this, we must be attentive.

'You will remember that last week James spoke to us about innocence. I would add this to what he so excellently said. We have been told to be, not only as harmless as doves, but also as wise as serpents. To live in innocence, or having fallen to return to the way, we need all the strength that we can muster – and to use our strength we must know where it lies. We must not, for instance, perform an act because abstractly it seems to be a good act if in fact it is so contrary to our instinctive apprehensions of spiritual reality that we cannot carry it through, that is, cannot really perform it. Each one of us apprehends a certain kind and degree of reality and from this springs our power to live as spiritual beings: and by using and enjoying what we already know we can hope to know more. Self-knowledge will lead us to avoid occasions of temptation rather than to rely on naked strength to overcome them. We must not arrogate to ourselves actions which belong to those whose spiritual vision is higher or other than ours. From this attempt, only disaster will come, and we shall find that the action which we have performed is after all not the high action which we intended, but something else.

'I would use here, again following the example of James, the image of the bell. The bell is subject to the force of gravity. The swing that takes it down must also take it up. So we too must learn to understand the mechanism of our spiritual energy, and find out where, for us, are the hiding places of our strength. This is what I meant by saying that it is the positive thing that saves. We must work, from inside outwards, through our strength, and by understanding and using exactly that energy which we have, acquire more. This is the wisdom of the serpent. This is the struggle, pleasing surely in the sight of God, to become more fully and deeply the person that we are; and by exploring and hallowing every corner of our being, to bring into existence that one and perfect individual which God in creating us entrusted to our care.'

Michael returned to his seat, his eyes glazed, feeling like a sleep-walker in the alarming silence which followed his words. He fell on his knees with the others and prayed the prayer for quietness of mind, which was at such moments all that he could compass. Laboriously he followed the petitions of Father Bob Joyce; and when the service was over he slipped quickly out of the Long Room and took temporary refuge in his office. He wondered how obvious it had been that he was saying the exact opposite of what James had been saying last week. This led him to reflect on how little, in all the drama of the previous days, he had dwelt upon the simple fact of having broken a rule. He recalled James's words: sodomy is not deplorable, it is forbidden. Michael knew that for himself it was just the how and why of it being deplorable that engaged his attention. He did not in fact believe that it was *just* forbidden. God had created men and women with these tendencies, and made these tendencies to run so deep that they were, in many cases, the very core of the personality. Whether in some other, and possibly better, society it could ever be morally permissible to have homosexual relations was, Michael felt, no business of his. He felt pretty sure that in any world in which he would live he would judge it, for various reasons, to be wrong. But this did not make him feel that he could sweep, as James did, the whole subject aside. It was complicated. For himself, God had made him so and he did not think that God had made him a monster.

It was complicated: it was *interesting*: and there was the rub. He realized that in this matter, as in many others, he was always engaged in performing what James had called the second best act: the act which goes with exploring one's personality and estimating the consequences rather than austerely following the rules. And indeed his sermon this very day had been a commendation of the second best act. But the danger here was the very danger which James had pointed out: that if one departs from a simple apprehension of certain definite commandments one may become absorbed in the excitement of a spiritual drama for its own sake.

Michael looked at his watch. He remembered now that he had arranged to see Catherine before lunch, having nerved himself at last to make the appointment. It was already time to go and find her. He knew that he must endeavour now to say something to her about Nick, to ask her to give him definite advice on how to make her brother participate more in the activities of the community. He did not look forward to raising this topic, or indeed to seeing Catherine at all, but at least it was something ordinary and patently sensible to do. He found himself hoping that Catherine might strongly advise the removal of Nick from the Lodge. He descended the stairs and glanced round the hall and put his head into the common-room.

Catherine was not to be seen; nor was she on the balcony or the terrace. Mark Strafford was sunning himself on the steps. Michael called 'Seen Catherine anywhere?'

'She's in the stable yard with her delightful twin,' said Mark. 'Brother Nick has at last decided to mend the lorry. *Deo gratias.*'

Michael disliked this information. He was a little tempted to postpone the interview, but decided quickly that he must not do so. Catherine might be waiting for him to, as it were, release her from Nick; and since he had at last, and with such difficulty, made up his mind to talk to her about her brother he had better not let his decision become stale. It would be a relief, anyway, to get that talk over, not least because he could then feel that, to some wretchedly small degree, he had 'done something' about Nick. He set off for the stable yard.

The big gates that led onto the drive were shut. Michael noticed gloomily, and not for the first time, that they needed a coat of paint and one gate post was rotting. He entered by a little gate in the wall. The yard, one of William Kent's minor triumphs, was composed on three sides of loose boxes surmounted by a second story lit by alternate circular and rectangular windows under a dentil cornice. It gave somewhat the impression of a small residential square. The stone-tiled roof was surmounted opposite the gates by a slender clock tower.

The clock no longer went. On the right side a part of the building had been gutted by fire, and corrugated iron, contributed by Michael's grandfather, still filled the gaping holes in the lower story. The yard sloped markedly towards the lake and was divided from the drive by a high wall. Now, in the heat of the day, it was enclosed, dusty, stifling, rather dazzling in the sunshine. It reminded Michael of an arena.

The fifteen-hundredweight lorry was standing in the middle of the yard just beyond the shadow of the wall, its nose towards the lake. The bonnet was open and from underneath the vehicle a pair of feet could be seen sticking out. Nearby, regardless of the dust, Catherine Fawley was sitting on the ground. Her skirt was hitched up towards her waist and her two long legs, crossed at the ankle, were exposed almost completely to the sun. Michael was surprised to see her in this pose and surprised too that she did not, on seeing him, get up, or at least pull her skirt down. Instead she looked up at him without smiling. Michael, for the first time since he had met her, conjectured that she might positively dislike him.

Nick came edging out from underneath the lorry, his feet disappearing on one side, his head appearing on the other. He lay supine, half emerged, his head resting in the dust. He swivelled his eyes back towards Michael who, from where he was standing, saw his face upside down. He seemed to be smiling, but his inverted face looked so odd it was hard to tell.

'The big chief,' said Nick.

'Hello,' said Michael. 'Very good of you to fix the lorry. Will it be all right?'

'What drivel,' said Nick. 'It's not very good of me to fix the lorry. It's shocking of me not to have done it earlier. Why don't you say what you mean? It was only a blocked petrol feed. It should be all right now.' He continued to lie there, his strange face of a bearded demon looking up at Michael.

Michael, still conscious of Catherine's stare, fumbled for words. 'I was just looking for your sister,' he said.

'I was just talking to my sister,' said Nick. 'We were discussing our childhood. We spent our childhood together, you know.'

'Ah,' said Michael idiotically. Somehow, he could not deal with both of them, and it occurred to him that this was one of the very few occasions when he had seen them together.

'I know it's wicked to chat and reminisce,' said Nick, 'but you must forgive us two, since it's our last chance. Isn't it, Cathie?'

Catherine said nothing.

Michael mumbled, 'Well, I'll be off. I can easily see Catherine another time.'

'All shall be well and all shall be well and all manner of bloody things shall be well,' said Nick. 'Isn't that so, Cathie?'

Michael realized he was a bit drunk. He turned to go.

'Wait a minute,' said Nick. 'You're always "off", confound you, like the bloody milk by the time it reaches me at the Lodge. If you want all manner of things to be well there's a little service you could perform for me. Will you?'

'Certainly,' said Michael. 'What is it?'

'Just get into the lorry and put the gear lever in neutral and release the hand-brake.'

Michael, moving instinctively toward the vehicle, checked himself. 'Nick,' he said, 'don't be an imbecile, that's not funny. And do get out from under that thing. You know the slope makes it dangerous, anyway. You ought to have put the lorry sideways.'

Nick pulled himself slowly out and stood up, dusting his clothes and grinning. Seeing him now in overalls and apparently doing a job of work Michael saw how much thinner and tougher he looked than when he had arrived: handsomer too, and considerably more alert. Michael also realized that these words were the first real words he had addressed to Nick since the day of his arrival. Nick, who had obviously angled for them, was looking pleased.

Michael was about to utter some excuse and go when the wooden door from the drive was heard creaking open once again. They all turned. It was Toby. He stood blinking at the enclosed scene, Catherine still sitting bare-legged and Michael and Nick close to each other beside the lorry. He hesitated with the air of one interrupting an intimate talk, and then since retreat was obviously impossible, came on into the yard and closed the door. Michael's immediate thought was that Toby was looking for him. He felt as if he were blushing.

'Why, here's my understudy,' said Nick. 'You might have had a lesson. But it's all over now.' Then turning his back on Toby he said to Catherine, 'Cathie, would you mind starting her up?'

To Michael's surprise, who had never associated her with engines of any kind, Catherine got up slowly, shook out her skirts, and climbed into the lorry. Watching her he had the feeling, which he had never had before, that she was acting a part. She started the engine. Nick, peering into the bonnet, surveyed the results. They seemed satisfactory. He closed the bonnet and stood for a moment grinning at Michael. Then he said, raising his voice in the continuing din of the engine, 'I think we'll take her for a little spin to make sure she's all right. Catherine shall drive. Come along, Toby.'

Toby, who had been standing uneasily near the gate, looked startled and came forward.

'Come along, quickly,' said Nick, holding open the door of the driving cabin, 'you're coming too.'

Toby got in.

'How about you, Michael?' said Nick. 'It would be rather a squeeze, but I expect someone could sit on someone's knee.'

Michael shook his head.

'Then would you mind opening the gates for us?' said Nick. He was sitting in the middle between Toby and Catherine, his arms spread out along the back of the seat so that he embraced the boy and his sister.

As in a dream Michael went to the big wooden gates and dragged them open. Catherine let in the clutch smoothly and the lorry swept past him in a cloud of dust and disappeared into the drive. A few moments later, as he still stood exasperated and wretched in the empty yard, he saw it reappear far off on the other side of the lake, roar up towards the Lodge, and vanish onto the main road.

CHAPTER 17

Toby rose from his bed and picked up his shoes. He had not undressed, and had not dared to go to sleep for fear of over-sleeping. His rendezvous with Dora was for two-thirty a.m. It was now just after two. He opened the door of his room and listened. The door of Nick's room was open, but snores could be heard from within. Toby glided down the stairs and reached the outer door. A movement behind him gave him a momentary shock, but it was only Murphy who had evidently followed him downstairs. The dog snuffled against his trouser leg, looking up at him interrogatively. He patted him, half guiltily, and slipped out of the door alone, closing it firmly behind him. On this particular expedition even Murphy was not to be trusted.

This was the night when Toby and Dora were to attempt to raise the bell. Since its apparently crazy inception this plan had grown in substance and complication; and Toby who had at first regarded it as a dream, had now become its business-like and enthusiastic manager. Just why Dora was so keen on something so dotty had not at first been clear to Toby. It was still not clear to him, but now he no longer troubled about anything except to please Dora: and also to overcome certain technical problems whose fascination had become evident to his mechanical mind.

On the day after his first conversation with Dora about the bell he had gone for another solitary swim. He had dived a large number of times investigating the shape and position of the object in detail. He had now no doubts, fired by Dora's certainty and confirmed by his own findings, that this was indeed *the* bell. Two colossal problems now faced him. The first was how to get the bell out of the water, and the second was how to effect the substitution of the old bell for the new which was to constitute Dora's miracle: both these tasks to be performed undiscovered and with no helper but Dora. It was a tall order.

Dora, who had clearly got no conception of how large and how heavy the bell was, seemed to think it all perfectly possible, and relied upon Toby's skill with an *insouciance* which both exasperated and melted him. Even though he knew it to be based on ignorance, her confidence infected him: he was infected too by her curious vision, her grotesque imagination of the return to life of the medieval bell. It was as if, for her, this was to be a magical act of shattering significance, a sort of rite of power and liberation; and although it was not an act which Toby could understand, or which in any other circumstance he would have had any taste for, he was prepared to catch her enthusiasm and to be, for this occasion, the sorcerer's apprentice.

It was the apprentice, however, who had to contrive the details of the sorcery. He had discussed various plans with Dora, whose ignorance of dynamics turned out to be staggering. The fact was, after some suggestions involving cart horses had been set aside, that the only motive power available to them which could have even a chance of doing the job was the tractor. Even then, as Toby tried to impress upon Dora, it was possible that they would be simply unable to shift the bell. The amount of muddy ooze inside it alone would double its weight; and the lower part of it might turn out to be thoroughly jammed in the thicker mud of the floor of the lake. Toby had attempted to dig the ooze away from it on his last diving expedition, but with only partial success. It was a bore that Dora could neither swim nor drive the tractor, since this meant that the bell could not be given an extra helping hand from below while it was being pulled from above.

'I'm afraid I'm perfectly useless!' said Dora, her hands about her knees, her large eyes glowing at him with submissive admiration as they sat in the wood having their final conference. Toby found her perfectly captivating.

The official plan for the new bell was as follows. It was arriving at the Court on Thursday morning. It would then be placed upon one of the iron trolleys which were sometimes used to bring logs from the wood, and it would thereon be attired with white garments and surrounded with flowers. So apparelled it would be blessed and 'baptized' by the Bishop at a little service planned to take place immediately after the latter's arrival on Thursday evening, and at which only the brotherhood would be present. The bell would spend the night of Thursday to Friday in the stable yard. On Friday morning shortly before seven o'clock, the time at which postulants were customarily admitted to the Abbey, the bell would be the centre of a little country festival, whose details had been lovingly designed by Mrs Mark, during which it would be danced to by the local Morris, serenaded by a recorder band from the village school, and sung in solemn procession across the causeway by the choir from the local church, who had for some time now been studying ambitious pieces in its honour, one indeed composed for the occasion by the choirmaster. The procession, whose form and order was still under dispute, would consist of the performers, the brotherhood, and any villagers who cared to attend; and as interest was rather unexpectedly running high in the village quite a number of people seemed likely to come in spite of the earliness of the hour. The great gate of the Abbey would be opened as the procession approached and as its attendants fanned out on either side of it on the opposite bank the bell would be unveiled during a final burst of song. After it had stood for a suitable interval, revealed to the general admiration, it would be wheeled into the Abbey by specially selected workmen who had a dispensation to enter the enclosure for the purpose of erecting the bell. The closing of the gates behind the bell would end the ceremony as far as the outside world was concerned.

Toby and Dora's plan was as follows. On Wednesday night they would endeavour to raise the old bell. For this purpose they would use the tractor which as good fortune would have it Toby was now being permitted sometimes to drive. The ploughing up of the pastureland had commenced, and since the beginning of the week Toby had been working on the pasture with Patchway. The evening departure of the latter usually took place with unashamed punctuality; it would be an easy matter for Toby, about whose activities at that hour nobody would be bothering, instead of putting the tractor away to drive it into the wood near the old barn. He had already cleared the branches and larger obstacles from the path that led through the barn to the lakeside, so that the tractor could be taken right through and almost to the water's edge. There it would be left until some time after midnight when Toby and Dora would meet at the ramp.

The tractor possessed a winch and a stout steel hawser with a hook at the end, used for hauling logs. With the hawser attached to the great ring which formed part of the head of the bell Toby hoped to be able to raise the bell, first by the winch and then by towing, and drag it into the barn. He had taken the precaution of sinking some stones and gravel at the foot of the ramp in case the bell should catch on the edge of the ramp where it ended under the level of the ooze. The danger at this point, apart from the unpredictability of the bell's behaviour, was that the sound of the tractor might be heard; but Toby judged that, with the south-west wind blowing as it had now been for some time, the noise was not likely to be audible at the Court, or if heard would not be recognizable. It might pass for a car or a distant aeroplane.

The next stage of the operation was no less complex. The large iron trolley on which the new bell was to rest had, fortunately, a twin brother. It was indeed the existence of this twin which made the plan feasible at all. Once the bell was inside the barn, the steel hawser would be passed over one of the large beams and the winch used to raise it from the ground. From this position it could be lowered onto the second trolley and made fast. The trolley could then, on Thursday night, without undue difficulty, be propelled along the concrete road which led beside the wood, sloping slightly down in the direction of the Court. The road led directly via the market-garden to the stable yard where the wood store was; and where the new bell would be, apparelled for its trip on the morrow. Here it should be possible for the bells to change clothes. The flowers and other garnishings of the trolley would conceal any small differences of shape which a sharp eye might notice between

213

the two twins. If the bells turned out to be of vastly different sizes this would certainly be a snag: but Toby, who had slyly discovered the dimensions of the new bell, and who had taken what measurements he could of the old, was confident that they were roughly of a size. The new bell, disrobed, would then be wheeled into one of the empty loose-boxes into which no one ever peered, and the operation would be complete. The most perilous, as opposed to difficult, part of it would be the last; but as the stable yard was a little distant from the house, and as none of the brotherhood slept on the side nearest the yard, it was to be hoped that no one would hear anything.

There was one final annoyance. The second iron trolley, which would convey the old bell, was in daily use in the packing sheds. Mrs Mark used it as a table on which she arranged her goods, before pushing it up to the back of the van for loading. If Toby were to remove it on Wednesday night its absence would be noted on Thursday. It must therefore be removed on Thursday night. A minimum of operations at the barn would, however, be left for Thursday. On Wednesday the bell would be lifted, by the hawser passing over the beam, to a point, measured by Toby, a fraction higher than the level of the trolley. A second hawser, which Toby had discovered in the store room, would then be brought into action, hooked into the bell at one end, thrown over the beam, and made fast in the fork of a nearby tree by means of a crowbar passed through the ring in which the hawser ended. The first hawser, which was attached to the tractor, could then be released and the bell left hanging. The tractor would be taken back to the ploughing very early on Thursday morning. The bell would spend Thursday hanging in the barn. Dora had collected a quantity of green boughs and creepers with which it might be disguised; but in fact discovery during that day was exceedingly unlikely. On Thursday night the trolley would be brought and passed under the bell. If Toby's measurements, including the allowance he he had made for sagging in the hawser, were exact enough the two surfaces would meet without interval; if his measurements were not quite exact the trolley could be lifted a little on earth and stones, or else dug into the floor of the barn, to take the rim of the bell. The hawser would then be removed and the bell would be resting on the trolley. This ingenious arrangement made it unnecessary to have the tractor in attendance on the second night.

The mechanical details of the plan aroused in Toby a sort of ecstasy. It was all so difficult and yet so exquisitely possible and he brooded over it as over a work of art. It was also his homage to Dora and his proof to himself that he was in love. Ever since the moment in the chapel when Dora's image had so obligingly filled out that blank form of femininity towards which Toby interrogatively turned his inclinations he had been, he felt, under her domination, indeed as he almost precisely put it, under her orders. The fact that Dora was married troubled Toby very little. He had no intention of making any declaration to Dora or revealing by any word or gesture what was his state of mind. He took a proud satisfaction in this reticence, and felt rather like a medieval knight who sighs and suffers for a lady whom he has scarcely seen and will never possess. This conception of her remoteness made the vitality of her presence and the easy friendliness with which, in their curious enterprise, she treated him, all the more delightful. She had for him a radiance and an authority, and the freshness of the emotion which she aroused gave him a sense almost of the renewal of innocence.

Strangely co-existent with the revelation of himself which, with daily additions, Dora was unconsciously bringing about, there was a dark continuing twisted concern about Michael. Toby avoided Michael but watched him and could not keep his thoughts from him; and his feelings veered between resentment and guilt. He had a sense of having been plunged into something unclean; and at the same time a miserable awareness that he was hurting Michael. Yet how could he not? His imagination dwelt vaguely upon some momentous interview which he would have with Michael before he left Imber; and there were many moments when he was strongly tempted to go and knock on the door of Michael's office. He had little conception of what he would do or say inside, but cherished, partly with embarrassment and partly with satisfaction, the view that Michael was in need of his forgiveness, and in need more simply of a kind word. Toby had, altogether, where this matter was concerned, a strong sense of unfinished business.

He made his way cautiously along the path beside the lake. The moon had not failed them and was high in the sky and almost full and the wide glimmering scene of trees and water was attentive, significant, as if aware of a great deed which was to be done. The lake, so soon to yield up its treasure, was serene, almost inviting, and the air was warm. He walked faster now, watching out for the figure of Dora ahead of him, almost breathless with anticipation and excitement. They had agreed to meet at the barn. He knew very well that there were a hundred things which could go wrong; but he burned with confidence and with the hope of delighting Dora and with a sheer feverish desire to get at the bell.

He reached the open space by the ramp and stopped. After the soft swishing sound of his footsteps there was an eerie silence. Then Dora emerged, taking shape in the moonlight, from the path leading to the barn. He spoke her name.

'Thank God,' said Dora in a low voice. 'I've been absolutely scared stiff in this place. There were such funny noises, I kept thinking the drowned nun was after me.'

A clear sound arose quite near them suddenly in the reeds and they both jumped. It was a harsh yet sweet trilling cry which rose several notes and then died bubbling away.

'Whatever was that?' said Dora.

'The sedge warbler,' said Toby. 'The poor man's nightingale, Peter Topglass calls him. He won't bother us. Now, Dora, quickly to work.'

'I think we're perfectly mad,' said Dora. 'Why did we ever have this insane idea? Why did you encourage me?' She was half serious.

'Everything will be all right,' said Toby. Dora's flutter made him calm and decisive. He paused, breathing deeply. The sedge warbler sang again, a little farther off. The lake was brittle and motionless, the reeds and grasses moving very slightly in the warm breeze, the moon as bright as it could be. It seemed then to Toby fantastic that in a moment there would be the roar of the tractor, the breaking into the lake. He felt as an army commander might feel just before launching a surprise attack.

He took a few steps into the wood. The tractor was there where he had left it, just outside the barn on the lake side. It was lucky that the barn had large doors opening both ways so that it had been possible to drive the tractor straight through. He had not dared to bring it any nearer to the water for fear its polished red radiator might be visible during daylight from the causeway. He quickly took off his clothes, and dressed only in his bathing trunks approached the tractor, shining his torch on it and checking the hawser and the winch. The winch had not been in use lately, but Toby had given it a good oiling and it seemed to be perfectly sound. He unwound a good length of hawser and looped it loosely round the drum. All this while Dora was hovering about behind him. At such a moment, attached as he was to her, he envied his medieval prototype who at least did not have to deal with both his lady and his adventure at the same time. For most of the operation Dora was useless.

'Just stand by near the water, would you,' said Toby, 'and do what I tell you.' He took a deep breath. He felt himself magnificent. He started the engine of the tractor.

A shattering roar broke the expectant moonlit silence of the wood. Toby could hear Dora's exclamations of dismay. He wasted no time but jumped on to the seat of the tractor, released the clutch, and let the great thing amble slowly in reverse toward the water. He felt love for the tractor, delight and confidence in its strength. He stopped it in the space near the top of the ramp and jumped off. He put the brake well on and began to drag a large log of wood across under the wheels. Dora rushed to help. He left the engine running, judging that a distant sound which continues is less likely to attract attention than an intermittent one. Then holding the end of the hawser, with its stout hook, he began to walk down the ramp.

The water was cold and its chilly touch shocked Toby, making him aware for a moment how completely he was entranced. He gasped, but plunged on till his feet left the stones and he was swimming, holding the hook in one hand. He now knew by heart the geography of the lake floor beyond the ramp. He felt he could almost see the bell. With the rhythmical sound of the tractor in his ears he dived. The hawser was heavy and helped to take him to the bottom, and his hand immediately encountered the mouth of the bell. Trailing the hook on the lake floor, the hawser running loosely through his fingers, he began to fumble towards the other end of the bell to find its great eye. As he did so a sudden consciousness of what he was doing came over him. He made as if to open his mouth and in a moment of panic shot up to the surface letting the hawser drop below him into the mud. Gasping, restored to the now terrifying scene of the moonlit lake and the roar of the engine, he swam back to the ramp.

Dora was standing with her feet in the water. She said something inaudible to him in frantic tones. Toby ignored her and began to drag the hawser in from the bottom. It came slowly, muddily. At last he had the hook in his hand again, and breathing steadily he swam out once more and dived. He grasped the rim of the bell and pulled himself towards it. With his next clutch he had his hand on the eye, his fingers slipping into the wide hole. Clinging onto the bell with one hand he approached the large hook with the other. With a sense of desperate joy he felt the hook pass through the hole. Then he rose, directing himself towards the ramp, and holding the hawser as taut as possible in his hand. He scrambled out. There was not much slack, he had judged the length needed very well. He pushed Dora out of the way and mounted the tractor. He geared the engine onto the winch and let it turn at a slow pace, first taking in the slack, and ready to switch off hastily if at any moment the bell seemed likely to pull the tractor into the lake. The hawser became taut, and he could feel the direct pull beginning between the tractor and the bell.

The winch came to a standstill. The engine roared, but the power was of no avail. Thinking quickly, Toby switched the power off the winch, moved the tractor a little away from the water, letting the hawser unwind, and brought it back to the tree-trunk in a new position. He switched over again to the winch and the hawser tightened. A heaving struggle began. Although the winch did not yet begin to move, he could feel a colossal agitation at the other end of the line. This was the moment at which the hawser was most likely to break. Toby sent up a prayer. Then he saw with incredulity and wild delight that very slowly the drum was beginning to turn. A fearful dragging could be heard, or perhaps felt, in that pandemonium it was hard to say which, upon the floor of the lake. Enormous muddy bubbles were breaking the surface. The movement was continuous now. The tractor was drawing the bell somewhat jerkily but steadily towards it as the strong winch turned. Toby could feel the great arching wheels braced against the tree-trunk. Like a live thing the tractor pulled. Then a grinding sound was to be heard: the bell must have reached the stony pile at the bottom of the ramp. Holding his breath Toby kept his eyes fixed on the point at which the thin line of the hawser, silvered by the moonlight, broke the heaving surface of the water. He felt a shock, which was probably the rim of the bell passing over the bottom edge of the ramp, and almost at the same moment, and sooner than he had expected, the hook came into view. Behind it an immense bulk rose slowly from the lake.

Hardly believing his eyes, yet chill with determined concentration, Toby waited until the bell lay upon the ramp, clear of the water, stranded like a terrible fish. He switched the power off the winch, and let the hawser fall slack, making sure that the bell was lodged securely on the gentle slope. Then he jumped down and began to pull the log away from under the wheels. A pale flurry seen from the corner of his eye was Dora still trying to help. He got back onto the roaring tractor, slipped the engine back into its normal gear, and very slowly released the clutch. The tractor bucked for a moment and then the great wheels began to turn and Toby saw the foliage moving past his head. He turned back to look at the bell. The rim was scraping hard on the stone and the upper end just clearing the ground. It jolted over the head of the ramp and the rim bit into the softer surface of the earth. Gathering beneath it a pile of earth and stones it followed the tractor into the darkness of the wood. Already Toby sensed the blackness of the barn roof above him, and he steadied the tractor across the floor and out through the wide door on the opposite side. When he judged that the bell had reached the middle of the barn he stopped the tractor and switched off the engine.

An appalling almost stunning silence followed. Toby sat quite still on the seat of the tractor. Then he breathed out slowly and rubbed his hands over his face and brows. He felt rather as if he would like now to crawl away somewhere and go to sleep. The last few minutes had been too crammed with experience. He began to climb from his seat and was mildly surprised to find that the extreme tension of his muscles had made him stiff. He got down and leaned over to rub his leg. He was amazed to find himself naked except for the bathing trunks.

'Toby, you were marvellous!' said Dora's voice beside him. 'You're an absolute hero. Are you all right? Toby, we've succeeded!'

Toby was in no mood for transports. He sneezed, and said, 'Yes, yes, I'm O.K. Let's look at the thing now. It'll probably turn out to be an old bedstead or something.' He stumbled past the dark shape in the middle of the floor and found his torch. Then he played the light upon it.

The bell lay upon its side, the black hole of its mouth still jagged with mud. Its outer surface, much encrusted with watery growths and shell-like incrustations, was a brilliant green. It lay there, gaping and enormous, and they looked at it in silence. It was a thing from another world.

'Well, good heavens,' said Dora at last. She spoke in a low voice as if awed by the presence of the bell. She reached out cautiously and touched it. The metal was thick, rough, and curiously warm. The thing was monstrous, lying there stranded upon the floor. She said, 'I had no idea it would be so huge.'

'Is it *the* one?' said Toby. He was amazed as he looked at it to think that it had been possible to make so large and inert an object obey his will. It was weird too that a thing so brightly coloured should have come out of so dark a place. He touched it too, almost humbly.

'Bring the torch closer,' said Dora. 'Paul said there were scenes of the life of Christ.'

They bent over the bell together, playing the light closely upon the vivid uneven surface. A little way from the rim it seemed to be divided into sections. Toby clawed with his fingers in the circle of light, pulling off encrusted mud and algae. Something was appearing. 'My God,' said Toby. Eyes stared at them out of square faces and a scene of squat figures was revealed.

'It must be!' said Dora. 'But I don't recognize that. Go on scraping. How grotesque they are. Yes, there's another scene. Why, it's the nativity for sure! Do you see the ox and the ass? And there are people catching fish. And all those men at the table must be having the Last Supper. And here's the crucifixion.'

'And the resurrection,' said Toby.

'There's something written,' said Dora.

Toby turned the light onto the rim of the bell. The words, interspersed with strangely shaped crosses, stood out clearly in the green metal. After a moment he said, 'Yes, it's Latin.'

'Read it out,' said Dora.

Toby read out 'Vox ego sum Amoris. Gabriel vocor. "I am the voice of Love. I am called Gabriel." '

'Gabriel!' cried Dora. 'Why, that was its name! Paul told me. It is the bell!' She looked up at Toby from where she was kneeling near its mouth. Toby turned the torch onto her. Her hair was wet with lake water and her cheeks were smudged with mud. A dark trickle was finding its way into the bosom of her hastily buttoned dress. Her hands laid upon the bell, she blinked in the light, smiling up at Toby.

'Dora!' said Toby. He dropped the torch on the ground where its curtailed arc of light continued to shine. Naked as a fish, Toby felt a miraculous strength twisting inside him. He, and he alone, had pulled the bell from the lake. He was a hero, he was a king. He fell upon Dora, his two hands reaching for her shoulders, his body collapsing upon hers. He heard her gasp and then relax, receiving his weight, her arms passing round his neck. Clumsily, passionately, Toby's hard lips sought her in the darkness. Struggling together they rolled into the mouth of the bell.

As they did so the clapper, moving within the dark metal hollow, struck violently against the side, and a muted boom arose and echoed away across the lake whose waters had now once again subsided to rest.

CHAPTER 18

Michael Meade was awakened by a strange hollow booming sound which seemed to come from the direction of the lake. He lay rigid for a moment listening anxiously to the silence that succeeded the sound, and then got out of bed and went to the open window. It was a bright moonlight night and the moon, full and risen high, cast a brilliance which was almost golden on the tranquil expanse of the water. Michael rubbed his eyes, amazed at the speed of his reaction, and still wondering whether he was awake or dreaming. He stood a while watching the quiet scene. Then he turned the light on and looked at his watch which said ten past three. He felt wide awake now and anxious. He sat on the edge of his bed, tense, listening. He had again that strange sense of impending evil. He sniffed, wondering if there were in fact some nauseating smell pervading the room. He remembered that just before he woke he had been dreaming of Nick.

He was too uneasy to sleep again. The noise he had heard – he was sure this time that he had really heard it – unnerved him. He had vague memories of stories heard in childhood of noises coming out of the sea to portend disaster. He got dressed, intending to make a tour round the house to see that everything was all right. Strange visions afflicted him of finding that the Court was on fire. He turned the light on in the corridor and walked about a bit. Everything was as usual and no one else seemed to be stirring. He went out onto the balcony and looked round him in the splendid night. He saw at once in the distance that there was a light on in the Lodge. Nick at least was up. Or Toby. He scanned the banks of the lake as far as he could see in either direction. All seemed quiet.

Then he noticed something moving, and saw that a figure was walking along the path that led from the causeway to the ferry. He was clearly revealed now, with a long shadow, the figure of a man walking purposefully. Michael felt an immediate thrill of alarm and apprehension. He watched for a moment and then hurried down the steps and across the terrace to intercept the night wanderer, whoever he might be. The man, seeing Michael coming, stopped abruptly and waited for him to come nearer. Straining his eyes in the moonlight, and almost running now, Michael approached; and then recognized the figure, with mingled disappointment and relief, as Paul Greenfield.

'Oh, it's you.' said Paul.

'Hello,' said Michael. 'Anything the matter?'

'Dora's vanished,' said Paul. 'I woke up and found her gone. Then when she didn't come back I thought I'd go and look for her.'

'Did you hear an extraordinary sound just now?' said Michael.

'Yes,' said Paul. 'I was just falling into a gorse bush at the time. What was it?'

'I don't know,' said Michael. 'It sounded like a bell.'

'A *bell*?' said Paul.

'I see there's a light on in the Lodge,' said Michael.

'That's just where I'm going now,' said Paul. 'I thought Dora might be there. Or if she isn't, I'd be interested to know whether Master Gashe is in his bed. Have you noticed those two rushing round together like a pair of conspirators?'

Michael who had indeed on his own account noticed this said, 'No, I noticed nothing.' They began to walk towards the ferry.

'Do you mind if I come with you?' said Michael. He too felt an intense desire to know what was going on at the Lodge.

Paul seemed to have no objection. They crossed in the boat and began to hurry along the path to the avenue. The light beaconed out clearly now. They passed out of the moonlight into the darkness of the trees and felt the firm gravel of the drive underfoot.

As they neared the Lodge they saw that the door was open. The light from the living-room, through the door and the uncurtained windows, revealed the gravel, the tall grasses, the iron rails of the gate. Paul, beginning to run, reached the doorway before Michael. He pushed his way in without knocking. Michael hastened after him, looking over his shoulder.

The scene in the living-room was peaceful and indeed familiar. The usual litter of newspapers covered the floor and the table. The stove was lit and Murphy was lying stretched out beside it. Behind the table, in his usual place, sat Nick. On the table there was a bottle of whisky and a glass. There was no one else to be seen.

Paul seemed nonplussed. He said to Nick, 'Oh, good evening, Fawley.' Paul was the only person who addressed Nick in this manner. 'I was just wondering if my wife was here.'

Nick, who had shown a little surprise, Michael thought, at his own arrival, was now smiling in his characteristic grimacing manner. With his greasy curling hair and his grimy white shirt, unbuttoned, and his long legs sticking straight out under the table he looked like some minor Dickensian rake. He reached for the bottle, and raised his eyebrows, possibly to express the slightly patronizing amazement, which Michael had often felt, too, at the frankness with which Paul revealed his matrimonial difficulties.

'Good morning, Greenfield,' said Nick. 'No, she ain't here. Why should she be? Have a drink?'

Paul said irritably, 'Thank you, no, I never take whisky.'

'Michael?' said Nick.

Michael jumped at his name, and took a moment to realize what Nick meant. He shook his head.

'Is Toby upstairs?' said Paul.

Nick went on smiling at him and kept him waiting for the answer. Then he said, 'No. He ain't here either.'

'Do you mind if I look upstairs?' said Paul. He pushed through the room.

Michael, who was just beginning to realize that Paul was in fact in a frantic state, found himself left alone with Nick. He cast a glance at him without smiling. He was fairly frantic himself.

Nick smiled. 'One of the deadly sins,' he said.

'What?' said Michael.

'Jealousy,' said Nick.

Paul's feet were heard on the stairs. He came blundering back into the living-room.

'Satisfied?' said Nick.

Paul did not reply to this, but stood in the middle of the room, his face wrinkled up with anxiety. He said to Nick:

'Do you know where he is?'

'Gashe?' said Nick. 'No. I am not Gashe's keeper.'

Paul stood irresolutely for a moment, and then turned to go. As he passed Michael he paused. 'It was odd what you said about a bell.'

'Why?' said Michael.

'Because there's a legend about this place. I meant to tell you. The sound of a bell portends a death.'

'Did you hear that strange sound a little while ago?' Michael asked Nick.

'I heard nothing,' said Nick.

Paul stumped out of the door and began walking back along the drive.

Michael stayed where he was. He felt very tired and confused. If Nick would only have stayed quiet he would like to have sat with him for a while in silence. But those were all mad thoughts.

'Have a drink?' said Nick.

'No thanks, Nick,' said Michael. He found it very hard not to look at Nick. A solemn face seemed hostile and a smiling face provocative. He cast a rather twisted smile in his direction and then looked away.

Nick got up and came towards Michael. Michael stiffened as he approached. For a moment he thought Nick was going to come right up to him and touch him. But he stopped about two feet away, still smiling. Michael looked at him fully now. He wished he could drive that smile off his face. He had a strong impulse to reach out and put his two hands on Nick's shoulders. The sound that had awakened him, the moonlight, the madness of the night, made him feel suddenly that communication between them was now permitted. His whole body was aware, almost to trembling, of the proximity of his friend. Perhaps after all this was the moment at which he should in some way remove the barrier which he had set up between them. No good had come of it. And the fact remained, as he deeply realized in this moment, for whatever it meant and whatever it was worth, that he loved Nick. Some good might yet come of that.

'Nick,' Michael began.

Speaking almost at the same time Nick said, 'Don't you want to know where Toby is?'

Michael flinched at the question. He hoped his face was without expression. He said, 'Well, where is he?'

'He's in the wood making love to Dora,' said Nick.

'How do you know?'

'I saw them.'

'I don't believe you,' said Michael. But he did believe. He added, 'Anyway, it's no business of mine.' That was foolish, since on any view of the matter it was his business.

Nick stepped back to sit in a leisurely way on the table, watching Michael and still smiling.

Michael turned and went out, banging the door behind him.

CHAPTER 19

'Well, and what happened then?' said James Tayper Pace.

It was the next morning, and James and Michael were in the greenhouse picking tomatoes. The good weather was breaking, and although the sun still shone, a strong wind, which had arisen towards dawn, was sweeping across the kitchen garden. The tall lines of runner-beans swayed dangerously and Patchway went about his work with one hand clutching his hat. Inside the greenhouse however all was quiet and the warm soil-scented air and the firm red bunches of fruit made an almost tropical peace. Today all routines were altered because of the arrival of the bell, which was due to be delivered some time during the morning. The Bishop was to make his appearance during the afternoon, and after the baptism service would partake of tea with the community, a meal which, in the form of a stand-up buffet, was being planned on a grand scale by Margaret Strafford. He would then stay the night and officiate at the more elaborate rites on the following morning.

'Nothing happened,' said Michael. 'After I met Paul I went with him to the Lodge. Toby wasn't there. We came away again and I went back to bed and Paul wandered off to do some more searching. When I saw him this morning he said that he went back to his room about three-quarters of an hour later and found Dora there. She said it was such a hot night she'd been for a walk round the lake.'

James laughed his gruff booming laugh and lined another box with newspaper. 'I'm afraid,' he said, 'that Mrs Greenfield is what is popularly called a bitch. I'm sorry to say so, but one must call things by their names. Only endless trouble comes from not doing so.'

'You say you didn't hear any noise in the night?' said Michael.

'Not a sound. But I'm so dead tired these days I sleep like

the proverbial log. The last trump wouldn't wake me. They'd have to send a special messenger!'

Michael was silent. Nimbly he fingered the glowing tomatoes, warm with the sun and firm with ripeness. The boxes were filling fast.

James went on, 'One oughtn't to laugh, of course. I can't believe anything serious happened last night. Paul is a dreadful alarmist and a chronically jealous man. All the same, we ought to keep an eye on things; and I think it's regrettable that they've gone as far as they have.'

'Yes,' said Michael.

'I'm sure Toby and Dora have done nothing but run around together like a couple of youngsters,' said James. 'Dora is just about his mental age anyway. But with a woman like that you can't be sure that there wouldn't be some gesture, some word that might upset him. After all, he's not like my young Eastenders. He's been a very sheltered child. A boy's first intimations of sex are so important, don't you think? And tampering with the young's a serious matter.'

'Quite,' said Michael.

'It's a pity,' said James, 'that we seem to have made so little impression on Mrs G. I wish she'd have a talk with Mother Clare. I'm sure it'd straighten her out a bit. That girl's just a great emotional mess at present. I feel we've let Paul down rather.'

'Possibly,' said Michael.

'And you know, we're fully responsible for the boy,' said James. 'He came here, after all, as a sort of retreat, a preparation for Oxford. Of course there's nothing seriously amiss in his rampaging around with Dora in a companionable way – but I think someone ought to put in a word.'

'Who to?' said Michael.

'To Dora, I'd say,' said James. 'Appealing to Dora's better nature may turn out to be a difficult operation. I fear that girl is a blunt instrument at the best of times – and also resembles the *jeune homme de Dijon qui n'avait aucune religion!* But even if she doesn't care about her husband's blood pressure she ought to show some respect for the boy. She should see *that* point. Suppose you gave her a little kindly admonition, Michael?'

'Not me,' said Michael.

'Well, how about Margaret?' said James. 'Margaret is such a motherly soul and Dora seems to like her – and maybe that sort of advice would come better from a woman. Why, here is Margaret!'

Michael looked up sharply. Margaret Strafford could be seen running along the concrete path towards them her full skirt flapping in the wind. Michael interpreted her portentous haste immediately and his heart sank.

Margaret threw open the door, letting in a great blast of chill air. 'Michael,' she cried, delighted with her commission, 'the Abbess wants to see you at once!'

'I say, you *are* in luck!' said James. Their two bright amiable faces looked at him enviously.

Michael washed his hands at the tap in the corner of the greenhouse and dried them on his handkerchief. 'Sorry to leave you with the job,' he said to James. 'Excuse me if I dash.'

He set off at a run down the path which led along behind the house to the lake. It was customary to run when summoned by the Abbess. As he turned to the left towards the causeway the full blast of the wind caught him. It was almost blowing a gale. Then he saw, looking across the other reach of the lake, that an enormous lorry had just emerged from the trees of the avenue and was proceeding at a slow pace along the open part of the drive. It must be the bell. He should have been interested, excited, pleased. He noted its arrival coldly and forgot it at once. He turned onto the causeway. He felt certain that the Abbess must know all about Toby. It was irrational to think this. How could she possibly have found out? Yet it was astonishing what she knew. Breathlessly, as he reached the wooden section in the centre of the causeway, he slowed down. His footsteps echoed hollow upon the wood. He had not expected this summons. He felt as if he were about to undergo some sort of spiritual violence. He felt closed, secretive, unresponsive, almost irritated.

At the corner of the parlour building Sister Ursula was waiting. She always acted watchdog to audiences with the Abbess. Her large commanding face beamed approval at Michael from some way off. She saw the summons as a sign of special grace. After all, interviews with the Abbess were coveted by all and granted only to a few.

'In the first parlour,' she said to Michael, as he passed her mumbling a salutation.

Michael burst into the narrow corridor and paused a moment to get his breath before opening the first door. The gauze panel was drawn across on his side in front of the grille and there was silence beyond. It was usual for the person summoned to arrive first. Michael pulled back the panel on his side to reveal the grille and the second gauze panel on the far side which screened the opposite parlour inside the enclosure. Then he straightened his shirt collar – he was wearing no tie – buttoned up his shirt, smoothed down his hair, and made a strenuous effort to become calm. He stood, he could not bring himself to sit down, looking at the blank face of the inner panel.

After a minute or two during which he could feel the uncomfortable violence of his heart he heard a movement and saw a dim shadow upon the gauze. Then the panel was pulled open and he saw the tall figure of the Abbess opposite to him, and behind her another little room exactly similar to his. He genuflected in the accustomed way and waited for her to sit down. Slightly smiling she sat, and motioned him to be seated too. Michael pulled his chair well up to the grille and sat down on the edge of it sideways so that their two heads were close together.

'Well, my dear son, I'm glad to see you,' said the Abbess in the brisk voice with which she always opened an audience. 'I hope I haven't chosen the most dreadfully inconvenient time? You must be so busy today.'

'It's perfectly all right, said Michael, 'it's a good time for me.' He smiled at her through the bars. His irritation, at least, was gone, overwhelmed by the profound affection which, mingled with respect and awe, he felt for the Abbess. Her bright, gentle, authoritative, exceedingly intelligent face, its long dry wrinkles as if marked with a fine tool, the ivory light from her wimple reflected upon it, reminiscent of some Dutch painting, reminded him of his mother, so long ago dead.

'I'm in a dreadful rush myself,' said the Abbess. 'I just felt I wanted to see you. It's been ages now, hasn't it? And there are one of two little business details. I won't keep you long.'

Michael felt relieved by this exordium. He had been afraid of being in some way hauled over the coals: and this was not the moment at which he wanted an intimate talk with the Abbess. In his present state he felt that any pressure from her would tip him over into a morass of profitless self-accusation. Taking courage from her business-like tone he said, 'I think everything's in train for tonight and tomorrow. Margaret Strafford has been doing marvels.'

'Bless her!' said the Abbess. 'We're all so excited we can hardly wait for tomorrow morning. I believe the Bishop is arriving this afternoon? I hope I shall catch a glimpse of him before he goes. He's such a busy man. So good of him to give us his time.'

'I hope he won't think we're a lot of ineffectual muddlers,' said Michael. 'I'm afraid the procession tomorrow may be a bit wild and impromptu. There's plenty of goodwill, but not much spit and polish!'

'So much the better!' said the Abbess. 'When I was a girl I often saw religious processions in Italy and they were usually quite chaotic, even the grand ones. But it seemed to make them all the more spontaneous and alive. I'm sure the Bishop doesn't want a drill display. No, I've no doubt tomorrow will be splendid. What I really wanted to ask you about was the financial question.'

'We've drafted the appeal,' said Michael, 'and we've made a list of possible Friends of Imber. I'd be very grateful if you'd cast your eye over both documents. I thought, subject to your views, we'd send the appeal out about a fortnight from now. We can cyclostyle it ourselves at the Court.'

'That's right,' said the Abbess. 'I think, for a cause of this kind, not a printed appeal. After all, it's something quite domestic, isn't it? There are times when money calls to money, but this isn't one of them. We're only writing to our friends. I'd like to see what you've done, if you'd send it in today by Sister Ursula. We can probably add some names to the list. I wonder what sort of publicity our bell will get? That might help in some quarters, mightn't it? I see no harm in the world being reminded, very occasionally, that we exist!'

Michael smiled. 'I thought of that too,' he said. 'That's why I don't want the appeal delayed. We won't have any journalists present of course. Not that any have shown signs of wanting to turn up. But I've prepared a hand-out for the local press, and a shorter one for the national press. I talked the wording over with Mother Clare. And I've asked Peter to take some photographs which we might send along as well.'

'Well done,' said the Abbess. 'I just can't think how you find the time to do all the things you do do. I hope you aren't overworking. You look rather pale.'

'I'm in excellent health,' said Michael. 'There'll be a let-up in a week or two anyway. I'm sure the others are working far harder than I am. James and Margaret simply never stop.'

'I'm worried about your young friend at the Lodge,' said the Abbess.

Michael breathed in deeply. That was it after all. He could feel a hot blush spreading up into his face. He kept his eyes away from the Abbess, fixing them on one of the bars beyond her head. 'Yes?' he said.

'I know it's very difficult,' said the Abbess, 'and of course I know very little about it, but I feel he's not exactly getting what he came to Imber to get.'

'You may be right,' said Michael tonelessly, waiting for the direct attack.

'I expect it's largely his own fault,' said the Abbess, 'but he is dreadfully out of things, isn't he? And will be more so when Catherine is in with us.'

Michael realized with a shock of relief that the Abbess was speaking of Nick, not of Toby. He turned to look at her. Her eyes were sharp. 'I know,' he said. 'It's been very much on my mind. I ought to have done more about it. I'll see to it that something *is* done. I'll put someone, perhaps James, quite seriously on his tail. We'll move him up to the house and just make him join in somehow. But as you say, it's not easy. He doesn't want to work. I'm afraid he's only putting in a little time here. He'll soon be off to London.'

'He's a *mauvais sujet* to be sure,' said the Abbess, 'and that's all the more reason for us to take trouble. But a man like that does not come to a place like this for fun. Of course he came to be near Catherine. But the fact that he wants to be near her *now*, and the fact that he wants to stay in the community and not in the village, are at least suggestive. We cannot be certain that there is not some genuine grain of hope for better things. And if I may say so, the person who ought to be, as you express it, on his tail, is not James, but you.'

Michael sustained her gaze which was quizzical rather than accusing. 'I find him difficult to deal with,' he said. 'But I'll think carefully about it.' He felt an increased determination not to be frank with the Abbess.

The Abbess studied his face. 'I confess to you,' she said, 'that I feel worried and I'm not quite sure why. I feel worried about him and I feel worried about you. I wonder if there's anything you'd like to tell me?'

Michael held on to his chair. From behind her the spiritual force of the place seemed to blow upon him like a gale. It was ironical, he reflected, that when he had wanted to tell the Abbess all about it she had not let him and now when she wanted to know he would not tell her. The fact was, he wanted her advice but not her absolution; and he could not ask the one without seeming to ask the other. Not that the Abbess would be tolerant. But he shied away almost with disgust from the idea of revealing to her his pitiable state of confusion. The story of Nick she almost certainly knew already in outline; what she wanted was to understand his present state of mind, and that would inevitably involve the story of Toby. If he began to tell the whole tale he knew that he could not tell it, now, without an absurd degree of emotion and without indulging in that particular brand of self-pity which he had been used to mistake for penitence. Silence was cleaner, better, in such a case. Looking down he saw, laid along the ledge of the grille, quite near to him like a deliberate temptation, infinitely wrinkled and pale, her hand, which had been covered with the tears of better men than himself. If he were to reach out to that hand he was lost. He averted his eyes and said, 'I don't think so.'

The Abbess went on looking at him for a little while, while he, feeling shrivelled and small and dry, looked at the corner of the room behind her. She said, 'You are most constantly in our prayers. And your friend too. I know how much you grieve over those who are under your care: those you try to help and fail, those you cannot help. Have faith in God and remember that He will in His own way and in His own time complete what we so poorly attempt. Often we do not achieve for others the good that we intend; but we achieve something, something that goes on from our effort. Good is an overflow. Where we generously and sincerely intend it, we are engaged in a work of creation which may be mysterious even to ourselves – and because it is mysterious we may be afraid of it. But this should not make us draw back. God can always show us, if we will, a higher and a better way; and we can only learn to love by loving. Remember that all our failures are ultimately failures in love. Imperfect love must not be condemned and rejected, but made perfect. The way is always forward, never back.'

Michael, facing her now, nodded slightly. He could not trust himself to utter any words after this speech. She turned her hand over, opening the palm towards him. He took it, feeling her cool dry grip.

'Well, I've kept you too long, dear child,' said the Abbess. 'I'd like to see you again in a little while, when this hurly-burly's done. Try not to overwork, won't you?'

Michael bent over her hand. Closing his eyes he kissed it and pressed it to his cheek. Then he raised a calm face to her. He felt obscurely that by his silence he had won a spiritual victory. He felt that he merited her approval. They both rose, and as Michael bowed to her again she closed the gauze panel and was gone.

He stood a while in the silent room looking at the bars of the grille and at the blank shut door of the panel behind them. Then he closed the panel on his side. How well she knew his heart. But her exhortations seemed to him a marvel rather than a practical inspiration. He was too tarnished an instrument to do the work that needed doing. Love. He shook his head. Perhaps only those who had given up the world had the right to use that word.

CHAPTER 20

The wind was blowing. Large piles of bulbous golden cloud passed quickly along the sky, obscuring and revealing the sun at short intervals. It was the sort of day which is gay in March but tiring in September. Dora was struggling with a white ribbon.

A sleepless night together with anxieties about the, it now seemed to her, colossal enterprise on which she had so rashly embarked had reduced Dora to a distracted state. The way in which, as she put it to herself, Toby had jumped upon her in the barn would at any other time have delighted her. The memory of his passionate childish kisses, still clear in her mind, moved her to tenderness, and she realized that she had not been unaware of the charms of that hard adolescent body and fresh uncertain face. But the excitement of Toby's brief embrace was swallowed up in her larger concern about the bell. She felt herself to be a priestess, dedicated now to a rite which made mere personal relations unimportant.

The scuffle in the barn had ended abruptly at the intervention of the bell. Neither of them could make out, having been absorbed in their activities of the moment before, how loud the sound had been. They decided it was probably not very loud, a mere murmur, and not to be compared with the full voice of the bell. All the same, a murmur from such a source was noise enough, and they waited anxiously in the silence that followed for any sound from the direction of the Court. As none came, they set to work at once on the next part of the operation which was carried out with a speed and efficiency which did Toby great credit. His only regret, which he expressed to Dora, was that she could have no idea how difficult what they had just successfully done had been. The bell now hung suspended by the second hawser a few feet from the ground. The hawser passed over the beam, out of the barn door, and its ringed end, pierced by a crowbar, was secured in the fork of a beech tree. The two conspirators had disguised the scene as best they could with twigs and creepers, and prepared to return to their beds. As they went, together this time, along the concrete road towards the Court Dora had taken Toby's hand in hers. Parting at the edge of the wood they faced each other in the moonlight. Trembling with nervous exultation, Toby took Dora by the shoulders and turned her until the moon shone upon her face. Amazed and delighted by her consenting passivity he contemplated her, and then took her in his arms, twisting her violently to receive his kiss and almost falling with her to the ground.

After these romantic adventures the next day had dawned somewhat soberly for Dora. Paul, who had searched for her in vain, and got his hand full of prickles from a gorse bush in the process, was not pleased with her when he returned to find her in bed; nor was he pleased when, after a brief sleep, they awoke at morning. He knew his wife's tastes well enough to suspect that she was not normally given to solitary communion with nature, especially at night, and he made no secret of finding her story of a moonlight ramble unconvincing. Nor did he hesitate to mention names in framing an alternative theory. Browbeaten before breakfast, Dora was in tears, genuinely sorry for Paul's distress, feeling herself for once unjustly accused, but unable to explain. More upsetting still, Paul then insisted on spending the morning with her: took her out for a walk which was a torment to both of them, and generally behaved to her as if she were his prisoner. This made it impossible for Dora to make contact with Toby, with whom, in the sweetness of their farewell last night, she had forgotten to make a precise rendezvous for the night to come. It also made it impossible for her to visit the bell, which she had intended to devote part of the day to cleaning, in readiness for its forthcoming dramatic appearance. The only time during the morning when Dora was left alone was for ten minutes when Paul was having a thorn removed from his finger by Mark Strafford. But Dora did not dare to look for Toby in that brief interval, and sat dejectedly in the common-room until Paul returned, still black with irritation and smelling strongly of Dettol.

Lunch went drearily. Everyone seemed to be on edge. Toby, who had clearly become aware of the wave of suppressed fury emanating from Dora's husband, looked subdued and avoided everyone's eye. Mrs Mark was fretting about the Bishop's arrival. Michael looked ill. Mark Strafford had been cast into a melancholy by the announcement of the auditor's visit, to take place next week. Catherine seemed more nervy than usual, and Patchway was cross because the wind had blown down all the runner beans. Only James lifted to the company a serene and cheerful face, diffused an atmosphere of robust and energetic confidence, listened with devout attention to Mrs Mark's reading from François de Sales, and seemed quite unaware that everyone else was not as carefree as himself.

After lunch Paul continued with maniac alertness to supervise his wife. Dora was by now thoroughly anxious about the night's arrangements. Retiring to the lavatory, she contrived to write a short note to Toby, which she put in a plain envelope and concealed in her pocket, saying: *Sorry I didn't make a date with you. Meet near the Lodge at 2 a.m.* This she trusted she would be able somehow to convey to the boy, pinning her hopes to Paul's well-known inability to spend more than a certain number of hours away from his work. Towards three she was glad to see him becoming restive; and half an hour later he made off in the direction of the parlours, having handed his captive over to Mrs Mark who had requested for help in the task of attiring the new bell.

This they were now engaged in doing. The new bell, set upon its trolley, was standing on the gravel outside the refectory. The refectory doors stood open, revealing the tables, decked for once with cloths, and laid for the buffet tea which the uncertain weather made it impossible to have, as Mrs Mark had originally pictured it, out of doors. With the help of members of what James called Patchway's village harem quite a creditable spread was toward. The bell had by this time been inspected and admired by everyone. Parked in the middle of the terrace, its smooth and highly polished bronze glowing in the intermittent sunshine like gold, it looked extremely strange, and yet charged with authority and significance. Its surface was plain, except for a band of arabesques which circled it a little above the rim, and the inscription, contributed by the zealous antiquarian, the Bishop: *Defunctos ploro, vivos voco, fulmina frango*. Upon the shoulder of the bell there was also written, and it gave Dora a curious feeling to see it, *Gabriel vocor*.

Over the bell, fitting it fairly close, was a garment of white silk. This garment had been fashioned by Mrs Mark out of some remnants of war surplus parachute material which she had in what she called her rag bag, a miscellany of vast dimensions. The material was heavy and slightly shiny. A cotton fringe, now frilled out upon the trolley, had been tacked to its lower end. At the top of the bell the white canopy, meeting at a point, turned out again and cascaded back down the sides of the bell in innumerable white ribbons which were to be tacked down, in a series of generous loops, and finally tied to each other at the bottom to form a scalloped border. Thus was simulated a bridal or first communion dress. If indeed the bell was being thought of as a postulant entering the Abbey, it was by modern standards somewhat overdressed; but at least it was customary for postulants to wear white. Dora, who thought Mrs Mark's confection had the coy demureness of a smart night-dress, noticed with relief that the garment was all of one piece and could easily be pulled off without disturbing its frills and flounces. Beside the bell stood a table with a damask cloth, to serve as an impromptu altar. Heavy stones kept the cloth in place. A considerable quantity of white wild flowers, collected by the village children, and which no one had had time to make into garlands, lay in a pile nearby, ready to be heaped onto the trolley at the last moment, their petals meanwhile being whisked off by the wind.

The ribbons were proving more troublesome than Mrs Mark had foreseen. The weather was partly to blame. The strands of satin, attached so far at the top only, streamed gaily away, flapping against themselves and each other with almost whip-like cracks, and gave to the bell more the appearance of a may-pole than of a bride. Gradually the recalcitrant ribbons were being attached to the silk, following the design of tiny crosses inscribed the night before in pencil by Mrs Mark, but even when attached the fluttering loops gave so much purchase to the wind that hasty tacking, especially if it was the work of Dora, was often pulled undone again. James had suggested pushing the trolley into the stable yard where it would be more sheltered, but Mrs Mark, now thoroughly in a panic and expecting the Bishop to arrive at any moment, preferred to have it left where it was, well in view upon the terrace.

Dora, more than usually butter-fingered with anxiety, fumbled with a ribbon. She had already had to undo it once all the way up to the top because of having inadvertently got it twisted. The ribbon was becoming slightly grey in her perspiring hands. The letter for Toby was still in her pocket and she would have excused herself from Mrs Mark for a moment in order to deliver it if she could have found out where Toby was; but this, in the hurly-burly, no one seemed to know. There was no sign of the boy. Dora trusted that he would surely turn up for the baptism service; and trusted equally that Paul, immersed in his studies, forgetting the time, would not, or at least would be late. As Dora kept looking up from her work to watch for Toby and Mrs Mark kept looking up to watch for the Bishop, things went ahead pretty slowly.

As they worked Mrs Mark was talking to Dora. It did not take Dora long, little as she attended to what was being said, to realize that she was being got at. Mrs Mark, on her own account or put up to it by somebody, was set to deliver a series of admonitions, and after a rather indirect beginning was now becoming positively frank. At another time Dora would have been furious. At present, however, the heavy responsibilities of her vatic role sufficiently distracted her, and a consciousness of innocence lent her detachment. It was true that she had let Toby embrace her, but the embrace had been incidental to a larger enterprise; and the implied charge of having actually pursued the young man did little justice to Dora's concern with higher matters. Virtuously indignant, Dora lent half an ear to Mrs Mark's clumsy and rather arch attempts to make a moral point.

'I hope you won't mind my saying these things,' said Mrs Mark. 'After all, it isn't as if we were all just on holiday here. I know you aren't used to this sort of atmosphere. But one must remember that little escapades which would be quite harmless in another place do matter here because, well, we do try to live a certain rather special sort of life, with certain special standards, you know. We live by rules ourselves and if our guests just don't there'll be chaos, won't there? It stands to reason. I know this sounds awfully dull and sober – and I'm sure your London friends would think we were a very stuffy lot. But trying to live up to ideals does often make one look ridiculous. And what I mean is this, that an inexperienced person may be quite upset by a sort of companionate friendliness in a member of the other sex, if he isn't used to that sort of thing. So we must be very careful, mustn't we? Oh dear, am I being terribly solemn?'

'Here's the Bishop!' said Dora, delighted to be able to terminate these rambling admonishments by the news that would throw Mrs Mark finally into a tizzy. A car had swung round out of the avenue and was to be seen speeding along the drive on the other side of the lake.

'Oh dear, oh *dear*!' said Mrs Mark, not sure whether to go on tacking ribbons or to rush back to take a final glance at the refectory. She dithered in the doorway, took off her overall, threw it under a chair, and then hurried through to call up the stairs to James who didn't appear to be there.

Dora stood by the bell, hands on hips, watching the car as it slowed down to cross the three bridges at the end of the lake. The car looked vaguely familiar. She supposed it was a common make. In the background she could hear Mrs Mark calling, and then moaning that just at the crucial moment *everybody* had disappeared. Dora watched the car serenely. She carried no responsibility for the success of the ensuing ceremonies, and indeed felt towards them much as Elijah must have felt when watching the efforts of the prophets of Baal.

The car was now coming towards them head on along the last section of the drive leading toward the house. Mrs Mark, still twittering, had emerged again onto the terrace. The car came up the slight slope towards them and stopped about thirty yards away. A figure got out. It was Noel Spens.

Dora's hands dropped to her side. 'Oh good Lord!' she said.

'It's not the Bishop after all!' said Mrs Mark.

'No, it's a friend of mine,' said Dora, 'a journalist. Oh God.' She set off at a run towards Noel.

Noel stood beside the car, one hand on the roof, smiling as if he had just called to take Dora out to dinner. She reached him, slithering to a standstill on the gravel, abrupt and savage as a small bull.

'Go away!' said Dora. 'Go away at *once*. Get into the car, for God's sake, before someone sees you, and go. I can't think what's possessed you to come here. I told you not to come. You'll ruin everything.'

'What a charming welcome,' said Noel. 'Keep your hair on, darling. I've no intention of going. I've come to do a job of work. I'm going to do a feature on this bell business. Don't you think it's an amusing idea?'

'No, I don't,' said Dora. 'Noel, use your *mind*. Paul's here. If he sees you he'll think I asked you, and he'll make the most beastly scene. *Please*, darling, go away. You'll only make awful trouble for me if you don't.'

'Look, sweetie,' said Noel. 'As you know, I usually behave with angelic tolerance where you're concerned. You may even have got it into your head that old uncle Noel doesn't mind what you do. You can just pop over to see him if you want to be consoled and pop off again when it suits you and he'll always be there waiting for you with a gin and martini. Well, that isn't altogether untrue; but somehow just lately I've found this role doesn't suit me quite so well as it used to. I've always acknowledged responsibilities where you are concerned; perhaps I've got some rights too. As you know, I was damn glad to see you the other day; and I was more than somewhat peeved when you cleared off. I don't usually yearn for what is not, I'm not that type. But I did feel I wanted to see you again soon – and I felt a little anxious about your curious state of mind. I thought those nuns might have been getting inside you. Then, oddly enough, my editor who knows the old Bishop who's coming down to bless your bell, got wind of this business quite independently and asked me to come. So I felt that in the circumstances it would be positively frivolous not to!'

'Oh, to hell with all that,' said Dora. 'The point is *Paul's* here. Can't you get that into your head? For Christ's sake go away before he sees you.'

'I'm fed up with hearing about Paul,' said Noel. 'Paul treats you disgustingly and you never really cared for him anyway. I think a little plain dealing with Paul wouldn't be a bad idea. I'm not sure that I won't give Paul a piece of my mind.'

'You can't be serious!' moaned Dora, distracted. 'You don't know what he's *like*. You've only seen him at parties. The Bishop will arrive any moment and then everyone will come and Paul will make a scene and I couldn't bear it!'

'You're a dreadful girl,' said Noel. 'You placate Paul until you can't stand it any longer and then you run away and then you get frightened and then you start placating him again. You must either knuckle under completely or else fight him. Quite apart from anything else, your present policy isn't fair to Paul. You won't really know whether you want to stay with him until you've fought him openly on equal terms, and not just by running away. And my guess is that once you start to fight you'll know you can't stay with Paul. And this is where I begin to get interested. You're unreliable and untidy and ignorant and totally exasperating but somehow I'd like to see you around the place again.'

'Gosh, you aren't *falling in love* with me?' cried Dora horrified.

'I don't use that terminology,' said Noel, 'so let's just say that I miss you. It's not out of sight out of mind any more, my girl.'

'Oh Lord!' said Dora. 'Look, Noel, I just haven't time for this just now. I'm terribly sorry, I do appreciate it and all that, and I know you're serious and I *will* explain, but the fact is I've got a plan on just now, nothing to do with Paul, and if things blow up over you it'll spoil it all – so do be an angel and go away. I *will* tell you all about it, only it's so terribly complicated. Do go, Noel, before something happens.'

'Sorry Dora,' said Noel. 'Just this once uncle Noel is going to do what *he* wants and not what *you* want. Where shall I put my car? I suppose I'd better leave the way clear for the Bish's Rolls Royce.'

'Now *you're* bullying me!' said Dora, almost in tears.

'Well, really,' said Noel. 'You call it bullying when I carry out my plan instead of yours. I almost sympathize with Paul. I think I'll drive into this yard, it looks a suitable place.' He got into the car, switched the engine on, and began to crawl round and through the open doors of the stable yard.

Dora watched him, despairing. She knew from his manner that he was quite determined to stay. It was no use pleading any further. This being so she must take some other steps to avoid an explosion. As it was, Paul would certainly be wanting to quarrel with her all night. But her immediate concern was to prevent a scene of open violence. Her own rites were after all to be the climax of the ceremony, and although a certain amount of chaos and failure in the preliminaries would not displease her she didn't want the thing to break down too badly; and in any case quite simply she feared the hideousness of Paul's anger exposed to the public view. She turned back along the gravel. There was the bell and there was Mrs Mark still tacking down ribbons, only two or three of which still streamed like banners. Dora's mind, attuned by brief practice to the exigencies of generalship, functioned. It was no good spending more time disputing with Noel. What time remained must be spent otherwise. How?

Dora's first instinct was to rush straight to Paul and tell him herself before he found out in some other way. Perhaps she could break it to him gently, calm him down, explain. She began to run along the terrace, passing Mrs Mark who looked at her inquiringly and started to say something. But before she got to the steps she was vividly picturing the scene and had changed her mind. As soon as Paul knew that Noel was here he would be deaf to any further commentary from her. Incoherent with rage and jealousy he would charge straight past her. She could never control him. Who could? She ran back again, once more passing Mrs Mark, who once more looked at her inquiringly and started to say something, and began to ascend the steps to the balcony. Noel, who had emerged from the stable yard, came across and began to pursue her up the steps, calling, 'Dora, can we fix somewhere to meet later on?' Dora paid no attention, rushed in through the hall and out into the corridor. She had decided to go and see Michael. It was just possible that Michael might make Paul see that, for the sake of the brotherhood, no public scene must be made on this day of all days.

Dora had never visited Michael's office, but she knew roughly where it was. When she found the door she knocked and bounded in without further ceremony. Her entry was so rapid that she had time to witness a little of the previous scene before its participants realized it had come to an end. Michael was sitting in a chair, leaning well forward, his elbows on his knees, his two hands extended. Toby was sitting on the floor just in front of him, one leg curled under, the other crooked up at the knee. One hand clasped his raised leg while the other was in process of making some gesture in Michael's direction. As Dora entered they both scrambled hastily to their feet.

'Oh hello, Toby,' said Dora, 'that's where you are, is it. I'm terribly sorry to bother you, Michael, but something awful has happened.'

Michael looked appalled. 'What?' he said.

'Someone I used to know has turned up, a journalist, to write about the bell. But when Paul finds out he's here he'll tear the place up. You must go and tell him not to.' This seemed to state the case.

Michael looked relieved. Then he looked at Toby. Toby mumbled something about 'Better be off now'. Dora began to say something to him but he went off without looking at her. Michael made to follow him, got as far as the door, and then came back looking confused and distracted. Dora was firm. Generalship was beginning to come to her. She said to Michael, 'Do you understand?'

'Yes, no,' said Michael. 'This man, this reporter is here now and you think Paul will make a jealous scene? Can't you persuade him to go?'

'He won't go,' said Dora, 'and it's no use your telling him to. What I want you to do is to prevent Paul from exploding. I'm going to tell Paul about it straight away.' She turned and set off again at a run. She could hear Michael's footsteps following her. They clattered down the uncarpeted stairs and out through the hall.

On the terrace, Noel was talking to Mrs Mark. They stopped to stare at the spectacle of Michael and Dora.

Noel said, 'Everyone seems to be in a terrible hurry today.'

Mrs Mark said, 'Oh Michael, don't go away, the Bishop will be here any moment!'

Michael who was down on the grass by now, ran back to reassure Mrs Mark. Dora kept on in the direction of the causeway. By the time she had reached the middle of the causeway and was almost out of breath she saw Paul emerge from the end door of the parlours. She started to wave to him frantically. As she neared the end of the causeway she saw a dark Rolls Royce coming slowly down the avenue from the Lodge gates.

Dora rushed up to Paul, who had quickened his pace when he saw her waving. She could see his frown from a long way off. 'Noel is here!' she cried.

'Who?' said Paul.

'Noel Spens,' said Dora. 'You know.'

Paul was tense and cool. 'You say,' he said, 'that Noel Spens is here. You yell this at me as if it were good news. He came to see you?'

'He came to report the bell business,' said Dora. 'Paul darling, don't get into a rage!'

'He came to see you,' said Paul. 'You invited him?'

'Of course I didn't invite him!' shouted Dora. 'Do you think I'm mad? He just came to interview people for his paper.'

'Well, I'm going to interview him,' said Paul. 'I'm going to give him an interview he won't forget!' He began to walk quickly across the causeway.

Dora followed, still talking and trying to hold onto his arm. The causeway was not quite wide enough for two people to walk side by side when disputing. The Bishop's car could now be seen in the distance crossing the bridges at the far end of the lake. Paul began to run.

At the end of the causeway Dora, who had been out-distanced, made a spurt and caught him up. As she did so she could see Michael running towards them down the grass slope from the house. Dora seized hold of Paul's hand violently and tried to pull him back, crying, 'Paul it's not my fault, I didn't want him to come! Don't spoil everything for the others by being furious now!'

Paul turned on her. He detached her hand from his with the other hand, and said to her quietly but baring his teeth, 'There are moments when I hate you!' Then he gave her a push which sent her flying back into the long grass.

Paul went on running. Michael converged on him, his arms spread out like someone who wants to prevent an animal from charging out of a field. Dora got up from where she had fallen in the grass, found her shoe which had come off, and began to run too in the direction of the terrace. The Bishop's car was just approaching the house. She passed Michael and Paul who had now met and came to a standstill. They both seemed to be talking at once. Dora did not think they needed her assistance.

The Rolls Royce came onto the terrace with the dignified condescension of a very large car moving slowly. It stopped at the foot of the steps, quite near to the bell. Mrs Mark, who had after all been left to hold the fort alone, rushed forward. James appeared a moment later on the balcony and began to hurry down the steps, falling over his feet. Noel lounged out of the refectory, eating a bun. Dora arrived panting and had to double up immediately because of an agonizing stitch.

The Bishop, who had apparently been driving himself, got slowly out of the car with the affable leisureliness of the great personage who knows that whenever and wherever he arrives he is immediately the centre of the scene. He was a big portly man with frizzy hair and rimless glasses, dressed in a plain black cassock and purple stock. His large fleshy face turned slowly, glowing with friendliness. He pulled a stick out of the car on which he leaned lightly while shaking hands with Mrs Mark, James, and Noel, and then with Dora, whom he was anxious not to exclude although she was hovering uncertainly in the background. Dora decided he took her for one of the maids.

'Well, here I am!' said the Bishop. 'I hope I'm not late? My charming chauffeur has abandoned me – a lady, I hasten to say, and also my secretary. The exigencies of motherhood called her to a higher task. She has three children to look after, that is not counting myself! So at much wear and tear to my own nerves and those of my fellow motorists I have driven myself to Imber!'

'We're so glad you've managed to come, sir,' said James, beaming. 'We know how busy you are. It means a lot to us to have you at our little ceremony.'

'Well, I think it's all most exciting,' said the Bishop. 'And is this exhibit A?' He pointed with his stick to the white ribbony mound of the bell.

'Yes,' said Mrs Mark, blushing with excitement. 'We just thought we'd deck it up a little.'

'Very pretty too,' said the Bishop. 'You are Mrs Strafford I believe? And you are Mr Meade?' he said to James. 'I've heard so much about you from the Abbess, bless her.'

'Oh no,' said James. 'I'm James Tayper Pace.'

'Ah!' said the Bishop. 'You are the man who is so sorely missed in Stepney! I was there only a few weeks ago at the opening of a new youth centre, and your name was often taken in vain. Or rather, not in vain. What an absurd expression that is, to be sure! Your name was mentioned, most fruitfully I've no doubt, and with positively devout enthusiasm!'

It was James's turn to blush. He said, 'We ought to have introduced ourselves. I'm afraid we make you a very poor reception committee, sir. This is indeed Mrs Strafford. This is Mrs Greenfield. Michael Meade is just coming across the grass with Dr Greenfield. And I'm afraid I don't know this gentleman.'

'Noel Spens, from the office of the *Daily Record*,' said Noel. 'I'm afraid I'm what they call a reporter.'

'Why, splendid!' said the Bishop. 'I hoped some gentlemen of the press might be present. Did you say the *Daily Record*? You must excuse me, I'm such a deaf old codger now, practically incommunicado on this side. May I ask if you were put on my track by my old crony Holroyd? I believe he now edits your distinguished rag.'

'That's correct, 'said Noel. 'Mr Holroyd got wind of this picturesque ceremony and sent me along. He sends you his greetings, sir.'

'An excellent fellow,' said the Bishop, 'in the best traditions of British journalism. I have always thought the Church was foolish to shun publicity. What we need is more publicity, of the right kind, of course. Perhaps I may say of *this* kind. What's that? No, I won't eat anything now, thank you. I'll just have the good old English cup of tea, if I may. Since my trip to America I value it more than ever. Then we might proceed perhaps to our little service, if the clans have mustered? And have the feasting afterwards. I see a board or two groaning with goodies in there.'

Michael and Paul had stopped again, just below the steps to the terrace, still talking. They began to walk back towards the causeway. Mrs Mark watched them with a look of despair, Dora with one of appalled apprehension. The Bishop was given a cup of tea. Noel chatted to him affably about members of the Athenaeum known to both of them. James stood beside them, smiling and rather shy. Father Bob Joyce, bearing with undignified haste what later turned out to be a stoup of holy water, placed it upon the table, and fussed round the bell, waving to the great man with the distant familiarity of one of the elect determined to let lesser men have their chance to be presented. Mrs Mark made little dashes into the refectory, keeping one eye on Michael, and keeping up an agitated discussion with Father Bob. Peter Topglass arrived with his camera, and joined the conversation with the Bishop, with whom it appeared he was already acquainted. Dora stood gloomily picking at one of the white ribbons on the bell. Her nervous plucking undid the tacking threads and the ribbon streamed out in the wind, which had not abated. Toby emerged, looking sulky, from the stable yard and was seized by Mrs Mark and introduced. James asked Mrs Mark for a cup of tea and was told in a whisper that they had better not start using the cups now as there were only just enough to go round once and no time to wash them up after the service. Patchway appeared and started complaining to James about the depredations of the pigeons until called to order by Mrs Mark and told to remove his hat. Catherine came down the steps from the house. She was wearing one of her London dresses and seemed to have taken some trouble with her appearance. A neat tight bun was fixed high at the back of her head and the curly locks which usually straggled over her brow had been cut short. Her face now seemed abnormally long and pale, and her smile, when she was presented to the Bishop, though sweet, was brief. She stepped quickly back and leaned against the balustrade, seeming to fall into a reverie, forgetting where she was.

'Well, dear friends,' said the Bishop, 'perhaps we could begin our little baptism ceremony. I gather you approved of my suggestions about the order of the service. I'm glad you didn't think I was being too archaic and popish! I think we might end with psalm a hundred and fifty, by the way. And I propose to leave out the Collect. I must say, I don't trust this sky not to pepper us with hailstones at any moment – so let us proceed at once. As my unfortunate congregation will have to kneel I suggest we descend from the gravel to the grass. I'm afraid my leech has prohibited genuflexion for me TFO, as we used to say in the army. Might I ask which of you are going to act as sponsors, or shall I say godparents, to the bell?'

'That will be Michael and Catherine,' said Mrs Mark. 'Please excuse me one moment and I'll fetch Michael.' She ran down the steps from the terrace.

Michael and Paul, still deep in conversation, were now walking back again from the causeway. Dora watched them anxiously. She avoided looking at Noel who was trying to catch her eye. They all descended the steps and stood about on the slope that led down to the ferry.

Mrs Mark was coming back with Michael and Paul. Dora disposed herself on the other side of the group from where Noel was standing. Michael was brought forward and could be heard apologizing to the Bishop. Catherine was ushered to the front. Mrs Mark was hastily attaching two very long extra ribbons to the bell. Then she hurried down and stood near Dora. Paul came up to Dora, looked her savagely in the eyes, his face screwed up to a point of suppressed fury, and then stood beside her, staring straight in front of him. The company disposed itself in two straggling rows with Michael and Catherine standing alone in front like a bridal pair. The Bishop mounted to the terrace. He took in one hand the two long ribbons which led to the bell. In the other he held an object, unfamiliar to Dora, which he dipped into the stoup of holy water. At a signal from Father Bob, the voices of James, Catherine, and the Straffords joined in the chant. *Asperges me, Domine, hyssopo et mundabor. Lavabis me et super niven dealbabor.* The Bishop began to cast the holy water onto the bell, making long dark streaks upon its white dress.

Dora observed with horror that Noel had come across and had somehow got himself next to her on her other side. She dared not look at Paul. She gazed glassily ahead, aware of the bell high above them on the terrace, its tent-like canopy audibly flapping. The sun came and went on the grass like a signal flash, and the wind tore at the Bishop's cassock, revealing a pair of smart black trousers beneath. The chant was ended, and the Bishop leaned forward to address Michael and Catherine. He said, 'What name do you desire to put upon this bell?'

After a pause, in a high and nervous voice, Catherine replied, 'Gabriel'.

The Bishop descended two steps and gave the ends of the white ribbons, one each, to Michael and Catherine to hold. Then he said, still speaking to them, 'Let us remember that the voice of Christ calls us at times to forsake earthly cares to sit at His feet and learn of higher things. Let this sign be consecrated and sanctified in the name of the Father and the Son and the Holy Ghost, Amen.' He ascended the steps again and faced his small congregation. 'The name of this bell is Gabriel. Now let us pray.' Everyone knelt down on the grass.

Paul reached out and took Dora's hand. He held it close, masterfully, pressing it without tenderness. Dora suffered this pressure for a while. Then it began to be hateful to her. She tried quietly to withdraw her hand. Paul held on. She began to pull. Paul gripped harder and twisted her wrist. Dora began to shake. A *fou rire* had got hold of her. She pressed her lips together so as not to laugh aloud. The Bishop's voice droned on. Tears of suppressed half hysterical mirth began to course from her eyes. With her other hand she reached into her pocket and pulled out her handkerchief.

With a handkerchief there fluttered out onto the grass the plain envelope containing the note to Toby. Dora saw it, was paralysed with horror, but could not stop laughing. She let go of her handkerchief which was immediately carried away by the wind. Paul, looking grimly ahead and still twisting her wrist, had not seen the envelope. With her free hand Dora spread out her skirt and petticoat to cover it. Then questing beneath them she tried to pick the envelope up to convey it back to her pocket. Her hand, involved in the fluttering folds of her petticoat, encountered another hand. It was Noel's. Noel's hand reached the envelope first and quietly removed it. For a moment, his face serenely lifted towards the Bishop, he held it at his side. Then he transferred it to his pocket.

Paul still stared ahead, oblivious. The rest of the community seemed to have their eyes closed. The Bishop with unfaltering voice looked down benignly, observing the by-play with the letter. He had seen odder things. Dora rearranged her skirt and clapped her hand over her mouth. It began to rain.

CHAPTER 21

Toby was in extremity. His thoughts and feelings swung to and fro in an unaccountable way which ten days ago he would not have been able to imagine. He deeply regretted having involved himself in Dora's crazy plan. It seemed to him now deceitful, silly, in thoroughly bad taste, and likely to end in some grotesque disaster. He would have liked to back out of it but did not know how. He was not unaffected too, by Paul's evident anger and by the faintly scandalized air with which he felt himself regarded by the other members of the community. He had not thought, when he sought in his need such particular help from Dora, that anyone else would be harmed or even concerned; he began now to see that his actions, in this quarter, had implications which he did not wish to sustain. On the other hand he felt excessively upset at the thought of doing anything which might destroy the sweet tenuous ambiguous bond which linked him now to Dora; and he hated the idea of letting her down. He longed to see her, and yet, because of the confusion of his thoughts, avoided her.

Meanwhile his feelings about Michael were swinging back the other way. The insidious fear about his own condition which had inspired Toby to think of Dora had not vanished but it had certainly faded. He was even a little reassured by what had passed between him and Dora. Indeed a sheer elation at having so successfully kissed her remained consolingly incapsulated in his distress. This left his mind more free to consider Michael once again as an individual and to feel their relationship for all its peculiarities as something real, interesting, even valuable. He began to be sorry for Michael and to speculate about Michael's state of mind. He began also to worry about Michael's opinion of him, and about how far the Dora business, which was turning out to be so much more extensive in various ways than he had expected, would damage him in Michael's eyes. His situation suddenly seemed intolerable.

Toby was a naturally truthful boy and had been brought up to believe that whatever mess one found oneself in one could always best get out of it by telling the truth. But truth-telling in this case, would be likely to prove difficult. What truth should he tell and to whom? He started to consider the possibility of going to Michael and telling him all about the plan for the old bell. The carrying out of the first half of the plan had been exciting; the carrying out of the second half seemed too onerous to bear. Toby simply could not see himself helping Dora to make the substitution of the bells; and this being so he rather cravenly felt that he was absolved from attempting it. Yet without Dora's sanction to abandon the plan, to betray her, who had so simply and completely relied upon him, was unthinkable too. Nor was there anyone in whom he could confide without by doing so effecting the betrayal. He thought of confiding in Nick; but he didn't trust Nick, and there was no one else. Patently, he told himself, what he ought to do was to go to Dora and tell her that he was giving up. This would not clear him of deceit, but it would at least be simple and more fair to Dora. But although he decided to do this several times during the day he did not go. Instead he went to see Michael.

Once he had set his feet on the way to Michael's room he felt as if he had entered a field of magnetic force. He could hardly stop himself from running. He reached the door, still uncertain what he was going to say. He knocked, and found Michael alone. Michael rose at once with a murmur of 'Oh, Toby!' which left little doubt of his pleasure at seeing the boy. But preoccupied perhaps by his own needs and problems he did not ask why he had come; nor did Toby feel any urge for immediate discussion since simply being in Michael's presence was so obviously an end in itself. He found himself sighing and smiling with relief. Michael sat down and looked at him solemnly for some time, as if he were memorizing his face. Then Toby, moved by some force which seemed to regulate his movements, sat down at Michael's feet and took hold of his hand. At that moment Dora came bursting in.

After this interruption Toby made himself scarce in the garden until it was time for the service, which he attended in a state of misery, indecision, and shock. When it was over he made off again, avoiding the social gathering in the refectory, and ran into the woods. A fine rain was falling and soon soaked him through but he paid no attention. He started off to visit the old bell, but changed his mind; he wished heartily that he had never discovered the rebarbative thing at all. He wandered about for nearly an hour, staring intermittently at the lake whose grey surface was pitted by the rain. Then he began to make his way back to the Lodge. He thought he would change his clothes and then go and look for Dora and tell her he could not go through with the plan.

Dripping wet and wretched he trailed into the living-room of the Lodge. It was already getting dark outside, and the un-lighted room was obscure and bleak. Toby stumbled in, kicking the newspapers aside. He fell over the recumbent Murphy and was half-way to the other door when he saw Nick sitting there in his usual position behind the table. He mumbled a greeting and was opening the door when Nick said in a clear voice, 'Wait a moment, Toby, I want to talk to you.'

Toby stopped and faced Nick across the table, startled by the urgency of his tone. He saw that Nick's bottle of whisky was bearing him company. A smell of drink pervaded the room, mingling with the chilly damp air from outside. The stove was out.

'I want a long and serious talk with you, Toby,' said Nick. He sounded drunk but determined.

'I haven't time now,' said Toby.

'You can spare me half an hour, dear boy. And in fact you will, whether you like it or not.' Nick got up from behind the table.

'Sorry, Nick,' said Toby. 'I've got to see somebody.' He realized that it might take a long time to talk Nick down, and he began prudently to back away towards the outer door. He would leave changing his clothes till later.

With a speed which took Toby by surprise Nick moved across the room and placed himself in front of the door. At the same moment he switched on the electric light. He surveyed Toby with his wide fixed smile. They faced each other.

Toby frowned, dazzled by the unshaded bulb. He said, 'Look here, Nick, don't be silly. I've got to go up to the house now. We can talk later.'

'Later will be too late my poor deluded child,' said Nick. 'You remember that I told you I would give you a sermon, the one the others didn't want to hear? Well, now is the time I am filled with the spirit. Take your pew!'

'Get out of the way,' said Toby.

'Come, come,' said Nick. 'Let's have no violence and cross words. Seek ye the Lord while He may be found. Only for that reason is time important. Sit down.' He gave Toby a sudden push which made him stagger back and sit abruptly in the arm-chair by the stove. Then, picking up the whisky bottle, Nick began to pull the table with one hand across the floor and jammed it noisily against the door. He sat upon it, drawing his legs up. He crossed himself.

'Nick, this isn't funny,' said Toby. 'I don't want to struggle with you, but I'm going out.'

'You'd better not struggle with me,' said Nick, 'unless you want to get hurt. Since you're in a hurry we'll cut out the hymns and prayers and go straight on to the sermon. In the name of the Father and the Son and the Holy Ghost. Dearly beloved, we are come of a fallen race, we are sinners one and all. Gone are the days in the Garden, the days of our innocence when we loved each other and were happy. Now we are set each man against his fellow and the mark of Cain is upon us, and with our sin comes grief and hatred and shame. What is there to lighten our darkness? What is there to ease our pain? Wait, there is a consolation and a remedy, the very Word of God, the dayspring from on high. A higher destiny and a higher joy awaits us than any which was known to our primeval pa as he lay blameless under the apple tree. It comes, it comes and it will make Gods of us all. I speak, beloved, of the joys of repentance, the delights of confession, the delicious pleasure of writhing and grovelling in the dust. *O felix culpa!* For had we been without sin we had been deprived of that supreme enjoyment. And see how miraculously our pain and our shame can be transformed! How sweet then our guilt, how welcome our transgression, which can bring on the pangs of so sharp a joy. Let us embrace our sin, beloved, and fall to couple with it upon the ground. Let us overcome our shame and turn our sorrow into joy, proclaiming our ill-deeds, kneeling and prostrating ourselves in the dust, and calling out for judgement, ravished, repentant, redeemed.'

'Nick, you're raving!' cried Toby, raising his voice to check Nick's increasingly loud and excited utterance. 'Let me out!'

'You shall stay to the end,' said Nick. 'The interesting part is just beginning. Do you imagine that I'm ranting in the void? By no means. What I have to say most intimately concerns each member of my congregation, and as you are its only member, apart from Murphy who is without sin, it most intimately concerns you.' He took a quick drink from the bottle. Toby had risen from his chair.

'Listen to me,' said Nick, speaking more rapidly and pointing his finger. 'Do you imagine I don't know all the tricks you are up to, Toby, all your little games? You treat me as if I were a piece of furniture, you think I don't notice what goes on under my nose – but I've made you a subject of loving study, Toby. And how you repay study, dear boy, believe me. So pure, so pretty, when you arrived, feeling yourself so good, belonging also to the communion of saints. What a pleasure that was, to be sure, it did my heart good to see you enjoying it all so much. But then what happens, what do we find? Our innocent, how quickly he learns. His head is turned, his vanity is tickled. He has found something more pleasurable now than religious emotion. A flirtation under the walls of a nunnery – what could be more thrilling? So first he plays the woman and then, to make sure he can do both, he plays the man!'

'Stop it, Nick, stop it!' cried Toby. He stood right before him with clenched fists and a burning face.

'I've seen you at it,' said Nick. 'I've seen your love life in the woods, tempting our virtuous leader to sodomy and our delightful penitent to adultery. What an achievement! So young

258

and so extremely versatile!' He drank some more from the bottle.

'Get out of the way!' said Toby. He was almost incoherent with distress and anger and fear. 'It's nothing to do with you.'

'Isn't it?' said Nick. 'After all, we're supposed to be looking after each other, aren't we? We are members one of another. You never bothered to look after me, but I take my responsibilities more seriously. I can hold the mirror up to you as well as the next man. What are you going to do about it? That's what I want to know. And what about your little frolic with the bell? Oh yes, I know all about the bell too, and that faked-up miracle you're planning with your female sweetheart.'

'Shut up!' cried Toby. He advanced on Nick and began pulling at the table. Nick uncurled his legs but still sat there laughing. Toby was unable to move the table.

'Wretched child,' said Nick. 'I told you you'd have to stay till the end. I wonder if you have any idea of the harm you're causing? To poor Michael for instance. But as for Michael his cup is filling and will soon run over, though not in the way the psalmist meant. Do you think you can play fast and loose like that with a religious man? Perhaps you think he smothers you with kisses and then goes to the Communion table with a light heart? You are busy destroying a man's faith, undermining his life, preparing his ruin – and even then you can't give it all your attention but start playing charades with a bloody bitch!'

'Oh stop, stop, stop!' shouted Toby. He plunged forward seizing Nick by the shoulder, meaning to pull him from his perch. Nick immediately gripped the boy about the neck and they fell struggling to the floor. Murphy began to whine and then to bark. Nick was the stronger.

'Shut up, Murphy, you're in church!' said Nick. Nick had now got one of Toby's arms twisted behind him and his knee braced in the boy's back. Toby's head was pressed lower and lower.

'Down, down, that's right,' said Nick in his ear. 'This is the confessional, only you needn't bother with your confession as I know it all. It's someone else you've got to tell the tale to, someone who hasn't heard it yet. The joys of penitence await you, Toby. Meanwhile, have a swig of this in remembrance of me.' He tried to turn Toby over, and reaching up for the whisky bottle poured a little of the whisky on to Toby's lips.

Like a spring released the boy began to struggle. The bottle fell between them and broke. They rolled across the floor up-setting Murphy's dish of water and rolling into the remains of his supper. Splashed with water, whisky, and gravy they fought among the chaos of old newspapers and broken glass. Nick was still the stronger.

Toby lay quiet. He was on his back now and Nick's face was above him. In this position they rested, both panting. Nick looked down at him and smiled. 'Poor child,' he said, 'it hurts me to do this, believe me it does. But I am made to be a scourge to certain men. You wouldn't understand. But at least I hope you've seen the point of my sermon. You're going to get up now and set your clothes to rights and then you're going to go like a good boy and make your confession to the only available saint, indeed the only available man, and that is James Tayper Pace. Up you get.'

Nick rose and Toby staggered to his feet, brushing down his clothing. He looked at Nick, dazed and appalled.

'I wish I could congratulate you on your truthful disposition,' said Nick, 'but the fact is that you have little choice. If by to-morrow you haven't had your little talk with James and told him everything I shall feel it my duty to make a statement. And by a happy law of nature, however low one wants to grovel one never paints oneself quite as black as the unpreju-diced and unsympathetic spectator can paint one. Another of the charms of confession. *Felix culpa, felix* Toby! Now go. And don't let your anger against me stop you from seeing that what I say is just. Go, go, go.'

Nick pulled the table away from the door and opened it. Toby stood for another moment, his hand raised to his face. Nick gave him a light push between the shoulders. He inclined forward as if he were going to fall and bolted out into the night.

CHAPTER 22

It was still raining but the wind had dropped. A soft sizzle of fine rain made the night more obscure and deadened all other sounds. It was after three o'clock.

Dora stood alone in the barn, close to the bell. She reached out every now and then and touched it, for company and to make sure it was still there. Earlier on, by the light of Toby's electric torch, she had attempted with soap, water, and a sharp knife to clean the bell. She had managed to prize away a good deal of mud and gravel, but many strange growths still adhering to the surface seemed to have the hardness of metal. For the last half-hour however Dora had done nothing but wait. She had arrived well before two, since for fear of being delayed by Paul she had not gone up to bed. Paul would know soon enough that he had misjudged her. She had hidden herself elsewhere in the house, dozing in a chair, and then had made her way through the rain to the barn.

At first she had been quite certain that Toby would come. Even though she had not managed to communicate with him during the day, he would know when and where to appear; and it had at least been agreed that he should bring the second steel trolley with him direct to the barn. When by half past two he had not arrived Dora had imagined that he might have had difficulty getting the trolley out of the stable yard, and she walked back that far to see. The stable yard was deserted and the trolley still in its place, though Dora noticed uneasily that there were two lights on in the house, one in her and Paul's bedroom, and the other in another room which she could not identify, James's or Michael's perhaps. She left the trolley where it was and rushed back to the barn, feeling sure that she would now find Toby there; but he was not there.

Dora was wearing a mackintosh and a scarf, but she was already wet through. Her sandalled feet were cold and muddy and the water had splashed up over the end of her dress which now clung damply to her knees, impeding her movements. She stood shivering in the barn, frightened by the darkness and the close blanket of the rain, awed by the proximity of the bell, and feeling increasingly sure now that Toby would not come. She wondered whether she should go and look for him at the Lodge.

It had not escaped Dora that Noel Spens must obviously have imagined that the letter which she had dropped was intended for him; indeed its contents were perfectly framed to sustain this illusion. It was therefore probable that Noel would present himself near the Lodge at two; and this thought had deterred Dora from going earlier to search for Toby. By now, however, Noel would have got tired of waiting and gone to bed. It was surely safe to go to the Lodge; and in any case anything was better than hanging round in the barn frightened out of her wits and chilled to the marrow. Dora set out along the path.

The moon was obscured and the path was full of obstacles, but Dora knew her way pretty well by now and was indifferent to the briars and brambles which dragged at her legs. She could feel the warmth of blood about her ankles. When she emerged from the wood she did not go round the house to the ferry but turned right across the causeway. The two lights were still on; and as she looked ahead of her across the water she saw that there was a light in the Lodge too. This made her extremely uneasy.

Dora began to run now, passing under the Abbey walls and away diagonally across the grass towards the Lodge. When she got near it she slowed down, avoiding the crunchy gravel of the drive and approached cautiously, laying her sodden feet quietly on the wet grass. She saw that the light came from the living-room of the Lodge; there was no light in Toby's room. She came cautiously up toward the window; it was a modern casement window set with small leaded panes and it was slightly open. Dora heard a murmur of voices. She fell on her hands and knees and crawled toward the window until she was almost underneath it. The voices could be heard clearly now, together with a clink of glasses.

'It would be hard to say whether or not it's supposed to be a joke,' Nick's voice was saying. He sounded drunk. 'With people like that you can never tell.'

'I'm sorry, Mr Fawley, but I still don't understand,' said another voice.

Chilled as she was Dora went a degree colder. The voice was Noel's. Incautiously she lifted her head to the level of the sill. Noel and Nick were sitting together at the table with the whisky between them. There was no one else in the room. Amazed and horrified Dora sank back and settled herself on a cushion of wet grass.

'You see,' Noel went on, 'this is in the technical sense such a good story that it would be a pity not to get it absolutely correct. And in any case I have a certain preference for getting things right. Even we newspaper men have our morals, Mr Fawley. Thanks, I will, just a little.'

'I've told you all I can,' said Nick. 'As for getting it right, who ever gets any story right? All you can do is mention a few facts, I don't suggest any more than that. What will happen tomorrow is anyone's guess. All I can promise you is a spectacle. I hope you've got a camera with you?'

'I'm sorry to keep on bothering you,' said Noel in the slow patient voice of a sober man talking to a drunk, 'and I know you must be frightfully tired, but do you mind if we go over it again? I'd like to check the notes I've made. You say that two members of the community, identity not disclosed, have found an old bell which used to belong to the convent long ago. And these two are planning what you call a miracle – the substitution of the old bell for the new bell. But what do they expect to achieve by this? After all, this is England, not Southern Italy. It sounds more like a practical joke.'

'Who knows what they expect to achieve?' said Nick. 'I'm sure they don't know themselves. Publicity perhaps. I told you this place was appealing for funds. And if you think it sounds mad, it's no more mad than believing that Jesus Christ was God and died to redeem our sins.'

'I can't agree,' said Noel. 'Belief is a highly selective business. And people will believe *that* who otherwise don't part

263

company with common sense. But never mind, let's get on with the story. You say that the plan won't now be carried out?'

'Unfortunately not,' said Nick. 'It was a beautiful plan, but one of the parties has lost his nerve.'

'I must say, you intrigue me,' said Noel. 'As you may have guessed, I feel no sympathy with an outfit like this. I don't think these people are consciously insincere, but they're just born to be charlatans *malgré eux*. I'm sure there are all sorts of little feuds and delusions in this crackpot community and I've certainly no objection to reporting them, without comment. If people want to stop being ordinary useful members of society and take their neuroses to some remote spot to have what they imagine are spiritual experiences I'm certain they should be tolerated but I see no reason why they should be revered. But as I say, I want to report and not to malign. What I was wondering, if I may ask it off the record, is what your motives are in telling me all this. Thanks yes. But fill up yourself.'

'There are moments,' said Nick, 'when one wants to tell the truth, when one wants to shout it around, however much damage it does. One of these moments is upon me. And now I shall go to bed. I advise you to do the same. You will have a strenuous and amusing day tomorrow.'

Noel began to reply. Dora got up hastily and started to run back the way she had come. The rain, heavier now, deadened the sound of her footsteps as she squelched through the grass. When she was nearly at the causeway she looked back. There seemed to be no one emerging from the Lodge; but as it was hard to see or hear anything except the rain she couldn't be certain. She ran across the causeway gasping for breath and turned along the lakeside path towards the barn. As she slowed to a walk she began to think. There was no mystery about how Noel was led to the Lodge and into the clutches of Nick Fawley. Her own letter had brought him there. As for how Nick knew about the bell, there need be no mystery about that either: she and Toby had made so much noise on the previous night, anyone *might* have heard, though in their excited optimism they had reckoned it as unlikely. Nick was, in any case, as she might have remembered, a bad sleeper and a night wanderer. He could easily have found his way to the barn and overheard herself and Toby running over the details of the plan just before they left the scene. Or he might just have seen Toby creeping out and followed him out of sheer curiosity. All that made sense; and by now it was hardly news to her that the plan would fail because one of the parties had lost his nerve. What appalled her was the idea, coming to her now fully for the first time, that this abortive fantasy would be reported, or misreported, in the newspapers and perhaps do great harm to the community.

Dora knew that if she had reflected more carefully on her plan she would have seen that it was bound to get publicity and bound to look, to the outsider, ludicrous or sinister. Its triumphant witch-like quality existed for her alone. Even Toby, she realized, had cooperated to please her rather than because he liked the plan. How could such a thing be understood by the outside world? Dora had become used to thinking of Imber as utterly remote, utterly cut off and private. Imber had retired from the world, but the world could still come to Imber to pry and mock and judge.

Dora reached the barn. She looked and listened. All was silent, all was as she had left it. She switched the torch on to the bell. It hung there, huge and portentous, motionless with its own weight. She switched the light off again and waited, wondering what to do. She came near to the bell which seemed now more and more like a living presence. She put her hand on its rim and felt again the rough encrusted surface and the strange warmth in it. She drew her hand up on to the squares, trying to tell by the feel which picture she was touching. Toby would not come. Should she carry out the plan herself? She could not do it alone, and in any case her desire to do it had vanished. The enterprise now seemed as cheap to her as it would shortly seem to the readers of the sensational press: at best funny in a vulgar way, at worst thoroughly nasty. Dora's heart swelled with remorse and rage. Why did Noel have to come here? The story would 'come out' in any case, but Noel's presence on the spot would ensure that it would be misreported in thoroughly picturesque detail. Dora knew what Noel could make of a story. She knew too the evasive mockery with which Noel would meet any plea for silence. More obscurely she grieved that Noel had been foolish enough to pursue and intrude in a way which seemed now to make it impossible for her to regard him as a place to escape to. In London his judgement of Imber had eased her heart. Here it was he who was under judgement.

But her more immediate thoughts concerned the bell. It was too late now to hope to keep everything dark. Was there any way of making the revelation less absurd, less damaging to Imber? Nick had told the story as if the projected miracle were the work of someone within the community; and this would probably be how it would appear: a crackbrained stratagem arising out of some schism in a society of lunatics. Yet it was she, and she only, who was responsible. How could that be made clear? Should she make a statement to the press? How did one make a statement to the press? She turned to the bell for help.

She pressed her palm gently against it as if supplicating. The bell moved very slightly. She steadied it and stood with both her hands upon it. Attending to it, she was struck again by the marvel of its resurrection and she felt reverence for it, almost love. When she thought how she had drawn it out of the lake and lifted it back into its own airy element she was amazed and felt suddenly unworthy. How could the great bell have suffered her to drag it here so unceremoniously and make it begin its new life in an out-house? She should not have tampered with it. She ought by rights to be afraid of it. She *was* afraid of it. She took her hands off it abruptly.

The hissing of the rain continued all round her, very soft, making an artificial silence more deep than real silence could be. The floor of the barn about her feet was sticky with the water that was still steadily dripping from her garments. Dora stood tense and listening. She put her ear near to the bell as if she half expected to hear it murmur like a shell that holds the echo of the sea. But from all the sound that lay asleep in that great cone not the faintest sigh was audible. The bell was quiet. Fascinated, Dora knelt down on the ground and thrust her arm inside it. It was black inside and alarmingly like an inhabited cave. Very lightly she touched the great clapper, hanging profoundly still in the interior. The feeling of fear had not left her and she withdrew hastily and switched the torch on. The squat figures faced her from the sloping surface of the bronze, solid, simple, beautiful, absurd, full to the brim with something which was to the artist not an object of speculation or imagination. These scenes had been more real to him than his own childhood and more familiar. He had reported them faithfully. They were familiar to Dora too, as in the light of the electric torch she looked at them again.

When she had walked slowly all round the bell she switched the light off. She was ready to drop with tiredness, chilled and stiff with the rain. It was all too difficult; she must go back to bed. But she knew this was impossible. She could not leave things wretchedly like this, unsolved and unmended; she could not leave the bell ambiguously to be the subject of malicious and untrue stories. As if it alone held the solution she could not bring herself to leave it, though tears of exhaustion and helplessness were warming her frozen cheeks. She had communed with it now for too long and was under its spell. She had thought to be its master and make it her plaything, but now it was mastering her and would have its will.

Dora stood beside it in the darkness breathing hard. A thrill of terror and excitement went through her, a premonition of the act before she consciously knew what the act would be. Vaguely there came back to her a memory of something that had been said: the truth-telling voice that must not be silenced. If it was necessary to accuse herself, the means were certainly at hand. But her need was deeper than this. She reached her hand out again towards the bell.

She pushed it a little and it moved. It was not difficult to move it. She felt rather than heard the clapper moving inside the cone, not yet touching the sides. The bell oscillated faintly, still almost motionless. Dora took off her mackintosh. She stood a moment longer in the darkness feeling with her hand how the great thing was shuddering quietly before her. Then suddenly with all her might she hurled herself against it.

The bell gave before her so that she almost fell, and the clapper met the side with a roar which made her cry out, it was so close and so terrible. She sprang back and let the bell return. The clapper touched on the other side, more lightly. Taking the rhythm Dora threw herself again upon the receding surface and then stood clear. A tremendous boom arose as the bell, now freely swinging, gave tongue to its utmost. It returned, its great shape scarcely visible, a huge moving piece of darkness. Dora touched it again. It was only necessary now to keep it swinging. The thunderous noise continued, bellowing out in a voice that had been silent for centuries that some great thing was newly returned to the world. The clamour arose, distinctive, piercing, amazing, audible at the Court, at the Abbey, in the village, and along the road, so the story was told later, for many many miles in either direction.

Dora was so astounded, so almost annihilated at the wonder of it, and by the sheer noise, that she was oblivious of everything except her task of keeping the bell ringing. She did not hear the sound of approaching voices and stood dazed and vacant when some twenty minutes later a large number of people came running into the barn and crowded about her.

CHAPTER 23

By the time Dora arrived the first part of the ceremony was over and the procession was about to start. It was about twenty minutes past seven. The rain had stopped and the sun shone through a thin curtain of white cloud, diffusing a chilly pale golden light. A white mist curled upon the surface of the lake, concealing the water, the top of the causeway just visible above it.

Dora had slept. Hustled back to the Court by Mrs Mark she had fallen into bed and become instantly unconscious. She woke again about seven and immediately remembered the procession. As she listened she could hear the distant sound of music. Things must have begun already. Paul was not to be seen. She dressed hastily, scarcely knowing why she felt it so very important to be present. Her memories of the night were confused and dreadful, like drunken memories. She recalled being dazzled by the light of torches, and seeing the bell, still swinging, revealed in their beams. A lot of people had surrounded her, pulling her, questioning her. Someone had put a coat over her shoulders. Paul had been there too, but he had said nothing to her, he was too transported at seeing the bell. He had not come back to their bedroom, so she assumed that he was still in the barn. They had divided the night's vigil between them.

Dora felt stiff and unspeakably hungry and miserable in a blank exhausted way. The air smelt of disaster. She put on her warmest clothes and went out onto the landing from which a window on the front of the house would command a view of the proceedings. An astonishing scene awaited her. Several hundred people, all completely silent, were standing in front of the house. They covered the terrace, crowded on the steps and balcony, and lined several deep the path towards the causeway. They had the expectant silence which falls during a ceremony when singing or speaking has momentarily stopped.

They stood there silent in the early morning, giving to the scene that sense of drama which is always present when many people are ceremonially gathered in the open air. They were all looking towards the bell.

The Bishop, dressed in full regalia, with mitre and crook, faced the bell which was still in place on the terrace. Behind him a number of little girls, clutching recorders, were trying to get out of the way of a number of little boys, wearing surplices, who were being hustled forward by Father Bob Joyce. The Bishop stood with evident patience, like a kindly man interrupted, and without turning round while the silent scuffle continued. The Bishop, as it turned out afterwards, knew nothing of the night's events. With his good ear plunged deep in the pillow he had not been roused by the clangour, nor had anyone chosen to tell him, so early in the morning, so improbable a story.

The little boys had by now successfully ousted the little girls, who were scattered along the edge of the crowd, casting anxious glances at their teacher. The situation of the Morris dancers was, however, even less to be envied. They had pressed forward in the wake of the choir under the impression that this was their moment. Complete with hobby-horse, tophatted Fool, and fiddler, armed with sticks and handkerchiefs, their legs decorated with bells and ribbons, they were conspicuous and self-conscious, not yet liberated and made triumphant by the Morris music and the dance. They had been told to start dancing shortly before the procession moved off and accompany it still dancing down to the causeway. But the great crowd had not been foreseen, and it was now plain that there was no room to dance on the terrace, nor could a space be cleared without asking several elderly ladies, who were pinned against the balustrade, to climb over and jump on to the grass. The Fool pressed forward through the choir boys to consult Father Bob. Father Bob smiled and nodded, and the fiddler who was standing at the back and reduced to a frenzy already by feeling that everyone was waiting for him immediately struck up with Monks' March. Some of the dancers began to try to dance, while others cried sssh! Father Bob frowned and shook his head and the fiddle music tailed away. The Fool fought his way back and gave some instructions, evidently discouraging ones, to his men. Father Bob tapped the Bishop, now looking more patient than ever, upon the shoulder, and the Bishop began to speak.

Dora could not hear what he said. Desperately anxious not to be left out she ran down the stairs and came out on to the balcony which was already black with spectators. She pushed her way towards the steps and managed to find a place from which she could see. The Bishop had stopped talking, and very slowly the bell was beginning to move. The trolley was pulled from the front and controlled from the back by two pairs of workmen, the men who had come with the bell and who would be permitted to enter the Abbey to put it up. They pulled solemnly on ropes which by an afterthought Mrs Mark had whitened with whitewash. The bell began to move across the terrace towards the slope that led down to the causeway. Immediately after the bell walked Michael and Catherine, followed by the Bishop, and then by the choir. Next, materializing from here and there in the crowd, came members of the brotherhood, all, as Dora observed, looking extremely haggard. After them came the disgruntled Morris dancers, walking not dancing, their bells jingling and white handkerchiefs trailing. After them came the recorder band with their teacher. After them the Girl Guides and after them the Boy Scouts. The tail of the procession was taken up by one or two minor dignitaries of the village church, who felt it their duty to process, and by those members of the general crowd who preferred the privilege of being in the procession to the excitement of seeing it. As they moved off people were clambering on to the balustrade or struggling up the steps to take photographs, cannoning into those who were rushing down the steps, or jumping off the terrace so as to get good places on the slope or the edge of the lake from which to see the next stage of the proceedings.

Dora stayed where she was. She could see well enough from there, especially now the balcony had emptied. She looked down at the still crowded terrace on which people were milling to and fro and saw that Noel had mounted on top of one of the stone lions at the foot of the staircase and was taking a photograph. This done he jumped off and started to run along by the side of the procession. The Girl Guides, who had been formed up near the gates to the stable yard, were just struggling through with a vigour which did credit to the quasi-military qualities of their organization, and it was difficult at this point to distinguish the procession from the crowd that surrounded it. Noel looked up and saw Dora. He beamed. Then he waved his camera case rhythmically to and fro and clapped his hands. Dora stared at this pantomime. Then it occurred to her that of course Noel was referring to last night. He must have been there; and that was how he felt about it. Dora smiled wanly and waved a feeble hand. Noel was pointing towards the lake. He wasn't going to miss his chance of another picture. Dora shook her head and he charged off through the mob. She could see him, head and shoulders above the others, outdistancing the Girl Guides and catching up with the head of the procession which was now nearing the causeway. The sun was beginning to break through its white veil and long scurrying shadows appeared on the grass. The choir burst into song. At the far end of the causeway Dora could see the great gates of the Abbey opening slowly.

She was alone now on the balcony. The crowd were mostly collected along the banks of the lake on either side of the causeway. The bell, moving slowly and smoothly, was going up the very slight slope from the bank to the causeway and came more fully into view. The sun shone, gilding its white canopy and gilding the white robes of the Bishop. The wind, less boisterous now, fretted the satin ribbons and ruffled the pale flowers with which the trolley was heaped. The Bishop walked stiffly, head a little bowed, leaning on his crook. The white surplices of the choir boys fluttered about them as they importantly raised their sheets of music. The bell was now on the causeway, moving more slowly over the slightly uneven stones. The other figures were following. The mist lay quiet over the water, still reaching to the top of the causeway, so that the procession, as they strung out on to the lake, looked as if they were walking on air. Dora leaned well forward to see better.

The choir broke into song. The more ambitious music was being reserved for the climax at the Abbey gate. Meanwhile, Father Bob's wishes had been over-ridden by local sentiment:

> Lift it gently to the steeple,
> Let our bell be set on high,
> There fulfil its daily mission
> Midway 'twixt the earth and sky.
>
> As the birds sing early matins
> To the God of Nature's praise,
> This its nobler daily music
> To the God of Grace shall raise.
>
> And when evening shadows soften
> Chancel cross and tower and aisle,
> It shall blend its vesper summons
> With the day's departing smile.

The singing continued. The Morris dancers, walking gingerly two by two, had by now left the shore, and the little girls were following, looking very cold in their white satin dresses. The bell was moving very slowly indeed and had almost reached the middle of the causeway where the wooden section was set in, commemorating the brave nuns of the sixteenth century. Dora's glance strayed to the crowd. She could not see Noel now. She spotted Patchway, who had declined to join the procession, and was standing stolidly at the back of the crowd in a place where he obviously couldn't see. Then something began to happen. Dora looked back quickly to the centre of the scene. A quick sigh went up. The choir boys' song faltered. The bell had stopped on the wooden boarding in the middle of the causeway and the workmen seemed to be scuffling round it. The Bishop had motioned the choir to move back. The procession was at a standstill. Raggedly the music ceased; and then in the murmur that followed a loud grinding sound was heard. The bell seemed to be tilting slightly to one side. An excited buzz arose from the crowd. Then very slowly the wooden supports sagged, the wooden surface sloped, the trolley inclined, and the bell, poised for a moment at an almost impossible angle, plunged sideways into the lake, taking the trolley with it.

The thing happened so quickly that Dora could hardly believe her eyes. There was the procession, still standing strung out on the causeway in the sun. There was the sagging hole in the centre, with two of the workmen marooned on the far side of it. The invisible water could be heard surging and gurgling. The bell had utterly vanished. A cry went up from the crowd which was half a groan and half a cheer. Those who had come for a show were getting their money's worth.

Dora ran down the steps and on towards the lake. Father Bob Joyce was hustling the procession back off the causeway, while at the shore end dozens of people were trying to push their way on. Someone, Dora could not see who, had fallen in. Shouts arose, and one of the choir boys was crying. The Bishop, conspicuous in the sun, was still standing where the bell had been, looking down into the water and talking to one of the workmen. The mist was clearing a little and the lake could be seen still churning away under the wooden piers, strewn with a circle of white flowers. Nothing of the bell or the trolley was visible above the surface. Several people by now had pushed past the Bishop and jumped the gap to survey the scene from the other side. The Abbey gates were unobtrusively closing once more.

Dora was fairly near to the lake by now, on the right-hand side of the causeway. At what had happened she felt intense horror mingled with excitement. She felt partly as if she must be responsible for this new disaster, and partly as if its magnitude made her own escapade pardonable by comparison. She came to the back of the crowd, watching her chance to get a nearer view. Then someone pushed very roughly past her. Dora said later that if it had not been for that violent shove she would not have paid attention and not have started to wonder.

She looked to see who the rude person was who had pushed her and saw that it was Catherine. Having got past her and out into the open Catherine began to walk away along the path that led beside the lake towards the wood. Dora looked back to the spectacle on the causeway. Then she turned thoughtfully to stare after Catherine who was some distance away by now and walking fast. No one had paid any attention to her departure.

It was very unusual, to say the least of it, for Catherine to push people out of her way; and what Dora had seen of Catherine's face was also rather unusual. Naturally she would be upset; but she had looked strange and distracted beyond measure. Dora hesitated. She was surrounded by people but no one that she knew was within sight. After a moment she began to pick her way back across the grass and followed along the path which Catherine had taken, keeping her in sight. Catherine quickened her pace and plunged into the wood. Dora began to run. Catherine had certainly looked very odd. All the same it was no business of Dora's. Yet she felt anxious and wanted to be sure that all was well.

Once in the wood she began to catch up. The path was thickly strewn with twigs and branches brought down by the storm. Catherine could be seen stumbling on ahead. Then she fell heavily, and by the time she had got up Dora was almost beside her. Dora called, 'Catherine, wait for me. Are you all right?'

Catherine was wearing an old-fashioned tennis dress, now scored with dirty marks from her fall. She brushed it down and began to walk on more slowly, ignoring Dora. She seemed to be crying. Dora, unable to walk abreast of her on the narrow path, followed, plucking at her arm and asking her if she was all right.

After a moment or two Catherine, brushing Dora off, paused and half-turning said, 'I am all right alone.' Her face had an odd staring look.

'I'm so sorry,' said Dora, not knowing whether to leave her or not.

'You see,' said Catherine, 'it *was* because of me. You didn't

275

know, did you? It was a sign.' She began to walk on.

Dora, seeing her face thought: Catherine has gone mad. This was the thought which had struck her at once when she had been rudely pushed aside, but which had seemed too fantastic to entertain. Catherine had seemed quite normal on the previous day. Surely people don't go mad suddenly. Dora, who had had no experience of mad people, stood frozen with fear and horror while the white figure of Catherine disappeared along the path.

When she had vanished between the trees Dora's instinct was to rush back to the Court for help. But then she decided that it was more important to pursue Catherine and persuade her to return. In that condition she might wander away into the woods and not be found. Dora was also moved by a desire not to make a fool of herself or make any more trouble. She might after all be quite wrong about Catherine, and to raise a false alarm when there was so much else for everyone to think about would be more than tiresome. She hurried forward and soon saw Catherine's white dress ahead of her.

It then occurred to Dora that they would soon be in the vicinity of the barn, and that Paul might still be there. This encouraged her and she ran on, once more calling Catherine's name. Catherine paid no attention and when Dora caught up with her the second time she seemed to be murmuring things to herself. Looking at that flushed distracted face Dora felt no doubt that her first instinct had been right. She seized Catherine's dress and at the same time began to shout for Paul. They came out into the open space by the ramp, Catherine hurrying and Dora holding on to her and shouting. There was no response from the barn. Paul must have left it; as it turned out later he had gone back by the concrete road to the Court to telephone a London colleague. Dora and Catherine were alone in the wood.

Dora gave up her shouting and said to Catherine, 'Do come back to the house now, please do.'

Catherine, without looking round, pushed Dora away from her, and said in a clear voice, 'For Christ's sake leave me alone.'

Dora, who was beginning to be a little incensed as well as

alarmed, said, 'Look here, Catherine, you're being silly. You come along with me.'

Catherine turned back at her, grinning suddenly with a smile that resembled the harsh unfading smiles her brother used. She said to Dora, 'God has reached out His hand. A white garment cannot conceal a wicked heart. There is no passing through that gate. Good-bye.'

They had passed the ramp now and reached a place where the path was very close to the edge, fringed on the lake side by tall rushes. An area of mud and green weeds lay between the bank and the clear water. Catherine turned away from Dora and began to walk into the lake.

She moved so quickly, plunging directly through the wall of rushes, that Dora was left standing, staring at the place where she had disappeared from view. A loud squelching sound came from beyond the rushes. Dora gave a scream and followed. Without hesitation she plunged through the greenery and gave another scream as she felt the ground give way beneath her. She sank in the mud almost to her knees. Catherine had managed to take another two steps and was farther out. Almost with deliberation, like a timid bather, she subsided into the gluey mess of weeds and muddy water, struggling to get farther from the shore. She lay sideways, the shoulder of her dress still strangely clean and white above the surface.

Dora called to Catherine, and then screamed again. But who would hear? Everyone was so busy and so far away. She reached out, trying to reach Catherine, lost her balance, and fell forward into the deeper water. The water splashed up over her face. Frenziedly struggling to keep her head up, she felt the slimy weeds dragging at her limbs. With a frantic effort she managed to draw her feet under her and sit in the mud with the water almost to her neck. Ahead of her Catherine was splashing. She had now sunk well into the water and seemed to be caught in the weeds, whose strands could be seen bound round one of her flailing arms. Dora reached forward and managed to catch Catherine by the hand. She shouted her name over and over again, and then screamed as loudly and piercingly as she could. She tried to pull Catherine back towards her.

The next moment she found herself being dragged forward. Catherine, resisting her grip, was pulling her out into the deeper water. Dora let go, but it was too late. She was now well away from the bank. Her feet trampled vainly in a bottom-less morass of watery mud and weed. She beat the surface with her hands, shrieking and swallowing water, her head thrown back, her arms half entangled. Something dark was unravelling on the water before her. It was Catherine's hair. As in a dream she saw Catherine's shoulder disappearing in the black ooze, her staring eyes cast upward, her mouth open. Fear of death came upon Dora. She fought desperately, gasping for air, but the weeds held her, seeming to drag her down, and the water was at her chin.

Then she heard a distant cry. Dimly, across the surface of the lake, she saw a black figure standing by the wall at the corner of the Abbey grounds, which ended a little way to the left on the opposite bank. Dora, in the last throes of terror, called again. She saw the figure beginning to disrobe. The next moment there was a splash. Dora saw no more; her own fight was near its end. Water streamed into her gasping mouth and the weeds now held one arm pinioned beneath the surface. Her feet trampled deeper in the gluey mud. She uttered a moaning cry of despair. A black tunnel seemed to open below her into which she was slowly being drawn.

'Don't struggle,' said a cool voice. 'Keep quite still and you won't sink any deeper. Try to breathe slowly and evenly.'

Dora saw, level with her face and strangely near, a head bobbing in the water, a boyish close-cropped head with a fresh freckled complexion and blue eyes. She stared at it, seeing it with a sort of mad clarity, and for the first moment she thought it really belonged to a boy.

Dora stopped struggling and found to her surprise that she was not sinking. The water lapped the bottom of her chin. She tried to breathe through her nose, but her mouth kept opening in terrified gasps. She saw with amazement, now that she was for a moment still, the two heads breaking the surface in front of her, the rounded head of the nun, who was swimming in the clearer water just beyond the weeds and cautiously edging in towards Catherine, and the head of Catherine, tilted over, her mouth and one cheek now submerged, her eyes glazed. With the same strange clarity Dora noticed that the nun's face was almost dry.

The nun was speaking to Catherine and was now trying to get a hold of her shoulders from behind and pull her out beyond the weeds. Catherine did not struggle. She was limp, as if unconscious. Dora watched. Catherine was being turned on her back. Her chin rose above the surface, her hair floated out behind her, and the nun was thrusting a white arm through it to hold her more firmly. A ripple reached Dora's mouth and she began to scream again. Her struggles recommenced, her breath came in staccato gasps. She was sinking now. The water seemed to pour into her, she began to suffocate.

She felt the warm muddy water rising upon her cheek. Then the next moment she heard voices, and two strong hands had seized her from behind. She was lifted from under the armpits. Rising a little from the water and turning, still struggling and gasping, she saw Mark Strafford's face close above her. He hauled her landwards, waist deep himself in the mud. Other hands took her there. She lay exhausted on the ground, the water running from her mouth. The shouts continued, and sitting up a moment later she saw James and Mark, both struggling well out, keeping a footing somehow in the mud, and raising the form of Catherine between them. Helpers plunging, linked together, from the shore, dragged them all to land. There seemed to be half a dozen people now squelching about on the muddy verge. Further out the head of the nun could be seen bobbing. She had relinquished Catherine and propelled herself back into the open water. She shouted something and began to swim round towards the ramp.

Dora collapsed again, lying face downwards on the grass. She coughed, spluttered, and moaned quietly with relief. Someone was asking her if she was all right, but she was still in another world. She listened without thinking that she might be able to answer, absorbed in the wonder of finding herself

279

alive. Suddenly someone leaned upon her and began pressing rhythmically on her back. Dora gurgled and sat upright. Giddiness overcame her and she covered her eyes, but remained sitting up, supported by one arm.

'She's O.K.,' said Mark Strafford. He transferred his attention to Catherine, but someone was already giving her artificial respiration. As Dora watched, Catherine rolled over with a moan, pushing her benefactor away, and sat up too. Her eyes were vacant, her white dress clung transparently to her body, her long wet hair coursed down over her breasts. She looked about her.

A grotesque figure was pressing forward. Dora stared at it in amazement: a short-haired woman, apparently naked to the waist, and dressed in black from the waist down. Then she realized that it was the nun in her underclothing. The nun leaned over Catherine, asking how she was, and then turned to smile at Dora. She was totally unembarrassed and accepted with a polite nod the coat which Mrs Mark was offering her. She seemed a young woman. Her freckled face was still almost dry.

'This is Mother Clare,' said Mark. 'You two seem destined to meet after all.'

Catherine had risen to her knees and was staring about as if looking for something. At that moment more voices were heard in the wood, and several more people appeared uttering questions and cries of amazement. Among them was Michael.

It was certainly a strange scene: most of the men muddied to the waist, two half-drowned women, and Mother Clare swinging the coat over her shoulders. Michael looked at it with the expression of someone who has had enough surprises and feels that this ought to be the last. But it was not the last.

As he advanced towards the centre of the group and began to say something, Catherine staggered to her feet. She advanced, grotesque with her long stripes of black hair, her mouth hanging open. Everyone fell silent. Then with a moan she ran at Michael. It seemed for a moment as if she were going to attack him. But instead she hurled her arms about his neck and seemed to cling to him with the whole of her wet body.

Her head burrowed into the front of his jacket as in tones of frantic endearment she uttered his name over and over again. Michael's arms closed automatically about her. Over her bowed and nestling head his face was to be seen, blank with amazement and horror.

CHAPTER 24

Paul paid the taxi-driver. He spent a moment or two working out the exactly appropriate tip. They went into the station. Paul bought the morning papers. They had arrived far too early for the train, as usual. They sat side by side on the platform, Paul reading the papers and Dora looking out across the railway. The sun shone upon a yellow mustard field and there was a haze over the low green tree-fringed horizon beyond. It was sunny again, but chill; the dusty illusions of late summer were giving place to the golden beauties of autumn, sharper and more poignantly ephemeral.

Dora had spent the rest of the previous day in bed. Everyone had been very nice to her; everyone, that is, except Paul. But the general concern had been for Catherine. Carried back to the Court, Catherine had remained throughout the day in a completely distracted condition. The doctor had been called. After administering sedatives he had shaken his head, spoken of schizophrenia, and mentioned a clinic in London. Late in the evening, after much debate and indecision, arrangements were made for Catherine to go as soon as possible.

Paul, in a condition not far from schizophrenic himself, had divided his energies between studying the bell and reproaching his wife. Fortunately for Dora's repose, the bell had claimed the larger part of his time; and very early that morning, after a long telephone call to someone at the British Museum, he had decided to travel to London by the ten o'clock train. This haste left no time for packing, and it had been decided that Dora should travel the following day, bringing the luggage. The larger suitcase, filled with Paul's notebooks, travelled with him. Dora was to do what she could with brown paper and string, and take a taxi from Paddington if necessary. The bell itself, the old bell, was also going to London, by road-rail container, for examination by experts.

Dora saw out of the corner of her eye that there was something about Imber in the paper. She did not want to see it. She stared ahead of her at the mustard field. Paul was reading it avidly.

After a little while he said, 'Read this,' and handed her the paper.

Dora glanced at it unseeingly for a moment, and then said, 'Yes, I see.'

'No, read it properly,' said Paul. 'Read every word.' He kept the paper held up in front of her.

Dora began to read. The article was headed – FAR FROM THE MADDING CROWD – and read as follows:

Few days in the history of religious communities, lay or otherwise, can have been quite so eventful as the last twenty-four hours at Imber Court, home of an Anglican lay community tucked away in the wilds of Gloucestershire. Event number one was the discovery, by two visiting members of the community, of an antique carved bell which had lain for many centuries sunk in the ornamental lake which surrounds the house. This bell is alleged to be the property of nearby Imber Abbey, Anglican Benedictine convent, which by an odd coincidence was just about to instal a modern bell. Rumour had it that the antique bell was to be 'miraculously' substituted for the modern bell at a quaint baptismal ceremony outside the Abbey. The miracle however did not occur, and those not in the secret were given a different surprise instead by (event number two) the pealing of the bell at dead of night, summoning them to a gathering in the woods more reminiscent of a witches' sabbath than of the sober goings on of the Anglican church.

More surprises were to follow. Next day, Friday, began ceremoniously, no witches in evidence. Blessed by a mitred Bishop the new bell processed slowly along the picturesque causeway which leads across Imber lake to the gates of the nunnery. Event number three took place, with dramatic suddenness, half-way across the causeway. The bell suddenly overturned into the water and sank without trace. Subsequent investigation suggested that sabotage, and not accident, was responsible for this disaster; and the finger of suspicion was pointed at one of the brothers.

Scarce, however, had this mystery been allowed to thicken when event, or catastrophe, number four ensued. One of the brothers, a sister this time, since the brotherhood embraces both sexes, who was shortly to proceed herself across Imber causeway to nunhood, became deranged and threw herself into the lake. Happily she was rescued quite unhurt by Miss Dora Greenfield, a visitor to the Abbey, with the help of an aquatic nun, who provided a unique spectacle by doffing her habit and diving in in her underclothes. The unfortunate would-be-suicide is receiving medical attention.

The Imber brotherhood, designed to allow laymen to have the benefits of the religious life while remaining in the world, has been in existence for less than a year. When not engaged in religious exercises it cultivates a market-garden. Why this recent outbreak of drama? A spokesman closely connected with the community mentioned schisms and emotional tensions, but members of the brotherhood were not anxious to comment, and assured us that life at Imber is normally peaceful.

The brothers are a self-governing body, subject to no defined ecclesiastical authority. They make no vows of chastity or of poverty. Who supports them? Voluntary contributors. An appeal for contributions is shortly to be issued, to be followed by a swelling of the numbers of brothers and sisters. The community occupies a charming eighteenth-century house in extensive grounds.

Well,' said Paul, 'have you read it all?'

'Yes,' said Dora.

'And are you pleased with your achievement?'

'Not very.'

'Not very? You mean you're a little pleased?'

'I'm not pleased at all.'

'I suppose you realize you've probably done permanent damage to these excellent people?'

'Yes.'

284

'Whose idea was it? Gashe's or Spens's?'

'Mine.'

'And you still say you had nothing to do with what happened to the new bell?'

'Nothing.'

'I wonder why I ask you questions when I never believe what you say.'

'Oh, do stop, Paul,' said Dora. Her eyes filled with unshed tears.

'I can't understand you,' said Paul. 'I'm beginning to wonder whether you aren't mentally ill. Perhaps you'd better see a psychiatrist in London.'

'I won't see a psychiatrist,' said Dora.

'You will if I decide you will,' said Paul.

The distant sound of the train vibrated on the still air. They both turned and looked down the line. The train was coming into view, a long way off. Paul got up and lifted his suitcase and advanced towards the edge of the platform

There was a commotion in the station yard. Dora looked round and saw that the Land-Rover had just drawn up outside. Out of it tumbled Mark Strafford, Mrs Mark, Sister Ursula, Catherine, and Toby. The train roared into the station.

Paul was busy finding himself an empty first-class compartment near the front with a corner seat facing the engine. Mrs Mark bustled Catherine straight through on to the platform, followed by Sister Ursula. Mark and Toby went to the booking-office. Mrs Mark saw Dora and piloted Catherine in the opposite direction. Mark followed his wife and gave her some tickets. Toby emerged, saw Dora, looked away, turned back, and waved half-heartedly, then got into the nearest carriage by himself. Mark and Mrs Mark spent some time finding a suitable carriage for Catherine. They found it and Mrs Mark pushed Catherine in and got in herself. They shut the door, and Sister Ursula stood by on the platform, talking smilingly to them through the window. Mark went back to look for Toby, discovered where he was, opened the door a little and stood with one foot on the footboard, talking.

Paul had stowed his things, opened the window, and leaned

there frowning at Dora. He said, 'I expect you at Knightsbridge tomorrow about three o'clock. I shall be there waiting for you.'

'All right,' said Dora.

'You understood all my instructions about the packing?'

'Yes.'

'Well, good-bye,' said Paul. 'I won't go through the farce of kissing you.'

'Oh Paul, don't be so beastly,' said Dora. The tears spilled on to her cheeks. 'Do say something nice to me before you go.'

Paul looked at her with cold eyes. 'Yes,' he said, 'you want me to comfort you now when you're in trouble. But last March, when I came home and found that you'd left me, there was no one to comfort *me* then, was there? Just you think it over. No, don't paw me. I'm not sexually attracted to you at this moment. I sometimes wonder whether I ever will be again.'

'Close *all* the doors, please,' shouted the porter, who had once been as far as Paddington.

Mark stepped back, shut the door, and stood laughing loudly at something he had just said to Toby.

'Paul, I'm so sorry,' said Dora.

'How absolutely not enough that is!' said Paul. 'I advise you to do some serious thinking, if you're capable of it.' He fumbled in his wallet. 'Here,' he said, 'is something you might think about. Bring it back to me in London. I always carry it with me.' He handed her an envelope. The whistle blew. The train began to move.

Paul pulled up his window at once and disappeared. Dora stood watching the carriages go by. She saw Toby sitting well back in his corner, his face twisted and anxious. As the carriage passed Dora waved, but he pretended not to see. Catherine and Mrs Mark were in one of the last carriages, and the train was moving fast by the time they reached Dora. Mrs Mark was looking at Catherine. Catherine looked at Dora, a quick peering unsmiling look with almost closed eyes. Then she was gone.

Dora turned towards the exit. Mark and Sister Ursula were just going back into the booking-hall. Before they disappeared they turned and smiled at her vaguely, evidently unable to decide whether to call her to join them. They went out and Dora heard the engine of the Land-Rover start up. It idled quietly. They were probably waiting for her to emerge.

Dora sat down again on the seat and regarded the yellow mustard field and the distant view of pale stubble and dark trees. It was less misty now. The engine continued to idle. Then the note rose, and she heard the wheels of the Land-Rover scraping the gravelly yard as Mark turned it sharply round. It roared away, out of the gate and down the road.

Dora got up and began to leave the station.

The station was just outside the village on the Imber side. A lane with high overgrown hedges wound away across the fields, and the footpath to Imber left it a quarter of a mile further on. Dora wondered whether to cross the line and go into the village. But there was no point in it, since the pubs would not be open yet. She turned into the dark tunnel of the lane. The sound of the train and the car had died away. A murmur accompanied her steps, which must come from a tiny stream invisible in the ditch. She walked on, her hands in her pockets.

Her hand encountered the envelope which Paul had given her. She drew it out fearfully. It would have to be something unpleasant. She opened it.

It contained two brief letters, both written by herself. The first one, which she saw dated from the early days of their engagement, read as follows:

Dear *dear* Paul, it was so wonderful last night and such absolute pain to leave you. I lay awake fretting for you. I can't wait for tonight, so am dropping this in at the library. It's agony to go away from you, and so wonderful to think that soon soon we shall be much more together. Wanting to be with you always, dearest Paul, ever ever ever your loving Dora.

Dora perused this missive, and then looked at the other one, which read as follows:

Paul, I can't go on. It's been so awful lately, and awful for you too, I know. So I'm leaving – leaving you. I can't stay, and you know all the reasons why. I know I'm a wretch and it's all my fault, but I can't stand it and I can't stay. Forgive this scrappy note. When you get it I'll be finally gone. Don't try to get me back and don't bother about the things I've left, I've taken what I need. Dora.

P.S. I'll write again later, but I won't have anything else to say than this.

This was the note Dora had left at Knightsbridge on the day she departed. Shaken, she reread both letters. She folded them up and walked on. So Paul carried them always in his wallet and wanted to have them back to go on carrying them. So much the worse for Paul. Dora tore the letters into small fragments and strewed them along the hedge.

CHAPTER 25

Since the events of the previous morning, Michael had been occupied. He had summoned the doctor to Catherine and interviewed him when he came and when he left and when he came again. He had spent some time, with Margaret Strafford, by Catherine's bedside. He had had speech with the Bishop and seen him off with such dignity as was possible in the circumstances. With Peter, he had investigated the wooden section of the causeway and discovered that two of the piers had been sawn through just below the water level. He had made arrangements by telephone with a firm of contractors who had agreed to come at once to repair the causeway and to recover the bell from the lake. He had interviewed the foreman who had arrived with tiresome promptness. He had answered some twenty telephone calls from representatives of the press, and talked to half a dozen reporters and photographers who appeared on the spot. He had visited Dora. He had taken decisions about Catherine.

In so far as Michael was thinking about anything during that day he was thinking about Catherine. The revelation made to him in the scene by the lake had surprised him so profoundly that he was still unable, in his mind, to pick the matter up at all. He was left, still gaping over it, horrified, shocked, full of amazement and pity. He had, in spite of himself, a reaction also of disgust. He shivered when he remembered Catherine's embrace. At the same time, he reproached himself, distressed that he had never guessed, or tried to guess, what really went on in Catherine's mind, and that when now some part of it had been made plain there was so little he could do. He tried to make his thought of her a constant prayer.

That Catherine had been in love with him, was in love with him, was something in every way outside the order of nature. Michael did not know how to put it to himself, the usual phrases seeming so totally inappropriate. He told himself, but

289

could not feel, that there was no reason why Catherine should not attach herself to him as much as to anyone else; he told himself too that, although the attachment was untimely, it was a privilege to be so chosen. He was not sure whether it made things better or worse to suggest that since Catherine appeared to be deranged her love was in a sense made null.

Her present condition certainly gave cause for deep anxiety. She had passed part of the day asleep. The rest of the time she lay on her bed weeping, addressing Michael whether he was present or not, reviling herself for various crimes which were never made clear, and raving about the bell. Nick, who had been told by the Straffords, came to her room soon after she was brought in. The doctor was already there and he had to wait. When he was admitted he sat dumbly beside his sister holding her hand, a dazed and stricken look upon his face, finding little to say. She for her part clung almost automatically to his hand or his sleeve, but paid him little direct attention, addressing to him her few sane remarks, which concerned opening or closing the window and fetching pillows. He was, perhaps, too much a part of herself to be, at that time, either a support or a menace. He spent a large part of the day with her, retiring only when she was asleep or when some other visitor was present, when he would walk alone round the garden near the house. He seemed profoundly upset but spoke to nobody; and indeed nobody had time, in the busy rush of that disorganized day, to speak to him. Michael passed him several times, and on the first occasion uttered some words of regret. Speaking to Nick was hideous; Catherine seemed to lie between them like a corpse. Nick nodded in reply to Michael's speech and went on his way.

It was late at night before the arrangements had finally been made for Catherine to go to London. Mrs Mark was to go with her, and stay with some friends nearby so that she could see her daily, if this was thought desirable, at the clinic. She promised to telephone Imber as soon as there was any news at all. When it was clear that it was really best for Catherine to go, Michael felt a craven relief. He wanted more than anything, at the present moment, that Catherine might go away and be looked after somewhere else. Her presence near him filled him with fear and with a sense of guilt which was vague and menacing, full of as yet unspoken indictments.

Falling exhausted into bed, Michael had soon discovered yet other worries to postpone his sleep. On the following morning, Imber would be in the headlines. However the story was told, Michael had no illusions about how the brotherhood would come out of it. After these catastrophes, to appeal for money would be, in the nearer future, impossible. Whether the whole enterprise was not now destroyed Michael tried to prevent himself from wondering. Time would show what could be salvaged and Michael was not without hope. What more occupied him now that he had contrived to remove to some distance the overwhelming thought of Catherine, was the overwhelming thought of Nick.

Peter Topglass had been the first to suspect that the descent of the bell into the lake had been no accident. He made his own investigations and then drew Michael's attention to the way in which the wooden supports had been tampered with. Michael and Peter mentioned their discovery to no one, but the reporters seemed to get on to it somehow. Michael was amazed at what Peter showed him; but once convinced that the thing was indeed no accident he knew for certain who had been responsible for it. He even, in some obscure way, and with an intuition which belonged to his present state of shock, guessed at Nick's motives. If Nick had wished to interfere with his sister's vocation he had probably been more successful than he expected.

The thought of Nick, once it came fully upon him, began to eat up Michael's consciousness; and about three a.m. he almost got out of bed to set out for the Lodge. He resolved to see Nick early the next day. With a sort of relief which at a deeper level was almost pleasure he felt that the catastrophes of the last days had as it were opened the pathway between him and Nick. At moments it almost seemed as if they had been designed to do that. To be able now so dramatically to see Nick both as criminal and as afflicted made it essential at last to destroy the barrier between them. Praying for him now,

Michael felt once more the elusive sense that God held them both, and held in some incomprehensible way the twisted strands of their concern for each other. Michael knew now that he *must* talk to Nick. In this extremity he must act fully the part of what he was, Nick's only friend at Imber. After so much that was appalling, no harm could now come of this, and the simple duty of speaking frankly and openly to Nick was finally set before him. Michael asked himself uneasily whether this duty had not in fact been set before him for some time if only he had used his eyes; but he left the question unanswered, and suddenly secure, relieved, positively glad at the thought of speaking with Nick tomorrow he fell into a sweet sleep.

The next morning opened with a full programme of cares and anxieties. Michael left the dispatching of Catherine to the Straffords, assisted by James, while he coped with further telephone calls, including one from the Bishop, who had been reading the morning papers and who was anxious that Michael should draft a letter to *The Times* designed to remove certain misapprehensions. It was nearly eleven o'clock before Michael had a moment to raise his head. When at last he felt that he could escape he left his office and set off down the steps and across the terrace. Nick had declined to travel up with Catherine. He had in fact not been pressed to by Margaret Strafford, who held a theory that Catherine was better without her brother for the moment; but he had announced in rather vague terms that he would follow her very soon. Michael expected to find him at the Lodge, probably in the company of the whisky bottle. He did not imagine that Nick would have the resolution or the sheer powers of organization required to leave Imber quickly.

As he emerged on to the terrace and saw how blue the sky had once more become and how warm and colourful the sunshine, he felt a stirring of hope and a sense that the horrors through which they had all passed would be dissolved and blotted out. All would yet be well. And as this sense of hope and of a healing providence came upon him he recognized it, without any distress or misgiving, as inextricably mixed up with his old love for Nick and the sheer joy of being once again upon the path that led towards him.

'Oh Michael, wait a moment!' said Mark Strafford from behind him.

Michael stopped and looked back, to see Mark leaning over the balcony above him.

'James wants to see you,' said Mark. 'He's in his office.'

Michael turned about. He had no wish to see James just now but with an almost automatic reaction he put first the claim of James's summons. The other matter was already seeming to him like a self-indulgence, a piece, after all, of his own private business. He came back up the steps. James's summons. As Michael climbed the stairs to James's office he reflected that it was unusual for James to summon him in this way. When James wanted to see him he usually looked for him and shouted his business out wherever Michael was to be found. He reached James's door, knocked, and went in.

The room was not large and was practically empty of furniture. A rickety table of much-scored oak was James's desk, with two canvas garden chairs, one on each side. Letters and papers filled boxes on the floor. Behind the desk a crucifix hung on the wall. The floor was unstained and uncarpeted, and the ceiling webbed with cracks. The resonant autumn sunshine showed abundant dust.

James was standing behind the desk as Michael came in, and running his hands again and again through his jagged dark hair. Michael sat down opposite him, and James slumped back into his canvas chair, making it groan and bulge.

'Catherine got off all right?' said Michael.

'Yes,' said James. He avoided Michael's eyes and fiddled with things on the desk.

'You wanted to see me, James?' said Michael. He felt preoccupied and in a hurry.

'Yes,' said James. He paused and fiddled the things back into their original position. 'I'm sorry, Michael,' he said, 'this is very difficult.'

'What's the matter?' said Michael. 'You look upset. Has anything new happened?'

'Well, yes and no,' said James. 'Look, Michael, I can't wrap this up and you wouldn't want me to. Toby has told me everything.'

Michael looked out of the window. He had again the strange sensation of *déjà vu*. Where had all this happened before? In the silence that followed the world seemed gently to crack about him, its appearance unchanged yet ready now to fall to pieces. Disaster is not quickly apprehended.

'What did he tell you?' said Michael.

'Well,' said James, 'you know, what happened between you. I'm sorry.'

Michael looked up at the crucifix. He could not yet bring himself to look at James. A quiet feeling of exasperation, which oddly accompanied his sense of total ruin, kept him sane and calm. He said, 'Very little happened.'

'That's a matter of opinion,' said James.

In the autumnal distance there was the sound of a gun being fired. Michael's mind reverted in a dazed way to Patchway and the pigeons. That real world was now very far off. He wondered if there was any point in giving James his version of the story. He decided there was not. Excuses and explanations would be out of place; and besides, he was without excuse. He said, 'All right. You've learned something about me, haven't you, James?'

James said, 'I'm terribly sorry,' twisting his things about on the table and pausing to examine his hand.

Michael looked at James now. In spite of the cell-like appearance of the room, dear James was not well framed for the part of Grand Inquisitor. Almost anyone else would have got some shred of satisfaction or interest from the scene. James got none. Watching his expression of pain and misery and his fidgeting Michael pictured for a moment how James must see him: the enormity of the crime and the disgusting and unnatural propensity which it revealed. James was right of course. Plenty had happened.

'When did Toby make this confession to you?' said Michael. He tried to calm his mind, to think about Toby instead of himself. To think about his victim.

'The night before last,' said James. 'He came to my room sometime after eleven o'clock. He'd been wandering round in the rain and was frightfully upset. We talked for hours. He told me all about the bell business too, I mean the other bell, and how he planned it all with Dora and how they pulled the bell out of the lake. But we didn't get along to that until the early hours of the morning. We spent such a long time on you.'

'That was good of you,' said Michael. The exasperation was gaining ground. 'What did you say to Toby?'

'I was pretty serious with him,' said James. He looked at Michael now with a level stare. A tiny flame of hostility flickered in the air between them and was gone. 'I thought he'd behaved foolishly, even in some ways badly, in relation to both you and Dora, and I told him so. After all, he'd felt badly enough about it himself to take this rather drastic step of making a confession – which I must say I thought a very sensible and admirable thing to do. And it had to be met with the seriousness which the case deserved. Anything else would have been too little.'

'Where's Toby now?' said Michael.

'I sent him home,' said James.

Michael jumped up from his chair. He wanted to shout and bang on the desk. He said quietly to James, 'You perfect imbecile.' He went and stood looking out of the window. 'When did he go?'

'He went this morning,' said James. 'I sent him off on the early train. The car taking Catherine picked him up at the Lodge. I'm sorry I wasn't able to raise all this with you yesterday, but there was so damn much happening. I had to make a decision. I decided it was better he shouldn't see you again. He obviously felt the thing was – you know, sort of messy and unclean. He'd tried to clean things up, for himself anyway, by telling about it. And I thought he should go while he felt, as it were, that he'd got back to some sort of innocence. If he'd stayed and had a talk with you he'd just have fallen back into the mess again, if you see what I mean.'

Michael drummed on the window. James was quite right in a way. But his heart ached terribly for Toby, sent away now with all his imperfections on his head, loaded with guilt, and involved by James's solemnity in a machinery of sin and repentance with which he probably had no capacity to deal. How typical of James to do the simple decent thing which was also so damned obtuse. By sending Toby away he had branded the thing into the boy's mind as something appalling; almost any other way of closing the incident would have been better than this one. Yet as Michael reflected how dearly he would have liked to be able to close this drama in his own way, he was not at all sure that his method would have been an improvement.

'Why am I an imbecile?' said James.

'There was no need to be so damn solemn,' said Michael. 'The real blame belongs to me. By sending Toby away you've made him feel like a criminal and made the whole business into a tremendous catastrophe.'

'I don't see why he shouldn't take his full share of responsibility,' said James. 'He's quite old enough.'

Michael looked away across the lake and down the great avenue of trees toward the Lodge. He said, 'I wonder why he suddenly took it into his head to confess to you?'

'Why shouldn't he?' said James. 'He was worried enough. I think what immediately made up his mind were some things Nick Fawley said. Apparently Nick knew all about it and reproached him and told him he ought to own up. First sensible thing Nick's done since he arrived, in my view.'

Michael continued to drum on the window. The slight dazzle from the lake hurt his eyes. He moved his head to and fro, as if to help his mind to take in what he had just heard. He was too appalled to speak. So Nick 'knew all about it'. His revenge could not have been more perfect. To have seduced Toby would have been crude. Instead, Nick had forced Toby to play exactly the part which Nick himself had played thirteen years earlier. Toby had been his understudy indeed. Michael had hoped to save Nick. But Nick had merely ruined him a second time and in precisely the same way.

Michael turned back to the desk and looked down at James, who had gone back to ruffling his hair. 'Well, that appears to be that,' he said to James. 'I'm sorry if I've seemed cross. I assure you I regard myself as very much to blame. There's no point in going into it now. Of course I shall resign or whatever one does and go away from Imber.'

James began to say something in protest.

There was a loud knock on the door and Mark Strafford came in. He looked pale, upset, and frightened behind his beard. He said, 'Sorry to barge in. I was down at the ferry and I heard a funny noise coming from the Lodge. I think it's Murphy howling in a very odd way. I wondered if there might be anything the matter down there.'

Michael pushed past him and took the stairs three at a time. He descended to the terrace, scarcely putting a foot to the ground, and began to run down the path to the ferry, his breath coming in loud gasps from sheer panic. Behind him he could hear the pounding footsteps of the other two. He reached the ferry well in advance, jumped into the boat, and cast off alone. The progress across the lake seemed to take an endless time, as the boat lazily rolled and pitched to and fro slowly propelled by the single oar, and as he dug savagely into the water Michael's glazed eyes could see, shimmering as in a glass, the figures of James and Mark left behind him on the landing-stage. He reached the other side and jumped out, and the boat immediately shot away, pulled vigorously back towards the house.

Michael stumbled on, still gasping, across the grass. The Lodge seemed immensely far away. He could hear quite clearly now the intermittent howling of Murphy. It was a terrible sound. He ran on, but by the time he got to the trees he had to slow down to a walk. His breath didn't seem to be coming properly. Leaning forward in an agony of anxiety he almost fell. He had to walk the last hundred yards quite slowly.

He was almost at the Lodge now. The door was open. Michael called Nick's name. There was no reply. Just outside the door he stopped. Something was lying in the doorway. He looked more closely and saw it was an outstretched hand. He stepped over the threshold.

Nick had shot himself. He had emptied the shot-gun into his head. To make quite sure he had evidently put the barrel into his mouth. There was no doubt that he had finished the job. Michael averted his face and stepped outside. Murphy, who had been standing over the body, followed him out whining.

James and Mark were approaching down the avenue at a run. Michael called to them, 'Nick has killed himself.'

Mark stopped at once and sat down on the grass at the side of the avenue. James came on. He took a look into the Lodge and came out again.

'You go and phone the police,' said Michael. 'I'll stay here.'

James turned and went back towards the lake. Mark got up and followed him.

Michael started to go in through the door but could not bring himself to. He stood for a while looking at Nick's hand. It was a hand that he knew well. He stepped back and sat down on the grass with his back against the warm stone of the wall. He had thought that Nick's revenge could not be more perfect. He had been wrong. It was perfect now. Hot tears began to rise behind his eyes and his mouth opened, trembling.

Murphy stood near him, shivering and whining, his eyes fixed on his face. He came up to Michael, and Michael stroked him gently. The landscape was blotted out.

CHAPTER 26

More than four weeks had passed and there was no one left now at Imber except Michael and Dora. It was late in October. Great sheets of various coloured cloud trailed endlessly across the sky, and the sun blazed intermittently upon the thick masses of yellow and copper trees. The days were colder, beginning usually with fog, and a perpetual haze lay upon the surface of the lake.

James and the Abbess between them had acted quickly. It had been decided to dissolve the community. James had departed back to the East End of London. The Straffords had decided to throw in their lot with a community of craftsmen who were attached to a monastery in Cumberland. Peter Topglass, urged and implored by Michael, had joined a party of naturalists who were just setting out for the Faroe Islands. Patchway had returned laconically to farm-labouring on a nearby estate. Michael stayed on to wind up the affairs of the market-garden and Dora stayed on with him.

Margaret Strafford was still in London with Catherine. Catherine had been having insulin treatment and was continually under the influence of drugs. She had not yet been told of her brother's death. Margaret wrote that there was no point in visiting her at present. She would let Michael know when there was some improvement and when a visit might be welcome. Meanwhile, Catherine was as well as could be expected. The doctors were not unhopeful of a complete recovery. The insulin was making her fat.

Dora, after appearing for some time to be about to go, announced, with a dignity and resolution which seemed new to her, that she would stay as long as she could be of any use. She seemed unperturbed by a large though diminishing number of long-distance telephone calls. At first, everyone was far too upset and preoccupied to think of suggesting that she should depart; later, she made herself indispensable. She fetched and carried, did errands by bicycle in the village, and washed and dusted and tidied unobtrusively in the house. The time came when, with the gradual departure of the others, she did more than this. By the time she and Michael were left alone Dora was doing the cooking and catering, as well as full-time secretarial duties. It turned out that she could type moderately well, and in the end she dealt entirely with the more routine correspondence, composing letters out of various formulae suggested by Michael.

They had been alone now for nearly a fortnight. Peter was the last to go; and even his departure was to Michael a relief. As for the others, his relations with them had become irrevocably wrenched and painful. Mark treated him with a clumsy kindness. but could not help being both curious and patronizing. While James followed him about with a look of such desperate compassion that he was quite glad for James's own sake when the latter departed to London. Although neither James nor Mark knew the details of Michael's history their imagination had been set in motion, and he had been unable to conceal from them his violent excesses of grief during the days following Nick's death. Their strange looks showed that they had drawn some conclusions of their own, and by the time they left their presence at Imber had become a torture to Michael. Dora's being there, on the other hand, did not trouble him at all. She was useful, she knew nothing, she guessed nothing, and she did not judge.

Dora, once she had made up her mind to stay, created her own role with energy; though even then there were one or two minor escapades. The beginning of October brought a spell of hot weather, and Dora announced that she proposed to learn to swim. By the time that anyone got around to telling her not to, since no one had time to supervise her and she must not go out alone, she had practically taught herself. She turned out, when put to it, to be a natural swimmer, buoyant and fearless in the water. Peter, and later Michael, went along occasionally to view her efforts and give some advice, and before the warm weather ended she had mastered the art quite adequately.

On Margaret's departure, Mark Strafford had taken over the cooking. Dora soon ousted him, however, and made up in zeal for what she lacked in talent. Her efforts were appreciated and she obviously enjoyed what she was doing. But the halcyon days for Dora came after the others had all gone, when she reigned undisputed over Imber. She took especial pleasure in Michael's domestic helplessness, and told him that she was delighted to cook for a man who didn't think he could cook better than she could. She kept the house reasonably clean and the office orderly and searched the gardens to find, in forgotten and uncultivated corners, autumn flowers that had been left there growing wild, and filled the hall and common-room with great bunches of dewy michaelmas daisies and aromatic chrysanthemums which brought back to Michael memories of childhood holidays spent at Imber.

Gradually the place was stripped. The market-garden was sold as it stood to a neighbouring farmer, and a good deal of the produce was lifted and removed at once. Bit by bit the furniture disappeared from the house, some of it returned by removal van to people who had lent it, some of it trundled vigorously away by Sister Ursula on a handcart to be taken into the Abbey. The causeway had been mended. The new bell had been lifted by crane out of the lake and unceremoniously bundled into the enclosure. It had by now been erected in the old tower, and announced its elevation in clear tones which reached Michael and Dora one morning as they were sitting at breakfast.

A curious dream-like peace descended on Imber. The distinction of days was unclear. Meals were served at odd times and often sat over lengthily. When the sun shone the doors were opened and the heavy table pulled out onto the gravel. The mornings were hazy, the afternoons damp and mellow, and the garden, with its dark lines of upturned earth, was oppressively silent. At night it was cold and the sky was clear and wintry with premonitions of frost. The owls hooted closer to the house. The sedge warblers were gone. And returning late from the chapel Michael would see the light blazing on the balcony and hear across the water the music of Mozart, played upon the gramophone by Dora who was showing a sudden new enthusiasm for classical music.

During this time a curious relationship grew up between Michael and Dora, something undefined and wistful which had for Michael a certain ease and *douceur*. Perhaps this was possible only because they both knew that the time was short. Amid many subjects of reflection Michael managed to wonder about Dora's future; and after a little time had passed he raised with her the subject of whether she oughtn't to go back to London.

Dora, when questioned, showed herself but too eager to discuss the whole matter with him, and so they discussed it. She told him that she had decided that there was no point in her returning to Paul, at any rate at present. She would only run away again. It was inevitable that Paul should bully her and that she should vacillate between submitting through fear and resisting through resentment. She was plain that things were mostly her fault and that she should never have married Paul at all. As things were, she felt that she would never manage to live with Paul until she could treat with him, in some sense, as an equal; and she had no taste for trying to improve her status by becoming precipitately and in her present state of mind the mother of his children. She felt intensely the need and somehow now the capacity to live and work on her own and become, what she had never been, an independent grown-up person. These views she uttered to Michael rather anxiously and apologetically, clearly expecting him to tell her that she ought to go back to her husband.

Occupying his mind as best he could with the problem of Dora, Michael felt no inclination to recall her sharply to her duties as a wife. He realized that his present views were perhaps heterodox, his vision distorted and his powers of judgement diseased. But he reflected again, and the picture seemed the same. When Dora said to him, her voice shaking with emotion, that 'everything to do with Paul was just the kiss of death', Michael saw with a dreary clarity what things would be like if she did return. Paul was much to be pitied, but he was a violent and bullying man, and although it was true that Dora ought never to have married him it was equally true that he ought never to have married Dora. Michael confined himself to pointing out to Dora that she did, after all, in some sense love Paul, and that her being married to him was a very important fact. It was also important that Paul loved her and needed her. Whatever plans she made for the immediate future she should keep alive the hope that she might return to Paul later if he should still wish it. Running away was worthless unless she could find herself a way of life which had dignity and independence, and in which she could win the strength needed to make her able to treat with Paul equally and stop being afraid of him.

What that way of life could be they discussed in the most practical terms. Dora had told Michael in a half amused way about her mystical experience in the National Gallery. Michael suggested that she should return to her painting; and Dora agreed, while insisting, as Michael indeed suspected, that she had a very meagre talent. Perhaps she could find a teaching job which would leave her time to go to an art school? Perhaps she could get back the scholarship which she had relinquished when she married Paul. The problem of where and how she could live arose too. Michael advised her to leave London. Dora at first declared that life out of London was impossible, but later saw the point of the idea and even found it rather exciting. When the discussion had reached this stage a providential letter arrived from Dora's friend Sally, to say that Sally had got a good job as an art teacher at a school in Bath, and had got her hands on quite a decent flat, and did Dora know anyone in Bath who might help her to find someone to share the flat? It then became obvious that Dora must go to Bath, and Michael conducted some correspondence for her to see if she could get a grant to help her to complete her studies in that city. A very small grant was forthcoming, together with some suggestions about primary school-teaching. This suited Dora excellently and ecstatic telephone calls passed between her and Sally.

Michael, reflecting later, was surprised at the efficiency with which he had helped Dora to organize her unorthodox future, considering how little thought he really gave to the matter. Perhaps his complete detachment from Dora, and a curious broken freedom brought about by his own state of mind, enabled him to act in a situation in which he would normally have hesitated or acted differently. He wondered if his counsels were wise; perhaps not even time would show. But he believed that he now knew Dora a little. She had talked a great deal about herself, and Michael glimpsed, in the stories which she told without bitterness of her unwanted childhood, some of the roots of her present being. No one had inspired her to place the least value on herself; she still felt herself to be a socially unacceptable waif, and what made her unpretentious also made her irresponsible and unreliable. Paul, with his absolute demands and his annihilating contempts and angers, was the worst partner she could have chosen. Dora was not altogether without hope of returning to Paul, and Michael hoped with her, although he was well aware that James had been right in calling her a bitch and that it was unlikely that her career of crime was at an end.

Dora of her own accord suggested that she might now have some talks with Mother Clare. She saw Mother Clare three times, and seemed pleased to have done so, though she was reticent about what had been said. They talked, of course, about their adventure in the lake, since which Dora had conceived a great admiration for the intrepid and amphibious nun; but they spoke too, Michael gathered, about Dora's future. He was glad to be able to conclude that the Abbey was putting no spanners in the wheel of his own plans for Dora, and had evidently not told her bluntly to return at once to her husband. He felt, in the case of Dora, too, that there was little point in forcing her willy-nilly into a machine of sin and repentance which was alien to her nature. Perhaps Dora would repent after her own fashion; perhaps she would be saved after her own fashion.

It was after they had been alone together for a while that Michael began to guess that Dora was a little in love with him. Something in her looks, her questioning, her manner of serving him, suggested this. Michael was touched, a little irritated, but in no way alarmed or repelled. He was grateful to Dora because he felt that she was a person to whom he could do no harm. There was something subdued and hopeless about her love which was perhaps new to her. Michael observed it, almost with tenderness, and did nothing to reduce the distance between them. He made her talk about herself, and quietly circumvented her clumsy efforts to make him talk about himself. Her unsuspicious and unsophisticated mind harboured of course no conception of his being a homosexual; and although Michael guessed Dora to be one of those women who regard homosexuals with interested sympathy he had no intention of instructing her. A little later he began to realize that she imagined him to be in love with Catherine. This was more upsetting. Michael was annoyed and distressed by Dora's continual probing references to Catherine, and her assumption that he was yearning to be summoned to Catherine's bedside. But again, he thought it better to leave her with that illusion. So they continued side by side, Michael knowing that he was causing Dora some unhappiness, but feeling that it was, for her, perhaps a novel and certainly a harmless variety.

For all that, perhaps partly because of it, Dora grew and flourished remarkably during those days. Michael felt this especially in the later time when there was a little less to do in the office, and he often found her out beside the lake, using as easel the old music stand from the Long Room, making water-colour sketches of the Court, of which she must have done, before she left, some three or four dozen. The weather was colder now, and though still cloudy yet often bright. Skies of dappled dove grey, streaky lemon yellow, menacing purple and limpid green appeared in Dora's pictures behind the silvery pediment of the Court. How wonderfully, Michael thought, Dora had survived. She had fed like a glutton upon the catastrophes at Imber and they had increased her substance. Because of all the dreadful things that had passed there was more of her. Michael looked with a slightly contemptuous envy upon this simple and robust nature until he remembered the last morning when he had been about to visit Nick and how well he too had thriven upon disaster up to the moment when he was vitally hurt.

One day a letter arrived from Toby. He was by now well installed at Oxford. Michael read his letter with relief. In awkward terms, Toby apologized for his hasty departure, and for his indiscretions, which he hoped had not caused too much trouble. He thanked Michael for his kindness, said how much it had meant to him being at Imber, said he was sorry to see from the papers that they were all moving, but hoped it would be just as good somewhere else. What mainly emerged, however, from the letter, and set Michael's mind at rest, was that for Toby the whole business was closed indeed. There was no sign of tormented guilt, no anxious brooding, no speculation about Michael's state of mind. The full significance of the happenings at Imber had happily escaped Toby, and he had no retrospective curiosity about them now. He was in a new and wonderful world, and already Imber had become a story. He had a marvellous old panelled room in Corpus, he told Michael. He had decorated it with pictures of the medieval bell taken from the *Illustrated London News*. His tutor was terribly impressed when he told him how he had discovered the bell! Murphy was very well, by the way, and settling down splendidly with his parents. He wasn't fretting any more. Hadn't it been a good idea of Peter's that he should take over Murphy? How terribly sad and shocking about Nick, he could hardly believe even now that it was true. Michael must come and see him at Corpus if ever he was going through Oxford and take a glass of sherry. Michael smiled a little over the letter and was glad of it. Perhaps he would go one day to see Toby, and to give Toby the pleasure of patronizing him a little, and of telling his friends afterwards that that was the odd chap he had told them of who once made a pass at him down at that place where he found the bell.

All these thoughts of Dora and Toby fluttered intermittently at the surface of Michael's mind. More deeply and continually he was concerned with other matters. The pain he had felt when he knew that Nick was dead was so extreme that he had thought at first that he could not survive it. During the first days he had been consoled only by the knowledge that he could still kill himself. Such pain did not have to continue. He could occupy himself only in things which concerned Nick, could only speak of Nick when he spoke at all. He searched the Lodge from end to end several times, searching for something, a letter, a diary, which he could construe as a message to himself. He could not believe that Nick had gone without leaving him a word. But there was nothing to be found. The stove contained charred paper, the remains perhaps of a final holocaust of Nick's correspondence, but it had all been thoroughly burnt and was beyond salvage. The house revealed nothing to Michael as, desperately and blinded by the tears which now started intermittently and without warning to his eyes, he ransacked Nick's cupboard and suitcases and went through the pockets of his coats.

During this time his love for Nick seemed to grow, in an almost devilish way, to the most colossal dimensions. At moments this love felt to Michael like a great tree that was growing out of him, and he was tormented by strange dreams of cancerous growths. He had the image of Nick continually now before his eyes, seeing him often as he was when a boy, seeing him in flight across a tennis court, agile and strong and swift, conscious of Michael's glance; and sometimes it seemed to him as if Nick had died in childhood. With these visions there came too an agony of physical desire, to be succeeded by a longing, so complete that it seemed to come from all the levels of his being, to hold Nick again in his arms.

Michael went to see the Abbess several times. Now, when it was too late, he told her everything. But there was nothing, at present, which she could do for him, and they both knew it. Michael felt himself responsible for Nick's death, as much as if he had deliberately run him over with the lorry. The Abbess did not try to take this responsibility from him; but she could not, either, help him to live with it. He went away, bent double with the pains of remorse and regret and the inward biting of a love which had now no means of expression. He remembered now when it was useless how the Abbess had told him that the way was always forward. Nick had needed love, and he ought to have given him what he had to offer, without fears about its imperfection. If he had had more faith he would have done so, not calculating either Nick's faults or his own. Michael recalled too how, with Toby, he had acted with more daring, and had probably acted wrong. Yet no serious harm had come to Toby; besides he had not loved Toby as he loved Nick, was not responsible for Toby as he had been for Nick. So great a love must have contained some grain of good, something at least which might have attached Nick to this world, given him some glimpse of hope. Wretchedly Michael forced himself to remember the occasions on which Nick had appealed to him since he came to Imber, and how on every occasion Michael had denied him. Michael had concerned himself with keeping his own hands clean, his own future secure, when instead he should have opened his heart: should impetuously and devotedly and beyond all reason have broken the alabaster cruse of very costly ointment.

As time went on Michael tried too to think of Catherine: poor Catherine, lying there drugged in London, with a terrible awakening ahead of her. He thought of her with great pity but could not purge from his mind the aversion which the idea of her still inspired. He dreaded the arrival of the letter which should summon him to see her. Perhaps he had found her existence, from the start, something of a scandal. Perhaps when Nick had first spoken of her he had felt jealous. He tried to remember. He found himself suddenly full of violent thoughts, wishing that it was Catherine that was dead instead of Nick, and strangely imagining that in some way she had destroyed her brother. Yet he pitied her, and knew in a cold sad way that till the end of his life he would be concerned with her and responsible for her welfare. Nick was gone; and to perfect his suffering Catherine remained.

The first agony passed and Michael found himself still living and thinking. Having at first feared to suffer too much, he later feared to suffer too little, or not in the right way. With strong magnetic force the human heart is drawn to consolation; and even grieving becomes consolation in the end.

Michael told himself that he did not want to survive, he did not want to feed upon Nick's death. He wanted to die too. But death is not easy, and life can win by simulating it. He cast about in his mind for a way of thinking about what had happened which left him finally without refuge or relief. He did not want for a single moment to forget what had happened. He wanted to use his intelligence about it. He remembered the souls in Dante who deliberately remained within the purifying fire. Repentance: to think about sin without making the thought into a consolation.

After Nick's death he was for a long time quite unable to pray. He felt indeed as if his belief in God had been broken at a single blow, or as if he had discovered that he had never believed. He absorbed himself so utterly, so desperately, in the thought of Nick that even to think about God seemed an intrusion, an absurdity. Gradually he became more detached but there was no sense of his faith being renewed. He thought of religion as something far away, something into which he had never really penetrated at all. He vaguely remembered that he had had emotions, experiences, hopes; but real faith in God was something utterly remote from all that. He understood that at last, and felt, almost coldly, the remoteness. The pattern which he had seen in his life had existed only in his own romantic imagination. At the human level there was no pattern. 'For as the heavens are higher than the earth, so are my ways higher than your ways, and my thoughts than your thoughts.' And as he felt, bitterly, the grimness of these words, he put it to himself: there is a God, but I do not believe in Him.

Eventually a kind of quietness came over him, as of a hunted animal that crouches in hiding for a long while until it is lulled into a kind of peace. The silent days passed like a dream. After his work he sat in the refectory with Dora, drinking innumerable cups of tea, while the petals of fading roses fell upon the table, diffusing a sweet weary smell of potpourri, and they talked of Dora's plans. He watched Dora, turning towards life and happiness like a strong plant towards the sun, assimilating all that lay in her way. And all the time he thought about Nick until it was as if he spoke to him endlessly in his thought, a continual beseeching wordless speech like a prayer.

Very slowly a sense of his own personality returned to him. The annihilating sense of a total guilt gave way to a more reflective and discriminating remembrance. It was indeed as if there was very little of him left now. He need not have feared to grow, to thrive upon disaster. He was diminished. Reflection, which justifies, which fabricates hopes, could not do so now for him. He pondered without intensity on what he was: his general grievance against nature, his particular wrong choices. One day no doubt all this would seem charged again with a vast significance, and he would try once more to find out the truth. One day too he would experience again, responding with his heart, that indefinitely extended requirement that one human being makes upon another. He knew this abstractly, and wondered if he would, in that time, do better. It seemed to matter very little. Nothing could mend the past.

No sharp sense of his own needs drove him to make supplication. He looked about him with the calmness of the ruined man. But what did, from his former life, remain to him was the Mass. After the first weeks he went back to it, crossing the causeway in the early morning through the white fog, placing his feet carefully on the bricks which seemed to glow beneath him in some light from the hidden sun, answering the summons of the bell. The Mass remained not consoling, not uplifting, but in some way factual. It contained for him no assurance that all would be made well that was not well. It simply existed as a kind of pure reality separate from the weaving of his own thoughts. He attended it almost as a spectator, and remembered with surprise the time when he had thought that one day he would celebrate the Mass himself, and how it had seemed to him that on that day he would die of joy. That day would never come, and those emotions were old and dead. Yet whoever celebrated it, the Mass existed and Michael existed beside it. He made no movement now, reached out no hand. He would have to be found and fetched or else he was beyond help. Perhaps he was beyond help. He thought of those against whom he had offended, and gathered them about him in this perhaps endless and perhaps meaningless attention. And next door, as it were, to total unbelief there recurred to him the egotistical and helpless cry of the *Dies Irae*.

> Quaerens me, sedisti lassus;
> Redemisti, Crucem passus;
> Tantus labor non sit cassus.

They got out of the taxi. Michael paid the taxi-driver for the double journey and asked him to wait to take Dora back to the Court. They went into the station.

It was yesterday morning that the letter had arrived for which Michael had been waiting. Mrs Mark informed him that Catherine was a great deal better. She seemed, in fact, to be more or less normal, though at this stage one could never say. Of course he must expect to find her much changed. She had not yet asked after her brother; it had been judged wise that Michael should be the one to tell her about Nick's death. His presence was therefore urgently requested in London.

Michael was at once eager to be off. His work was done now at the Court. Nothing detained him. He spent the day packing and making telephone calls and arranged to leave next day on the early train. Dora was to leave by a later train which would take her, with only one change, to Bath. She telephoned Sally to expect her late the following evening.

Dora, who had watched with anxiety the arrival of any letter from Mrs Mark, knew by Michael's excited agitation, even before he told her, that this must be *the* one. She had waited sadly, but with a sense of the inevitable, for the ending of her time with Michael. She loved him with a quiet undemanding hopelessness. After so much pain and violence his very inaccessibility was consoling. And she could not bring herself to be jealous of a being so rare and so unfortunate as Catherine.

She had not regretted her decision not to return to Paul. With immense relief, and the sense of a load taken off her, she welcomed Michael's support. She wrote long explanatory letters to Paul. Paul replied with angry screeds, telegram ultimatums, and telephone calls which always ended abruptly with

311

one or other of them banging down the receiver. Paul had, for some reason perhaps connected with Michael, spared her his arrival in person. He announced to her, more clearly than ever before, his philosophy. There were no two ways about it. She was the type of woman who was made to vacillate between teasing and submitting. He had had enough of her teasing. It was time for her to submit. This was in fact what she really wanted to do, and she would find that this was where her true happiness lay. Independence was a chimera. All that would happen would be that she would be drawn into a new love affair. And was it right, because she knew that he would wait for her indefinitely, that she should inflict upon him, indeed upon both of them, these continual and pointless sufferings? He was aware that when she had some new fantasy in her head she was cold and ruthless, but he appealed to her common sense and to any remembrance that she still had of how much she had loved him. And by the way, could he now have back those two letters he had given her?

Dora was moved but not profoundly shaken by these communications. She pondered over them and answered them with clumsy attempts at arguments. She also replied at length to a letter from Noel. Noel apologized for having bothered her by appearing at Imber. He realized now that it had been unwise. He was sorry, if she was sorry, that the place had been made to look so ludicrous in the press. But there it is, facts will speak. His own article had been fairly moderate. He was sorry too, subject to the same proviso, to hear that Imber was folding up. However, it was also good news since it meant that Dora would soon be back in London, and when, oh when, should they meet? She owed him a lunch. He had meant it when he said he missed her. He was missing her at this moment.

Dora replied that she was not coming to London. She would see him at some later time. For the present she wanted to be left alone. She felt a nostalgia for the ease of his company; but she no longer had the feverish urge to escape into his world. She attempted to turn her thoughts away from Paul, away from Noel, away even from Michael. It was not easy. She packed her things and collected together the paintings she had made in the last few weeks. She went to bed exhausted. She imagined, as she imagined every night, Paul sitting alone in his beautiful Knightsbridge room, beside the white telephone, wanting her back. But her last remembrance was that on the morrow Michael would be leaving her, and when they met again he would perhaps be married to Catherine. She wept herself to sleep, but they were quiet and comforting tears.

The morning was foggy as usual. They walked along the platform and sat down on the seat. The fog curled in slow tall breakers across the track and the fields opposite were invisible. The air was damp and cold.

'Have you got a winter coat?' said Michael.

'No. Well, it's at Knightsbridge,' said Dora. 'It doesn't matter. I'm not a cold person.'

'You'd better buy one, you know,' said Michael. 'You can't get through the winter in that mackintosh. Do let me lend you some money, Dora. I'm not short.'

'No, of course not!' said Dora. 'I shall make out very well on the grant, now I've got that part-time teaching job as well. Oh dear, I wish you weren't going. Anyway, your train's sure to be late with this fog.'

'I hope it won't be too late,' said Michael. 'Margaret's meeting me at Paddington.' He sighed deeply.

Dora sighed too. She said, 'You packed my pictures all right?' She had given him three of her sketches of Imber.

'They're flat on the bottom of my case,' said Michael. 'I do like them so much. I'll have them framed in London.'

'They're not worth it,' said Dora, 'but I'm glad you like them. I can't really paint.'

Michael did not contradict her. They sat silently for a while, looking into the fog and listening for the train. The day was blanketed and still.

'Don't forget to give the key to Sister Ursula when you go,' said Michael.

'What will happen to Imber, anyway?' said Dora. 'Who does it belong to? Funny, I never wondered this before. It seemed as if it just belonged to us.'

'Well, in fact, it belongs to me,' said Michael.

'To *you*?' said Dora, turning to him. She was amazed. And in the instant her quick imagination had seen it changed, the garden radiant with flowers, the Long Room decked and carpeted, the house filled and warmed and peopled, made into a home for Michael and Catherine and for their children. It was a painful vision.

'It's the old home of my family,' said Michael, 'although we haven't been able to live there for a good many years. What will happen to it? It's going to be leased indefinitely to the Abbey.'

'To the Abbey?' said Dora. She drew a small sigh of relief. 'And what will they do with it?'

'Live in it,' said Michael. 'They've needed more space for a long time.'

'So it'll actually be inside the enclosure, the whole thing, the house, the lake, everything?'

'Yes, I suppose so.'

'How perfectly dreadful!' said Dora.

Michael laughed. 'It's a just reversal of roles,' he said. 'In the old days the Abbey used to be a curiosity in the grounds of the Court. Now the Court will be a curiosity in the grounds of the Abbey.'

Dora shook her head. She could not think how Michael could bear not to live there even if the place fell down about his ears. The distant sound of the train was heard booming through the fog. 'Oh dear,' she said. 'here's your train.'

They got up. The train came into the station.

Not many people were travelling, and Michael soon found an empty carriage. He stowed his suitcases and opened the window, leaning out and looking down on Dora. She seemed ready to burst into tears.

'Come, come,' said Michael, 'cheer up!'

'I know I'm silly,' said Dora, 'but I'll miss you so much. You will write, won't you, and let me know your address?'

'Of course I will,' said Michael. 'I'll be in London till January, and then in Norwich till the summer. Anyhow, I'll let you know where I am.' He had taken a temporary job at a Secondary

Modern school for the spring and summer terms.

'I'll write,' said Dora. 'I may write, mayn't I?'

'Of course,' said Michael.

'Do give my love to Catherine,' said Dora. 'I do hope she'll be all right.'

'Surely I will,' said Michael.

They remained looking at each other, trying to think of something to say. Dora was aware of his hand on the edge of the window. She wanted very much to cover it with her own hand, but did not do so. She wondered if she would dare to kiss him when the train was leaving.

'I never thanked you properly about Bath,' she said. 'I couldn't have managed it without you.'

'Oh, that's all right,' said Michael. 'I'm so glad it worked out. Give my greetings to Sally!'

'I will!' said Dora. 'You know, I quite look forward to it. I've never been in the West Country. I wonder how I shall get on. What does one drink there?'

Michael made a wry face. 'West Country cider,' he said.

'Isn't it nice?' said Dora.

'It's nice,' said Michael, 'but very strong. I shouldn't take too much of it, if I were you.'

'I shall telephone Sally to get in a large jug,' said Dora, 'and tonight we shall be drinking your health in West Country cider!'

The whistle blew, and the train gave a preliminary jolt. Blushing violently, Dora stood on tiptoe, drew Michael's head down gently, and kissed him on the cheek. He looked surprised. Then he kissed her forehead in return. The train began to move, and in a moment he had disappeared, still waving to her, into the fog.

Dora drew out her handkerchief and walked slowly back to the taxi. She shed some tears and a sweet sadness pierced her heart. Anyway, the kiss had gone off all right. She got into the taxi and told the taxi-man to drop her at the entrance gates.

As she walked down the avenue of trees the fog was clearing, and the Court became visible opposite to her, its pillars and copper dome clear-cut and majestic in the sunshine, a light radiant grey against a sky of darker moving clouds, rising above the still misty levels of the lake. Only the windows seemed to Dora a little dark and blank, like the eyes of one who will soon be dead.

When she got to the ferry, the boat was still on the other side and invisible in the fog. She drew upon the line and felt it coming heavily and sluggishly towards her. It emerged into view and came bumping up against the landing-stage. Dora got in and was about to propel herself across. Michael had taught her how to use the single oar. Then a new idea occurred to her. A second oar was always kept for emergencies, upon the landing-stage. Dora picked it up. She fitted the two oars into the rowlocks, and then undid the painter that joined the boat to the two sides of the ferry. No one would be coming across that way now.

She got in and sat down, trying the oars gingerly. She used to know how to row. After a certain amount of splashing she found that she still knew. The oars dipped and the boat moved away slowly over the surface of the water. Delighted, Dora released her breath and sat enjoying the gliding motion and the silence of the misty lake, broken only by the dripping of water from the blades. The mist was becoming golden. Now it began to clear away, and she saw the Court and the high walls of the Abbey toward which she was drifting. Behind the Court the clouds were in perpetual motion, but the sky was clear at the zenith and the sunshine began to warm her. She kicked off her sandals and trailed one foot in the water over the edge of the boat. The depths below affrighted her no longer.

She looked at the Court. She could not help being glad that Michael and Catherine would not live there, and their children and their children's children. Soon all this would be inside the enclosure and no one would see it any more. These green reeds, this glassy water, these quiet reflections of pillar and dome would be gone forever. It was indeed as if, and there was comfort in the thought, when she herself left it Imber would cease to be. But in this moment, and it was its last moment, it belonged to her. She had survived.

She drew in her foot and began to row slowly along the lake.

From the tower above her the bell began to ring for Nones. She scarcely heard it. Already for her it rang from another world. Tonight she would be telling the whole story to Sally.

Bestselling British Fiction in Panther Books

GIRL, 20	Kingsley Amis	40p	☐
I WANT IT NOW	Kingsley Amis	35p	☐
THE GREEN MAN	Kingsley Amis	30p	☐
THE RIVERSIDE VILLAS MURDER			
	Kingsley Amis	50p	☐
THAT UNCERTAIN FEELING	Kingsley Amis	50p	☐
THE EXPERIMENT	Patrick Skene Catling	40p	☐
FREDDY HILL	Patrick Skene Catling	35p	☐
THE CATALOGUE	Patrick Skene Catling	35p	☐
THE SURROGATE	Patrick Skene Catling	40p	☐
THE DECLINE OF THE WEST	David Caute	60p	☐
GEORGY GIRL	Margaret Forster	25p	☐
THE FRENCH LIEUTENANT'S WOMAN			
	John Fowles	75p	☐
THE SHY YOUNG MAN	Douglas Hayes	40p	☐
THE WAR OF '39	Douglas Hayes	30p	☐
TOMORROW THE APRICOTS	Douglas Hayes	35p	☐
A PLAYER'S HIDE	Douglas Hayes	35p	☐
THE GOLDEN NOTEBOOK	Doris Lessing	£1·00	☐
BRIEFING FOR A DESCENT INTO HELL			
	Doris Lessing	60p	☐
A MAN AND TWO WOMEN	Doris Lessing	60p	☐
THE HABIT OF LOVING	Doris Lessing	50p	☐
FIVE	Doris Lessing	60p	☐
WINTER IN JULY	Doris Lessing	50p	☐
THE BLACK MADONNA	Doris Lessing	50p	☐